DO NOT REMOVE
CARDS FROM POCKET

The Dixie Association

Donald Hays

SIMON
AND
SCHUSTER
New York

Copyright © 1984 by Donald Hays
All rights reserved
including the right of reproduction
in whole or in part in any form
Published by Simon and Schuster
A Division of Simon & Schuster, Inc.
Simon & Schuster Building
Rockefeller Center
1230 Avenue of the Americas
New York, New York 10020
SIMON AND SCHUSTER and colophon are
registered trademarks of Simon & Schuster, Inc.
Designed by Irving Perkins Associates
Manufactured in the United States of America

1   2   3   4   5   6   7   8   9   10

Library of Congress Cataloging in Publication Data

Hays, Donald.
    The Dixie association.

    I. Title.
    PS3558.A865D5   1984   813′.54   83-27178
    ISBN 0-671-47564-9

Grateful acknowledgment is made for permission to reprint material
from *Doc Ellis: In the Country of Baseball* by Donald Hall with Doc Ellis,
copyright © 1976 by Donald Hall, reprinted by permission of Coward,
McCann and Geoghegan; and from *The Collected Poems of Kenneth Patchen*
by Kenneth Patchen, copyright 1942 by New Directions Publishing
Corporation, reprinted by permission of New Directions.

There are no Arkansas Reds. There is no Dixie Association. There is a
Little Rock, but I have altered it to suit my purposes. There is an
Oxford, Mississippi, but it is not in Williams County, nor is it, any
longer, dry. This is all made up.

For my father, who taught me the game
For Mike O'Bryan, who pointed me toward the park
And for Patty, my love, who always paid for the lights

But down
Again, there'd be millions of people without
Enough to eat and men with guns just
Standing there shooting each other.

So he wanted to throw something
And he picked up a baseball.
—KENNETH PATCHEN, "The Origin of Baseball"

In the country of baseball the magistrates
are austere and plainspoken. Many of its citi-
zens are decent and law-abiding, obedient to
their elders and to the rules of the community.
But there have always been others—the
mavericks, the eccentrics, the citizens of inde-
pendent mind. They thrive in the country of
baseball.
—DONALD HALL, "The Country of Baseball"

Part I

1

I was in my cell packing my shit in a cardboard box. It was during the morning unlock and I had the place pretty much to myself. The place was the third floor of cellblock C, #54. As of that day, the tenth of April, two days before we were to open the season against the Selma Americans, I'd watched four years and a week crawl past me since justice's chauffeurs had driven me back to the Oklahoma State Slam for my second jolt. I was ready to see how I'd stand up under another dose of freedom.

I didn't have any trouble fitting my stuff in the box. All I had was three or four dozen paperback books, eight or ten letters, a few newspaper clippings, and a contract. Lefty Marks had sent me some of the books, most of the letters, and the contract, which promised to pay me a minimum of $600 a month plus room and board to play baseball for the Arkansas Reds. Julius Common Deer had clipped the articles out of the *Arkansas Chronicle* and mailed them to me. He'd printed "March 15" in neat letters at the top of the one I liked best. The headline said: LEFTY MARKS SIGNS ARMED ROBBER.

He not only signed me, but he got me sprung nearly three months early. It was easy to figure how he did it—we were overcrowded—but I wasn't sure why he did it. I'd never met him and he'd only seen me play once. That was in late February over at Norman when we played Oklahoma University in the annual gawk-at-the-thieves exhibition. I did jerk the ball around that day. But that one game and young Julius Common Deer's word were about all he had to go on. It's true I'd hit .477 with power and played a solid first base during my seasons in the McAlester pinstripes. That didn't mean much though. They didn't let us play outside the penitentiary over once a month, and the few first-rate pitchers we saw lacked the nerve to brush any of us back. I wanted to believe Lefty just had a sharp eye for talent. But I had to figure it was more likely that he was desperate for players. And then, too, it must've occurred to him that a thief on the field would put fans in the seats.

"Well, Hog. I sure hate to see you leaving us. But I expect you'll be back before we get to missing you good. You ain't the kind that can keep from stepping on his dick." Homer Stamps, a huge, fat, vicious thug that had been born in a prison guard's uniform, filled the open doorway to my cell. His smile made his jowls wobble.

Any other day there'd've been no percentage in messing with Homer. He made you suffer for it sooner or later. But I was on my way out and figured he wouldn't have time to get serious revenge. "Anything you want me to tell your wife before I skip town?" I asked him. "She smuggled me a note asking me to stop by this morning. Ordinarily I got no truck with her kind, but when you've done without as long as me, the sap backs up on you and your judgment goes."

He lumbered over to me and threw one of those big, slow rights that's not much good unless you've got somebody holding the man you're aiming at. I ducked under it, slipped to one side, and laughed while the force of the punch pulled him past me. I could've fought the son of a bitch in an outhouse without him ever landing a blow.

"Just kidding, Cap'n Stamps," I said. "I know a God-fearing gentleman like yourself wouldn't keep a woman that had one of them nasty gashes between her legs." I'd seen his wife three or four times at the mercy shows the state gave us once in a while to make themselves look good—Merle Haggard, Johnny Paycheck, David Allan Coe. She was a big, sad-eyed, horse-faced woman that looked to be about ten years free of the moon. Homer probably used her to practice his right on.

He worked his face into that killer-guard look he was so fond of. "You better hope they don't bring your sorry ass back here, Durham. What you been through up to now will seem like a barn dance up against what I'll put you through then."

"Hell, Homer, I'm a pro ballplayer now. You ever hear of any-body arresting a ballplayer when he's in his prime? Two or three years from now you'll be watching my life story on TV. 'Pride of the Slammer: The Hog Durham Story.' Maybe they'll let you play yourself. I don't believe anybody else could do you justice."

"Haw, haw," he snarled. "Get your shit together, hero. It's time to go see if the garbage truck's come."

I picked the box up off the bunk and followed him out of the cellblock, across the yard, through a couple of gates, and into Receiving and Release. The guard behind the storeroom counter there gave me a suit of clothes and the property envelope that had the stuff in it they'd taken off me four years earlier. All there was was an old yellow plastic comb that had about half its teeth missing, a cheap wallet that was empty except for a picture of a girl named Anna Lee Yancey I'd lived with in Stilwell some the last few months I was out last time, and a twenty-one-jewel Bulova I'd lifted off some display counter in Tulsa. I ran my hand across the edge of the comb and most of the rest of the teeth broke off. Anna Lee had married twice that I knew of since I'd seen her last, and she hadn't been much to me anyway—just a place to hole up in. But the watch still worked. I slipped it on. I figured I might need it to pawn sometime.

The cheap brown lightweight suit was as much too big for me as mercy is for a warden. But a man can get himself killed wandering around outside in a set of slammer blues, so I went ahead and took cover in the suit.

That was the fourth time I'd been in that room—twice coming and twice going. Going's easy. It's the coming in that sticks in your craw. And sitting there on that bench getting ready to walk again, I thought about those times and what I'd done to bring them on. The first jolt was for cattle rustling, not quite six years earlier. I'd gone into that line of work when I was nineteen and had been at it five years when they nailed me. The first three-and-a-half years I'd teamed up with Julius Common Deer's father, Ice, who could do wonders with a damn rope. Indians are the only cowboys left. We drove a few head of them huge, helpless Santa Gertrudis off the Kerr ranch, but usually, to be safe, we went further away to get our stock—up to Oologah and Talala and Nowata, over to Pawnee and Gray Horse and Pawhuska, down to Vamoosa and Bowlegs and Wolf. We'd put a steer in the back of Ice's old GMC pickup and a couple more in the horse trailer we had hitched to the back. Then we'd drive them back home and sell them to this little half-breed named Bingo Montana whose Tahlequah meat house sponsored the semi-pro ball team I played for and Bingo managed back then. Everything considered, he paid us a fair price, and we did all right for ourselves. But having a family to think about cut down a good bit on the joy Ice would let himself take from thieving. And finally he took what he'd saved up and bought himself a Jersey cow, a couple of Hampshire hogs, and a dozen laying hens and took to raising corn.

The work was lonesome after that and chancier. But I kept it up because I was good at it and it beat working. Anyway, they caught me one night with a load of prime beef, and since I'd been in trouble a couple of times for petty shit when I was a kid, they didn't fuck around with me. They trotted me across a courtroom and then hauled my young ass straight to McAlester. I got out after doing a year and took a job screwing the little legs on the bottom of couches at the Southland Furniture Factory in Fort Smith. I stood for a few months of that before going across the river to Van Buren one Friday afternoon and sticking up the People's Bank and Trust Company. I drove off in a stolen Mustang with over $3,600 and a feeling that Pretty Boy Floyd wouldn't've made a pimple on my ass. I figured next time I'd set fire to some mortgages.

They caught me in Muskogee less than seven months later. I walked into this liquor store on Choctaw aiming to buy me a fifth of J.T.S. Brown, but there wasn't anybody in there but this oleo-assed clerk and I was already drunk and I thought, Well, what the hell? The banks are closed. All I had with me was a Buck knife, but I hauled it out and flipped it open and let him have a good long look at it. He gave me the money without so much as whining and the heat met me at the door and gave me a lift down to the county slam, where I sobered up. They'd had the store staked out. My job was the sixth one pulled there in the last ten weeks. They charged me with all six of them and a man like me seldom has a good alibi. The public defender plea-bargained me out of two of the counts. I couldn't draw much comfort out of the fact that I had gotten away with the bank job.

When I had the suit wrapped around me and cinched up good at the waist, the Receiving and Release clerk called me over and handed me fifty dollars and told me the other fifty they owed me was sitting in the parole office in Little Rock. I made a show of counting the fifty.

"That'll buy you a night's drunk and a nigger whore," Homer Stamps said. "After that you'll have to take up rape."

"You boys would be surprised at how easy it is to get a woman if you're not puss-gutted and stupid," I said.

Homer started toward me, but the clerk said, "Just get him out of here. The quicker we get rid of him, the quicker we'll get him back."

I worried that some Arkansas cop would be standing in the outer waiting room with a warrant for me, but nobody was there except the trusty that had the receptionist job, and he waved us on through.

We went out a glass door and down a hundred feet of sidewalk and then Homer gave the o.k. sign to the gatehouse kings and they buzzed open the iron between me and the world.

When I set foot on the outside, it wasn't jubilation I felt, or anything like it, but a doubt that fluttered in my belly until it came within a moth's breath of being fear. Serving time doesn't make you fit to do anything but serve some more. But I couldn't afford to let myself screw up again. One more jolt and I'd be a habitual. And that's life, sweet Jesus, without parole.

2

Julius Common Deer sat in the cab of a late-model army-green three-quarter-ton Ford pickup that had "Columbia County Cooperative" written on the door I could see. All I knew about that cooperative was that Lefty's way of running it was what had started people calling him a Communist. But it didn't matter to me if Lefty was Castro's blood brother as long as he was giving me a chance to make a living playing ball, which is easier than stealing, a damn sight safer, and sometimes—when the wind's right and your blood's jumping and you got your eye on a hard one coming in fat—almost as exciting.

I walked across the highway and around the truck and got in and set my box of books between me and Julius. "Let's stretch some white lines between us and this hole."

He started the engine. "Nice suit you got," he said.

"Fits all sizes," I said. I leaned forward and got out of the coat. Then I took it by the shoulders and stretched it out in front of me until it damn near blocked the view before us. "It might come in handy," I said. "We can spread it over some poles and hold a revival under it." I wadded it up and laid it on top of the box.

Julius laughed and pulled out on the road, heading north up 69 toward Checotah. "You're liable to see some revivals when we get to Little Rock," he said. "They're holding singing conventions in the parking lot right outside the stadium. Some days they make it hard for us to get in and practice. They think the devil's running the team. Lefty's just his stand-in."

"Christians are the salt of the earth," I said. "Nothing grows where they've been."

Lefty's last letter had warned me about the riled crusaders at Arkansas Field. His advice was for me to stay as far clear of them as I could. And when I *had* to be around them—at the ballpark, for instance—I ought to keep my mouth shut, just get through them as quickly and gently as I could. But I didn't figure I'd be able to keep clear of them long. I'd already gotten a letter from some fool Little Rock preacher named G. Forrest Bushrod, who told me if I'd stay clear of Lefty and let Jesus in my heart his church would set me up with a room and a broom. I wrote back saying that a voice I'd recognized as God's had come to me in the night and said:

> Pop and glide. Pop and glide.
> See the ball before you stride.

I'd love to be able to sweep out the church and testify to all the fans there, I told the preacher, but since the Lord had took to talking to me like an old batting coach, I figured I'd better play ball.

But if Lefty's advice was pretty much worthless (I'd learned a long time ago that you couldn't stay clear of the faithful) and the preacher's was just something I could draw a laugh out of, I had gotten another piece of advice that worried me some. It was in a letter from Ice, who wrote about as often as Ayatollah Khomeini went out for spareribs. Ice said he couldn't ride down with Julius and meet me when I got out because that same morning he was supposed to be at the Tahlequah courthouse, where Joseph Hum-

mingbird would be tried for killing a deer out of season. Ice
thought there might be trouble over it and advised me to stay out
of Tahlequah for a while, being as I was on parole.

I thought Julius might be able to tell me a little more about
what was going on there, so I asked him why the law had just now
arrested Joseph Hummingbird for something he'd been doing
every couple of months for years.

"Dad told you then," he said. He didn't seem to want to say any
more and that made my suspicions worse.

"Ice isn't in trouble too, is he?"

"No," he said, relaxing some. "Him and some of Joseph's friends
are just going down there to see if they can help him out."

"They're wanting to spring him in plenty of time for him to bless
the corn, I guess." About ten years ago Joseph had come back
home with a piece of paper some school in Texas had given him
that said he was a genuine Baptist with a license to preach. He
showed it to some government agency and they gave him enough
money to build a combination church and community center beside a little fork in the road called Cherokee Springs about fifteen
miles east of Tahlequah. As soon as he got the church up and
painted, he swapped the Holy Ghost off for the Great Spirit—
started chanting to put the spring in new-planted corn, dancing to
suck the rain out of the summer sky, and pouring a stew concocted
of roots and herbs and such down folks to cure everything from
ringworms to dropsy. He wouldn't eat anything but corn, beans,
tomatoes, squash, melons, and venison. The law hadn't ever liked
Joseph, but he'd always had enough of a following to make whoever was having a turn at playing sheriff leery of running him in. It
had to've been the game warden that arrested him, of course, but
since he hadn't done it before, I had to figure he wouldn't've done
it now without getting the sheriff's go-ahead. Joseph must've done
something more than kill another deer or they'd've just gone on
letting him chant in peace. One kind of religion is as good as another for keeping the Injuns down.

But whatever was happening, Julius didn't seem to feel like
talking about it, so I let it ride. The day was warm and bright and
had just enough breeze in it to air it out good, and I didn't want to
spoil it by chewing on Cherokee County politics. I laid my head
back against the seat and let the wind blow over my face and

watched the world roll past my window. Things had turned green
and started to flower and I didn't notice any fences I couldn't've
jumped over.

I don't know but what I wouldn't've been content to ride along
like that all the way to Little Rock, but once Julius realized I was
letting go of Joseph Hummingbird, he started telling me about
Lefty and the team. Christ, I'd known him all his life and I
couldn't remember ever hearing him go on so about anything. He
made the Arkansas Reds sound like the '27 Yankees and Lefty like
a cross between George Orwell and Earl Weaver. He said the Reds
had three former big-leaguers, some good young guys, and a big
San Blas Indian that was going to set the world on fire. And Lefty,
who knew more baseball than Ted Williams, was wise and fair and
a friend to the poor. He wasn't just giving us a pennant to win; he
was offering us a cause to serve. Lord God, paradise was just up the
road.

Because Lefty had sprung me, I was ready to show him some
gratitude. And you had to admire him for having been the only
one-armed man ever to play in the big leagues, even though he did
it during World War II when everybody but queers and cripples
was off shooting foreigners. But I thought Julius was getting a little
carried away with his praise. Hell, there may be some folks out
there fool enough to be saints. But I figured the best way to play it
was to take it for granted that anybody that seemed like one was
running a carpet game on you. So by the time we'd ridden the
highway about halfway across Lake Eufaula, I'd decided Julius
was blowing his hopes up so high somebody was bound to let the
air out of them. It looked to me like I'd be doing him a favor by
taking the pump away.

"We may be good," I told him. "I got no way of knowing one
way or the other. But I wouldn't stake my ass on it if I was you.
Them old big-leaguers you talked about are nearly done for or
they wouldn't be in Little Rock. And anybody any older than you
that was really good would've been signed by a real team. What
Lefty's got is a collection of has-beens and wet-dreamers. God
knows, we both owe him for the chance he's giving us. You know
what it means to me, and for you it's a way not to end up in one of
them swaybacked shacks in the Cookson Hills trying to feed a fat
wife and a half-dozen whining kids. The thing for a kid like you to
do is not to worry much about the team but to look out for his own

self. If you hit .300 and play a good center field, somebody'll sign you up and move you to a higher league."

"You don't have to be an asshole to hit .300."

"It don't hurt."

"It's good to see how prison has brightened your outlook."

I looked out the window on my side and saw a pair of fat fishermen in one of them big bass boats that sell for about the price of a local politician.

"I'll tell you what, Hog," Julius said through a friendly but too confident grin. "It won't take more than a few days for even you to start trusting Lefty. You'll do it in spite of yourself."

"Maybe so. I guess it'd be nice. Right now there's not three people I got much trust in. One of them's an old man named Shakespeare Creel that was my cellmate back down there in McAlester. And the other two are you and Ice. And I wouldn't give a kid as young as you a chance if you weren't Ice's boy." I gave his grin back to him then. "Around anybody else I try to keep a close eye on my ass. I'd just as soon not have to walk around with somebody's dick hanging out of it."

The truth was that it wasn't really trust I felt for Julius but that kind of protective feeling you get for a kid you've seen grow up and don't want to watch anything bad happen to. He was as talented a young ballplayer as I ever saw and I wanted him to learn quick just what that talent could and couldn't do for him. When the little bastard was twelve years old, he started playing for a semi-pro team that Horace Roasting Ear ran at Nycut. You could tell even then he had a chance to play his way out of them flintrock hills. There used to be Cherokee teams scattered all over that country and I guess over the last six years Julius had played for eighteen or twenty of them. They played every Saturday and Sunday and whichever nights during the week they could scrounge a field with lights, starting at the end of February and playing on into the middle of November. Teams that had everything on them from half-grown kids to old men playing on nothing but memory and whiskey; teams that played in everything from cow pastures to some of the old bush-league parks still standing thirty years after TV and the La-Z-Boy recliner took the heart out of Class-D ball. The best players would go with whoever offered them a uniform, a ride to the game, and maybe a chance to win a little pocket money in a tournament. A team might play one week and fold the next. So if you were good, your loyalty wasn't to any team but to yourself and the game. I thought that was the way it ought always to be.

At Checotah we pulled into a little ptomaine palace and got ourselves a bag of cheeseburgers and a couple of RCs and after we got back on the road, heading east on 40, the talk came easier between us and we laughed together some, the old con and the young buck, innocent in such different ways.

I sung a few bars of "I Hear Little Rock Calling" when we crossed the Arkansas line and then when we passed the Van Buren exit, I did the chorus of "So Long, It's Been Good to Know You."

From there the highway follows the river valley east and a little south. The world seemed to open up in front of us and close in behind—which was just what I wanted it to do. I jawed with Julius and let the road signs fly past, enjoying the fool feel of freedom I got from putting road between me and McAlester.

We pulled off the road at Conway and traded the Exxon boys a day's wages for a fresh tank of gas and then rolled on into Little Rock about suppertime. I talked Julius into letting me get us a motel room. He told me it wasn't but a twenty-minute drive south to where the team was staying, but I felt like getting something to eat and sucking down a few beers and seeing what the night had to offer in the way of gash. Besides, I wanted to see my parole officer first thing in the morning and get that out of the way. Julius finally agreed to the room but not until after he called Lefty and checked in.

"I want to be back by ten," he said. "Lefty told me there was something on the news we ought to see."

"Cuba invade Florida?"

"It's Joseph Hummingbird."

"You little bastard."

We got some good ribs at a spook joint Julius knew about and then hit several bars where we put away some beer and shot some nine-ball. I kept an eye cocked for something in heat, but it was a Tuesday night and there didn't seem to be many women loose. One we talked to showed some interest, but that was in Julius. I might've had too much meat on the end of my line. Julius could've had her, but he let her go. It was easy for him to be particular.

A little before ten we got a couple of six-packs and went back to the motel. In the room Julius tuned the TV to a Tulsa station they got on the cable, and we stretched out on our beds and cracked us a beer apiece. Channel 6 news started off with a story on a Broken Arrow car salesman who spent a good part of the afternoon standing on top of the Oral Roberts Prayer Tower threatening to jump. He finally let himself be talked down by a tenor with the World Action Singers, who prayed over him a minute and then turned him over to the cops and the bughouse boys. Next, they showed one of the former Oklahoma governors being released from a federal golf course prison in Florida. He said he'd been born again in the slam and was going to start spreading the gospel. Then, after a Kerr-McGee commercial, it was Joseph Hummingbird. There was a helicopter shot of the Cherokee men that had surrounded the courthouse and then a closer view given by a moving camera. The outside row of bucks sat facing out on the rock wall that ringed the courthouse lawn. Another row stood behind them looking toward the courthouse. Each of the Cherokees carried a hunting rifle. The lawn was empty except for a couple of deputy sheriffs standing in the shade of the Will Rogers statue. A reporter explained that the Cherokees were afraid the law was trying to deprive them of their traditional hunting and fishing rights. He stuck his microphone into several of the braves' faces but got only Chief Joseph stares in reply. Next, we saw the reporter on the courthouse steps interviewing the county prosecutor, an asshole that called itself J. Reilly Whitsett, who said he'd just witnessed an outrageous miscarriage of justice. "Joseph Hummingbird is guilty of hunting out of season, resisting arrest, disturbing the peace, and, as you can see, inciting to riot. But this court allowed itself to be intimidated and freed Mr. Hummingbird on a technicality. The law in Cherokee County is being held hostage." He stomped off then, to the country club probably, where folks know what the law was written for.

Joseph Hummingbird came out the door with several of his friends, all of them silent and rigid and righteous. The newsman hurried over to him and asked whether he considered being freed on a technicality a victory. Joseph wore buckskin pants and a red T-shirt that had AIM written across the chest of it in big black leters. He anwered the man in Cherokee.

The weather was next. Julius got up and shut down the TV. I remembered my beer and took a long pull off of it.

"Christ, I wish I'd been there," I said.

"I know." He looked kind of hangdog. "But there wasn't any need for you and there might've been trouble."

We were quiet for a minute. I killed my beer.

"Well," I said, "it's been a black day for the Lord's troops. They had to let go of me, and then Joseph Hummingbird comes at 'em head-on and runs 'em over."

"It's a sign," Julius said.

"A man that believes in signs is going to spend most of his time lost."

3

A little after eight the next morning, Julius dropped me off at the parole office, just across the street from the capitol building, and they made me wait nearly an hour before they let me see the man that had my other fifty dollars. Sitting there in one of them green plastic chairs that sticks to your back, I took to grinning like a castrated half-wit any time one of the secretaries looked up at me. I tried to make my mind get a good hold on the idea that whenever the notion struck them these folks could ship me back to the can for farting too loud.

Even after I got in the man's office, I had to wait a few minutes while he diddled some papers. But that was all right. It gave me time to size up the man I'd be dancing the slammer tease with. He had brown hair that hung down to his collar, a soft, pale face that was starting to sag, and the tired, red-rimmed eyes of a man that works too hard doing a shithook job. He wore a brown corduroy suit, a green knit tie he'd loosened some, and an old wrinkled piss-yellow shirt. I knew that when he got up off his padded rolling chair and came out from behind his big gray metal desk so I could see him good, he'd be wearing a pair of suede desert boots and pretend to be the kind that cared. I'd hoped they'd run all of them out of Arkansas.

He finished with the papers and hid them in a folder and walked around to me and stuck his hand out. He was as heavy as me, but mushy, would've lasted about as long in a good fight as a spastic at a rattlesnake roundup. "I'm Randy Mantis. I'm pleased to meet you, Donald. Sorry we had to keep you waiting."

I took his hand. "Hog," I said.

His head jerked back just enough so that I could notice the movement. "Pardon me?" Some of the charm had quit his voice.

I smiled like a young coon in a red Buick and said, "Hog. I been called Hog all my life. Donald just don't fit right."

He walked back around behind his desk, sat down, and opened the folder again. "Oh, yes. Here it is. There is a notation that some of your fellow inmates referred to you as Hog. But often, as I'm sure you're aware, a name which might be appropriate in prison is much less so elsewhere. Now that you're back in society, you might want to consider dropping it."

"Hog suits me." I let it go then, figure I'd clam up and let him get through the "Let's Be Friends" spiel I knew he was primed to deliver. They memorize it in counseling class.

When he was ready to sing, he pushed his chair away from his desk, propped his feet up, locked his hands behind his head, and worked his face into a picture of social concern. "Donald," he started in. "Or, uh, Hog. Pardon me. We're going to be seeing each other regularly for a couple of years and I'm certain there'll be times I'll have to tell you things you might prefer not to hear. Therefore I think it only fair that you be told something about me and my attitude toward my work."

I looked him straight in the eye and shut my mind off to him. It was an old song that never had appealed to anybody but them that sung it. So I let the tune hum past me, nodding at him once in a while when the drone died down.

After what I'd guess to be about five minutes, he took his feet down, scooted his chair back up, put his elbows on his desk, leaned toward me, and gave me his old square-shooter look. "I want you to remember that it's not the brave man who gives up and pulls a gun, it's the coward. And once you begin learning to make your own way, you'll find there's a great satisfaction in it." He leaned back again, satisfied, the sermon seasoned and served. "I'd like us to be friends, Hog."

"I won't let you down," I said in a voice you could've boxed up and sold.

"Good. That's what I want to hear."

He took a pack of cigarettes out of his shirt pocket and offered me one. I took it even though it was the kind that has the filter the smoke can't get through. I was being polite. I had a pack of Luckies right there in the pocket of my slammer farewell suitcoat. Mantis gave me a light and asked me if I'd seen the morning paper. I hadn't, so he gave me the sports section of the *Arkansas Chronicle* and told me to read the column at the top of the page. It was by a jacked-up fool named Wilbur Haney and the gist of it was that Little Rock would be better off with no professional baseball team at all than with one run by Lefty Marks. He called Lefty a Socialist troublemaker who had spent the last twenty years trying to compensate for being one-armed. He went on to say that sports in Arkansas had always meant the Arkansas Razorbacks—young, apple-cheeked student-athletes playing for the glory of their state. It would be a shame to have that image spoiled by a man who shouldn't be allowed to manage an American baseball team. If he wanted a team, why didn't he get one in Cuba, where he belonged? There was a little box down below that said that Reverend Mutt Samples, a state senator from Smackover, had called for a special session of the legislature to investigate Lefty Marks.

I handed the paper back to Mantis and put my cigarette out in his ashtray. "The first game's tomorrow," I said.

Mantis studied me a few seconds, then nodded once and looked down and opened my folder back up. "Your file says that you worked as the purchasing agent's clerk for the last two years of your term. There is also reference to the fact that you did a considerable amount of reading."

"Yessir. I can read and cipher." I'd taken and kept the clerk job because I could make a little side money at it. And once I'd gotten to be cellmates with Shakespeare Creel, he'd taught me that reading was about as good a way as we had of forgetting time.

"And you wrote some poetry, I believe?"

"Yeah. There was this poet from Tulsa named Sterling Slaven that used to come down once in a while and run a workshop. He wasn't exactly Yeats and I wasn't either." Slaven was a little wasted, goateed, whisky-eyed, sponge-bellied, bald fucker. He used to come and stick his nose in the dirt of our lives, then go home, wipe it off on a sheet of typing paper, and sell it.

Mantis let me see his Good Samaritan smile. "I think this indicates a pattern that implies something important about your personality, don't you?"

"If you want to get by in stir, you got to figure some way of taking your mind off where you are and how long you're going to have to stay there. Some guys lifted weights and some took up the guitar. I read books and played baseball. Playing baseball is what I do best." I knew damn well what Mantis was sliding his way around to.

He put his elbows on his desk and folded his hands together in front of his neck. "I think in the long run your intellectual pursuits will prove more beneficial to you. You're over thirty—quite old for an athlete. And no matter how well you perform for the team here in Little Rock, you have absolutely no chance of making a career of baseball. At the very best, all you can look forward to is a year or two of minor-league ball. It's a dead end for you, Hog. That's hard, I know, and I don't enjoy saying it, but I think you'll agree I owe it to us both to be straight with you." He stuck his thumbs out and hooked them under his chin. "At this point in time, I don't think it would be in our best interest to allow you to play for the Reds." He leaned back in his chair and crossed his legs.

"You own one of the other teams?" I stood up. "I believe I'll see me a lawyer. Ole Lefty sounds like the kind that might could steer me to a good one. You boys made me a promise you're trying to back out of now, and I might just, by God, win this one. Thanks for the smoke. I think you got fifty dollars of mine." Yeah, they can ship you back for farting, but the time comes when you just got to go ahead and let one rip.

When you have to deal with government office scum, it never hurts to mention a lawyer. Mantis waved a fairy hand at me. "Please sit down, Mr. Durham. Allow me to finish."

I laid my hands on his desk and pushed my face toward him. "If you're going to slap me in the slam for playing baseball, then do it, by God. It ain't the end of the world. If you're not, then cough up the fifty bucks. I'll send you the box scores once a week."

"I have no intention of slapping you back in the slammer, as you put it. That is, if you can keep from assaulting me here in my office." I was a little surprised at how calm and sure of himself he sounded—but then we were on his reservation. "I can do it, of course. Parole can be revoked at any time, with or without cause. But I'm sure you're familiar with those provisions." He stopped there, waiting for me to sit down, I guess. I held my ground. He heaved up a sigh and shook his head and went on. "Oklahoma released you into Lefty Marks's custody. They're overcrowded and you'd served good time there. So I don't think they investigated Marks the way they should have. But it's done and now we're in a bind. We'd much prefer you didn't play for this team. But if you insist on it, we'll let you. At least for a while. Now would you please sit down?"

I sat down. "What else is there to say? You don't want me to play, but you'll let me. I want to, so I'm going to. There it is."

"I'm going to try to talk you out of it."

I laughed out loud at that. "Have at it, cowboy."

"All I ask is that you consider an alternative we've arranged for you." He spoke a little too high and fast so he stopped a minute and put the record on the right speed. "You don't have to reach a decision on it today. We've persuaded the city library to offer you a job driving a bookmobile. It doesn't pay much more than enough to live on, but it would be a start in the right direction. Plus, we can get you enrolled at Little Rock University beginning in the summer session. They'll give you a loan covering books and tuition, and you can work toward a degree in library science—or whatever you might choose. But with your clerking experience, that course of study should be no problem for you. The library will arrange your driving schedule around your class hours."

I started to give him the answer he deserved, but he showed me his palm. "Just hear me out." I'm sure he knew he'd lost, but a man that's got a job's got a job. "I know this can't seem as glamorous to you as being a baseball player. But without even taking the politics of the situation into account, it would be much more practical for everyone concerned. Especially for you, Hog. It would put you in the real world. The other way you'd be hiding from reality in ballparks, almost as closed off from everyday life as you would be in prison. This way you'd be firming up your future; the other way you'd just be frittering away the present. And you've already done too much of that."

"Thanks a lot," I told him. "It'd be a dream come true for me. It's why I went into crime in the first place. To get enough loot to set up a library of my own. Hog, the librarian. Got a nice ring to it, don't it?"

"Well," the man said, his face settling back into his business frown, "I suppose reason was too much to hope for. A man who's been irresponsible all his life won't change in one day. So you go on and play for your team. But let me tell you this. All we need is for you to make one mistake that has nothing to do with baseball and we're off the hook. And you'll have plenty of chances to make that mistake. We haven't completed our investigation yet, but I think it's safe to say that most of the men you'll be living and playing with are not model citizens. And there are three women living in that house also, hardly nuns, I daresay." He stopped long enough to give me a smirk. "I estimate you'll last maybe a month in that situation, six weeks at the outside." He got an envelope out of one of his desk drawers. "Here's your money. Enjoy it."

It was the first time I'd heard of the women and I was about to ask him to tell me more when I caught myself. I wondered why Julius hadn't told me about them. Maybe he was afraid I'd roar straight out to the house and go frothing through the door. He had a little streak of gentleman in him. But anyway, I got up and took the envelope and stuck it in the back pocket of my McAlester tuxedo and walked to the door, where I turned around and said, "Come out to the park and watch me play. I won't disappoint you. Lord God, can I hit! In a month, six weeks at the outside, everybody in town will be talking about me."

"That's what I'm afraid of," he said. "Check back in here before the team leaves town."

"Give that bookmobile job to the next man," I told him. "He might need it."

I walked a few blocks north and went into a bar called Friday's at Third and Victory. I had a beer before calling a cab and another while I waited.

The cabdriver was the kind that took the job for the fellowship of it. He asked what I was doing going out to Arkansas Field. I told him I played for the Reds.

"No shit! What kind of team you guys going to have?"

"Don't know. I ain't worked out with them yet."

"I ain't no Communist," he told me, "but I been a ball fan all my life. And to tell you the truth, I can't help but get a charge out of the way your boy Lefty Marks has been putting the prod to this damn church-foundered burg. It ought to be a helluva year. The bastard's supposed to have everything playing for him from wild Indians to armed robbers."

4

The God-and-Country junkies were jumping up and down sing-ing brush arbor hymns just outside the chain-link fence in front of Arkansas Field. Most of them were women—their poor fool hus-bands out shoveling shit in the sun so these dried-up bags would have the leisure to wander around howling at the devil. I expect they gave the Old Boy a laugh.

When he saw them, my new pal, the cabdriver, said, "Look at them. Born again and again and again. I'm counting on you boys to do it up proud for all us drunks and backsliders."

He drove right up in their midst and they hushed and waited to see if we'd been washed in the blood. He stuck his head out the window and said, "Any of you holy rollers need a ride home?"

That kind of took them aback for a minute, but then one of them hollered, "My home is on high," and started singing "We're Marching to Zion." The others chimed in with a vengeance.

I told the cabbie, "Well, if a man expects to be a real hitter, he's got to learn to come through in the clutch." I got out and started toward the gate.

They didn't really try to stop me, just slow me down enough to be sure I got a stiff dose of their fool song. I took it easy wading through them, never pushing but never stopping either. I've never hit a woman that didn't need it, but if I'd been absolutely free then, I might've cold-cocked one of them Christer twats. They were all around me screeching that damn hymn in my ears, their faces twisted up with the glory of the moment and years of reli-gious suffering. The Lord keeps shitting on them that lack the sense to wipe it off. They get used to it and mistake it for the an-swer to their prayers.

But I knew that Mantis would like nothing better than for me to slug one of these skirts, so I let them rave at me without having to suffer for it. Several of them had written messages on placards that they had stapled onto stakes and were fanning the air with. Shit

like "Save Our City" and "Keep Communism Out of Our Parks"
and "Vengeance Is Mine, Saith the Lord."

The gate was locked when I got to it and there was a big cow-
faced woman backed up against it that looked like she might be a
sister to Homer Stamps's piece. The singing stopped, praise God.
In a voice that would've shriveled God's own cock, the heifer asked
who I was and what was my business with the Communists inside.

"I'm Brother D. W. Durham. The Death Row Evangelist."

She looked at me like she'd caught me writing limericks in the
Book of Revelation.

"Maybe you've heard of me," I said. "I'm the one that led Gary
Gilmore to the Lord on his way to the firing squad. I'd like to bring
the Word to the sinners inside the park."

There wasn't a sign of light in her brimstone eyes. "The gate's
locked, mister."

I reached out and put my left hand on her right shoulder as
gently as I could and still move her over to one side. "A locked
gate's no obstacle to a Christian, sister," I told her.

I jumped against the gate and then climbed over the son of a
bitch. It wasn't but about ten feet high and going over a fence like
that was something I'd been hankering to do for four years.

After I came down on the other side, I didn't look back at them.
I went down a sidewalk until it came to a runway that led me up
into a grandstand behind home plate. It felt good in there, like a
church sanctuary during the week. From where I was I could tell
that God's gashes had commenced butchering another hymn. But
I couldn't quite make out which one it was—maybe "Praise the
Lord and Pass the Ammunition." I just tried to shut them out of
my mind as best I could. That's all you can do. They're here and
they're going to stay awhile—scared shit of living and calling the
damn misery down on anybody that's not.

What I did as soon as I got up in the grandstand was to see how
far it was out to the fence. Three hundred ten down the line in
left—easy pickings even though the wall looked to be twenty feet
high. I guess the fence was so close there because that part of the
field was rubbing against the Orval Faubus Freeway. They
must've known I was coming because between the fence and the
freeway there was a high screen to keep the balls from landing in
somebody's front seat. The wall angled back pretty quick from

dead left. It went to 355 in left-center, 385 in straightaway center, then curved back to 360 in right-center, and 355 to the right-field pole. A little ways beyond the right-field wall was some kind of drainage ditch and just the other side of that was the southeast corner of the city zoo. A 500-foot shot might get you a buffalo.

I was a little surprised at how good the place looked. No games had been played there in the last two years—well, maybe some kind of city Holy Joe little league crap, but nothing regular. I found out later that Lefty had talked the team into doing most of the remodeling themselves. They resodded quite a bit of the field, put a coat of paint over everything but the ground, and just generally nailed down anything that was coming loose. The walls were a deep green, the seats a bright red. And my eyes are as blue as the Irish Sea. I was just as glad I missed all that labor.

The grandstand was about thirty rows deep and curved around behind the field from first to third. There was an upshooting roof that would shade most of the grandstand seats in the afternoons. Directly behind home plate at the top of the grandstand was a little white press box and an old organ. Down either line past the grandstand were the bleacher seats, and there were four rows of box seats in front of the grandstand. The box seats were just the kind of metal folding chairs people sit on at card games and church socials. I noticed that it couldn't be more than thirty feet from home plate to the backstop. That was going to prove a help to us because we had two old catchers that were both pretty good except for the fact that neither one of them could move fast enough to scatter his own shit.

I sat down in one of the seats next to the aisle about halfway up the grandstand and just kind of reared back and half-shut my eyes and started making up newspaper headlines: DURHAM WINS GAME WITH TAPE MEASURE SHOT. HOG SNORTS AGAIN. RUSTLER LEADS REDS TO CHAMPIONSHIP. It wasn't until the team came out of the clubhouse and started setting up for batting practice that I reminded myself that the main difference between wet dreams and dreams of glory is that with the second kind you didn't get the kick at the end. But baseball is a dreamer's game, I guess, and the glory you can get from hitting a ball may be the only kind there is.

I went down and stood behind the batting cage and told some of the boys who I was. None of them seemed to think it was the second coming. Maybe they were worried about their wallets back in the clubhouse. But whatever the reason, they just kind of grunted at me and shied away.

I looked around for Lefty, but unless he'd sprouted a new arm, he wasn't anywhere on the field. Julius was in the outfield shagging flies and when he saw me he trotted in and asked how it had gone with the parole officer. I told him I was another fifty dollars closer to my first million and still on the loose.

There was a big black kid on the mound throwing smoke. Ordinarily in batting practice, they just lay it in there, but the season started the next day and this was real pitching. And Julius told me Lefty didn't think gimme batting practice did a hitter any good unless he was just trying to fix some flaw in his stroke.

What these guys were doing was giving the black kid mainline jolts of confidence. The only time they hit him at all was when he tried his curve on them. You could see it coming: he cocked his wrist too much and too early. The kid was Franklin Brown, who you're likely to be reading more about when he makes the big time in two or three years. Before the year was out he would give up on the curve and learn to throw a slider that could make Hank Aaron look like a faggot with a fly swatter. But there in the spring all he had was the fastball and though you could hear it whistling when it came in and it had a hop on the end of it, I knew I could hit it. You come at me hard, I got you. It's the change that's apt to get me.

But there was no way I could get into the clubhouse and get a uniform on before Brown finished his turn on the mound. And anyway, Julius said Lefty was in there talking with some businessmen and politicians. I didn't want to get caught in the middle of another Baptist hop, so I stayed where I was.

When Julius was hitting, I rode him a little—nothing rough, just the kind of horseshit you do with your friends. He hit Brown fairly well, nailing that here-I-come curve ball every time and even ripping some of the fastballs. But Brown had him popping up a lot. I kept telling Julius he'd be a home-run hitter in an elevator shaft. When his turn was about up, he walked out of the cage and handed me the bat.

"Let's see if you're as good with a bat as you are with a knife."

I knew it was his way of doing me a favor, letting the boys see me hit the fastball. But I wasn't real sure about going up there in my street shoes and my slammer charity suit. I'd talked my way into a corner I was going to have to hit my way out of, so I laid my jacket down on the grass and took the bat.

Brown blew the first one right by me. It was a high, tight hard one that rode up and in on me some. I swung from my heels and my feet came out from under me and I ended up laying on my ass looking as thunderstruck as a gang-banged cheerleader. It handed the boys a good laugh. I heard one of them yell, "Get up and run, Durham. The cops are coming."

It didn't take me long to shut them up. Brown got the next one out over the plate and I caught it on the money part of the bat. It was still rising when it left the park, cleared the screen and most of the freeway. I turned around and told them to send their damn cops after that in a helicopter.

I knew there was no place to go but down after a lick like that, so I got out of the box and gave Julius his bat back. The boys were a lot friendlier with me then, slapping me on the back and kidding me about falling on my ass and allowing as to how the wind had carried the ball out of the park. I handed the bullshit right back to them, saying that I had a little crick in my back that kept me from taking my full swing and anyway I hadn't got good wood on the ball and had had to muscle it out. I told them I felt a little ashamed of taking advantage of a kid that didn't throw any harder than Brown. They hoo-hawed with me and I began to feel like I was part of the team. I figured I'd be all right unless some of their money started disappearing. But there was no getting around that. I was going to be a prime suspect the rest of my life.

The hitter after me was Jefferson Mundy and he was the best one I saw that day. He was a long-muscled, six-foot spook, as black as a judge's heart, and he sprayed line drives all over the field. My shot had probably taken some of the music out of Brown's hummer, but there was no denying that Mundy was a hitter. I started to think maybe Julius had been right—maybe we did have a shot at winning.

Watching him made me anxious to get a uniform on. I wanted it to start right then, get out on the field and dig my spikes into the ground. I decided that if the businessmen were going to be all day with Lefty I'd just have to go ahead and let them have a look at me.

Julius followed me toward the dugout and asked what I thought about Mundy.

"He's a hitter," I said.

"And he's the best shortstop you ever saw." Julius said it like he'd just sewed up an argument.

"Maybe so," I said through a grin. "I forgot what a good one looks like. The shortstop I played with for the last four years had a lot of range and quick hands and a damn rifle arm, but there were times in the late innings when something would throw his concentration off and he'd butcher anything that bounced his way. He was a guy named Skillet Huffor that had beat his wife to death with a frying pan."

I went on down into the dugout and through the door at the home plate end. The clubhouse was crawling with merchant-looking scum, all at the far end of the room sitting on wooden stools they'd gotten from the locker stalls that lined the two long side walls. Lefty was standing up facing them. Next to him was a red-faced, bulb-nosed, curly-headed man that was sitting in the whirlpool tub. All of them were in front of the tiled wall that blocked off the showers.

As soon as he saw me, Lefty started toward me. He was wearing a gray sweatsuit he might've bought back when Jesus was still an apprentice seaman. He just let the left sleeve flap.

He said, "Hog Durham." Somehow he managed to make it sound kind of dignified.

I said, "Lefty."

We shook hands. He had a helluva grip. He was around six feet tall and had a head full of half-gray hair. I couldn't see any fat on him. He had the lines a man his age has to have around his eyes, but other than that the skin was tight on his face—nothing sagged. His blue eyes were the bright, steady kind I was used to seeing on sharp cons. All but a trace of the romance had gone out of them, but they weren't cold.

He led me over to the other guys. When he got to them, he said, "Hog, I'd like you to meet some of the city fathers."

I told him I just wanted to get a uniform and some spikes and swing a bat. But he had a number he was set on doing.

The first one he introduced me to was a middle-sized thief a few years older than me whose body was starting to meander south on him—needed a couple more hours a week at the Racquet Club. Like the rest of them, he had on what I figured was a top-of-the-barrel merchant outfit.

"Hog, this is Jess Godley, the mayor of Little Rock." The mayor stood and shook my hand. I guess it was a habit he'd had too long to get over all of a sudden. And he did it the way a politician does—like he was trying to wipe something off on me without me catching him at it.

"That's really his name. Jess Godley," Lefty said. "It was God's way of telling him to go into politics. It may get him elected governor someday. Right mayor?"

The mayor kept his ambitions to himself. The man in the tub snorted.

"Let's see now. Who's next? Oh, yes. Of course." He went over to a steak-fed white-headed guy that looked like he'd probably lied his way into many a respectable cunt. "This is the Reverend Dr. G. Forrest Bushrod, pastor of the First Baptist Church and Investment Corporation out at Scavenger Heights. He is also lifetime chairman of the Little Rock Interdenominational Alliance of Ordained Vigilantes." The preacher didn't say anything, but his eyes were sending Lefty to hell.

"We've corresponded," I said. I was starting to enjoy it some, though I'd still rather been out getting in my licks.

"And this gentleman is Conrad Welch or Welch Conrad, I can't remember which. He's the city attorney." He was showing me a short, neat, candy-assed wimp.

"Welch Conrad." The mouthpiece said it like he was reading it off a list.

"Ah, yes," Lefty said. "Formerly of the firm of Takem, Shakem, Breakem, and Stakem."

The mayor stood up and said, "We don't have to sit still for this. The man refuses to listen to reason. We have other options."

"No thanks to you, Jess," Bushrod said. "Let him entertain his convict. He's not hurting anyone but himself. We're not finished here."

"Thank you, Reverend Dr.," Lefty said. "I was praying you wouldn't abandon me just as I am." Then he gave a little nod in the direction of the audience he was insulting and told me, "These others are just lower members of the same species—city councilmen, little preachers."

"What the hell? Just give me a sweatsuit." I was starting to think maybe my parole officer had something.

"Christian politicians," Lefty went on. "An oxymoron of course. But here they are. They've come over to put the fear of God in us. Somehow it got out that I'm not a member of the Fellowship of Christian Athletes and these gentlemen want to fry me for it. They're saying that if I don't play this game their way, they're not going to let me use the field. But my lawyer—he's the Jew in the baptistry there, Barry Rotenberg"—Lefty jerked his thumb toward the whirlpool—"tells me that if these boys keep screwing with me, we'll sue the shit out of them. By the time we get through I might be able to buy me a big league club."

He put his arm around me then and looked out at the oxymorons. "Gentlemen," he announced, "as some of you have already guessed, this is Hog Durham, my first baseman."

The city attorney decided to fire back. "I recognized him from his mug shots. And I've discussed his case with his parole officer."

Naturally, I thought. Just another case of two government dogs taking turnabout licking each other's ass. But I kept from saying it. Lefty was doing more than enough talking.

What the lawyer said must have made Lefty realize that even if they couldn't do anything to him just then, they had a vice around my nuts.

"Gentlemen," he said, "I need to give Mr. Durham his equipment. I'll be back to hear the rest of your threats in just a few minutes. Meanwhile, you might enjoy trying some of them out on Mr. Rotenberg. His people are long accustomed to Christian charity."

There was a door just the other side of the shitters at that end of the room and I followed him through it. He walked to the middle of the room we'd entered and pulled the chain that was hanging from the light. Then we went back and closed the door behind us. It was just a storeroom, wide unvarnished wood shelves lining all the walls. It smelled of old leather, stale air, and forgotten dust. A big net hammock was stretched across the far end of the room. Lefty saw me looking at it and said, "Eversole sleeps there. A strange man, but he could pitch us to a pennant."

"Eversole?"

"You'll meet him soon enough."

He took two uniforms off one of the shelves and said, "The whites are for home, the grays for the road. The way things are going we might ought to reverse it."

When he handed me the uniforms, he said, "I want to apologize for what went on out there, Hog. The bastards made me mad. I was thinking more about insulting them than protecting you. It won't happen again. You have my word on that. I'll do what I can to protect you."

He was something. When he looked you in the eye like he did me and talked in that steady, earnest voice, you couldn't doubt but that he was telling you the truth—the kind of man you had to watch out for or he'd have you sticking your nuts in a grinder for some cause you didn't know or care the first damn thing about.

I held up one of the uniform tops and looked at it. It was the old-fashioned kind—cotton, no horseshit decoration, just "Arkansas Reds" on the chest and the number on the back. "I got them cheap from the Albuquerque Conquistadors," Lefty said. "They're going to double-knits and neon tops." He threw me some stockings and sanitary hose.

I caught them, looked at them a second, and then made myself say, "I thank you for springing me. I'm owing you."

"It was easy. Your time was about up. And they were already being sued for packing too many prisoners in there. Here are your spikes. The caps are over there behind you. Pick out one of these sweatsuits to work out in. I think Julius took your first-base mitt out with him. We have some cups, but you'll have to get your own jocks if you don't already have some."

"I'll buy a few before tomorrow. I donated my old ones to the state of Oklahoma."

I got a sweatsuit and started undressing. Lefty leaned against the shelves across from me. "Maybe if I stay in here long enough the sons of bitches will leave," he said.

"I doubt it. The preacher looked like he had another sermon in him."

"He doesn't have another sermon," Lefty said, "just the one he never tires of delivering."

I pulled the sweatpants on over my underwear. I could make do without the jock until the next day. Hell, I was sixteen before I wore one, and my cods were at least as important to me then as they are now.

"Listen, Hog, I want to say a couple more things and after that I'll keep my nose out of your business unless you need my help some way." He was going to go on, but I interrupted him.

"Man, I won't stick anybody up as long as I'm playing for you. I may just be good for one year of pro ball, but I want that year. I'm not going to fuck it up."

"That's not what I was going to say. Or not exactly. I just wanted you to know that I'm aware of what they're putting you through. About three days ago your parole officer called me into his office. What's his name? Mantis?"

"Yeah."

"I think he may be all right," Lefty said, and it made me wonder about his judgment. "But he's under a lot of pressure. He told me he'd found you another job. He asked me to let him have a chance to offer it to you without me interfering. I gave him my word. If you want that job, take it. No hard feelings. Your chances of staying free might be better that way. This posse's going to come after us with everything they have. You've probably got more to lose than any of us."

"I don't want the goddam job."

"Good. If they decide to revoke your parole, I'll do everything I can for you. I can make them look bad. I can raise all kinds of hell. But watch yourself. Because the truth of it is if they're determined to go through with it, I can't stop them."

I had the sweatshirt on by then. "I know. I know it better than anybody. Leave it lay. It's my worry. I'm going to play ball. If they want to jerk me back to the slam, they're going to have to come drag me off the field. I'll go in my uniform."

He got up and walked over to the door. "You know, the better you hit, the better your chances of staying free. The publicity will protect you."

"That's the case, I'm sprung forever."

I went out on the field then where I was safe—or felt safe, though I knew better. And I ripped that baseball, Jack, rattled the fences, brethren, put five of them out of the park, one of them going even further than the one I hit in my street clothes, plumb over the damn freeway Orval Faubus had had built in honor of himself.

It wasn't a bad start, though it jacked me up more than was sensible. There were people that wanted to box me up and cart me off, people that had the legal right to do it. And if they'd've come for me right then, I'd've just been standing there, my mind watching that ball sailing over the screen and the freeway again and

again. You do what you can. I wanted to believe a man could do
wonders with a swing of the bat.

5

About half an hour after I finished my batting show, Lefty led
the preachers and politicians to the gate and reunited them with
the parking-lot choir, which perked up and started screaming
"Bringing in the Sheaves."

We spent the next hour or so taking infield and shagging flies. I
shared first base with a tall, pit-headed left-hander named Mike
O'Bryan, who told me he quit a job climbing poles for Old Mother
Bell to play for the Reds. He wasn't bad at catching the ball, but
there was no telling when he'd take a notion to fire one up in the
stands. He said he'd sat on them poles so long it had screwed up his
aim. I'm not exactly an acrobat around the bag myself, but I hang
on to anything that comes to me. And though my arm's not what it
used to be—a couple of riled bucks like to ripped it off me after a
snooker game six years ago at the Paradise Lounge in Fort Gibson,
Oklahoma—you don't need much arm to play first base. O'Bryan
did have a pretty portside swing, but I'd've bet a grand against a
used rubber he couldn't hit with me. He might get to start the first
game or two because he'd been here working out for three weeks
before I arrived, but I knew the first-base job would be mine before
the week was out.

I tried to size up the rest of the infield while we worked out. On
second we had a wiry, leather-faced, sour-looking little guy named
Worm Warnock. I doubted if he could hit his weight divided by his
hat size, but he looked like he could do the job in the field. And
maybe he could bunt. Over at third Rainbow Smith wasn't exactly
Brooks Robinson. He was quite a bit fatter than he was quick and I
could see that he got his name from the way his throws traveled to
first. But he'd been up with Oakland during a couple of their good
years back before Charlie Finley tried turning Alameda Stadium
into a funeral home. Since it was clear he didn't get that far with
his glove, you had to figure he could hit. And he had put several
out during batting practice—nothing like I'd done, of course, but

not bad. With him and me at the corners we'd have power, even if we were a little short on grace.

And we could leave the grace, by God, to Jefferson Mundy. He was everything Julius had said he was. He had the kind of speed and hands the Lord gives a lot of black kids in place of a decent chance. And even from deep in the hole he sent the ball on a line to first. Lefty had managed to sign most of the players on this team either because they were old or were twisted in some way, but he'd nailed four young ones, good ones that were on the way up—Julius and Mundy and that pitcher Brown and another black kid out in right named Atticus Flood. I thought at first that those four kids just hadn't used their heads, hadn't known any better, but the truth of it was that on a good day Lefty could talk the Pope into opening a whorehouse.

And the main show during that part of practice was Lefty's one-armed juggling act. Other than him we didn't have any coaches, so he hit grounders to us while a deaf Cajun relief pitcher named Dummy Boudreaux hit flies to the outfielders. Lefty would lodge the meat end of the fungo bat in between his right jaw and shoulder, then toss the ball up high enough to get his hand back on the bat and start it moving toward the ball. And he hit sharp grounders that went right where he wanted them to. After he got through with us, he called Dummy off and hit some to the outfielders so they could work on their throws to the bases. He smashed the fuckers too, sometimes bouncing them off the wall and giving us a chance to work on relays. He must've been something to see in his prime. But I bet the guys he played with hated his ass. Nobody likes to get showed up by a cripple.

Right after infield most of the team headed in to the showers, but I felt like taking some licks against the pitching machine, so me and Julius went over to the cage on the other side of the right-field bleachers and took turns at it for about a couple of hours. It's a good way to get your swing in a groove, but batting in a cage like that takes a lot of the joy out of hitting. You got screen all around you and no matter how good you hit the ball, it's not going over seventy feet. What I do is try to hit shots up the middle and put dents in the machine.

I could've hit till dark, but because I like to feel the wood against my palms, I wasn't wearing a batting glove and I figured I better quit before my hands got chewed up. So we went in and I took a hot shower, which I enjoyed as much as anything I'd done since leaving McAlester. I'd taken a shower that morning before going to see Mantis, but that was in the motel and I'd had to stand in a little half-assed bathtub with the curtain drawn and I'd had to just about double over to get my head wet because the nozzle struck me about cock-high. So this was the first real shower I'd had in over four years. In the slam the water was cold, you had to pay for soap, and there might be as many as fifty cons trying to get under five nozzles. Sometimes you got as much sweat on you as water.

I couldn't find a towel when I got out of the shower so I went into the storeroom to get one. That gave me my first good look at Jeremiah Eversole. He was laying naked in that big hammock that was stretched across the room. Though it was built for two people, Eversole damn near filled it. He had shiny black hair that hung nearly to his shoulders and framed his big, round face. He was forty-six years old then, but you couldn't tell it. He looked like something time wouldn't have much effect on. What you noticed was the size of him—at least six-five and upwards of two-fifty and none of it waste. I didn't often see a man I was sure could rip me apart, but I knew that if I ever went after Eversole I'd be carrying at least a bottle with me.

It surprised me that he was reading. Maybe it shouldn't have— since most people figure I have to sign my name with an X—but it did. It was a thick hardcover book, but with him laying crosswise to me I couldn't see the title of it when I first came in.

He didn't seem to mind that I'd come in there, just glanced over at me once and went back to the book. All I could come up with to say to him was, "Lefty said you stayed in here."

"Yeah."

"I need a towel."

He pointed at them.

I had to go under the hammock to get to the towels and that gave me a chance to read the book's title. It was *Darien Massacres: Pedro de Avila and the Conquest of Panama.* Down at the bottom of the spine were those numbers libraries put on their books, so I knew Eversole had either checked it out or stolen it. My guess was that he didn't carry a library card.

I was to spend a good part of that season trying to figure Eversole out and there's a lot I still don't understand. But I learned this much. His mother was the daughter of an American navy officer

that was stationed in Panama. And she spent at least part of at
least one night rolling around with a San Blas Indian buck because
Eversole was what come of it. And I guess he remembered where
he'd come from and what had been done to his kind because as far
as I could ever find out he just had this one book and the only time
he ever read it was on the day before he·was scheduled to pitch.

I got a couple of towels and went back under the hammock and
was about to leave when I thought—Shit on it. He's not going to
kill me for telling him who I am. I walked back over to him and
held out my hand and said, "I'm Hog Durham."

He turned his face toward me and there wasn't any expression
on it except that cold look of confidence a man has when he knows
that after all he's been through there's nothing you can do to hurt
him or please him or even surprise him much. He nodded at me.
"The robber," he said, like he approved.

"Yeah," I said. "Keep your doors locked."

He took my hand. It felt like an honor.

6
―――

The supper Dummy Boudreaux concocted us out of chicken and
rice and various table scraps was enough to make a man think
Cajuns were God's chosen kind, and the house Lefty'd bought us
from the state after they'd had to close it was so grand and white
and on such a high hill that you might've expected the niggers to
be waiting the table for us instead of eating at it with us. But I
couldn't really appreciate either the house or the cooking for wondering where the women were. On the road out from the park,
Julius had finally told me some about the three of them—a dyke
mechanic, an ex-cheerleader that had taken too many tumbles,
and a blonde-headed, long-legged teenager that could make your
cock rear up and recite the Pledge of Allegiance. Now my old cock
had never learned the pledge, but it could do the minute waltz all
night long and was in dire need of a partner.

Until about six months before the team moved in, the home had
been a shelter for various kinds of hard-luck women—battered
wives and unmarried mothers, teenage girls yearning for the fast

life and middle-aged saloon queens yearning to get out of it. But then the state legislature, running low on money and figuring the last thing they needed to pay for was a rest home for fast women, had shut it down. So Lefty, who, when he needs to be, is nearly as sharp with a dollar as old man Rockefeller and all his scavenging spawn, hustled up to Little Rock and offered to take the place and its shame off the state's hands cheap. The place was an old but well-kept white-frame three-story, thirty-room house sitting on a barbered oak- and maple-shaded lawn and surrounded by ten acres of pine hills fifteen miles south of Little Rock on the road to Hot Springs. All through that year we kept the big varnished wooden sign with its fancy burnt-in letters hanging over the front door. "Arkansas Home for Women," it said. I imagine it's there yet.

Julius wasn't saying why the women had stayed on. Of course it was easy enough for me to make lewd guesses. The mechanic had once been a professional wrestler that called herself Amazonia and my bet was that she was staying there at least partly because the other two women were easy to pin. And those two probably either liked being pinned or couldn't get out from under Amazonia. Still, they could've moved out and got their own place. So I couldn't help but think there was something about living with a houseful of baseball players that appealed to them. And I didn't care what they did with Bobbie Sampson, a.k.a. Amazonia, as long as they could turn around and hit from the other side.

Since Julius had told me the women were on the Reds' payroll, I'd expected them to be doing the cooking and housekeeping for us, but they were off somewhere that evening, and anyway Dummy Boudreaux loved to cook and if he'd set his mind to it he could've made a glutton out of Mahatma Gandhi.

We ate off a long oak table that had a bench on each side of it and a straight chair at each end. Fifteen people were sitting there that night and there was room for more. I'd met them all that afternoon, of course, but there were still a few names I hadn't quite gotten hold of. As we ate I thought again what a strange crew we were. Guys from eighteen to twenty-one and then again from thirty-two or -three to forty-some. Nobody in his middle twenties, when a ballplayer ought to be at his physical prime. We were all playing for this team out of either innocence or desperation. Hasbeens and wet-dreamers, I'd told Julius. And I think I was right.

We talked some about the Selma Americans, the team that was coming into town the next day to open the season. They had been Dixie Association champions the last two years and were expected to win it again. They were the closest thing to a dynasty the league had known. Now and then one of the other teams would come up with a good crop of players and take the pennant, sometimes even twice in a row. But those players tended to move on, up and out, north to the big clubs, and whatever team they'd played for in this league had to pretty well start over. But Selma was home-owned, not hooked up with any major-league organization, and for the most part was able to keep the same team year in and year out. Even the few players that went from Selma up to Triple-A or the majors usually came back home a few years later to play out the string. So while other teams in the Association often had more raw talent, Selma had more experience and made fewer mistakes. And they played hard. Their manager and majority owner, Bull Cox, who was also the county sheriff there though he had to delegate most of his authority during baseball season, wasn't a man that took losing with much grace.

Sitting just to my right at the table was a bald, fat knuckleballer named Bullet Bob Turner who had pitched in the big leagues for a dozen years and nearly as many teams. He had a stack of baloney sandwiches and a quart of Coors in front of him. He said, "I've known old Bull for a lot of years. We played together on that Selma team when I was just a curly-headed kid and he was in his last year as a player. He was a little hard to get along with sometimes, but he ain't a bad guy. Y'all better watch your asses if a fight breaks out. Old Bull is one that'll damn sure take up for his players. Ain't afraid of a circle saw." He picked up one of his sandwiches and took a bite that would've strangled a normal man. He saw me watching him swallow it and must've thought I was longing for baloney. "There's plenty of meat in the icebox. You don't have to eat that coon-ass food if you don't want to."

"This'll do," I told him. "And I could go forever without any more baloney. Like to foundered on it when I was a kid. Horse cock, we used to call it."

"Suit yourself."

Lefty wasn't about to let a discussion of Bull Cox's character end with Bullet Bob's admiring description of the man's bravery. "I've had some previous dealings with Sheriff Cox myself," he said. "I was in Selma during the marches and I watched the fat bastard beat on a lot of heads. One of them was mine."

"He was doing his job," Bullet Bob said. "You got to leave a man room to do his job. That's something not many do-gooders understand."

"There may be good in him," Lefty said. "But every time it raises its head he takes a whack at it with his nightstick."

"He's changed some." Bullet Bob spoke with his mouth full of baloney. "They even got a colored boy playing for them now."

"The league requires him to have at least one, so he found him a relief pitcher that he'll use every fifth Sunday. If he's changed, he's done it recently. Just two years ago I helped some people down there set up a cooperative like the one we have in Magnolia. About the time they got it working, it burnt down. There was insurance but not enough and quite a few of the people shied away after that. The word was that people's houses would be the next thing to burn. Everybody is pretty well convinced that Bull is a good hand with a match."

"They built that shed theirselves; they probably wired it bad. Nigger-rigged it."

Across the table, Franklin Brown stood up and glared at Bullet Bob.

"Aw hell, Frank," Bullet Bob apologized. "I meant nothing by it. Just a slip of the tongue. It's a saying I growed up hearing." For a second his eyes met Brown's, then moved back down to his sandwiches. "I was raised wrong, I guess." He gave a short laugh at that, but I couldn't tell whether he was laughing at himself for telling the truth or for lying. He had the kind of big, round, unwrinkled face that's hard to take much sense from. I was thinking that him looking away from Brown like he did meant that he was at least a little afraid, but the next thing he said made me doubt that. "Fuck it. I apologized. Why don't you set down now? You're shading my food."

"Go on and sit down, Frank," Lefty said. "That meat'll go bad if he doesn't finish it quickly." Lefty was smiling, but it was his professional smile.

Franklin was probably glad to sit down. I don't mean that he couldn't've whipped Bullet Bob. That would've been easy. Though Turner would've probably just got back up and finished his baloney and beer when he came to. What it was was that Franklin had jumped up too quick over too little and knew it. Still he had to say something. "Man, I don't care what you think. Just try to keep from saying it."

It was Jefferson Mundy, sitting right there by Franklin Brown and every bit as black, that finally poked a hole in the tension. "If he wins some games for us, he can say anything he wants to. Them white mothers won't hit that knuckleball either."

"Can't nobody hit it when it's right." Bullet Bob was as solemn as a foot-washing Baptist talking about the wages of sin.

We ate for a while after that without saying anything. I waited until I'd cleaned my plate before asking Lefty about that co-op he ran in Magnolia.

Dummy Boudreaux, who was sitting at the end of the table nearest the kitchen, scooted his chair back and went in and got three pies off the stove. "Rhubarb," Lefty said. "Dummy and I just got it out of the garden this morning."

Rhubarb makes good pie anyway and Dummy could've made a good one out of horse apples. While we ate the pie, Lefty told me about his co-op.

"We started it with the money I got by suing the college down there for firing me. At first it was just a produce shed where the small farmers could always sell their crops. Most of the farmers that brought produce to us were black, especially in the beginning. We had two big trucks then and we'd haul the food to Shreveport or Dallas and make a good profit on it. But we held that profit back and early in the winter after our first summer of business— that was '71— we notified the people who had been selling to us that we had made a profit that summer and that we were going to have a meeting and turn that profit—all of it—back to them. Most of them came and got their share of the profit and we mailed shares to the ones that didn't come. We told them all that this was a business *they* owned—all of them together. The people who worked at the shed would be paid a decent salary, and the farmers who raised the food would be paid a fair price for it. And whatever profit we made above that would always be divided equally among all of us. We were a genuine farmers' cooperative. The small farmer was dying down there, like he is everywhere. But by banding together they gave themselves a new chance. We own farm equipment in common. Our farmers don't have to mortgage their homes to buy a new tractor or a hay bailer. They can use one of those that belongs to us all."

"It worked, then?" I said. "It's still working?"

"Oh yeah. It works. It wasn't always easy. Not because the idea was ever wrong, but because there were a lot of people down there that didn't like it—businessmen, politicians, preachers—the same gang that always yells communism whenever the poor seriously try to help themselves. We beat them in Magnolia because we stuck together and because the idea we had was simple and right. We have a whole fleet of trucks now and a grocery store and a cannery and a meat-packing house and a couple of years ago we started our own school. None of us are rich, but then nobody ought to be."

I laughed at that, not out of scorn and not because it was wrong, but just because he was so serious about it.

The pie was gone by then and when Lefty paused some of the boys started clearing their dishes off the table and carrying them to the sink in the kitchen. "It's your night to do the dishes," Bullet Bob Turner told me. "The rest of us has all done 'em at least once. You got to take your turn."

That was all right with me. I wouldn't've wanted to make a living at it, but I didn't mind standing my turn. "I hope you got some gentle soap," I said. "I'd hate to get my hands chapped up. The women always seemed to like to have a smooth hand rubbing 'em up."

"Wear gloves," Lefty told me.

"With the dishes or the women?"

"Both."

Lefty leaned against the counter and talked to me while I washed the dishes. The main thing he wanted to tell me was that he was going to start O'Bryan at first base over me in the opening game.

"Fair enough," I told him, rinsing a plate. "All I want's a chance. After four years of getting paid in chits and dreams, just drawing $600 a month will hold me a while and, before long, I'll be your first baseman."

"Well," he said. "I've seen you hit." That had been that day at Oklahoma University. The schoolboys had beat us 6–3. They had this tall, whip-armed left-hander named Snake Teague that struck out fourteen of us, including me once. But the other three times up

I hit two doubles and a home run and drove in all our runs. Though I'd known Lefty was somewhere in the stands and kept looking up there trying to pick him out, I never could. But it wasn't much more than a week later that I got a contract from Lefty.

"Your getting me sprung early will keep you in my good graces a while. And when I start hitting, even O'Bryan will tell you to give me the job."

He looked at me a minute, shook his head once, and said, "We need to find some way to help you rebuild your confidence."

"A good woman would do the trick. I need one I can ride like a racehorse and whip like a runaway slave."

He smiled in spite of himself. "Everybody wants to be loved." He pushed off the counter and started toward the dining room.

He was about to the door when I said, "I was wondering. How come you got fired down at that school in Magnolia?"

He turned around and looked at me and then looked down at his feet and ran his hand back through his hair. "Oh, I led some anti-war marches on campus, disrupted the ROTC parades, did some work for the NAACP. Most places it wouldn't've been enough to get me fired. That was 1969, after all. But in Magnolia, Arkansas, they thought I was Che Guevara. They might've been able to get by with firing me if they'd been smart about it. But they fired me for incompetence, and when I took them to court they had a hard time convincing the judge that it took them fifteen years to discover it."

"You did better in court than I ever did."

"I was a college professor and I managed to get a couple of liberal organizations to go together and hire me a good lawyer—Rotenberg, the one you met today. But still we lost the first round. That was in the Federal District Court in El Dorado. The judge there was an old seg named Oren Hawkins who had spent about thirty years in Congress and then retired to the federal bench. We won in St. Louis, at the Court of Appeals. First time I'd been in St. Louis since I'd quit playing ball."

Well, you ask Lefty a question, you get a damn answer. Too many years of teaching, I guess.

When I finished the dishes, the women still hadn't come back from wherever they were and I thought about going up to my room and reading or playing solitaire or jacking off or whatever it is free men do in their spare time. But I'd spent too much time closed up in a room with my dick in one hand and my heart in the other, so I went out and wandered around the grounds for a while, walked the fencerow like I sometimes used to do with my grandfather when I was a kid living with my mother and her folks on their hill farm just west of Short, Oklahoma.

Blackberry vines clustered along most of the fencerow and wherever the vines died out, shoots of poke salad came up thick through the ground under the rusted barbed wire, down where the birds had shit the seeds. If the trees here hadn't been mostly pine, I might could've actually made myself believe I was back on that upland childhood farm, and when I came to the half-acre garden at the northeast corner of the place, the juices of memory really came undammed. I climbed the hog-wire fence around the garden and then walked up and down the rows. The English peas were up and blooming. The tomato plants had just been set out—the stakes were in the ground, but the plants weren't big enough to tie yet. There was a good stand of string beans, about four or five inches high, planted in the same rows with sweet corn, whose stalks the beans would later climb on. But it was the cucumber plants, barely out of the ground, that I knelt over. I remembered the time—I was about twelve, I think—we harvested a crop of my grandfather's cucumbers and loaded the bushel baskets of them into an old flatbed truck he'd borrowed from one of the neighbors and headed into Fort Smith to sell them at the Farmers' Co-op. They were fine cucumbers, long and dark green, just barely resembling the squat, mushy fuckers the supermarkets are full of now, and the old man was proud of them, as he had a right to be since him and his two mules and his wife had done it all, plowing and planting, fertilizing and hoeing. (He used to joke that my grandmother was the best hoer in Sequoyah County and she'd lean on her hoe a minute and let out that short, high laugh of hers and say, "Now ain't you the card, Luster Grange, ain't you the card?" like maybe it was the first time she'd ever heard him say it.) Anyway, the Co-op wouldn't buy those cucumbers. They had contracts with the riverbottom farmers and didn't want to diddle around with my grandfather's little load. So we drove to the other shed in Fort Smith and to the two in Van Buren and then east to Ozark and then back west again to Alma and north up 71 to Fayetteville, selling a bushel here and there to a grocery or a roadside stand, taking a left on 62 and riding on through Prairie Grove and Lincoln, still stopping and trying but doing it without hope now, doing it only because we were there and had nothing more to lose, then turning south on 59 and back into Oklahoma again, heading home, and in the end, the circle come full, the old truck's one headlight guiding us through the midsummer darkness, we stopped at neighbors' houses and gave the crop away except for the few bushels we threw over into our hog pen. We hadn't talked during the last part of our ride, but when we'd finished dumping all the cucumbers, the old man leaned against a corner post and said, "It's a good year for cucumbers and maybe hogs, but it's hell on truck farmers."

It was as close as he ever came to figuring out the market, though he managed to hold on to that place and scratch a living off it until his back went out on him about six years later. He didn't have either the money or the insurance to fix it, so he pulled a rocking chair up next to his empty fireplace and sat down and looked into the ashes and slowly wiped the last thirty years out of his mind. He died there, rocking in his youth, an idiot. And I could've had the farm then and the damn cucumbers and hogs, but I wanted another way and easier money and so hustled my ass to the pen.

I stood up and looked down the rows again and tried to figure what my grandfather would've thought about what Lefty'd done down in Magnolia. The old man thought a person ought to stand on his own two feet and so he shied away from organizations, especially ones that anybody, right or wrong, might call Communist, but I think he might've sold that load of cucumbers to Lefty and then knocked the living shit out of anybody that didn't like it. It's damn sure what he ought to've done. I decided then and there that if Lefty was doing what he said he was doing with that outfit in Magnolia, it was something simple and important and right. And what that thought made me do was wonder why he was here now wasting his time with a baseball team.

It was way past dark by the time I quit mooning around over them cucumbers. And I might've stayed out there till morning if I hadn't heard the car pull up in the driveway. I thought it must be the women coming home, so I hurried to the house and went in the back door. Several of the boys were in the big living room drinking beer and listening to Woodrow Ratliff play his guitar and sing. I just got sat down good when the women came through the front door. Bobbie Sampson was the first one through. She was wearing jeans and cowboy boots and a blue work shirt and looked like she might've come as close as anybody there except me to giving Eversole a good match. I'd been prepared for a full-blood dyke and she looked the part. But I judged the two that came in behind her to be prime pieces. Pansy Puckett, the older one, around thirty, the fallen cheerleader, was a light-haired woman that had on a short skirt and a knit top and looked like she'd had so many good times they'd started running into bad. I pegged her for the kind of woman that could make six inches of old cock feel like Aaron's rod. She did look a little worn, but that might've been because she was standing beside as choice a slit as I'd ever laid my calculating eyes on. Susan Pankhurst was tall and long-legged and blond-headed and had eyes the color of Colorado sky: Hitler would've made her his poster girl. She wore a Saint Louis Cardinal T-shirt, gym shorts, and a pair of running shoes. When He finished putting this one together and stepped back to take His first good look at the finished product, the Lord must've given some consideration to repeating His Virgin Mary Act. And I might've hopped her myself then and there if four years of self-abuse hadn't taken so much of the spring out of my legs.

They had a spic reliever with them. He was carrying a suitcase in one hand and dragging a duffel bag with the other. His name was Gonzalo Pinzon and he was tall and had dancer's muscles and was handsome if you don't mind light brown. His clothes were cheap and loud, the kind a color-blind half-wit might wear. Tight orange pants, shiny, pointy-toed black loafers with little silver bells over the insteps, and an imitation-silk palm-trees-against-an-ocean-sunset shirt. His suitcase had a sticker across one side of it that said: "Castro Blew It."

"They found me," he told Lefty, and showed us a perfect set of teeth. He let go of both the grip and the bag and sat on the floor by them.

"Carney?" Lefty asked.

"No. Well, yes. But he sent another man after me. Cesar Ratoplan. Vice president in charge of personnel for Elysian Land Development. He was waiting outside the park this afternoon. I ate dinner with him. He paid. Shrimp at Confederate's Landing. He tried to make me go back." He spoke without an accent, but his voice was a little musical and his hands did a slow dance while he talked, a dance done for its own sake, a dance which took your attention away from the words—or their meanings anyway. He was drunk.

"He must've been pleased by the way you dressed up for the occasion," Lefty said.

" 'You're disgracing yourself and your kind,' Ratoplan says to me. I used to wear this costume to the office sometimes so they'd send me home. 'You can't sell real estate looking like an idiot,' my stepfather would say. 'We need to attract the lower classes,' I'd tell him. 'No. We must be an example to them,' was his answer. He loved to talk about the moral obligations of a businessman. I need a drink."

Nobody jumped to get him one. "Everybody loves a drunk," Pinzon said. He went to the refrigerator and came back with a quart of Turner's Coors. "Salty beer. Brewed from the purest Mexican blood." He held the bottle out at arm's length and said, "To a free Cuba. Down with Fidel Castro. Up with G. Harold Carney and Cesar Ratoplan." He put the bottle to his lips and turned it up. Beer ran down his chin and neck and watered the palms on his shirt.

For a minute it looked like he was going to fall over. Lefty got up and offered to show him to his room. But about the time Lefty got to him, Pinzon rallied and roared off again.

" 'Fuck it,' I told Ratoplan. 'I'm not going back. You can have Miami. Cut it up and sell it over and over again.' Ratoplan watched me get drunk on Cuba libras. He left that place but not the town. He knows where I was staying. That's why I've got to stay here." He turned and spoke directly to Lefty, who was standing just a couple of feet from him then. "Don't let him in. Always wears a three-piece suit with a flag in the lapel. Oils his words. Says he won't leave town until he can take me with him. Bastard'll be at the game. Hates baseball." He turned his face away from Lefty and looked across the room at me. "You know Castro was a pitcher? Medium speed, fair curve. Dime a dozen."

I decided he might be worse than drunk—he might be crazy. But I went along. "At his age," I said, "he ought to develop a trick pitch. A knuckleball or a fork ball or something."

"Won't do it," Pinzon told me. "Still thinks he's a flamethrower." He laughed way too long and hard at that. Then he faltered again. His head sagged and his legs went limp on him. Lefty reached over and kept him from going all the way down.

"Been going too long," Pinzon said. "Got to crash." But he wasn't quite ready to give it up. He told Bobbie Sampson he was sorry he'd caused them to miss the fish fight.

"We were leaving anyway. The men were pawing Susan."

He looked at Susan. "No wonder," he said. He took another drink of the Coors and handed the bottle to Lefty. He waved a slow hand at us. "See you at the game, boys. Let's win one for old Ponce de Leon. I'm going to go up and tidy my room and pass out." But then he caught another wave and started rolling again. "Beware, my friends, of Ratoplan. A vicious bastard. A well-tailored scumbag. A credit to his race. *Viva la raza.* Beat Selma. It's us against them and they're everywhere. Do we have gunports in our rooms? Pray for Sergeant Fulgencio Batista, alone in Spain, Franco dead. Hand me the bottle, man. The night is young and my heart is full." Lefty held on to the bottle and Pinzon went on without it. "We are but columns of blood. The game's the thing. It's all a dream. Let's play our hearts out, comrades. It's all that matters. I have seen the night and it is black. The sun is sinking over Miami. You cannot see the sky for the planes. What is the price of land here? Is property theft? Love the earth, throw the hard one up and in, the curve down and away. That is all I know and all I need to know. For, lo!, the magic man is shooting smack in Yucatan. And there is no plan but Ratoplan."

He could've went on a while as far as I was concerned. I was enjoying it. But that was as far as he could go then. Lefty took him by the arm and said, "Come on, Gonzalo. There's a game tomorrow. You might have to pitch."

Pinzon said, "Bless you, pure heart," and followed him away. Susan Pankhurst picked up Pinzon's suitcase and duffel bag and started after them. "I'll help you with that," I said.

"I can handle it. Anyway, I need to talk to Lefty."

I let her go and went over and joined Pansy Puckett on the couch. I gave her my Jack Nicholson grin, the one that says what I do may not be right but it ought to be fun. "Don't I know you from somewhere? What's a nice girl like you doing in a place like this? You have an interesting face. Intelligent eyes. Do you believe in the equality of the sexes? Could I have the honor of being your escort to the slammer ball?" I guess I was inspired by Pinzon's manic rant. But I had sense enough to keep my voice down, just leaned over and whispered absurdities to her.

She gave me a nervous smile. "You're the one from, uh, Mc-Alester?"

"Yes, ma'am," I said. "Hog Durham, armed robber, freed at last, at your service. Armed and dangerous."

"You look safe to me."

I didn't remember anybody telling me that before and I felt like I'd been insulted. "Vasectomy, 1975," I told her, and put a look of mock sorrow on my face.

"I haven't heard that line in quite a while." She let me get a good look at her eyes. They were green and friendly. She painted around them. "I bet you've got kids scattered all over Oklahoma." She touched my arm. Soft, gentle woman fingers. I almost asked her to go upstairs with me right then.

"Maybe. But if I do, the youngest one has to be going on four years old."

Across the room, Jew Bernstein, a left-fielder, asked Bobbie Sampson where she'd found Pinzon. "The Tank," she said. "Susan and Pansy hadn't either one ever been there. They'd heard me talk about the fish and wanted to see the place, so when I got through working on the bus this afternoon I took them into town. We ate some barbecue at Hoot's and took Pansy out to the mall to buy a watch and it was still way too early to go to The Tank, but the girls were anxious so we went on anyway. Gonzalo was in there and already acting crazy. I'd seen him at the park and knew he was on the team even though he wasn't living here. I saw I'd better get him out of there before he landed in jail or got hisself killed. And anyway, there were a couple of guys there that started grabbing on Susan as soon as she walked in, her not having on any more clothes than she does. In fact, that's what finally convinced Gonzalo. He wouldn't listen to me, but when I got Susan to ask him to come with us he went right along. We were just going to take him home, but he said his place wasn't safe any more. He didn't even go into the place when we took him there—it was an old duplex on Battery Street. Had his bags packed and under a shrub in the backyard. He had me drive down the alley and then stop a couple of houses down from his place. He snuck back like a thief and got the bags. Then he ranted and raved all the way here. Kept talking about his stepfather and Castro and that woman who's going to swim to Cuba again. It was hard to make sense out of any of it."

Lefty had come back downstairs about halfway through Bobbie's spiel. He stood in the doorway until she finished it. Then he said, "He'll be fine now." He came over to the couch and sat on the other side of Pansy. "Play us something, Woodrow. Your guitar's gathering dust."

Ratliff played "It Ain't God That Made Honky-Tonk Angels" and it would've made Kitty Wells proud to hear him. I knew the words and had a woman beside me to serenade, so I sang along with him. And I thought about all the slammer nights when me and old Shakespeare Creel filled that last hour before lights-out with hillbilly songs. We would sit on the edge of that bottom bunk—his—and he'd pick his guitar and I'd either blow my mouth harp or just sing. And when it was right we'd forget where we were and how we got there and just be two men and the song. It would take their damn bell and a half-wit guard to jerk us back into time. And I can remember laying there in the dark thinking that that hour out of time was the best you could expect. There is no salvation, just relief. Nothing is ever all the time.

Bullet Bob Turner was thinking too, but it wasn't about music—though he could've had a honky-tonk angel or two flapping around way back in his mind. He was wondering about time though. Pansy Puckett looked at her new watch and told him it was 8:34.

"It ain't too late yet for them fish," Bullet Bob said. "They don't start it till about ten. I got 'em timed." He took his quart from between his legs and stood up out of the rocking chair. "Anybody want to ride in with me and get rich?"

Nobody did.

"To hell with you then. I'll go upstairs and get Stump and Joe Buck."

While Turner was upstairs, I got Bobbie Sampson to tell me what it was they did at The Tank. It was a riverside dive in Little Rock and every Wednesday night at ten the bartender there took a fat goldfish out of its aquarium and dropped it into one with a big hungry piranha. The drunks bet big money on just how long it would take the piranha to finish off the goldfish. The odds changed with every bite.

Jew Bernstein said, "Bob'll go there and blow whatever's left of that big-league pension check that keeps him in beer and gambling money. He's a damn idiot, but he's still got that knuckleball."

"The simple life. You can't beat it," I said. I figured next chance I got I'd be down at The Tank throwing my money at them fish too. But not that night. I needed me a good woman bad.

I guess explaining The Tank to me made Bobbie want to go back, because when Bullet Bob came down with the two catchers, she asked if she could go with them.

"I ain't particular," Turner told her.

"That's no shit," Stump Guthrie agreed.

They headed for the door. Lefty said, "The game's at two tomorrow, remember. We need to be there by noon at the latest."

Bullet Bob turned around and said, "I thought we was free men."

"You are. But we might need you to pitch tomorrow."

"My butterfly works best when it's got a hangover," Turner said, and he and Stump Guthrie went on out the door.

Bobbie Sampson looked at Lefty and shrugged and then followed them out. But Joe Buck Cantwell hung back a minute and said, "I'll keep an eye on him."

"I don't care how drunk he gets," Lefty said. "He can pitch hungover. He did it for years. Just keep him out of trouble."

Cantwell nodded and walked into the night.

Things went pretty easy after that. We sat around and drank a little beer and Pansy drank some rosé wine and listened to Ratliff pick and sing. He knew a shitload of Woody Guthrie songs and I got him to do "The Ballad of Pretty Boy Floyd." About half an hour after Turner and the others left, Julius and Susan came downstairs together, looking right pleased with one another. They went down to the far end of the room and sat on the carpet next to the easy chair Dummy Boudreaux was in. Dummy offered her the chair, but she turned him down. He seemed happy to have two such fine-looking, well-nourished young folks sitting beside him.

And they did look like they belonged in a magazine or on the cover of one of them trash romances the Baptist women get their kicks out of in beauty shops. The tall, long-muscled, raven-haired buck and the golden-haired, ivory-skinned, turquoise-eyed maiden. I decided they'd been screwing—or if they hadn't yet, they would be soon. And God knows I envied the Cherokee bastard. She looked like the kind you'd want to stay inside of forever.

And what made it worse was that Pansy seemed to be hot for Lefty. She kept talking to him with a kind of moonstruck cheer-leader voice about the team and about his work. I had decided earlier that my best shot that night would be with Pansy—Susan being the kind, I figured, a man like me either had to work his way up to or jump on the spot. But now I was beginning to think I had no shot at all—one of the women being an Indian lover and the other a stump freak.

What was still giving me hope was that Lefty didn't seem much interested in her—not in the way I was, I mean. Maybe he'd had her and didn't want any more, or maybe he just didn't care for cheerleaders, or maybe—and I figured then that this was the maybe closest to truth—he wanted to stay above this kind of car-rying on—a Puritan without a God. But whatever his reasons, he made it clear—to me, if not to Pansy—that he didn't intend to enter the bareback riding event that night. He talked to her, an-swered her questions politely enough, but I could see him pull away when she touched him, almost flinching sometimes, espe-cially when she laid hand to his stump. And after a while she was laying her palm on his poor parody of an arm every time she spoke to him. She did it gently and let him move away from it, but still I thought it might be her way of punishing him for not paying her the right kind of attention. So I waited and smiled and kept pour-ing her glasses of that rosé she seemed to like so much.

Ratliff had gotten down to playing the songs he liked best, old union songs—"Union Maid," "1913 Massacre," "The Ballad of Joe Hill," "Solidarity Forever," "The Ludlow Massacre," and suchlike. Not exactly courting music. I thought about going up and getting my mouth harp and maybe blowing some kind of hard-up lover tune to show Miss Pansy my soul, but I was afraid she might be gone when I got back and my soul would be all I'd have to see me through the night. And I'd already spent too much time alone with that son of a bitch.

Patience paid off for once. About ten-thirty Lefty stood and stretched and said, "Old fielders never die; they just drift out of the park."

"And old radicals have to get their sleep. Otherwise they'll drift into liberalism," Jew Bernstein kidded him.

Lefty laughed a little at that and said, "The Lord looks after drunks and children, but we agitators have to look after ourselves."

He walked out of the living room and into the dining room. Without saying a word to Julius or anybody else, Susan Pankhurst got up off the floor and followed him. It was the second time he'd left the room that night and the second time she'd followed him. She caught up with him at the foot of the stairs. I could hear talking but couldn't make out words. My first thought was that maybe they were making plans for later in the night and that maybe that was why he hadn't been any more than polite to Pansy Puckett. Now, of course, if I'd've taken the time to clear my head and think straight about it, I'd've seen better than that even then, might've even figured out what it really was Susan and Lefty were talking about. But my mind had a coat of backed-up jizz over it then and the world looked kind of come-stained to me. Hell, seeing all the attention Lefty was getting from them women made me wonder if I hadn't overprized my left arm all my life.

"Let's have one more round and call in the dogs," Jew Bernstein said.

I went into the kitchen after the drinks, hoping to overhear some of Susan and Lefty's talk. But all I got was the end of it.

"That's fair enough," she told him. "I'll be ready. All I ask is a chance."

That should've told me right there what they were talking about, but it didn't. She had her back to me. I had my eye on her ass. It wasn't a bad way to look at the world.

"You'll get that chance," Lefty said to her, and gave her a father's smile. Then he looked over at me. "Enjoy yourself tonight, Hog."

He was on his way up the stairs before I took my eyes off Susan and started trying to think of an answer. But what he said and the way he said it convinced me that my drought was going to end that night. I asked Susan if she wanted a beer. "We're just going to have one more."

"I'll share one with Julius."

I brought the beers in and then took Pansy's glass back and gave it another squeeze of the grape. Before I sat down again I picked my beer up and held it out in front of me like Pinzon had done and said, "Here's to old Babe Ruth and all the women that loved him."

After we drank to that, Bernstein got up and made a toast of his own. "Here's to Sandy Koufax, who wouldn't pitch a World Series game on Yom Kippur."

Then it was a game everybody had to play.

"To Big Chief Allie Reynolds, who cut down many a paleface," Julius Common Deer said. "And to Johnny Bench, the half-breed from Binger."

"To Satchel Paige and Cool Papa Bell and Josh Gibson and all those who weren't allowed through the front door and to Jackie Robinson, who came through it with his spikes high," Woodrow Ratliff said.

"To Babe Didrikson Zaharias and all those who might've made it if they'd seen a chance," Susan Pankhurst said.

"And here's to the Arkansas Reds," said Pansy Puckett, the old cheerleader resurrected in her. "May they tear the Dixie Association apart."

"Amen, sister," I said.

Dummy Boudreaux hadn't been drinking with us—I guess because he couldn't hear what we were drinking to. But when we'd all had our say, he stood and put the bottle to his mouth and sucked it dry. He did it so fast it seemed like a trick—the bottle full one second, empty the next. Then he gave us a nod and a grin and left. Maybe it was his way of toasting Dummy Hoy and Dummy Taylor and all the guys that played but never heard the applause. But whyever he did it, he did it in high style. I'd only seen one other man that could kill a beer like that, a guy named Tugboat Sidebottom that used to win bets doing it at the Branding Iron in Fort Smith. And, Lord God, old Tugboat must've weighed 500 pounds—took his baths in Lee Creek and his showers in the damn Robo-wash. But Dummy was a normal-sized man, not near as big as me.

"Christ," I said, "I could take that deaf son of a bitch in a bar and make both of us rich."

"That's nothing," Pansy told me. "He can do it with a quart."

"He does it when he's feeling good, as a tribute to the company," Jew Bernstein said.

We finished our beers and the four of us men started carrying empties into the kitchen. We stood around the refrigerator a minute and talked about the next day's game. Ratliff and Bernstein were more curious about the reaction of the people of Little Rock than about what might happen in the game itself. Would we draw a crowd? Would they support us? Would the demonstrators be there early trying to stop us from getting through the gate?

"Once it starts," I said, "it'll be just like any other game. The game takes over. It's outside of time."

"I don't know," Ratliff said. "Ours may be different." But he looked a little surprised that I'd said something that might be taken as philosophical.

Susan Pankhurst came into the dining room, waved good night to us, and went upstairs.

"God can do wondrous things with Gentiles," Jew Bernstein said.

"He must've let Solomon help him with that one," I said.

I didn't want Pansy to think I'd forgotten her, so I started back toward the living room. Ratliff and Bernstein followed me to where the stairs came down into the dining room. Ratliff said, "I guess I'll go sing myself to sleep."

"Not too loud," Bernstein joked. "It's hard for me to sleep with those massacres going on."

I stood at the foot of the stairs a minute figuring Julius surely had sense enough to clear out with them. But he had something to say first.

"Be careful," he whispered. "She's looking for a husband."

I laughed at him. But when I talked I whispered too. "Shit, Julius, she's like me. She just takes it a night at a time. Why else would she be in there waiting?"

"You got it all figured out, don't you?" There was an edge in his voice. "And maybe you're right. But I think she's getting tired of having to take it the way you want to give it to her."

"One more night of it won't hurt her."

She was still sitting there in the middle of the couch when I went back in to her. "I should've gone up with Susan," she said. And her eyes filled with a sadness that came close to pity. But I couldn't tell if it was for her or for me or for us both.

I stood in the middle of the room, looming over her. "Do you know how long it's been since I was alone in a room with a woman?"

"Yes," she said. "I know." She tried to smile, but it just kind of scarred up the sadness. I thought maybe she was putting on an act.

"Would you like some more wine?"

"No. I don't need that."

I took a step toward her.

"No," she said. "Wait."

"Let's take a walk. I'll tell you a story. I won't hurt you. Won't touch you if you don't want me to." I wasn't sure how long I could keep a fool promise like that, but I didn't want to spend the night standing in the middle of that room.

We walked together through the dining room and then the kitchen and went out the back door. The moon was nearly full and I found the way without any trouble. I didn't touch her until I lifted her over the fence into the garden. In that light I could see curiosity on her face and maybe a little fear but not the sadness anymore. I led her by the hand over to the cucumber hills and told her that story about my grandfather. About halfway through it she took her hand out of mine and put her arm around my waist. And then I put mine around her, trying not to seem urgent about it, trying not to let the nearness of her upset the flow of my story, which was working so well.

When I finished it, she stood quiet long enough for me to start thinking about my next move, which wouldn't've been nearly as smooth as that last one. But just before I came on, she looked up at me and said, "I guess I ought to tell you one now."

"If you want to." But I was hoping we wouldn't spend the night trading stories.

"I was raised in El Dorado. My daddy drove a truck for Murphy Oil and after me and my brother Jimbo were both in school Momma got a job as a checker at the Piggly Wiggly store. They told me and him all the time we were growing up how they wanted something better for us, how they wanted us to get an education and live a different kind of life from theirs. Jimbo was three years older than me and played ball all the way through school and was pretty good at it but not good enough to do anything with it after high school. And he wasn't interested in going to college if he couldn't play ball there." She stopped there and said, "Lord, I'm just going on."

"Go on some more. I want to hear the end of it." The end of it, of course, is exactly what I wanted to hear. "You're doing fine. It's not right to quit right in the middle of it."

I guess she wanted to be sure I was at least interested enough to listen to her story all the way through, because she went on then and finished it without another break.

"Well, anyway, Jimbo joined the Marines right after high school and right after he got out of boot camp they sent him to Vietnam.

That was in October of 1967. I was in my senior year of high school. He got killed in January of 1968 at a place called Khe Sanh. A little sliver of metal went through his heart. They sent us the body and a bunch of those medals they gave you for getting killed. Daddy and Momma buried the body and hung the medals up on the wall and then just closed up. Went to work and came home and shut the hurt inside themselves and the hurt was so big it ate up everything else. They looked a little bit older every evening when I came home from school.

"I was head cheerleader then and going with this guy named Garland Sagely, who had been the quarterback on the football team, and he'd take me parking out on a salt flat just off Highway 7 between El Dorado and Smackover. We'd make out for a while, but I'd always start crying about Jimbo and make Garland take me home before he got what he wanted. I think now that Garland was the kind that things came too easy for, girls and sports and everything. His daddy was a lawyer and Garland had a big white Thunderbird he drove around town in. Anyway, he took my crying for three or four weeks and then didn't see me again for a while after that. Even at school he'd just pass me in the halls without saying anything and he moved away from me in the classes we had together. But then one Wednesday night in April he came by the house about suppertime and asked me if I wanted to go for a ride. I went because I liked Garland—or thought I did—and because I felt kind of bad about the way I'd carried on with him and because everything was dead in that house and I was afraid that if I didn't do something I was going to be dead too. He took me straight out to the salt flats and that time I didn't stop him, didn't cry that time until it was over. He put his pants back on and drug me into that Thunderbird and drove me back toward home. I slumped down naked in that red bucket seat and held my clothes up to my face and sobbed. Just before we got back to town he turned off on a dirt road and drove down it a ways and got me out and took me again right there by the side of the road just a little before dark. And that second time it was the other way around—I cried until he finished with me and then stopped. I put my clothes back on finally and got back in the car because there wasn't anything more he could do to me and I sat up stiff-backed and straight-necked and hard all the way home. And it was him that was crying then, saying he was sorry and that he'd lost control and that he wasn't really that way.

But I knew he wouldn't ever come back again and that I'd just be a story he'd tell, laughing probably. And so I made myself not care about any of them. And it was a long time before I let myself care enough about anything or anybody to cry again or to say no. Because nothing mattered to me and sometimes the men felt good for a minute or two and if they didn't that didn't matter either."

If I'd been in my right mind I'd've just led her up to her room and let her be. A sensible woman wouldn't tell such a story to a stranger, especially one that had just got out of the pen. But I guess I was feeling a little like Garland Sagely must've felt—this was one night that wasn't going to go by without me getting laid. And sometimes your right mind isn't the best place to be anyway. So I went down to my knees and pulled her down with me—she didn't resist, it wasn't like I had to force her—and I looked at her and she was dry-eyed—still beyond crying, maybe—and I said, "Well, don't say no now. Jimbo's gone past any recalling and Garland Sagely right now is probably sleeping next to a wife he can't stand in a big house he bought with shyster money. And so it's just me and you and the darkness left and all the light there's going to be is what we can make on our own."

"I don't want it not to happen. I just want it to matter."

"It matters." And God knows that was the truth. But what I'd thought was going to be an easy piece had turned out to be something else. I wasn't quite sure what yet, just knew that since the piece was still there, I'd still take it. I'd deal with the other later—when I had to.

She put her arms around me and brought her face next to mine. "You talk nice for a criminal," she said. And if there was sadness in her voice I couldn't hear it any more.

"In the slam," I told her, "you either learn to talk or shut up. I wasn't in long enough to learn the hard lesson."

"Shut up," she said.

We lay down together on the cool, damp earth. And we made music that night, Miss Pansy and I, played several renditions of the old song that has made and ruined many a fine musician, the one that Shakespeare Creel used to call Adam's *Unfinished Concerto for Two Strangers*.

Part II

7

There must've been over 3,000 people inside the park for the opening day game—I have to guess because Lefty didn't count heads—and probably another couple of hundred outside with their placards and their hymns. And I imagine that a lot of the ones inside were still waiting to hear the national anthem when Jeremiah Eversole started the season with the pitch that had been illegal in baseball since the last time Burleigh Grimes threw it. It came in hard and dropped at the last instant like a silver dollar in a slot machine. The Selma Americans had their kid shortstop, Jimmy Stennis, leading off and he stepped toward the pitch in good shape, started his bat, then, seeing the break too late, tried to check his swing. But failed. Strike one.

I was sitting in our dugout between Lefty Marks and Joe Buck Cantwell, who wasn't catching because of a little bruise on the elbow of his throwing arm. "There ain't been a game here in two years and the bastard starts it off with a spitter," Cantwell said.

"He just knows the one way," Lefty said.

Eversole's second pitch tailed toward the kid's chin. Stennis leaned in and then jerked back so hard he fell on his surprised young ass. He got up slow and took his time dusting himself off before venturing back into the box, time enough maybe to pray for a straight fastball or an honest curve. Eversole just stood out there with his foot on the rubber and waited. He wasn't going to be fazed by any prayer that kid knew. Stennis didn't have a saint's chance at a political convention. He swung hard at two more good spitters without coming within a foot of either of them. Pissed off, embarrassed, and fired up by the sounds of the holy rollers outside, the kid yelled "Goddam Communist" at Eversole, who didn't blink an eye, though communism, being a white man's scam, was probably as alien to him as any other doctrine.

"Go back to Momma, kid. Tell her they don't play fair in Little Rock," Cantwell jeered at Stennis.

"They think that kid's a good prospect," Lefty told him. "They think he'll be in the big time in two or three years. He may be one of the few that gets out of Selma."

"You couldn't tell it by the way he looked against Eversole," Cantwell said.

"He probably won't be able to hit Eversole in five years, when he's twenty-six and Eversole's fifty-one. But that won't matter. The kid'll be making more a year than Eversole's made in his life."

Cantwell laughed. "Life ain't fair, is it, Lefty?"

"Not yet." And Lefty said it without laughing.

I leaned back and finished the hot dog I'd made myself while I was working the grill. We didn't charge admission, but we sold food and drinks—hot dogs and hamburgers, popcorn and peanuts, cokes and beer. Lefty wasn't the first person who figured out that the secret to getting by in the minors is to get people into the park even if you have to let them in free. If you get enough of them in, you can make good money just selling them beer. Hell, that's how bars stay in business. And we sold the stuff ourselves, stood in the concession stands in our uniforms and steamed the dogs and grilled the burgers and drew the drinks and took the money. Pansy and Susan and Bobbie stayed there all through the game and some of the players that weren't in the game at a particular time helped them out. And before the game we watered the dirt part of the infield ourselves and rolled the chalk down on the foul lines and around the batter's box. And there would be times that year when the rain would come and the whole bunch of us, the ones in the game and the ones on the bench, would grab the tarp and cover the infield. It was a fair enough system, I guess, considering we had a few guys that were better groundkeepers than ball-players.

Eversole wasn't one of them, though. And sitting on the bench marveling at him, I wondered how he fit into Lefty's system. He should've been pitching in the big leagues, but according to Lefty, they didn't like his general attitude and after he cold-cocked his manager and two of his coaches in a bar fight after a game at Indianapolis, the bosses blacklisted him. But still he'd been pitching in

Mexico and had to've been making more down there than he was here. Somehow Eversole must've let himself be convinced that by helping Lefty he'd be taking a kind of revenge against the system that had shut him out.

I'm sure the boys from Selma were wishing Eversole had been pitching anywhere that day but Little Rock. Their second hitter, little Punch Lurleen, who had led the league in hitting a couple of years earlier, got his bat sawed off in his hands by Eversole's in-shooting fastball and just stood at the plate looking like a Mormon at a freaker's ball while Eversole picked up the slow roller—which hadn't gone near as far as the fat end of Lurleen's bat—and threw him out at first.

Next up was their first baseman, Axe Heflin, a big, red-faced rawboned free-swinger. He took a spitter for a strike and then hung in tough against that fastball and so took it in the ribs. He let out a yelp that sounded more like it came from a faggot auctioneer than from the tough Klansman he was supposed to be. But then he got his voice under control and snarled and threw down his bat and started toward the mound. He didn't take but a couple of steps though before he realized that if he was going after Eversole he ought to've taken the bat with him. Even then I'd've bet that Eversole would've jammed that bat fat-end-first up Heflin's ass and spun him around on it. Something like that must've entered Heflin's mind too, because he came to his senses and trotted down to first, growling and holding his ribs. Selma's trainer came out on the field and sprayed some painkiller on the bruise.

Cantwell said, "That lunatic Indian's liable to get us in a fight or two before the season's out."

"Maybe not," Lefty said. "You notice Heflin backed off. I don't think he's in the habit of that."

"They'll just take it out on the rest of us. Somebody's liable to just turn around and club me or Stump over the head with the bat. Course, unless they was a low-ball hitter they'd miss Stump."

Pick Maddox was batting cleanup for the Americans, and Eversole's first pitch to him was another high, tight, hard one. Though it didn't look like it missed the corner by more than two or three inches, Maddox jumped away from it like it was a hand grenade. That brought old Bull Cox out of the Selma dugout to discuss the situation with the umpire.

The dugouts weren't more than fifty feet from home plate and

we were sitting close to the home plate end of ours and anyway
Bull had the kind of voice that carried. We didn't have to strain to
hear him. "You need to tell the son of a bitch that killing ain't
legal in American baseball."

"That last one wasn't much off the plate, Bull." The umpire
wasn't near as loud as Cox, but I could make out what he was saying.

"I guess old Pick was just practicing his steps in case the ballet
comes to town." And Bull did a little jig to show what he meant.

"I can't say what he was doing. I'm not a batting coach."

Most of the fans were standing by then and jeering at Bull. He
seemed to enjoy it. I figured he was one of those guys that stayed in
the game because he loved to put on a show and a baseball diamond was the only stage anybody would let him on any more. He
turned to the crowd, showed them his tobacco teeth, and tipped
his cap. When he turned back around to the umpire, he said, "This
place has been going to shit ever since they elected a Rockefeller."

"Sit down now, Bull," the umpire told him. "You've put on your
show."

"Somebody's got to try to entertain these folks. They ain't had
no fun since Eisenhower sicced the army on them." The voice was
lower now but still loud enough for me to hear. Then Bull jerked
the smile off his face and set his jowls. "But I come out here on
business too. If you ain't up to keeping that half-breed from taking
my boys' heads off, maybe I can figure something out for myself."
He looked over at our dugout then and wagged a finger at Lefty,
who responded with the two-fingered sign that can mean either
peace or victory. Bull used a slow swagger to get him back to his
dugout. Just before he sank back down out of their sight, he lifted
his cap to the fans again. It brought him a round of applause.

"Goddam," Lefty said. "I'm losing this crowd to a man who believes in apartheid."

But Eversole started winning them back for him right quick. He
struck Pick Maddox out on three spitters that came down like the
law on a poor man.

We didn't have any regular base coaches, of course. It was another thing we took turns about doing. During this game Speck
Anderson, a utility infielder, took third and Bullet Bob Turner got
first. Turner looked like he'd jumped into that tank with them fish
the night before, but he waddled out to first eagerly, probably fi-

guring he was doing the fans a favor by giving them a gander at an old big-league veteran like himself. Some of them did recognize him and he got a little hand. He gave them his half-wit hero's grin and a fat man's bow and then joked around first base with Axe Heflin.

In our dugout Stump Guthrie was bitching to Joe Buck Cantwell. "From now on you catch him. I don't give a shit about that little bruise on your elbow. It's awful funny you got it the night before you were supposed to catch Eversole. The cocksucker. I give him a signal, he nods, then throws whatever the hell he wants to. It ain't worth it." He talked in a semi-whisper, making sure Eversole didn't hear him.

Lefty and Cantwell and Stump and I all looked down to the far end of the bench where Eversole was sitting. On his big round face he wore a scowl that looked like part of his inheritance. Nobody sat within five feet of him.

"He looks like he might be considering taking up cannibalism," Stump Guthrie said.

"Just go down there and explain the situation to him," I joked to Stump. "If he don't like it, punch his face in." A wise man would've put good money on Eversole pinning both Jacob and the angel.

"I'll just cut my throat instead. It'd be easier on me," Stump said.

"Hell, Stump, you can catch him," Lefty said. "You just have to get yourself ready. If we're going to take him out for not communicating, we might as well cut him, period. You can handle him. It's not like he has all that many pitches. He just throws the shave and the shower."

"You don't have to take *him* out. Take *me* out."

"I'll talk to him," Lefty said. "And Joe Buck can catch the last couple of innings if you're still wanting out. Just thank God all you have to do is catch Eversole. Pity the poor bastards having to try to stand in and hit him." He went down and sat next to Eversole and talked to him for a couple of minutes. I saw the big man nod a time or two. But then Stump had said he'd nodded at him too.

While that was going on, Jefferson Mundy, our lead-off hitter, dodged two fastballs thrown at his shins. I recognized the strategy from when I was a kid. I used to play for a Babe Ruth team, Stout Realty in Fort Smith, where the coach, one of those guys that claimed he would've made the majors if he hadn't hurt his arm in the service, would tell our pitchers to shake up a white man by throwing at his head and a nigger by going for his shins. It seemed clear that Bull and his Americans believed in the old ways.

But the third pitch to Mundy was out over the plate and he hit a rope to the right-fielder.

"Good lick," Lefty told him when he came back.

"Shit," Mundy said.

Stump Guthrie, who I guess had resigned himself to a night of misery, leaned forward and spit a gob of juice from his twist onto the dugout steps. "I wonder what kind of league they got down there in Mexico that would put up with that maniac for twenty years."

"The boys I knew that played in it said it was bang up, Stump," Cantwell told him. "They know how to keep a heathen like Eversole in his place. But up here we're obliged to treat him like a human being." After he spoke Cantwell took off his cap and scratched his bald head.

"It may be a bad mistake," Stump concluded.

Just past us, in the home plate corner of the dugout, Jefferson Mundy commenced to thrash the water cooler.

Lefty walked over to him. "You keep hitting line drives and most of them will fall in. You keep kicking coolers and you'll be back down in Magnolia overhearing people say you had the talent to make it but not the sense."

"I wanted that first one," Mundy said. But he let the cooler be.

The kid was just nineteen and hadn't made enough outs yet to get used to it. He and Atticus Flood and Franklin Brown had carried the Colombia County Co-op team that Lefty had coached to a pair of Arkansas high school championships. And that's why the three of them, who were all genuine prospects, ended up on the Reds.

Jew Bernstein fouled to first for the second out.

Atticus Flood, who Lefty had batting third, fouled a pitch off his hands and then like to've ruptured himself missing a change-up.

"He guesses too much," Cantwell said.

"Sometimes he guesses right," Lefty said. "And he's going to see a lot of fastballs hitting in front of Smith." What he was saying was that when they got behind Flood most pitchers would feed him fastballs rather than risk walking him and having to face Rainbow

Smith with a man on. And what I figured was that when I got into the lineup I'd be batting third and fattening up on them fastballs.

Then Flood stepped into an outside fastball—one that you can bet your sister's cherry that Jigs Thurmond, the Selma left-hander, meant to waste—and sent it into the gap in right-center. The ball took a Mexican hop off the fence and by the time the Americans got it back into the infield, Flood was standing on third.

"And he can run," Lefty told Cantwell through a smile.

But that was it for a while. Rainbow Smith reached a little for one of Thurmond's curves and flied to straightaway center. It was as close as either team came to scoring until the seventh.

Lefty spent most of the middle innings up in the stands passing out programs—he called them manifestos—and jawing with the fans. I wandered up there a time or two myself. Sold some dogs and brew and kept an eye out for an available woman. There were some up there sunning their legs, but they seemed to be doing that for its own sake rather than to get a rise out of a man. They were there to enjoy the game or the weather or to be with a boyfriend while he enjoyed them and it all looked so innocent I just let it be. Anyway, my night with Pansy had considerably eased the pressure my cock had been putting on my brain. So mostly what I did in the grandstand was to try to see what the fans were like, what they thought of us and whether they'd come out in spite or because of all the publicity and all the stir being raised on our account. It pleased me that as best I could tell more than a few of them had come simply because we were putting on a game they liked to watch. It was a bright spring afternoon, a good day to start a season, and a lot of old diehards that had seen some great players perform in this park were grateful for another chance to watch the slow, graceful unfolding of this American game. I don't think most of them cared in the beginning whether we were Fascists or Communists or atheists or Moslems.

Lefty had made sure these fans got in without too much trouble. They'd had to run the holy rollers' hellfire gauntlet, of course. But Lefty had seen to it that the Christians didn't actually block the gates. He told their preacher, the Reverend Dr. Bushrod, that he and his congregation had every right to make asses of themselves wherever they wanted to, but if the Christians physically stopped anybody from entering the park, he—Lefty, I mean—would sue them and that by the time he got through with them he'd have turned their church into a Marxist reading room. One of the things almost everybody knew about Lefty was that he'd sued the University of Southern Arkansas and won a pretty penny from them. And one of the things Lefty knew about respectable Americans was that the threat of a lawyer scared the living shit out of them.

But once Lefty got the fans in, he couldn't leave them alone. He'd taught too long, tried too long and too hard to change the way the world was run to just sit back and let them watch a baseball game. I thought I understood what Lefty was doing and what caused him to do it, but my opinion was that those fans had a right to be just fans instead of having to hear Lefty tell them how the team worked and why Eversole had never been given a chance to make the majors. But people listened to him. I guess there were probably some there more interested in Lefty than in baseball. After all, he'd had his name in the paper several times. And he went on and on, from fan to fan, friendly enough, I guess, and always talking in that calm, reasonable voice that could soothe you into agreeing no matter what it was saying.

But this was Lefty's dream and I told myself he had the right to go about trying to make it real however he wanted to. And as far as I could tell, he didn't run any fans off. I even noticed some of them dropping change into the red donation buckets we'd hung on posts here and there around the stands.

During the bottom of the fifth I was peddling beer in the bleachers down the right-field line just above our bull pen and I saw a spic that had scrubbed up and hid inside a three-piece suit that would've looked fine at a senator's funeral. He was sitting in the first row and leaning forward with his hands on the railing. He wasn't watching the game but was laying his cold, black eyes down hard on something else. After I studied him a minute, I saw that it was Gonzalo Pinzon he was trying to spook. Pinzon was up off the bench and a little ways down toward the fence from the Chamber of Commerce greaser, who he was making a show of not paying attention to. He and Franklin Brown were kind of dog-assing around together, showing off their pitching motions to one another using an imaginary ball. Pinzon bloated his belly out and did an imitation of what must've been Luis Tiant drunk. The tailored spic never took his eyes off Pinzon or the glower off his face. And I guess Pinzon finally got tired of trying to ignore him because after he'd run out of pitching motions he walked over to the railing and asked the fans if any of them had a silver dollar they'd lend him for a minute and when nobody responded he went over to the man who had to be the one he had called Ratoplan and told him, "Give me the one you keep for luck."

The man hesitated but, caught by surprise, forked it over. Then Pinzon got two baseballs and did a juggling act with them and the dollar. Whatever else Pinzon had done with his life up to then, he'd spent a lot of time throwing things up in the air and catching them when they came down. He was good at it. He caught and released balls behind his back and between his legs and reversed the direction of their flight from left to right and then from right to left again. It beat anything of that kind I'd ever seen, but then the circus didn't do a big business in the Cookson Hills when I was a kid.

It's hard to judge time in a case like that, but Pinzon must've carried on for several minutes. The bleacher fans applauded all during the last part of it. I carried my tray of beers down close to the railing so I could watch Ratoplan's face and hear if he said anything to Pinzon when it was over. I kept my eyes on him as much as on Pinzon because he was the one I was most worried about. I wanted to know what the power was he was holding or trying to hold over Pinzon. I thought he must be either pretty confident or pretty desperate to be shadowing Pinzon in public. His expression didn't change during the juggling. He kept that unmoved stare on Pinzon the way a man will on a kid he has seen show off in the same way too many times.

When he was done, Pinzon gave the dollar back to Ratoplan and said, "Why don't you put it in one of the donation boxes? Keep baseball alive in Little Rock."

Ratoplan stood and put the dollar back in his vest pocket. "Quite a cute routine you have, Gonzalo," he said. "Pointless, of course, but it makes more sense than baseball."

"Can't you hear Miami calling?" Gonzalo asked him.

"Not yet," Ratoplan told him. He stared at Pinzon, gave him a bored smile, then turned and walked away. I followed him along the aisle and watched him walk up the ramp that led to the exit. He carried himself like a young banker, straight and brisk and single-minded, diverted by neither the people nor the game. He was the kind of man three-piece suits were invented for.

I went back down into the dugout then. It was the top of the sixth. Lefty came down a half-inning later.

"They swallow the line?" I asked him.

"Oh, it'll take a while," he laughed. "I have to deprogram them."

He had to be pleased with the way the day had gone. The holy rollers hadn't managed to do much more than add a little color to the game and so far the city had laid off completely.

We sat through the top of the seventh without saying a word, each of us admiring the way Eversole handled the Americans. He wasn't fancy, just raised his left leg and pushed forward with his right and poured the ball home, cut all the waste from his motion so that he was left with just grace and power. Grease and power, I guess you could say.

"We may lose the rest of them but we ought to win most of the ones he pitches," Joe Buck Cantwell said.

"He does have amazing control for an anarchist," Lefty said.

Selma hadn't gotten but one solid hit—a double to left-center by their catcher, Iron Joe Talmadge—and two scratch singles— one a little flare over first and the other a roller down the third-base line that Rainbow Smith fell on his face trying to bare-hand. But we only had six hits off Jigs Thurmond and nobody had come through in the clutch for us yet.

But then with two down in our half of the seventh, Julius walked and Lefty sent me up to hit for Stump Guthrie. I paused just outside the batter's box, tapped my bat against my cleats a time or two, and helped myself to a lungful of air. The crowd was so quiet I didn't have any trouble hearing the razzing the boys from Selma were giving me. Bull stood on the top dugout step, giving me the lawman's knife. "Better hit quick, Durham, and get gone. Believe I hear a siren blowing yonder."

I stepped into the box and touched the outside corner of the plate with the tip of my bat. From his catcher's squat, Iron Joe Talmadge said, "Everything's pretty well nailed down here, Durham. I don't see a thing you could make off with."

"Aw," I said, "I'm just trying to keep you boys diverted while my partner cleans out your clubhouse."

"If he's as slick as you, he'll be doing time right quick."

Jigs Thurmond threw me a good curve and I fouled it off, realizing as I swung that it would have been smart to look at a pitch or two.

"Got a little hitch in your swing," Talmadge told me. "Probably comes from having to look over your shoulder all the time, don't you reckon?"

"Probably so," I said. "Lot's of times there's some asshole behind me running off at the mouth."

"A man like you can always use a good talking to."

I took Thurmond's second pitch, another curve, for strike two.

"A little hitch ought not keep a man from swinging entirely," Talmadge said. "I know it's tough out here on your own and all, but you got to keep trying."

"I don't know," I said. "Maybe I better hang it up. Looks like ole Jigs is way too tough for me."

"Well, I guess you could get even by holding him up after the game."

"Not worth the trouble. Wouldn't get nothing but a picture of his poor ole wife and a Klan membership card."

Thurmond aimed the 0-2 pitch at my chin. I leaned back and let it sail by, then stepped out of the box to straighten my helmet. "Better pull that hat on down over your face," Bull Cox yelled. "Somebody's liable to recognize you."

When I got back in the box, Talmadge said, "How'd you make out in the pen, Durham? They tell me a lot of you boys turn queer."

"Why you asking?" I said. "Looking to be buggered?"

The ump called time, walked around Talmadge, pulled a whisk broom out of a pocket, and, while sweeping off the plate, told us to keep our wit to ourselves.

When time was back in, Thurmond fed me the curve he thought he had me set up for. But I was expecting it and, besides, he hung it some and got it a few inches over on my side of the plate and, Christ, I tattooed the son of a bitch, jerked it over the wall and the screen and out into the afternoon traffic. I stood at the plate a few seconds, admiring my work, then turned back to Talmadge and said, "Tell ole Jigs he's giving that curve away. Cocking his wrist way too soon."

I took my time circling the bases and when I got back around to home my teammates were there to grab my hands and slap my back and head and ass and I could hear the fans yelling for me and I saw Bull sling a helmet against his water cooler and, Lord, it was all I could do to keep from taking another trip around the bases.

In the dugout even Eversole came over and nodded and shook my hand and grunted thanks.

"It's nothing beside what you been doing," I said. He nodded again and went back to his place.

Home runs do for me what fires did for Nero—I felt like fiddling. I was grinning like a cowboy in a whorehouse and thinking that after a day like this I might end up out in that garden with Pansy and Susan both. "This is easy time, boys," I said. "It's enough to make a man turn his back on crime."

"Now don't go saying something you'll have to take back later," Julius Common Deer joked.

Lefty reminded us that there were still two innings to go and that we ought to save some of the celebrating for when it was over. But I don't think anybody in the park thought Selma was going to score two runs off Eversole that day. I slapped Lefty on the back. "Hell, Lefty, a man ought not to make a habit of waiting to celebrate. You got to either celebrate when you're ahead or learn to celebrate losing."

"Slammer wisdom," he said.

In the top of the eighth Bull Cox roared out of his dugout and asked to see "the goddam swampball that savage is throwing." He said, "My boys is wet just from the spray they get when it passes by." He must've figured his only shot at winning was to get Eversole thrown out because he yelled out at him, "Throw me the ball, wild man." Eversole threw a mean spitter that looked like it was going to hit Bull in the nuts but at the last minute zipped down into the dirt at his feet and skidded off to the side. The umpire probably would've thrown Eversole out of the game then and there, but that's when Bull really started raving. Even beside himself like he was, he knew better than to go after Eversole, so he turned his tongue on the umpire and Joe Buck Cantwell, who had gone in to catch for Stump Guthrie. The umpire took it for a while, didn't toss Bull until he called him a "damn, faggot, Christ-killing Communist." And that pissed him off so he either forgot about Eversole or let him stay in just to spite Bull. Eversole made the most of it, too, striking out the last four Americans as easy as if they'd been Boy Scouts.

While Bull was ranting and foaming, Lefty announced over the loudspeaker that a flatbed truck full of fresh vegetables had just pulled up at the main gate. There was cabbage and sweet peas, carrots and leaf lettuce, asparagus and rhubarb. It was provided by the Columbia County Food Cooperative. Anybody needing vegetables was welcome to them.

He hadn't yet started giving away meat.

8

"I'd prefer you weren't accompanied by your entire gang on these visits. As of yet you're the only one I have authority over," Mantis told me when his secretary, confounded by our number and high spirits, buzzed him out of his office. I didn't have to wait that time. It was nine o'clock on a bright Monday morning, the day after we'd ended our first home stand by beating Selma for the third time in four tries, and the whole busload of us had pulled up in front of the parole office. Lefty had walked in with me, and several of the boys that were curious about the workings of justice followed. The rest stayed in the bus sleeping off celebration liquor or reading about theirselves in the *Chronicle*. When I got through doing my regularly scheduled slammer tease, we'd be off to Oxford to take on the Fury.

"We wanted to demonstrate the high esteem Mr. Durham's co-workers hold him in," Lefty said. "Isn't that right, fellows?"

Jew Bernstein, Woodrow Ratliff, Julius Common Deer, and Franklin Brown, who were standing right behind us, smiled and nodded at Mantis. Bullet Bob Turner had already spotted the water cooler and was over there trying to loosen his tongue from the roof of his mouth. Morning wasn't his time of day. It took about five gallons of water to wash that glue off his tongue and I suspect that if it hadn't been for his devotion to his pitching he would've just started back in sucking down beer every morning as soon as he came to. But his knuckleball was every bit as good as he said it was. He had won one game against Selma and saved another. Six innings of relief without yielding a run.

"I believe old Hog hits the fastball about as good as any man I ever played with," Jew Bernstein told Mantis.

"He's been an inspiration to us all," Woodrow Ratliff said, straight-faced.

"I'm sure," Mantis said, his voice full of strained, piss-ant sarcasm.

"And as the man into whose custody Hog was released," Lefty said, "I want to report that he has been showing up for work regularly and doing an exemplary job. We've only used him as a pinch hitter so far, but he's hitting .750. Three for four with a home run and a double. The home run won the opening day game for us. And all of his hits have come in the clutch." You might've thought I was Babe Ruth minus his appetite for hot dogs and beer.

"Uh huh," Mantis nodded. "I read about it. I believe the headline was EX-CONVICT RIPS AMERICANS."

"Very unfortunate." Lefty puckered his lips and made a little smacking sound. "Sportswriters are a notoriously melodramatic lot. And then I'd like to think the Selmans were being a bit presumptuous when they named their team. Wouldn't you?"

"You call your team the Reds," Mantis shot at him.

Lefty raised his hand to the side of his head and scratched a couple of times like a bad actor playing somebody that was having to stop and think. "You believe that ill-considered? Intimations of bolshevism?" He rubbed his chin. "Maybe so. But, you see, my grandfather, old Zachariah Marks, came down to Arkansas from Cincinnati in a wagon in 1903. He became a staunch Arkansan, but he never forgot his Ohio roots. Consequently my people have always rooted for the Cincinnati teams. Pardon the pun. I thought about calling this team the Redlegs, but you have to pay more for lettering that way."

"I'd like some coffee," I said. I figured that would bring Mantis's attention back to me. And I'd noticed Bullet Bob wander over to the Mr. Coffee machine and commence fiddling with it.

"Too much to drink?" Mantis asked me. I'm sure he was glad for the chance to jump on somebody besides Lefty.

"No. A little sleepy is all. I was up at dawn working in our garden. I'm an old farm boy. I like to feel the raw earth beneath me." And the truth was that Pansy liked it too. We hadn't missed a night rolling in that garden since we'd started. She like to've drained me of all my sap the night after I hit that game-winning shot. I would've liked to've had her on a bed, but she said she thought our shacking up together right there in the home might cause dissension on the team. In some ways she was a prize woman, but in others she hadn't ever gotten over being a cheerleader.

"If you'll drag your friend away from the coffee machine before he dismantles it, I'll have Julie brew some coffee. But I don't think we're equipped to satisfy an entire baseball team." Mantis pointed his thumb toward Turner, who was pouring coffee straight out of a can into one of them paper filters. "And if we're through with the character references, I'd like to speak to the parolee in private." He turned and started toward his office.

"Don't mind us," Lefty said. "I just thought that this little peek under the hood of the great engine of justice might keep my boys from sticking their hands in the motor."

Mantis stopped, turned back around, motioned toward Bullet Bob again, opened his mouth to say something else to Lefty, but then gave it up, let it be, slumped a little, and went quickly into the safety of his office.

I followed him, remembering that Lefty had promised never again to risk letting his tongue get me in trouble. Though he wasn't nearly as rough-edged with Mantis as he'd been that day with the preachers and politicians, he was still playing the same game. I was hoping that he understood the workings of their system well enough to know exactly how much he could get by with. But I wasn't sure. I had to wonder sometimes whether his disgust for them was something he couldn't always control. In my position, about all I could do was trust him and pray he wouldn't charge them up to the point where they'd fry me just to singe him.

Mantis sat down in his bureaucrat's swivel chair and laid his hands out on his desk and studied them. I pulled up the stooge's seat for myself. Without looking up he asked, "Was bringing the whole team Lefty's idea?"

"I had the appointment and I'm here."

He gave me a hard look, which meant that I could see prison bars at the back of his eyes. "Hog," he said, and now he used the name without fussing, like he'd decided to quit pretending it didn't fit, "I'm not particularly impressed with the fact that you can get a baseball team to follow you into my office. I want to make it clear to you that I will not be intimidated."

"There's some damn good players among them. I was surprised. We might just set this league on its ass. You think that coffee might be ready?"

"Julie will bring it when it's ready. This is not a cafe." He looked down again, picked up a pencil, and started drumming the eraser end against his desk top. For a minute it was like the hand was on its own. Mantis watched it like it was somebody else's as the drumming got quicker and louder. Then he stopped himself, let the pencil fall, watched it roll until it stopped against the edge of the ink blotter, and said, "It's generally best for a convict to keep his name out of the paper."

"Ex-convict," I reminded him.

"As of now."

"Now's what matters." I lit up a Lucky.

Looking right straight down at his desk, he said, "If you played for a, shall we say, less controversial team, the publicity would be good for everybody concerned. But I'll be frank with you. The way it is now our office is under a lot of pressure."

"Then I'm glad I've got a parole officer that won't be intimidated."

"I will not be intimidated out of serving the public good." He looked up and gave me that McAlester stare again. "When it becomes clear that the public good would best be served by returning you to prison, we will return you to prison. The public good wouldn't figure so prominently in this case if you hadn't decided to play for the Reds."

"You never can tell. I might've been a twisted librarian. I might've drawn dirty pictures in the margins of Nixon's memoirs. I might've sweet-talked little girls into the back of the bookmobile and given them a gander at my goddam pride. God knows what a man right out of prison might do when you give him a van and the run of the town. This way I'm off the streets a lot more."

He closed his eyes and put his hands together in front of his mouth. He wasn't ready to cart me back to the can yet or he wouldn't have kept fooling with me, but he had something he wanted to tell me or something he wanted to threaten me with or he would've just told me to clear the hell out. I took a final drag off my cigarette and he opened his eyes and watched me stub the butt out in the ashtray on his desk. Then he lit one of his cancer-proof jobs.

"I suppose it would be absurd for me to tell you it's not too late to reconsider," he said and let out a thin stream of smoke.

He didn't say it like a question, so I didn't bother to answer. I was wondering how a man like Mantis might react when he was under pressure from all sides. How long would he stand up under it before he put me away to get himself some relief? And then I understood what maybe Lefty had known from the start, that we had to convince him that the hell he would catch for letting me roam the southern wilds with this alien baseball team was nothing compared to that he'd get if he had me bound and gagged and hauled back to the hole. I'm sure things would've been a little easier for Mantis if the *Arkansas Chronicle* had been a different kind of paper. But it was old and liberal and out of place. They left their sports section to Wilbur Haney, who used it mainly to promote the University of Arkansas Razorbacks. He despised the Reds and everything we stood for and didn't hesitate to say so in print. But their staff editorials sounded as liberal as a Yankee Democrat speaking to an NAACP convention. Just the day before, one of their editorials had said that "Lefty Marks and his Arkansas Reds are a welcome and much needed addition to the heretofore rather provincial world of Arkansas athletics." They even came right out and praised Lefty for providing ex-convicts a chance to make a place for themselves in society. So if Mantis sent me back to the slam for anything short of sticking up another bank, he'd be praised in the sports section and damned on the editorial page. And Lefty was certain to do all he could to keep the publicity coming, for, good or bad, it was apt to put people in the ballpark. I knew there had to be a line, though, beyond which Mantis and his bosses would decide to ignore the papers and Lefty's Jew lawyer and follow their hearts—which would mean damnation for any parolee that didn't suck ass.

"We've gotten off to a bad start, Hog, you and I," Mantis said, getting off to a bad start again. "I'm willing to try to reconcile myself to the fact that for the time being at least you're going to play baseball for the Reds. What I wish you'd try to understand is that maybe I can help you do that without getting yourself into trouble."

"Next time up I'll strike out and dedicate it to you."

"You're making it hard for me to be tolerant," Mantis said.

"If it's easy it's not tolerance. I wonder about that coffee."

"Perhaps your friend has broken the machine. I'm almost done. Let's finish."

"Or perhaps Julie has been lured onto the bus."

"Or dragged, more likely." He allowed himself a smile in honor of his wit.

"The kind you have to drag aren't worth the trouble. They wear themselves out getting there."

"A very public-spirited view," he said, and quickly held his arm out and showed me his palm. "Enough." I agreed with that.

He put his cigarette out and studied the ashtray a minute. "I want to get this said without interruption." He straightened his back and looked me in the eye and then raised his aim to a few inches above my head. "Part of my job is to find out what I can about the people you associate with. To that end I've had routine checks run on all the people listed on the Reds' roster. Most of them seem to be more or less acceptable, though our check is by no means complete yet. There is only one that might be seriously objectionable."

"Lefty Marks."

"Gonzalo Pinzon. He spent a year in the Florida Boys Industrial School. Car theft. Unauthorized use of credit cards. Resisting arrest. Possession of a controlled substance."

"He got stoned, stole a car, and charged a crate of potato chips." I was a little surprised at first that it was Pinzon he was warning me about, but it didn't take much thinking to realize that it made sense. Eversole had spent a good part of the last quarter-century in Mexico and anyway probably steered pretty well clear of society when he could and society steered pretty well clear of him the rest of the time. Bullet Bob might've slept with the city a night or two for public drunk, but that's all. Oh, it's possible Lefty been in custody long enough to have his picture taken and sing a verse or two of "We Shall Overcome," but that shit don't count, that's not real time. Pinzon was loud and smart and Cuban—the kind, I imagine, that keep the Miami jails in business. But there was still the one thing that made me wonder. "I thought he came from a rich family."

"His stepfather is a real estate tycoon. His real father owned a nightclub in pre-Castro Cuba. He apparently fell off his boat when he and his family were fleeing Havana. Gonzalo was just an infant then. The evidence is that he hated his stepfather from the time his mother married him in, let me see"—he picked up a sheet of official paper and looked at it—"yes, 1961, until about two years ago. Then he went to work for his stepfather's company, Elysian Land Development, and within six months he was a vice-president.

"Prior to that and even after he served the year in reform school he was arrested several times—drunk and disorderly, disturbing the peace, and once for breaking and entering. But except for that one time in Juvenile Court he was never brought to trial. His stepfather always intervened on his behalf, made restitution, whatever. Why, I don't know."

"Love," I said, but what I figured was that Pinzon had something on the old man. "Is that all?" I stood up. "Thanks for the tip."

"He's high-strung and violent. The Miami police found him extremely abusive. I can't order you not to associate with him at all because, unfortunately, you're on the same team. But you don't need his kind of trouble on top of everything else. Stay away from him as much as you can."

"We're back in town on the seventh of May. I'll see you sometime after that."

"You'll see me on the morning of the seventh at nine o'clock. You will not bring your team with you."

"Lefty might have something to say."

"Tell him to call."

"He hates the phone company."

The guys were sitting around the waiting room drinking coffee. Julie was over at the machine brewing up another batch. Bullet Bob stood beside her with an empty cup in his hand.

"I passed," I announced. "Let's hit the bricks." We left the coffee brewing.

When I got on the bus I went straight back to Pinzon and sat beside him. I wanted to get a line on what the slick son of a bitch had in his head.

9

Late that night a voice said, "Hog! Hog!" and a hand shook me and a bell went off and I raised myself up out of the long, bad dream I'd been having in my bed on the second floor of The Caddies' Rest, an antebellum Mississippi mansion that a man named Jason Commerce had turned into a nice little hotel. The voice and hand were Lefty's and the bell was in Pinzon's alarm clock. Pinzon had decided he wasn't in pitching shape yet and was going to start running in the middle of the night. When we'd got into our beds that night, he'd asked if I'd mind if he set his alarm for about two in the morning. I said that over the last four years I'd got used to hearing bells and anyway waking up to one and knowing that I could go right on back to sleep would probably make me feel good. But coming out of a dream that way, hearing first a voice and then an alarm clock, startled me some. I sat bolt upright and shook my head and then saw Lefty standing by my bed, the hall light reflecting off his hair like a damn halo. A second later I noticed Bullet Bob behind him, in the doorway, swaying heavily back and forth, like he was dancing to some slow, drunkard's song. But if there was music in his head it wasn't getting out his mouth.

Pinzon got out of bed and went over to the sink and started washing his face. Lefty asked me to come out in the hall for a minute. I pulled on a pair of jockey shorts and went out there. My first thought was that Bullet Bob had slipped out in the team bus and run over somebody.

"Pop Stone called me a few minutes ago," Lefty told me. "There's been a fire at DeForge Stadium. Eversole was sleeping out there and he caught the man who set the fire and held him until the police came. But apparently one of the cops made him mad and he hit one of them. Pop Stone told the sheriff that Eversole was one of our players and talked him into holding him there until we can get down and maybe straighten things out. I'd like you to come with me to the field. Eversole seems to trust you."

"If Eversole trusts me it's because he thinks the cops don't. And I don't know if I can stand there with a straight face and tell him he ought to be sorry for hitting a cop." I was still about half asleep, but I had sense enough to know I wasn't the world's best hand at reasoning with the law.

"It ain't really the cops," Bullet Bob said with a wet grin. "It's just ole Jim Tom Grimm. I used to play ball with him. Threw hard but not much control. He wouldn't arrest a ballplayer."

I couldn't quite make sense of that, but Lefty explained. "Grimm's the sheriff here now. He and Bob were out together earlier tonight." That made sense. In a dry county like this one was, you buy your beer from the sheriff. And that's why it made sense too for Lefty to be bringing Bob, drunk as he was, with us.

"We played together in both the Three-I League and the Carolina League. Lord, the times we had."

I stood there a minute figuring I ought to just say no and go back to sleep, but I was curious as to what a man would look like after Eversole hit him and anyway couldn't keep down an urge to be there when whatever was going to happen happened.

When I went back into the room to get dressed, Pinzon was sitting on the edge of his bed lacing up his running shoes, a pair of bright orange jobs that looked like they could've been part of the official ghetto Olympic outfit. While I was getting into my hippie convict uniform (tennis shoes, jeans, and T-shirt—I had actually found and bought a T-shirt in Little Rock that had Property of the Oklahoma State Prison written on the front of it, but I decided against wearing it that night), Pinzon did some stretching exercises.

He walked out into the hall with me, and Bullet Bob said, "Holy Christ, a bathing beauty."

"I don't like dry counties," Pinzon said. "I'm going to run to Memphis to get a drink."

"Bring some back," Bob told him.

"I'm still not sure how much good this kind of running will do your pitching," Lefty said. So they'd talked about it before.

"It can't hurt," Pinzon said.

As soon as he set foot in the yard Pinzon took off toward the golf course next to the hotel. The rest of us walked to the bus. "You drive," Lefty told me. "It's not a job for a one-armed man."

The Caddies' Rest was a mile or two south of Oxford on what they called the Old Taylor Road, and DeForge Stadium was built on a rise above one of the bends of the Mottstown Highway five or six miles northeast of town. But we had to drive right through town to get there and it must've taken nearly a half-hour. Now and then Bullet Bob would get some wind and rear up and butcher a line or two of some honky-tonk song.

Since there were no legal bars, we didn't see a soul on the streets at that time of night. The main drag was mostly a long string of instant hamburger huts and factory chicken stands with churches in between them. It looked like a lot of the people here got their kicks saying grace over Big Macs. I knew better of course. It's the places where good times are outlawed that the wildest times are had.

There were a couple of cop cars in the stadium parking lot and we pulled up beside them. Three guys that had been leaning against the fence next to the ticket booth came up to us. One of them had a uniform on. "Sheriff Jim Tom Grimm," he said, and stuck a big hand out at Lefty, who shook it and said, "Lefty Marks." Lefty tilted his head toward me. "This is Hog Durham. And I believe you know Bob Turner."

The other two guys introduced theirselves as Pop Stone, the manager of the Fury, and Stephen Gabbard, their owner. Stone was a pleasant-looking man with bushy white hair. He wore a pair of khaki pants and the tops to his pajamas. Gabbard was younger and leaner than Stone and a lot more solemn. I figured him for either a lawyer or a preacher. It turned out that he made his living lawyering but would preach to you any time he saw the chance.

When we had finished the handshaking horseshit, Bullet Bob asked Grimm what the hell was going on.

"One of your boys got out of hand," Grimm said. "Big ole buck Indian. Said his name was Eversole and that he pitched for you guys, but we couldn't get shit out of him other than that."

"Where is he?" Lefty asked, but the sheriff had decided to do his talking to Bullet Bob. It was easy to see that Lefty had brought Bob along so we'd have somebody on our side the sheriff would be comfortable talking to, but I still wasn't sure I wanted to have Bob interpreting for me.

"He was as naked as a nigger at a stud auction when we got here and he had Colonel Sanders Flemson tied to that light pole yonder with his own overalls," Grimm told Bullet Bob. "Miz Flemson had called us and said that Sandy had got loose again, so we come right down here because that damn half-wit has been trying off and on for years to burn the stadium down. The fire was out when we got here and wasn't ever much to start with and everything would've been all right if your Indian hadn't've cold-cocked poor ole Lump."

"Lump Wingo?" Bullet Bob said, and his face seemed to brighten some. "Ain't he the one that come up to see you play that time in Des Moines and me and you and him got drunk in the Sportsman's Bar after and he got to rubbing on the wrong skirt and had to lay the bouncer out with a cue stick. If I remember right we ended up passed out in a graveyard."

"That's him," Grimm said. "His momma had just died then.

He's a damn fine lawman now." He started toward the main entrance to the stadium and motioned for us to follow. I'd smelled beer on him before, but it wasn't until I watched him half swagger and half stagger that I realized he was damn near as drunk as Bob.

While we were walking along, Lefty asked Pop Stone about Colonel Sanders Flemson. Pop said he was the thirty-one-year-old idiot son of Jay Gould Flemson, who owned about half the town and ran a bank that once or twice a year threatened to foreclose on the other half. "They like grand names. Colonel Sanders was born Jefferson Davis Flemson, but some years back J.G. went to court and had it legally changed. Did it mostly out of spite against his wife, I think, but the name did fit. Colonel Sanders is unnaturally fond of fried chicken. Sandy doesn't have good sense—doesn't have much sense at all, as a matter of fact—and Mrs. Flemson comes from an old family and refuses to allow her own blood to be locked away. And the boy is more or less harmless. They have a Negro boy that watches over him some during the day and when he's not there they have a little rig they hook one end of to a tree and the other to the idiot's leg. They give him about twenty feet of running rope, but he tends to wind himself around and around in the same direction until he's pinned himself against the tree." He laughed at the thought of that, then shook his head. "I guess it's sadder than it is funny, but I'm not sure."

Stephen Gabbard didn't seem to see much humor in it. "It's a complicated story, but the essence of it is that the father is a mercenary tyrant and the son is neglected and handicapped and has learned to fight back in just one way: strike a match. One of these times when he escapes from his room at night, he'll do some serious damage."

We went through the ticket gate and then turned left following a walkway around the back side of the third-base grandstand. There weren't any lights on inside the gate, but we found our way by the ones in the parking lot. Near the far end of the grandstand, the deputy sheriff was sitting on the walkway with his back against the block wall. Just to the other side of him was a wooden door.

"Your Indian's in there," Grimm said. "Gimme that flashlight, Lump."

The deputy handed it to him and when he did he lifted his face and turned it in such a way that it caught the light. He probably wouldn't be able to open his left eye for about a week, but other than that I couldn't tell that he'd suffered much damage. Eversole must've put the fear of God into those two fuckers, though, or they would've busted that door down and went in after him before it ever occurred to them to start calling people and asking for help or advice or whatever it was they wanted from us.

"I'll show you where that Flemson pinhead tried to start a fire," Grimm said. "He didn't do six bits' worth of damage." He waved the light around, but that didn't do much more than indicate the general direction. It was easy enough to find the place on our own. It wasn't but about ten feet beyond the door. The idiot had piled some leaves and twigs against the block wall and laid a foot-long piece of 2×4 across the top of the pile. He had managed to get the fire started, but that's about it. He had blackened a few feet of the wall's green paint and littered the walkway some, but apparently that had been enough to rouse Eversole.

Stephen Gabbard borrowed the flashlight from Grimm and took a closer look at the damage. After a minute he handed the light back and said, "The day will come when he'll learn what will burn and what won't and there'll be hell to pay."

"Odds are that whatever he burns, his daddy will be part owner of," Pop Stone said.

It seemed like all of us were putting off any discussion of what was to be done about Eversole, but when we got back to the door Lefty asked Grimm straight out what he planned to do.

"I damn near shot the son of a bitch." Then he commenced to tell the story over again. "When we drove up we heard some noise and come over here and seen poor ole Colonel Sanders strapped to that pole and howling like a damn Yakima Indian and your buck standing here with his arms across his chest and his pecker waving in the breeze. For a minute I thought he was some kind of giant queer or something. We yelled to him that we were the police coming up to check out the situation, but he didn't pay us no mind, didn't give the least sign of even hearing us. We finally come up behind him real careful, figuring he might be crazy, dangerous crazy, not just stupid like that poor, howling half-wit Flemson. He must've heard us coming, because we made sure we made plenty of noise so as not to startle him, but he just stood there as still as a courthouse statue. Lump got right up behind him and stuck his gun in his back. That damn Indian jumped like a ten-dollar whore at a hundred-dollar offer and spun around and knocked ole Lump out colder than a two-day turd. Then before I could draw a bead on him he was inside that door."

"He ain't no queer. I can tell you that," Bullet Bob said.

"No. I never seen one hit like that." Grimm reared his head back and let out a big snort. Then he looked over at Bob again. "You remember that one we picked up in Charleston and got it drunk and took its clothes off and tied it up to that statue of John C. Calhoun?"

When Bullet Bob and Grimm quit laughing, I said, "Eversole lost his hearing in Vietnam." I knew I was taking a chance. Bullet Bob could have contradicted me before he even realized what I was trying to do. But I didn't see that we had much to lose. And despite what some people tell you, most of the time the best way to deal with the cops is to look them straight in the eye and tell them the biggest lie you can think of.

Lefty gave me a quick, sideways, doubting look, and Bob opened his mouth and said, "Hell . . . ," but I cut him off before he could get anything else out.

"He had his back to you, didn't he?" I asked Grimm.

"Yeah, but . . ."

"He can talk," Lump Wingo said. "He told us his name and said he was a baseball pitcher. He didn't have no call to sucker punch me."

"He can talk," I said. "He just can't hear. And any time he knows somebody's talking to him he gives them his name and occupation."

"Shit," Wingo said. "Why didn't he just say he was deaf instead of running off and hiding like he did?"

"He'd just hit one policeman who'd stuck a gun in his back and he saw another one drawing a bead on him. He took cover. I'm surprised he even told you his name."

"Well, he done that through the door," Grimm said.

"He must've figured you'd call us and we'd be able to explain to you," Lefty said, falling in with the lie.

Grimm stared at me, his red-rimmed eyes hard and mean. "You better not be feeding me a line of shit, Buck."

It was time to flesh out the story. "Eversole was with the Twenty-sixth marines in Khe Sanh in the late winter of '68 when things was bad. They were dug in there and the Cong threw everything they had at them day and night for weeks. Eversole got to be good friends with a kid named Mickey Herr from Waycross, Georgia. Well, one day something went in the Herr kid's head and he climbed up out of the bunker and took off across the field toward the jungle. Eversole says the kid was yelling, 'Come and get me, motherfuckers. Let me see your faces.' The kid had got about a fifty-yard start before Everosle realized what was happening and took off after him. The kid ran a little ways further and the shelling started in again. They were big shells coming from a long ways away, so they weren't aiming at the kid. He just happened to be out when they started in. Eversole says that one of the shells hit right in front of the kid and blew the earth right out from under him. When Eversole got to him, the kid wasn't much more than a piece of meat, but Eversole picked him up and started back to the bunker with him. On the way back Eversole was knocked off the ground by a shell that hit a little ways off to one side of him. He didn't get hit by any of the shrapnel but the concussion knocked him out for a few minutes. When he came to, he picked his friend's body up and carried it the rest of the way back to the bunker. He ain't heard a thing since that shell knocked him out."

They were quiet for a minute, the way you'd like an audience to be right after you tell them a good story. All I lacked right then was somebody in the background humming a few bars of the Marine Hymn.

Finally, Grimm remembered he had a job to do and looked straight at Bullet Bob and asked him, as solemn as the pope on Good Friday, "Is this man telling us the truth or just jacking us off?"

I'm not sure Bullet Bob even knew what he was doing by then. He may have gotten so carried away with my story that he decided to believe it, but whatever it was that was going on in his head he stared right at his ole friend and saved our asses. "It's the God's truth, Jim Tom, the God's truth."

I knew then that unless Eversole opened the door and told us to hold the noise down, we were out of trouble.

Grimm said, "Well, I'll damn-sure have to say he didn't ever act like he heard us. And I guess Lump'll live. What do you say, Lump?"

Wingo wasn't quite ready to let it go. "How the hell come after what all them Communists done to him and his friend he hooked up with an outfit like yours that all the papers say is Communist?" he asked Lefty.

"We are *not* Communists," Lefty told him without blinking. "We are anarcho-syndicalists."

"Hell, Lump," Grimm said, "you know better than to believe all that shit the papers say. There ain't no such thing as a Communist baseball team."

"Fuck it," Wingo snarled. He stomped off toward the parking lot.

"Lump don't take to having the piss knocked out of him and not being able to do nothing about it," Grimm explained. "You can't blame him. You boys ought to tell your Indian to stay clear of trouble from here on out. He won't get but this one warning. Bob here knows me to be a man of my word. He can tell you I ain't shitting you."

"Damn right," said Bullet Bob, like he was proud to know such a man.

"Well, then." Grimm said it the way a man does that thinks he just done a hard job well. He nodded at Lefty and me. "Glad I met you boys. I think you'll find that Oxford is a quiet law-abiding town, contrary to what you might be led to believe from this evening. Then Grimm said, "I go to work bright and early. Them that's coming with me better come on." He started away from us.

"Sheriff Grimm." Stephen Gabbard spoke in a voice he might have used on a hostile witness.

Grimm stopped and heaved a big sigh before he turned around. "Yes, Mr. Gabbard." I couldn't tell if the words had more weariness or disgust in them.

"What are your plans for Colonel Sanders Flemson?"

"I took him home. I already told you that. Mr. Flemson has agreed to take care of any damages."

It was the first time I'd thought about that. I knew something about how the cops operate and why and I realized then just how lucky Eversole had been. The damn sheriff had taken Flemson home and then driven around and picked up Stone and Gabbard and all the while Lump Wingo had been alone here with his swollen eye and his gun and Eversole. Grimm had been giving him his chance to get revenge. I didn't know whether it was fear or pain or maybe even decency that kept Wingo from busting the door down, but I was sure it was a good thing for him and Eversole both that he didn't.

"Yes, Jay Flemson can do that easily enough," Stephen Gabbard told Grimm. "But you might remind your friend that he does not own this stadium. I am responsible for it. And you can inform him also that the next time his idiot son trespasses on this property, I intend to press charges."

"You'll lose," Grimm told him.

"Eventually, I shall prevail," Gabbard said. And then, to Lefty, "I'd like you to give my thanks to your pitcher for capturing the moron arsonist."

"He'll be pleased," Lefty said.

"Now, Sheriff, I'll take that ride home. That is, if you think you can stay on the road."

"Take your chances, lawyer."

Grimm led us out, looking like his name, but walking straighter than he had on the way in. Bullet Bob caught up with him after a few steps, and by the time they were in the parking lot they had each other laughing again.

Gabbard walked a few steps behind them, and Lefty and Pop Stone and I brought up the rear. Pop asked Lefty who he was going to pitch tomorrow. Lefty told him Eversole.

Pop Stone gave us a big friendly smile. "Aw, that poor, deaf Indian," he said. I thought he was going to laugh, but he kept it in.

Lump Wingo was sitting in his car waiting to make a final statement. When he saw us coming toward him, he started his car, roared its motor, and shot off into the night, throwing gravel behind him.

"Used to be a stock car driver," Grimm said.

Gabbard and Stone got in the back seat of Grimm's car and we waved good night to them. Bullet Bob waited while Grimm finished some tale or other, and I thought for a minute that he and the sheriff might spend the night cruising the town together. But after he rewarded Grimm with a big laugh, Bob waddled to the bus and climbed on.

We followed the sheriff's car out of the lot and onto the highway back to town. Bullet Bob said, "Ole Jim Tom's come back to his hometown and made a good life for hisself. You got to hand him that."

"It makes a man want to stop and take stock of things," I said.

"You won't think none the lesser of me if I wait till morning to start in on it, will you?" Bob asked me. "I believe I'll just hang it up for the night, right now." He slumped down in his seat and let his eyelids fall to. About a mile down the road we went around a curve and Bob rolled onto the floor. "Fuck," he groaned, and started to pull himself back up. But then he thought better of it and let himself lie.

Lefty and I laughed a little and then Lefty said, "It's a good thing he didn't pass out earlier. He saved our asses tonight."

"I thought I did all right myself," I said. "Didn't you like my story?"

"You're a good ole boy, Hog, but you damn-sure like to juice things up."

10

Pinzon's alarm went off again at eight o'clock that morning. He had put it on top of the chest of drawers clear over on the other side of the room so he'd have to get out of bed to shut it off. I rolled over and tried to go back to sleep but couldn't do it. I heard him in the bathroom brushing his teeth and washing the sleep out of his eyes and gargling. I went in there and took a piss.

"Want to make some money?" he asked me.

"Nah. I'm rich."

"I'm going to go over to the golf course and fleece some merchants. You can be my partner."

"I don't play. Besides, I need to go back out to the field and talk to Eversole." I headed back toward my bed.

"Suit yourself," Pinzon said when he came out of the bathroom. "It's easy money. We'll play best ball. You won't ever have to hole a putt."

I was tempted, but I didn't know if I wanted to be part of a hustle I wouldn't be in charge of. Still, I probably would've went if I hadn't been set on going out to talk to Eversole. "Maybe tomorrow," I told him.

"There may not be anybody that'll play me tomorrow."

I puffed my pillow up and propped my head on it and got a book Lefty had loaned me off the nightstand. The name of it was *All God's Dangers*. It read like a smart man talking.

"How do I look?" Pinzon asked me when he was dressed. He had on a pair of peach-colored double-knit pants and an orange Ban-Lon shirt. His shoes, his socks, and his belt were white. He had his hair slicked back.

"Like an ignorant greaser," I told him.

"Perfect." He walked to the closet and got two clubs, a five-iron and a putter, out of his duffel bag.

"You won't need a caddie."

"Just to carry my money back for me." Saying the word "money" must've prompted him to check his roll. He took some bills out of his wallet and ruffled them under my nose. "How much you think I have, Banker Durham?"

"I'd say three or four hundred dollars if I didn't suspect you had ones sandwiched in between them two twenties."

He gave me a big wide-eyed grin. "Meester, the mahn from the hotel says thees Tanglewood bery, bery good golf playing, but say too I need monney. I show heem monney." He ruffled the roll again, making his quick hands look nervous. "He say, 'They let you play then.' I play manny, manny years in Mehico. Play bery good. You show me United State golf like Hock Neekles? I haff two club."

He had me laughing by then so he stopped. "That may be over-doing it," I said.

"You ever been to one of these places?"

I shook my head.

"It's hard to overdo." He picked the two clubs up again and lifted the business end of the putter to his lips and kissed it. "God bless America," he said, and went out the door.

A couple of minutes later I was still lying in bed wishing I'd gone with Pinzon when someone knocked at my door. I figured it was Lefty wanting me to go with him to talk to Eversole, but it was Pansy. She had on some denim shorts and a little light green knit top that showed off her tits.

"You always open the door naked?" she asked. But she seemed to like what she saw.

"My momma told me to put my best foot forward." I opened

the door wider, let her in, and locked it behind her. She went over and sat on the edge of my bed.

"Maybe you ought to borrow one of Pinzon's outfits. He looked cute," she said.

"I don't want to hide my bushel under a light."

She picked my book up and looked at the cover. "Is this good?"

"It starts off good." I took it from her and laid it on the night-stand.

"I missed you last night." She sounded like she was sixteen.

"Another thing my momma taught me was that it's sometimes smart to play hard to get."

I sat beside her. My old cock was rising. She looked down at it and tried to keep a serious look on her face. "Your momma might've been awful smart," she said, "but she never taught you to be hard to get. And she was wrong about that best foot too. You're way shy of that."

"A man has to make do."

"And a woman."

We made do.

When we got through, I told her I needed to go to the field to see Eversole. She sprung up like a German soldier. "Lord," she said. "You made me forget to tell you. He's not at the field. Somebody shot him in the arm last night."

"Which arm?"

11

When I finally got myself out of Pansy and dressed and down-stairs, the lobby and the verandah both were full of Reds milling around and speculating as to what might've happened to Eversole. I looked for Bullet Bob, but he wasn't there, hungover probably and maybe a little shamed over having lied to Grimm, his old side-kick and current liquor source.

Woodrow Ratliff told me what little there was that could be known then. Lefty had woke him that morning about daybreak and said Eversole had been shot in the arm and was in the county hospital. Lefty had got Dummy Boudreaux up then and they'd ridden in the bus to the hospital. Lefty had told Woodrow to keep the rest of us here. The bus would be back in time to get us to the game that night.

"Pinzon was down here a few minutes ago," Ratliff said. "He said you and Lefty and Bob went out to the field last night to get Eversole out of trouble for hitting a cop. You think this is part of the same business?"

"I don't know." But it hadn't occurred to me that anybody other than Lump Wingo might've done the shooting. I was even kicking myself in the ass for not having seen it coming, not staying at the field and standing guard.

I knew that if Lefty had wanted my help that day he'd've asked for it, but I figured this was as much my affair as his. If I was partly responsible for Eversole getting shot, the least I could do was go to the hospital and try to find out exactly what had happened and what was being done about it. So before Ratliff could ask me any more questions, I went through the big dining room and into the kitchen and out the back door. Pansy saw me slipping away and followed me. She caught up with me in the backyard and touched my elbow.

"What're you going to do?" she asked.

"Think. And I need to be by my myself to do it. You go on back upstairs and play with your dildo or something." I had worked myself around to being pissed at her for screwing me before saying anything about Eversole.

She stared at me a minute and I watched the color go out of her face and come back red. Then she opened her hand and drew it back quick and I knew she was going to slap me. I could've stopped her easy enough, but I figured I needed hitting and thought I could take any lick she could throw, so I just stood there and took it.

"Asshole," she said.

I thought she might cry, but she wouldn't let herself. She turned and walked away from me, hurrying the first few steps and keeping her head high and straight, but then slowing to a normal pace and slumping a little. Watching her, I realized something dangerous had happened without me knowing it. She had gone beyond just being a woman I could have most any time the urge caught me and she was handy. It wasn't a thought that pleased me, but I went after her anyway and caught her and gripped her arm hard enough to keep her from jerking away while I apologized. I explained some about Eversole and said I was sorry for taking it out on her. Then I let her arm go. She was through trying to get away.

When I finished, she said, "I'll try not to ask too much of you, Hog. But don't treat me like a ten-dollar whore."

I nodded and did my damnedest to smile. "I never won any prizes for manners. You might ought to raise your sights."

She reached up and touched the place on my cheek where she'd hit me. Her eyes were bright and wet. I couldn't help feeling like some cow-eyed idiot. "I never won any prizes for my aim," she said. "I just have to take whatever falls." Then she went back inside.

I climbed the honeysuckle-covered rock fence that went around the backyard and then I cut across the cow pasture to the road that led to town. Walking along, I thought how it was that things got complicated whenever you had a woman more than a night or two at a time. Sometimes it seemed like the more you found out about a woman, the less you knew her. What I'd generally done before was to get up and leave any time I felt dog lust changing into something else. I thought I had some understanding of dog lust. But, Christ, who knew about the other?

I'd gone half a mile or so down the Old Taylor Road and been passed by three cars when a man in a Ford pickup that was pulling an empty horse trailer stopped for me. He said his name was Freeman Quick and that he was on his way to buy a quarter horse from J. G. Flemson. "You know him?" he asked.

"Heard of him."

The wind-cured skin on his face fought against the grin he tried to crease it with. "I've finally skinned him. I been buying and selling livestock in a small way for nigh onto thirty years now. I do all right at it, but the one man that always gets to me is J. G. Flemson. A sensible man would've given up trading with him years ago, but I got a streak of muleheadedness in me that won't let me quit till I've slickered him once. This is the time." He let out a big snort and popped his right hand against the steering wheel. "Where you headed?"

"County hospital. Got a friend laid up there."

"Bad?"

"Don't know yet."

He took a right off the main drag and said, "The hospital's up here a piece. It ain't much out of my way."

I hadn't been with him long enough to be anything but a little bit sorry for him. He had as much chance of skinning Flemson as a Cherokee does of getting elected pope. He was too eager and talked about it too much. I thought I might could help him out. "I ain't been in town but a couple of days," I said, "but from what little I've seen and heard, this Flemson must own just about everything in town. You must've done some sharp conjuring to come up with a way of skinning him."

It was all the prodding he needed. "Yessir," he said. "But a lot of it was just luck and keeping my eyes peeled. You see, Flemson's got this quarter horse—well, he calls it a quarter horse but it ain't no more than a quarter quarter horse, if that." He jerked his head back a notch or two and blew a gust of air out his nose. "It's a damned old half-lame spayed mare that he got somewhere for nothing probably and brung home hoping it'd be something that idiot boy of his would like fiddling with. But from what I've heard tell, the boy never done nothing but try to set the mare's mane afire. Another man would've just kilt it or sold it for dog food, but Flemson's got to try to make money off it. So anyway, for about six months now he's been coming around trying to sell it to me. Wanted $200 for it. 'It's a quarter horse,' he tells me, 'and tame as a lapdog. The perfect horse for breaking a kid in on. Be just the thing for that grandson of yours,' he says. Well, I just laughed at him and let him go on, not having the least notion of ever buying that pore swaybacked mare. But I sold a couple of yearling calves to a feller just south of Bethlehem the other day and he starts telling me how his woman's been on him to get a gentle saddle horse for their boy. He's a banker or lawyer or some such thing that runs his farm so he can take it off his taxes and don't have no more idea what a saddle horse is worth than a damn bubble dancer would. So I tell him I think I can get him one for $350 and he lights up like a Chinaman at a rice festival. I tell him the one I got's kinda old and a little stiff-jointed. But he don't care. Just wants to get his wife off his ass."

I could see the hospital just up ahead. "So you're going to make a quick $150?"

"Well, not quite. I waited a few days hoping Flemson would

come back out to the place trying to palm that mare off on me again, but he didn't and I was afraid the deal would fall through if I didn't get it done quick. So I had to call Flemson and ask if he still wanted to get shut of that mare. He said he thought he might could still bring hisself to sell it, but his boy was getting fonder of it by the day and he didn't see how he could part with it now for less than $250. I'd already figured the phone call would cost me, but I'll still be a hundred dollars to the clear, so I took the deal."

He pulled up to the curb in front of the hospital. I just started to open the door and get on out, but I thought I'd seen through the carpet game Flemson was running and I decided to explain it to Quick in return for the ride. "It's none of my business," I told him. "And I might be wrong about this, but I think Flemson may be getting to you again. I suspect him and that Bethlehem banker or lawyer or whatever he is have ganged up on you. Flemson's a banker too, ain't he? And Bethlehem's not far from here. You can bet your ass and one of your nuts the two of them know each other. Them kind all slop at the same trough. So if it was me, I wouldn't give Flemson my money till I got the $350 from the other guy."

After I stepped out of the truck and onto the sidewalk and shut the door behind me, I stuck my head back in the window. Quick had both hands on the top part of the steering wheel and was staring straight ahead, through the windshield, seeing nothing. "I thank you for the ride," I told him.

He never turned to look at me and I had to strain some to hear what he said. "It ain't ordinarily my way to pay no heed to outsiders' advice. But I thank ye for it anyway. I'll turn it over in my head." I nodded once and pulled my head back. Then he raised his clutch foot and let the truck jerk out into the middle of the street, just missing getting ass-ended by some squash-headed fraternity-looking wimp in a Trans Am. When the Pontiac scholar honked at him, Quick, who must've been looking for an excuse to hit somebody, stopped his pickup and got out and headed back after the boy. But it don't look cool to get dragged out the window of a shining silver road-sucking chariot by some damn scrub-dirt farmer, so the wimp threw it in reverse to give himself some room and then shoved it down into low and screeched around Quick and the truck both, shooting up a brave middle finger as he passed.

Quick stood out in the street and cussed for a minute and then looked over at me and said, "The little son of a bitch probably got that Pontiac from Flemson Motors. It won't last him long." He didn't laugh or even smile. He wasn't saying it to be funny. It was just a way of letting me know that Flemson stuck it to everybody it'd reach.

A blue-headed old woman came up behind him in a new-looking beige Dodge and honked. He looked at her once before quick-stepping back to his truck and taking off. I figured he'd go ahead and punish himself by finishing up the deal he'd made with Flemson.

Eversole wasn't there. The information girl sent me to admissions, the admissions girl sent me to the emergency room, the emergency room girl sent me to the fourth floor, and the ward clerk there pointed me to the jail. Once they'd had Eversole doctored up good, the sheriff had come and hauled him away. No, the wound wasn't serious, she said. Just grazed his left forearm.

I had sense enough to know that I was apt to stir up more shit in Grimm's cage than I'd cover. But I've always had more curiosity than sense and more gall than either. So I went on.

"Well, by God, there he is. The goddam Vietnam expert." Jim Tom Grimm stood behind a counter that, with the walls, squared off a corner of the room. There were two doors in the room besides the one I'd come in. The one in the wall straight across from me was heavy and metal and painted gray. The other one was to my left, a few feet down from where the counter joined the wall. It opened into Grimm's private office. I could hear voices coming through that door. The only people in the main office were me and Grimm and the dispatcher, a blubber-butted, burr-headed, idiot-eyed kid that didn't look far out of high school. He sat next to Grimm reading a paperback book he had propped against his radio.

"Ain't you got another yarn for us, Buck? We could use us one now. Time's gone a little slack on us since we got your bud Crazy Horse penned up good." He smiled, but his eyes kept that cold, buzzard look that's as much a part of a sheriff's getup as his badge.

"What you got Eversole charged with?"

"He ain't deaf."

"Well, let's see now. He ought to get out in five years. Ten at the most."

"Depends on what kind of shape the Flemson boy's in when we find him."

"What the hell are you talking about?"

"Take a guess at it, Buck. Make you up a story to suit the occasion. Have a few shells go off here and there to give it some color."

I stood quiet for a minute, thinking. Grimm stared hard at me, never letting justice's dry grin slip off his face. The dispatcher still hadn't looked up from his reading. I figured he must've come to a killing or a screwing.

"You mean to say it wasn't Wingo that did the shooting?" I asked.

"Your renegade was just winged. Ole Lump can hit a gnat's ass flying. Down here, we train our lawmen right."

"Blessed are the straight shooters," I said, "for they shall run the county."

"Amen, cowboy."

I saw that if I kept jawing with Grimm I was going to win me a bed next to Eversole's. "I just came to see Lefty," I said. "He in there?" I pointed to the door the voices came through.

"Last I saw of him, that's where he was headed."

He let me take a couple of steps toward his private office.

"I don't seem to recollect giving you a invitation." He looked down at the dispatcher. "How about you, Harmon? You give ole Buck here a special invite?"

Harmon raised his head and studied me with his big, lightless eyes like he was trying to come up with the right answer to a hard question. "No sir," he finally said, and then dove back into the paperback.

"I wonder then what it is that possesses a man to try going in where he ain't been invited." He scratched his head, doing his best to imitate a man thinking. "Draw you up a chair, Buck, and see if you can't come up with a tale that'll clear my mind about that. A man in my line needs to learn all he can about motive."

I went on over next to the door of his office and leaned my back against the wall. "I believe I'll stand," I told him. "God knows what might happen to a man that was to doze off in a place like this."

"Well, now, you might just have something there, Buck. We do get some lowlife passing through here."

"I expect they like the company."

"One of the things a thief that wants to stay in business ought to learn to do is watch his mouth."

He was right about that. I shut up, focused my eyes on the wall across the room from me, and tried but failed to make sense of the few words I could hear slipping past the door. The wall seemed like it might make some sense, though. So I walked over and started looking at the pictures Grimm had covered it with. Grimm riding at the head Honorary Posse of Williams County. Grimm making arrests. Grimm triumphant in the middle of a patch of marijuana. Grimm proudly shaking hands with a healthy, beaming George Wallace. And several old pictures of Grimm in various baseball uniforms, Des Moines and Charlotte, Wichita and Selma. In the Selma picture he was standing beside a young, sober Bullet Bob Turner.

"Interested in history, are you, Buck?"

"It whiles away the time." I didn't look at him, just kind of edged my way on down the wall until I came to a framed letter signed by Jimmy Carter thanking Grimm for helping to get out the 1976 vote in Williams County.

Grimm had to've been watching me read it. "Ain't that something?" he said. "I drove more niggers to the polls than Lincoln freed."

"Must not've had one running for sheriff."

"I don't get much opposition."

I turned and looked at him then—the muleshit smirk, the rubber eyes. "Apparently not," I said.

He took a key ring out of his pocket and handed it to the dispatcher. "Harmon, why don't you run over to Emily's Grill and have her fry me up a couple of burgers and on your way back pull me a Co-Cola out of the box down the hall."

"Yessir." Harmon finished a page, turned a corner of it down to mark his place, laid the book on the counter, and left.

When he was gone, I walked over to see what the book was that had entranced him so. *How to Become a Prayer Warrior* by Dr. J. Raymond Whiteside. I'd heard of Whiteside. He rode point for a lynch mob out of Asheville, North Carolina, that called itself the Christian Caucus. So I'd been wrong earlier about ole Harmon; it wasn't a killing or a screwing he'd come to in his reading, but a saving or a damning.

"Good Christian boy, Harmon," Grimm told me. "Daddy's the Reverend Killegrew down at the First Baptist Church."

"Must get in the way of your liquor business," I said, knowing better.

"Well, now, to tell you the truth, ole Harmon ain't the smartest fucker that ever lived, but then it don't take no engineer to talk on that radio."

"No," I said. "He fits right in." I started back to the wall pictures.

"Whoa up there, Buck," Grimm said. I turned around to face him. "I sent Harmon out so I could talk straight with you. I been told by them that know just where it was that you got your education. And I'm beginning to get some notion of just what kind of team it is your man Lefty's running. That ain't either here or there right now, though I'm damn-sure keeping it in my mind. But I don't much cotton to being made a ass out of. You made up that war story to cover your teammate and I can understand that. Maybe the big red son of a bitch is a helluva pitcher and I've seen the time I'd've maybe done the same thing you done. But me and ole Bob Turner's been through firefights and shitstorms together and I want you to let him know I don't appreciate him tacking his Amen onto the ass end of that lie you told me last night."

"He was just drunk," I said.

"Being drunk don't give a man call to shit on his friends."

"I'll tell him that. It'll be his lesson for the day."

"You do that, Buck. And let him know he might ought to be looking a little sheepish tonight when he comes by for his dose of liquor."

We both let it go then. I studied the rest of the pictures and thought about how folks had managed to keep things seeming about the same by letting them change just a little at a time. Grimm drove blacks to the polls so they could vote for men that only a few years before would've driven them away from the courthouse with shotguns and firehoses. But then, what the hell? It's a free ride and maybe a jar of whiskey. And most every time that'd get my vote too.

J. G. Flemson was the first one of them to come out of Grimm's private office. He was a small, spare man with big eyes. He wore what looked to be an expensive suit, but it didn't seem to hang quite right from him. To him it was probably just the kind of uniform he had to wear to play his kind of game. You couldn't say his face was handsome or ugly either, just a face that did its job, another part of the uniform. It didn't look like laughing would come easy to it.

Lefty and Stephen Gabbard followed him over to Grimm. Lefty saw me and shook his head, saying nothing. Gabbard held his head stiff and cocked back some and almost seemed to be holding his breath, as if he didn't like the smell of things around him.

"Let the Indian go," Flemson said to Grimm. I had sidled up close enough to be sure of getting an earful.

Grimm looked first at Flemson, then at Lefty, then back at Flemson. "What about Sandy? Hell, we can't . . ."

"Let the Indian go." Flemson said it slower that time, stopping a beat after each word.

Grimm punched the intercom button. "Lonnie, bring the goddam Indian up."

"Which one?"

"Jesus, Lonnie. How many we got? I tell you what. You just bring up ever' man we got that ain't either a white man or a nigger."

"Oh, him."

Flemson left without saying another word. Grimm watched him going, nodded a couple of times, and said, "The big ones think different than the rest of us."

"Those kind don't think," Lefty told him. "They scheme."

"Whatever you want to call it, it pays good," Grimm came back.

I asked Lefty what they'd had Eversole charged with in the first place.

"Unauthorized alteration of the trajectory of a county projectile and suspicion of misplacing a prominent mongoloid." He raised his eyebrows when he said it and he used his professor's voice.

Gabbard laughed—or chuckled really, very civilized. Grimm said, "It does a pore ole farm boy a world of good to hear the quality talk."

We heard the key turn in the metal door. The door opened out toward us and Eversole came through. He had on his Reds uniform without any of the socks. His bare feet were in tire-tread sandals. A fat, bald man whose nose was just a heavy scar with a hole on each side of it stood in the doorway and said, "Here he is. Welcome to him." He pulled the door to and slid back down to his hole.

Eversole stopped in the middle of the room and glared at Grimm, who matched him eye for eye a second or two and then turned his face on Lefty. "Your boy's got purty eyes," he said.

"I suppose that's why you can't stay away from him," Lefty said.

Eversole walked over and put both hands on the counter and leaned his big face over at Grimm. "Keep away," he said. It sent a chill through the room.

Grimm didn't say anything until just after Eversole had gone out the door into the hallway. Then he cracked his vigilante grin and spit "You betcha, Buck" through it.

Lefty and I went on out then, leaving Gabbard to trade threats with Grimm. We caught up with Eversole about halfway down the hall and again I asked what the hell had happened.

"One of them shot me," Eversole said. He looked down at me and though his face didn't change much, I thought I saw something dance in his eyes and I wondered if maybe he wasn't enjoying all this.

We went out a side door and met Harmon Killegrew carrying Grimm's bag of burgers across the lawn. He had to step off the sidewalk to let Eversole by. He gave us a big white Christian Caucus smile and said, "Have a nice day. God loves you and so do I."

"That won't do me any good," I told him, "unless God's a woman."

"Don't pick on cripples," Lefty told me a few steps later.

"Hell, they're all cripples. That's why they use Jesus for a walking stick."

"That's all right," Lefty said. "You can't blame them for that. You have no right to object until they start using Him for a club."

Dummy Boudreaux was waiting for us in the bus, which he'd parked in a lot a block south of the square, just behind Flemson and Son's Baptist Book Store. Eversole wanted us to drive him back to the ballpark, but Lefty said no. "Hell, they may have an ambush set up out there."

Dummy drove the bus out of the lot and into the street.

"I'm pitching tonight," Eversole announced.

"If the arm's all right," Lefty said.

I said, "Aw, hell, Lefty. A man don't need but one arm to play baseball."

"There's only been one who did it," Lefty laughed. "And he was a helluva man."

Eversole sat up straight in his seat and looked out at the passing town the way a Union soldier might've done in another century. Lefty and I, sitting together in the seat just behind Dummy, kept sneaking looks over at Eversole. I don't know what Lefty was thinking, but I was wondering how it was that Eversole had come to mistake a baseball diamond for a battlefield.

When we were clear of town and back on the Old Taylor Road, I finally got Lefty to tell me what he knew about what had happened. Eversole either didn't know or just wouldn't say who had shot him, didn't seem to even pay us any attention when we discussed it right there beside him. Lefty still thought it might've been Lump Wingo, but Wingo had alibis, of course, several of them. And you had to suspect Colonel Sanders Flemson too. He'd escaped from his room after Grimm had driven him home—had busted out a window and climbed down a tree apparently. He still hadn't been found. That was why they'd arrested Eversole. Flemson and Grimm had figured the idiot had gone back after Eversole, shot poorly, and then got beat to death or dragged down to the river and drowned.

"Why'd they let Eversole go then?" I asked.

"Gabbard made Flemson call Jason Commerce a few minutes ago from Grimm's office. Commerce admitted that his daughter—Candy Jo, I think her name is—had stolen his new pickup truck." Lefty stopped there, shook his head, and laughed.

"So? What's that got to do with this?"

"It seems that the Commerce girl and the Flemson boy run off together every once in a while. Gabbard says it goes way back."

12

And what did all that gunsmoke and cussing come to? Well, nothing, right then. Eversole went right ahead and did what he'd've done if there hadn't ever been a shot fired. He stepped up on the mound that night and blew the damn Fury away. Just before the game, I saw him pour some rubbing alcohol into his wound, cover it with gauze, and then wrap an Ace bandage around it. If it bothered his pitching, you couldn't tell it. He had a perfect game until the bottom of the sixth when he hit their catcher, Boon Lions, in the ribs with a brushback pitch. Quincey Coldfield, their shortstop, broke up the no-hitter in the seventh with a little humpbacked single to right. They got a run in the ninth when Jumping Joe Easter doubled, stole third, and then came home on Sam Feathers's sacrifice fly. But by then we'd already gotten four runs off their ace, Popeye Cobb. I drove in two of them myself, a second-inning double off the wall in left-center. Rainbow Smith hit a solo homer in the fifth, and two innings later Julius Common Deer tripled Jefferson Mundy home from first with our last run. It was the first game I started, and I did all right, getting that clutch double and a walk in four trips. But it was Eversole's show, the way it would be every time he pitched.

But we beat them without Eversole too, winning two of the other three games in spite of the fact that, after Eversole, the best job we got out of any of our starting pitchers was the one Franklin Brown turned in. And he gave up four runs in six and two-thirds innings. We won with our hitting, our fielding, and our relief pitching. And "relief pitching" is just a general way of saying Bullet Bob Turner, who saved two games, Brown's and Pinzon's. We were six and two when we left Oxford, and Turner had either won or saved four of the six.

So we didn't have but two real pitchers then—a starter and a reliever—and were playing .750 ball anyway. It was early, of course, but I'd seen what was supposed to be the league's best team—Selma—and another—Oxford—that usually finished in the upper division, and I felt fairly certain that if I didn't get thrown back in jail and Eversole didn't get killed and Bullet Bob didn't die of alcohol poisoning and the goddam Christians didn't blow up the whole busload of us, we'd be in the pennant race all the way. I didn't come to that judgment because we'd won six of eight. You can't tell anything by that. Hell, the worst team in a league will win around 40 percent of its games and on a good weekend might sweep a series from the best team. Two years ago Grambling College beat the Yankees in a spring exhibition game. In baseball, it takes a season for a team's heart and talent to prove themselves and even then it might be a gust of wind or a bad hop or an umpire's call on a low strike or a bunt that stays just fair or rolls just foul that decides the whole shit-amaree. What you can be sure of is that if you have heart and talent, you'll be there at the end with a chance. I'd been playing baseball on teams since I was ten and I knew a player of talent when I saw one. We had several—pitchers like Eversole and Turner, sluggers like me and Rainbow Smith, a receiver like Joe Buck Cantwell, and the young ones that had all the gifts—speed and grace, the strong arm, the quick bat, the sure eye—kids like Julius Common Deer, Jefferson Mundy, and Atticus Flood that were going to be improving a little every day for about ten years. I was less sure about our heart, but I reasoned that most of us were flakes of one kind or another and some of us were old flakes, persistent flakes, thirty- and forty-year-old flakes that had turned their backs on almost everything but baseball and flakery. And to my way of thinking, folks that have kept being flakes as long as some of us had have to have heart, for, Lord God, you're always trying to weave some wired-up jalopy in and out between the limousines in the funeral procession and knowing all the while that the best you can get out of it's a laugh, that sooner or later one of them sleek, fat fucks is going to hit you, and that when they do they'll just stop a minute and toss you in the hearse and bury you under the banker and find a relative of yours somewhere in the procession to bill for the service. I thought we had that kind of heart, misfits' heart, and that we would fit together, for a season, anyway, because most of us knew we couldn't fit anywhere else.

The three days after we sprung Eversole were good ones, late mornings, porchswing afternoons, and ball-game nights. Pop Stone came over every afternoon and him and Lefty and some of the rest of us would rock out on the verandah and swap yarns. Pop told us some about Candy Commerce and the Flemson moron. When Candy was around and relatively stable, Colonel Sanders stayed pretty content, but she'd been married twice and once had run off to Mexico with an outfielder named Julio Rivera and she had days when she'd go most anywhere and do most anything with most anybody. And when she wasn't playing, she was praying, traveling back and forth between whoredom and Christendom. So the idiot spent about half his time either whining or mastering the art of arson or both. Pop could tell a good story and I felt damn near civilized sipping from a cold glass of tea and dragging on a Lucky and talking and laughing. And it did me good to hear Lefty telling stories just for the joy in it and not troubling himself with whether a lesson could be taken from them.

The games didn't draw too well. I doubt if 75 people showed up

Thursday night, and there weren't but two or three hundred for the Friday- and Saturday-night shows. We had our best crowd on Sunday afternoon, but even then I doubt if we drew as well as the First Baptist Church had earlier that day. But they seemed like decent enough fans. They rooted for the home boys without getting on us much. And they actually gave Eversole a hand when he finished his game.

And usually, even Sheriff Grimm, selling beer and whiskey out of the trunk of his squad car in the parking lot after the games, showed us only the backslapping, hoo-hawing side of his good ole boy personality once we got Eversole out of his jail. Maybe the old ballplayer still in him let him see how much Eversole meant to us, let him see that a pitcher like that was damn-sure worth telling a few lies for. I don't know what kind of explanation Bullet Bob gave him, but it must have satisfied Grimm, because I saw the two of them laughing together outside the clubhouse right after Eversole's game. It could've been that Grimm just needed or wanted the money we paid him for liquor and knew it was good for business to laugh a little with your customers. But I suspected he was biding his time, playing the good-timing, bullshitting redneck until he got a clear shot at us. Whatever it was that moved him, though—greed or cunning or love of baseball or just one fool's simple need for another one to drink and jaw with—he watched all the games and later, when the parking lot was about empty and the stadium lights were off, he'd be out there doing business out of the ass end of his car. And he had liquor store prices, too, which surprised some of the Reds and caused a few of them to think of him as an honest man performing a public service. But I'd dealt with enough sheriffs in enough dry counties to know that the liquor you buy from them is what they've confiscated from some poor fucker that's drove off somewhere and carried it back.

Nobody likes having a few beers after a game more than I do, Lord knows, but I figured it'd be smart for me to stay clear of Grimm and anyway I didn't want to give the son of a bitch any of my money, so I decided to teetotal it until we got to Memphis. But that didn't last but one night. After the second game of the series, I was walking to the bus with Pansy and Pinzon, who'd been the winning pitcher despite giving up six runs in seven innings. Grimm had backed his car right up next to the door of our bus so that none of us would have to go out of our way for liquor. He and Bullet

Bob leaned against the side of the car, each of them holding a Falstaff, the rest of the six-pack sitting just below the blue misery beacon on top of the car. About half the team was already on the bus. I wanted to join them, but Grimm felt like talking.

"Damn fine piece of womanflesh you got there, Buck."

"I thank you, sheriff," I said. I let Pansy get on the bus ahead of me and started to follow her on.

Bullet Bob said, "You ought not to hold no grudges against Jim Tom, Hog. He's a man that's got a job to do and done it."

"I won't argue that," I said.

"Aw, come on, Buck. Have a beer on the county. The way you bruised that apple tonight, you got one coming. It makes a man wonder why you ever took up thieving."

I'd jacked a room-service hummer out of the joint with a couple on in the eighth and before that I'd stung a pair of flat curves for singles. "I learned to hit the curve in the slam," I said.

"Maybe I ought to haul some of the Fury over to Parchman then." He reached behind him, got the beer off the car, and freed a can from the plastic six-pack cuff. "Have a beer on a sheriff. It might improve your outlook."

He held the Falstaff out to me and I took it, figuring that would be the quickest way of getting shut of him. Lefty came over and asked Grimm if he had a lead on the Flemson boy yet.

"He took his horse with them," Grimm said. "Man named Freeman Quick was jumping around the square all afternoon telling folks he'd've skinned Jay Flemson good if Flemson hadn't've hid that horse on him. Nigger named Roskus Versh that pumps gas for Major French out by Spaniard's Bend said Candy and Colonel Sanders stopped in there early this morning and had the horse in the back of the truck. Said they put $18.68 worth of ethyl and six of them big thirty-cent Baby Ruth bars on Jason Commerce's Gulf credit card."

"Didn't they get theirselves a R.C.?" I asked.

"They did. They paid cash for it." Grimm said. "I'm in favor of letting them go and hoping to God they get on the hell out of Mississippi. But that was a brand-new four-wheel drive GMC they drove off in and Jason Commerce ain't about to give it to his daughter."

"Not to mention the horse," I said.

"A man did get shot," Lefty reminded him.

"Hell, coach, that buck ain't hurt none. You seen how he throwed tonight. That bullet just fired him up. You ought to be grateful." Grimm laughed again.

"It's the God's truth," Bullet Bob agreed.

"God works in wondrous ways," Lefty said. Then he started to the bus and I sucked my beer dry and followed him, leaving Bullet Bob to the badge and the night.

Standing in the bus doorway, I heard Grimm say, "Hey, Buck, me and ole Bob's headed out to a little skin parlor the other side of Lena's Grove. You're welcome to come along if you care to. Bob says you're all right once a man gets to know you some. I'll get you special rates."

"I got all I can handle for the time being," I told him. "You boys go on ahead. But you better keep an eye out for the law. You can't never tell when them bastards'll take a notion to start raiding the pussy markets."

Bobbie Sampson, who was driving for us, pulled the door to behind me.

13

We split four with Memphis and took three of four from Nashville. We were hitting so good that some nights our pitchers would give up six or eight runs and we'd still win it for them. Myself, I was geting hits the way God makes poor folks—one right after the other. Up to then, I'd averaged .471, 24 for 51, with five home runs and nine doubles. And one of the doubles would've been a home run if part of the right-field fence in Memphis hadn't been burned down. Since it would've been dangerous for the right-fielder to go chasing off into the night after a fly ball, Lefty and the Memphis manager, Luther Ray, agreed that for that first night anything hit either through or over that fifteen- or twenty-foot gap would be a ground rule double. They thought it'd save arguing over whether the ball would've cleared the fence or not. They just did it for the one game. The next day the grounds crew threw up a makeshift plywood stretch of fence, nailed a Jax Beer sign to it, and went back to regular rules. But sure enough, I came up in the first inning of that first game, Mundy on first with a single in his pocket, and this fireball kid pitcher they got named Howie Tellico threw me a gopher about four inches to my side of the outside corner and I stepped into it and hit it with everything I had. The son of a bitch looked like it was still going up when it cleared that gap in right-center. I hadn't quit cussing when they finally talked me into going back to second base. Lefty came out and argued that a ball hit that far ought to be a home run no matter what, but Luther Ray held that an agreement was an agreement and couldn't be altered just on account of logic. The handful of fans got quite a kick out of it. And when I got back to second, the Memphis infielders commenced to ride me some, telling me I needed to learn to get around on the ball and such. And even our boys rolled around laughing in the dugout like a bunch of school kids. Now, I take a particular pride in my home runs—especially ones hit that far and to the opposite field—so it took me a few minutes to see any comedy in this, but it did come to me. I'd probably hit me three or four 500-foot home runs before the year was out, but a 500-foot double is a once-in-a-lifetime job.

"Why is it," I asked Julius after Rainbow Smith had driven me home with a standard double, "that ever' time the good Lord is moved to take a crap I happen to be standing directly under Him?"

I laughed and he did too. He said, "It was as clean a double as I ever saw."

There'd been a fire in Nashville, but that one had just charred up five or six rows of the third-base bleachers. When I saw that fence in Memphis, the first thing that came to my mind was that Flemson kid and the hard-on he had for matches. But I half-dismissed that, figuring that whatever other problems the Commerce girl might have, she surely had sense enough to keep her idiot friend from wandering around setting fire to ballparks. But the fire in Nashville made me wonder if she wasn't actually helping him. I asked Lefty what he thought about it and he gave me a wiseacre shrug and said that maybe the Christers were right about us after all. The Lord did seem to be hankering to give us a taste of fire.

But anyway, when Bobbie Sampson headed our bus out of Nashville at about one in the morning on the first of May, we stood at the top of the league, 11 and 5, a game and a half above Selma. Plaquemine, our next stop, was 500 miles, or, as Bullet Bob said, ten quarts, away. In the afternoon before the last game of the

Nashville series, a bunch of us had chipped in and bought three of them big green plastic trash barrels and put them on the bus and filled them with ice and beer. We figured to make the trip a celebration.

And we did—most the way. We hadn't got all the way out of the Fugitive Field parking lot before Woodrow Ratliff hauled out his guitar and commenced tuning up. Then I got my mouth harp out of my duffel bag, and as Bobbie guided the bus out of Nashville and onto the Natchez Trace Parkway and followed that south out of Tennessee and across the very northwest tip of Alabama and then headed diagonally across Mississippi, Tishomingo to Woodville, we picked and blowed and sang our way back through fifty years of country music, from John Prine and Billy Joe Shaver and some of them east Texas cocaine outlaws back to Doc Watson and Merle Travis and Patsy Cline and Kitty Wells to Lefty Frizzell and Hank Snow and Ernest Tubb and Hank Williams through Roy Acuff and all the way back to ole A. P. Carter. There was some we couldn't do because we lacked the hands and the instruments to do them justice—Flatt and Scruggs and Bob Wills and Bill Monroe—and, of course, we didn't really do any of them justice if you looked at it with a cold eye. But Ratliff could play the shit out of that Gibson he had and after all my years of practice in the Slammer Conservatory I was passable on the mouth harp, and maybe the best thing about most of them songs is that just about anybody that takes a notion to can sing them. We must've sung "Will the Circle Be Unbroken" for forty-five minutes, and I think at one time or another everybody on the bus—even the blacks, who probably would've preferred some Detroit soul—got out in the aisle and stomped at least a step or two. Well, everybody but Eversole and Bobby Sampson. And once when I looked back at Eversole, I caught him smiling. Bobbie had to drive, but she sung along and kept time by slapping her right palm against the steering wheel. Even Dummy Boudreaux, deaf as a blackjack post, felt the energy of it. He went back and held his hand out to Susan Pankhurst and she got up and did a little jig with him and when they finished she hugged him and then kissed him on the mouth and ole Dummy grinned like a banker fondling mortgage papers.

Ratliff started wearing out down toward the deep end of Mississippi, and about sunup he put his guitar down and laid his head back. I hated to see him quit. I felt like I could've sung my way on down into Mexico. The music and the laughter and the bus cutting through the Mississippi night had given me as sure a feeling of freedom as I'd had in God knows when. It wasn't as exhilarating as that time I drove out of Van Buren in a stolen car with three big sacks of a bank's money riding on a seat beside me. But I'd done that out of desperation, defiance, a need to do something that mattered, one way or another. This singing had nothing of desperation in it, or defiance either, unless you want to say that anything done just for the joy that's in it is an act of defiance, that all singing and dancing, laughing and fucking are ways of pissing on doom.

Ratliff wasn't the only one tired. When the music stopped, most of the others began nodding off. Pansy laid her head on my shoulder and fell into a kid's trusting sleep. Bullet Bob threw a neon orange Houston Astro blanket out in the aisle and rolled over on top of it. Julius and Susan, in the seat straight across from me, slept sitting up, under a quilt, leaning into one another with their heads resting together—the blonde and her dark meat or the buck and his pale squaw. Maybe—but love, it looked like. Lord God, love. It scared me a minute, looking at them and thinking about myself. Thinking how when you felt innocence rising up in you, you had to push it down hard enough to keep it from making a plumb fool of you but not hard enough to kill it because it's what makes a man matter. And thinking then that maybe a man with as many miles and scars on him as I had would be doing the brave thing by not pushing at all—to feel the happy fool starting to take over in me and to know what it was and what it would do and then to just let it be, leave it grow.

It was on up in the morning when 61 carried us into Baton Rouge, where we crossed the Mississippi. A few minutes later we were in Plaquemine and then through it. A parish road led us out into what the signs said was Bayou Chalin. We took a right off that road onto a private drive that had been built up out of the swamp. About a mile down that we came to a gate guarded by a foreign-looking man that was nearly as tall as Eversole and probably 25 pounds heavier. He wore a uniform he might've taken off an opera soldier—tassels on the shoulders, gewgaws on the chest, a sword on one hip, a gun on the other, and a rifle slung across his back.

Bobbie stopped the bus and Lefty stepped out and talked to the gussied-up thug, who kept his hand on his pistol all during the conversation. When Lefty finished, the guard went over to his shed and said something into his telephone. Then he hung up and came out and opened the gate. We drove through and I turned around and watched him lock it behind us.

"Arise, ye soldiers of the revel!" Pinzon stood and yelled. "We've let the bastards capture us."

14

After another quarter-mile or so, we came to Fort Saint Ignatius. The concrete wall surrounding the garrison must've been fifteen feet high and nearly half that thick. A pair of surly-looking guards stared down at us from behind their parapet. The iron-gray gate opened out and Bobbie drove us in. The inside grounds had been completely paved over except for a little green space around the big two-story white stucco house that stood in the middle of the yard.

We got out of the bus and an old man and a young woman came through the door to the glassed-in porch and walked toward us. The old man was Pumpsie Narvaez, who'd been running this parish since about the time Hitler sunk his claws into Germany. The years had weathered him some, but I couldn't see that they'd bent him at all. He wore a loose white summer suit, a pale-blue shirt, a string tie, and a wide-brimmed straw planter's hat. At seventy-two—which is how old Lefty later told us he was—Pumpsie was still barrel-chested, rope-muscled, and flimflam-eyed. All he had for a left ear was a hole with a little lump behind it. I kind of admired the way he let it show, refusing to grow hair down over it. The woman beside him made me think of the way Dolly Parton might look if Dolly was about a foot taller and the hair she piled on her head was black instead of blonde. In other words, Pumpsie's piece had a nice wide mouth and tits the size of a baby's head.

"It ain't much, boys," Pumpsie announced to us with the sweep of an arm, "but I call it home."

"We'll try to make do," Lefty told him.

Pumpsie walked up to Lefty and took his hand—didn't put his out and wait for Lefty's, just reached down and lifted Lefty's and started pumping. "Lefty Marks," Pumpsie said, sounding serious and proud. "I saw you play in Shreveport in '19 and '42. You were with Houston. I never will forget it. You went 3 for 4. The first two was bunts and a man couldn't've rolled them out there by hand any prettier and the last was a double you damn near made the third baseman eat when he came up the line on you. And then towards the end of the game you throwed out some poor fuck that tried to score from third on a short fly to left. Beat anything I ever saw." He dropped Lefty's hand.

Lefty nodded several times. You could see that pleasure had been surprised onto his face.

But Pumpsie went on. "I've heard tell you've soured some since. Gone pink and maybe even plumb red. But I want to come right out here and now and say that that don't mean ratshit to me. A man plays whatever game he can squeeze the most good out of. And as long as you don't mess with mine, I'll lay off of yours. I invited you to bring your boys down and stay here with me because I admired the gumption you showed that day in Shreveport. You give me half a chance and I'll show you a good time."

"Yes," Lefty said, "I remember that day. They had a young left-hander. Name was Joe Fred Hopper, I believe. Smoked it, but hadn't yet had time to develop much else. And I could always handle that hard stuff. A couple of years later I heard that Joe Fred had gotten killed in France."

"Well," Pumpsie said, "damn curve wouldn't've done him no good anyhow then." He looked back at his woman and said, "Mary Belle, come up here and get you a head-on gander at the only man that ever one-armed his way to the big time. Us cripples got to stick together. I'm the only one-eared man that ever ran Plaquemine Parish."

She had on a long black wrap-around skirt and a lacy white blouse that she'd buttoned all the way up to her throat. Her blue eyes sparkled and her teeth shone and I figured she'd laid waste to more good men than U. S. Grant. Pumpsie watched her with a proud owner's eye and I couldn't keep from thinking that there's any number of things worse than being an old fool.

"Lefty Marks, this here's my woman, Mary Belle Loudermilk. Dances a week or two a month down in the Quarter under the name of Connie Lingus. Maybe we can arrange for you to catch her act some night before the season's over."

Mary Belle gave Lefty her hand and curtsied and let the sun

catch her smile. She didn't look much over fifty years younger than
Pumpsie.

"Pleased," Lefty managed to say. He let go of her hand without
kissing it.

"I'm honored, Mr. Marks," Mary Belle said, all milk and honey
poured over a jigger or two of Spanish fly.

Pumpsie let us get an eyeful of her before he spoke again. Then
he addressed the whole team. "I expect you boys are saying to
yourselves: 'Well now, how did that old fart get him a woman the
like of this here?' It's a fair question, I'll grant you. So I'll give you
the answer. It's money and power that does it, boys. Money and
power." He stopped a second and nodded solemnly. "That and
having a cock the size of your throwing arm."

Most of us laughed—short and nervous-like, but laughter. Then
Mary Belle, looking as philosophical as a woman made like that
can, said, "No. It was just the money and power. And then, there's
nothing like an old man for foreplay."

"Aye God, Lefty," Pumpsie snorted. "What can you do with
them? You take 'em in off the street and feed 'em and give 'em
some moral training and first thing you know they're trifling with
your manhood. I'm an old man, unnaturally sensitive. I don't
know how much more of it I can stand."

"Ah, poor Pumpsie," Lefty said. "Child of the heart."

"That's what everybody says." Pumpsie threw an arm around
Mary Belle. "What say you and your boys follow us in out of the
sun? I'll have ole Tiboy stir us up a pot of something or other. I got
more food in there than you can say grace over."

Bullet Bob finally came to enough to ask a question. "What the
hell happened to your ear?"

Pumpsie, mocking sadness, looked at the ground and shook his
head a time or two. "It was my sweet, fat wife, Renée—gone these
five years. Keeled over at dinnertime, face down, in a plate full of
red beans. I told ole Tiboy, 'It's the way she'd awanted it.' Back in
1948 she caught me curled up asleep with a naked dancing girl
name of Amber Heat wrapped around me and before I got woke
up good she had my ear in her hand. I've thanked God ever since
that that's all she took. A sweet woman she was, but fat as a pen-
sioned whore. And vile-tempered and lazy, God rest her soul.
Worst housekeeper you ever saw. Ever' time I went to piss in the
sink it was full of dishes."

15

When I'm old and gray and sailing toward the old folks' home, bring me a dancing girl and a splint for my cock.

I admired the way old Pumpsie refused to have any part of a graceful old age. Grace was for artists and Christians. Pumpsie wanted noise and movement, food and music, women and whiskey.

Pumpsie had built his fort back in the early '60s to give himself room to lock up all the freedom riders he expected to come down trying to civilize his rich, wet, one-parish Confederacy. He figured, too, that if it came right down to it he could hole up there with his little army and his g-string harem and make a glorious last stand.

I got all that from Lefty. Pumpsie didn't talk politics, didn't bother to explain himself, just told jokes and poured bourbon, grabbed women and ate crayfish. He'd talk ball with you or swap tales about neon nights, but the fort was just there and the parish was his. That was understood. You could like it or move on. It was just that American. He was a lecher and a thief and maybe he needed killing. I wouldn't've wanted to have stayed long enough to have become part of what he ruled. But there was blood in him and laughter. Outlaws may be as bad as merchants at running things, but they throw better parties. I enjoyed myself, for no longer than I was there.

I wondered some about Lefty though. "What's a man like you doing in a place like this?" I asked him one afternoon over a piece of holy meat pie.

"Couldn't resist," Lefty said. "I've heard stories about the place since just about the day he started building it. When he invited us, I gave in to my curiosity. A man needs to see how the other half lives." Half his mouth smiled and then he stuck a bite of the pie in it. "They eat well," he said.

I wondered, too, about Mundy and Flood and Brown. But they seemed to do just fine, and as far as I could tell Pumpsie didn't even notice them. Lefty said that when he'd written to accept the invitation he'd been careful to let Pumpsie know that the blacks would be coming with us. Pumpsie'd replied that he'd been raised on brown sugar, that a baseball team wasn't nothing without color, and that he'd always wanted to visit Africa.

His team wasn't worth a warden's promise, but he made more money off it than any other owner in the league. It wasn't as much a baseball team as a gambling scam. I heard that back in the '50s they even had betting windows right at the stadium. Fans bet on everything from the outcome of the game to the number and kind—home run, triple, double, single—of hits a player would get. You could bet on how long a pitcher would last, how many hits or runs would come in a particular inning—damn near anything. If you liked a long shot, you could lay your money on a no-hitter. About twenty years earlier the league office had forced Pumpsie to shut down the betting windows. He'd done that, but the gambling went on. Fans could play their hunches in the office of the Narvaez Land Company up till an hour and a half before game time, or they could just wait until the game started and bet from their seats. The ushers were bookies.

The league office ignored the gambling. The Pirates drew over a million fans a year. The league needed them. In 1963, when the Milledgeville Peacocks came within a prayer of going under, Pumpsie loaned their owner, Regina Pope, enough to keep herself afloat. And it was understood that Pumpsie would do the same for any of the other owners—just so long as they didn't try to gum his game up with their rules.

Lefty explained it all to us in the clubhouse, trying to prepare us for the first game. He even read us part of a letter he'd gotten from the Commissioner of the Dixie Association, Judge Lee Stuart Jackson. It said: "You will undoubtedly discover that certain of the methods utilized by Mr. Narvaez in the operation of his franchise are somewhat unorthodox. Some of these methods, I hasten to add, would not be tolerated if utilized by the owner, or owners, of any of the other of the Association's various franchises. One would do well, moreover, to keep in mind the incontestable fact that life in Plaquemine is in many ways influenced by strong residual elements of a foreign culture. What the fans there find acceptable might conceivably elsewhere be considered an outrage. I can, however, categorically assure you that the sanctity of the games themselves remains inviolate."

"What the hell does that mean?" Bullet Bob asked.

"These crackers and coon-asses bet on every pitch," Pinzon explained, "but they won't throw the game."

And they didn't throw the games, I don't guess. They weren't good enough to have to bother with that. They'd never won the league championship. They finished over .500 about once every ten years. They'd never had a player that went up to the big leagues. They had a helluva good time.

While we were taking batting practice before the first game, I saw Pinzon go over to the stands and hail an usher. I asked him how much he'd bet and what on. He said he'd wanted to put a hundred on Eversole throwing a no-hitter, but that players weren't allowed to bet.

It worked out for the best. He'd've lost his hundred.

Eversole set the Pirates down in order for five innings—fifteen in a row, twelve of them K's. But we were so far ahead by then—13–zip—that he lost interest, quit bothering to throw hard and stopped loading the ball up. Now, the Pirates weren't outright spastics. A couple of them—Castro Corrado and S. O. Russell—were actually ballplayers, didn't quite have professional talent, but came close. You groove one to them, they'll hit it. So by the time the game was over, Eversole had given up five hits and two runs.

I think it depressed him to pitch in a game all the competition had been wagered out of. Before his games he steeled himself for battle. The battle turning out to be a carnival confused him. He couldn't let himself join in the fun, but he couldn't fight either. He just kind of shrugged his way through the last four innings. Probably he'd've rather been back in Oxford, dodging bullets.

And God knows it was hard to make yourself believe that winning mattered there. Pumpsie's parishioners, who had packed the double-decked stadium, cheered or booed, rejoiced or cursed according to how their bets turned out. In the top of the third I hit one out—altogether we hit eight that night—and the folks whose money said I'd do that gave me an ovation.

Pumpsie started his grandson, Louis-Ferdinand Narvaez, that game and left him in nearly five innings. By then he'd given up 11 runs, 6 home runs, 14 hits. He didn't walk anybody. All Louis-Ferdinand had was a big windup, more than his share of gall, and a sense of humor. He'd rear back, kick his leg up above his head, grunt like a weightlifter, push towards home, and let loose a fastball that a good sprinter could've run alongside of. Oh, he'd try a curve now and then, but they just spun a little different than his fastball. Even the outs we made were the kind that bruise a fielder's hand.

But it wasn't for getting shelled that Pumpsie jerked his grandson. It was for not being able to stand up any more. When Pumpsie finally went to the mound, Louis-Ferdinand was sitting on the rubber taking in a standing ovation. A lot of the fans must've made good money betting on Louis's gopher, and maybe the rest were just applauding endurance—I don't know.

Louis-Ferdinand was the worst pitcher they had. But they didn't have one I couldn't've hit when I was sixteen. Their best one—a serious, sad-eyed man named Gunner Wise—threw the ball damn hard and held us to eight runs in the third game. His trouble was that his curve just bent a little instead of jumping like a good one will and that his fastball, hard as it was, came in straight, no sink or rise or tail. When you hit it, it was apt to be gone for a while.

I remember standing out by second after sending a double howling to the wall in the seventh inning of the fourth and last game of that series and looking up at those two decks full of gamblers and wondering how these bastards ever won a game. And they did win some—usually played about .300 ball. Then when I turned it over and looked at it good it wasn't hard to see. Part of it was that they gradually sucked you into their way of doing things. The game was an excuse for folks to get together and have some laughs and maybe win some money. So the ballplaying tended to get sloppy. But the big reason, I'm sure, was that, if he cared to, a visiting pitcher could make a sight more money there by losing than by winning. It would've been easy enough to get around the rule against players betting. Hell, I could've sent Pansy down to the Land Office to place bets for me. The odds against Plaquemine winning were 3–1. You're a pitcher getting through the month on a bush league check, you'd be tempted to bet that check on Plaquemine and do what you could to give them the game.

But during that first stay, none of us ever went in to Plaquemine except to play ball. Pumpsie kept us pretty well entertained out at the fort. We'd drive in and win an easy game of an evening, then go back out to the fort and eat and drink and maybe walk outside once or twice and holler into the Louisiana night. Good ole boys drinking and snorting. I even liked laying in that cell Pumpsie had for me to sleep in. The slammer architecture—the bunk beds, the concrete floor, the rusted, lidless commode, the one bare bulb, and the little, square window, too high to reach, too thick to break— laid my past out all around me, without threatening me. It was strange, I guess, how that made me feel free.

Pansy slept with me in that cell, and it set her too to thinking on my past and worrying over our future. The night before we headed back to Little Rock she asked me what I thought would become of us. I said I didn't know. I said I just liked the way she felt laying up against me. I said it was dark outside. I tried to think of something funny to tell her. I said I didn't know.

The most dangerous thing you can do is to care.

16

The morning after we got back to Little Rock I went downtown to let Mantis shoot another government fix into me. A pair of shaved, hungry-looking cons had their heads together in the wait- ing room—plotting a job, probably. But I didn't have a chance to get in on the conversation. I'd no more than got sat down before Julie buzzed Mantis and he told her to send me right in.

"Good to see you, Hog," he said, hiding behind a salesman's smile. "Have a seat."

I did. Then I lit up a Lucky. He pushed a white ceramic ashtray across the desk at me. In the middle of it there was a picture of a big red razorback pig, snorting smoke.

"I thought maybe Lefty would accompany you again." He sounded pleasant, like he was talking about some old boy both of us had known and loved since we were all kids together.

"I rode in with the team, but they went on down to the field. This is a working day."

"I see," he said. "I wanted a word with him. But I can call."

I didn't know what the hell was going on in his head, but I kept from asking. I figured Lefty could handle it.

Mantis rocked forward and rested his forearms on his desk. "I see you guys are in first place."

"God's been sleeping."

He smiled again. He said, "Well, it is true that the Reverend Bushrod and his followers have directed their energies elsewhere. For the two of us, that's good news."

"We're back in town now though. Sitting ducks again."

"But I do think we can hope you've become somewhat respectable. You *are* leading the league. Fifteen and five, I believe, isn't it?" He picked the sports section of the *Chronicle* up off his desk. "Yes. Three full games ahead of Selma. I don't think anyone expected you to do this well. It's gratifying to know that in spite of everything else the Reds are a legitimate baseball team."

I asked him who was leading the American League West.

He checked the standings again. "Seattle. A game and a half over Chicago."

"They won't be there long."

He thought a minute, then nodded. "Well taken. But my point isn't that the Reds will win the pennant. Only that you play well enough to belong in the league." He leaned back in his chair and tilted his head to the left. "And you, Hog. I must admit I seriously underestimated your talent."

"I could always hit. It was armed robbery I never quite mastered."

"But hit like this? How could anyone have known you were capable of hitting the way you have been? Even after only twenty games, a .500 average is very impressive."

"Five twenty-one," I told him. "Thirty-seven for 71. Eight home runs. Twenty-three RBI's." I figured he was trying to set me up for some kind of fall, but I didn't see how it could hurt to give him my numbers. They love statistics. "Just cruising right along on my way to the Triple Crown," I said.

"I honestly hope so. Nothing would make us look better." He ran an index finger along an eyebrow. "The Triple Crown. That's really something. Do you truly think you have a chance at it?"

"No."

He waited for more, but I wasn't giving it to him. What you give them now they'll hit you with later.

"Well," he said. "We can hope."

I snuffed the stub end of my Lucky on the razorback. "We done? I got to make a living."

"Not quite." He studied the ceiling a minute. It was them soft white squares. I thought he was readying himself to throw the rope. But he put it off a while. "Let's see. You're playing Milledge-ville today, aren't you? They've been fairly solid the last few years. Colorful manager."

"A man like me wonders why a man like you went to the bother of doing all this research."

"My job," he said. "By the way, I understand you ran into a lit-tle trouble in Oxford."

"They winged our ace."

"Jeremiah Eversole, isn't it?"

"Helluva sinker."

"I received information from a Williams County deputy sheriff alleging that you misrepresented the truth to an investigating offi-cer."

"They couldn't've stood the truth pure." I reached into my shirt pocket for another Lucky, then decided against it. "You got the cuffs ready for me?"

He laughed. I went ahead and had the Lucky. He rode his chair over to his filing cabinet, opened a drawer, and took out a sheet of paper. "This is the deputy's report." He put it back. "I want you to understand that I do my job thoroughly."

"I never doubted it."

He scooted himself back over to his desk. "After I received the deputy's information, I called the sheriff down there. His opinion was that you were only trying to protect a friend and teammate you believed to be innocent." He leaned back in the chair and crossed his legs.

I gave him a bored look and he showed me the smile again.

"Actually," he went on, "all I wanted to say to you about what went on in Oxford was that we were fortunate the papers here didn't carry anything about it. The *Chronicle* has been printing nothing about you except the Dixie Association standings—not even box scores. They may not have intended it this way, but they couldn't have done you a bigger favor. All the baseball fans here know now is that you're in first place. Unless Lefty intentionally stirs things up again, the Reds will simply be another minor league baseball team. As for the Reverend Bushrod, he's working full-time to get John P. Schicklgruber elected to the Senate." Mantis looked at his watch.

"Yeah. I saw their picture in the paper this morning." The *Chronicle* picture, front page, had shown Bushrod and Schicklgruber waving bibles and facing a gaggle of the riled-up born-again in front of the Asher Avenue Adult Book Store and Peep Show. Schicklgruber had been the congressman from northwest Arkansas for six or seven terms. He took all the godly stands—favoring bombs and oil men, opposing niggers and fuck films. I figured he was a shoo-in.

"Well then," Mantis said after a pause. "This has worked out better than either of us had a right to hope. I'm quite optimistic. The team's doing well. You're doing even better. In fact, I'm wondering if you don't belong in another, higher league. At your age you need to rise as rapidly as you can. There's a possibility I can help you do that."

I got up. Jesus, they'll tell you anything.

"Just a minute," Mantis said. "I'm serious about what I said. You've convinced me that you are a baseball player. I'm certain you'll continue to do quite well playing for the Reds this year. But what about the future? Do you actually mean to tell me you would turn down a chance to play for a better team? It's possible I can get you that chance. Surely even Lefty would advise you to accept such an opportunity."

"You just want me out of town," I said. "And I like it here. Springtime. All churches and roses."

I turned and started for the door.

"Sit down." He said the words loudly and stopped for a beat in between them, the way you would if you were giving a command to a balking dog.

I turned around and gave him a grin. "That's better. At least we've quit playing like we're here trying to help each other out."

He reached out with his left hand and pressed his intercom button. "Julie, has Mr. Ratoplan returned?"

"Yes, sir."

"Send him in, please."

I was still standing in the middle of the office when Ratoplan came in, unwrinkled, upright, stiff, and cold. The iceberg spic. A perfect gray suit covered his hard brown body. Styled black hair rolled back over his skull. He looked at the world through dark, narrow eyes.

"Cesar Ratoplan," Mantis said. "Hog Durham."

"Howdy, Pancho," I said.

Mantis told Julie to bring in another chair.

"I won't detain you more than a few moments, Mr. Durham," Ratoplan told me. "I merely wish to tell you something of the history of our mutual colleague, Gonzalo Pinzon." The voice was low, calm, confident. He'd educated the accent out of it.

Julie dragged a chair over to Mantis's desk. Ratoplan thanked her. She left. He sat down, crossed his legs, straightened the crease in his slacks. I stood where I was another minute, thinking about leaving. But he had me hooked and knew it. I wanted to hear the story. I walked back over to my chair and sat down.

Ratoplan recited the facts. Pinzon's father, Juan, had owned a casino in Batista's Havana. When he heard Castro coming, he put his family and his money on his speedboat, set his bodyguard at the controls, and headed for Florida. Somewhere between Havana and Key West Juan fell over the side and drowned. Ratoplan said there was no evidence that anyone had pushed him over. Gonzalo and his mother, Margarita, who'd been a stripper in the Pinzon casino until she'd hooked the owner, went on to Miami. Two years later she landed herself the sixty-year-old Miami millionaire real estate tycoon named G. Harold Carney.

Ratoplan flicked something I couldn't see off his britches leg. I sucked in a stiff dose of the Lucky and then blew out some rings. Ratoplan pulled once at his left earlobe, pursed his lips, and went on. "Whatever one might think of Margarita and her motivation, not even Gonzalo doubts that G. Harold Carney fell in love. The marriage revitalized him. He became a vegetarian, forswore tobacco and alcohol, and spent an hour each morning pedaling an Exercycle he had installed in his office. Today, an octogenarian, his heart is sound. Prior to the marriage, Hal had merely been a dedicated capitalist; afterward he became an energetic fanatic—and I do not use that word pejoratively. He devoted himself completely to a specific goal—the liberation of Cuba."

Ratoplan stretched his neck, touched the knot of his tie, and kept going.

"Gonzalo was a boy of five when his mother married Hal. But he was already beyond her control. She was not meant for motherhood. So Hal, denied a son for so long, immediately assumed the bulk of the responsibility for Gonzalo's rearing. Unfortunately—and for reasons best left to psychiatry—Gonzalo seems always to have resented his stepfather. But Hal never gave up on him. He believed his cause to be greater than himself and he knew that God had not allowed Moses to enter The Promised Land. Therefore, he tried unceasingly to train Gonzalo to be his Joshua.

"But during his teens Gonzalo evinced no ambitions other than to become either Lucky Luciano or Juan Marichal. Many times during those years Hal rescued Gonzalo from either the streets or the jails to which they led. So when he first noticed Gonzalo's interest in baseball, he encouraged it, thinking it preferable to, say, car theft or drug smuggling. However, it became increasingly evident that Gonzalo was not outgrowing his interest in that somewhat adolescent sport. In fact, the older Gonzalo grew, the more seriously he seemed to take the sport. Something obviously had to be done. When Hal realized just how seriously Gonzalo was taking the game, he hired a scout to evaluate the boy's talent. I say 'boy.' Gonzalo was nearly seventeen. It was only two months prior to his arrest. The scout was a professional. We were assured he was the best in the area. Magpie Malone."

"Oh, yeah," I said. "Pitched for the Cardinals and Giants back in the '30s. Journeyman curveballer. Talked out loud to himself all the time he was pitching. Great American."

"The very man," Ratoplan said. "His assessment was that Gonzalo's talent was, by professional standards, no better than marginal. Now, G. Harold Carney is committed to excellence. He had Malone deliver his scouting report directly to Gonzalo. He pointed out to Gonzalo that the best he could reasonably hope for from baseball was a few dull years pitching before sparse crowds on a procession of backwater diamonds. Gonzalo did not react well. He left. Two months later Hal received a call from the police. Hal loved Gonzalo too much to allow him to ruin his life either on the diamond or on the streets. Therefore, he did not stand in the way of the juvenile court. Gonzalo served a year in the reformatory."

"Your tale's getting a little tough to swallow, Pancho," I said. "It's hard to see even a lunatic land developer sending his boy to the slam just to keep him off the pitcher's mound."

He gave me a slow, confident nod. "You see, Mr. Durham, to a man like G. Harold Carney frivolity is tantamount to sin. It is a waste of time and energy, a shirking of one's moral obligations. Life is not a game. It is a serious business."

"You apply logic to life," I said, "you get sadness and subdivisions."

Ratoplan glanced at his shoe, then back up at me, then went on as if I'd said nothing. "Prison did Gonzalo no good. He had to learn the hard way. He worked out with weights, gave up drugs, and ran several miles a day. All for the wrong reason. As soon as he was freed be began playing baseball again. He pitched extremely well during his last year of American Legion ball. At the end of that year he signed a contract with the Cleveland Indians. He pitched three years in their organization, never winning half his decisions, never rising above the Carolina League. Magpie Malone had been right. Gonzalo was not offered a contract for a fourth year. So then when Hal went to him and offered him a job with our company, Gonzalo accepted. We thought he had finally grown up. When he left us early this February, he was a vice president of our Elysian Land Development Company."

"He could be selling swampland to old folks and taking potshots at Castro and instead here he is again, slinging curve balls at grown men." I stopped and gave them a wise nod. "It's what's wrong with the world."

"There's more truth in that than you realize," Ratoplan said, showing me one of his soft, clean palms. "But I have no desire to argue. I've come to ask a favor of you. We want Gonzalo to come back home. I think you can help persuade him. If you can, G. Harold Carney will reward you generously. We can guarantee you a good position with the company. I'm told you're an excellent minor-league player. Should you wish to continue in that line, I'm sure Hal could arrange to have you added to the roster of one of the Florida teams. He is well connected with several of the general managers. Mr. Mantis here assures me that if and when the time comes he can and will make the necessary legal arrangements."

"Nice fellow, that Mantis," I said.

Ratoplan went on as if he were negotiating the terms for a contract with another businessman. "I'm authorized to give you a $2,500 bonus for accepting employment with our company. For your first year, you would be paid a salary of $1,500 a month."

"I see. You Florida freedom fighters want to get Gonzalo back in your outfit, and ole Nightstick Mantis there just wants to get me the hell out of Dodge. You boys like the taste of one another's ass?"

"Just a minute," Mantis began.

Ratoplan interrupted him. "Our offer of employment is contingent, of course, upon your persuading Gonzalo to return to Miami.

I'm far from certain you can accomplish that. But when Gonzalo is suffering through a mood like his current one, you're the type of man he listens to. And if you fail, nothing is lost."

I stood up. "Well, boys, it's been educational. I do appreciate your offer, Pancho. But I'm flush just now."

"Think it over," Ratoplan said, cold as a banker at a foreclosing. I knew then that I'd done just about what he'd expected me to.

As I walked out, I heard Mantis telling me I was a fool, that there was nothing immoral about Ratoplan's offer, that it offered me a secure future. I shut the door behind me and walked past Julie's desk and out of the place and onto the streets, thinking of all the times I'd had to sit still while some licensed fool told me that life was a serious business, that I had to learn to accommodate myself to reality. You play by their rules; it is a business. I use you, you use him. I got a dollar, you got a dime. So fuck 'em all, I thought. All those immaculate, methodical realists that aren't but another scam or two away from ruining the world.

17

I hadn't got out of the office good when Ratoplan pulled up beside me in a silver Imperial that was as long as a boxcar. I looked over, saw who it was, and kept walking. He eased past me, parked the car next to the stop sign at the corner, and got out. He waited for me there at Third and Victory, under the red-and-white awning over the door to Friday's.

I could've lost him right then—turned back and went in and out of alleys and buildings until I'd shed him. But I knew he'd corner me sooner or later. Hell, I had to show up for ball games and meetings with Mantis. I'd hooked my life to a schedule. It made me easy game. And anyway, it was Mantis that worried me, not Ratoplan. I didn't think Ratoplan could do much to me other than jack up his bribe. I was wrong.

I walked up to him without changing my pace.

"They don't allow no peddlers here, Pancho," I said. "Spoils folks' appetites."

I took a step toward the door and he laid a hand on my shoulder. I stopped, looked down at it, then up at him. "Right now I can't think of anything I'd enjoy more than ripping that pretty arm off of you and then carrying it on out to the park and taking batting practice with it."

He moved the hand, but not out of fear. "I am not the man you take me for. I have been in fights. I do not lose."

"It's high time then. A few scars might make you human."

He cocked his head a little to one side and let a corner of his mouth start upward as if he might, someday, smile. I was surprised at how easy he held himself, at how god-awful sure he seemed, there on the street, in the open, just the two of us.

"There's no advantage to having scars," he said. "They reopen too easily. Take yourself, for instance. A man with your past is always vulnerable."

"Oh, but praise the Lord, Pancho, I've done my time and seen the light. All there is up ahead of me now is good roads and green lights."

"Possibly. But there is that unsolved bank robbery in Van Buren. A thing like that could cloud a man's future."

Even then he didn't let himself smile, but I could tell by the sharpshooter's glint in his eye that he was enjoying himself. He was a man that had found his calling. I did what I could to keep surprise and anger off my face.

"Van Buren is a tight, ugly little place," I said, giving him a big horseshit grin. "A church on every corner. No liquor. Christian women. A man looking for a good time there might have to take to bank robbery."

A college-age girl came out the door and walked between us. She'd squeezed her ass into fifty dollars' worth of jeans and wrapped her tits in a Rolling Stones T-shirt. I watched her walk around to the parking lot and get in her Grand Prix.

"Your type?" Ratoplan asked.

"I don't know nothing about cars."

"That model is flashy," he said, "but cheap." Then he motioned toward his own car. "I'm going west. The ballpark's on my way. We'll have to discuss this matter sooner or later."

He did take a fool's pride in his car. "Quiet motor," he said after starting it. "I could have flown from Florida, but this is an absolute joy to drive." I fired up another fucking Lucky and waited for him to work his way into the next verse of his civilized little blackmail song.

He glided over into the right lane, cruised past an old Volkswagen, and started in. "As you say, Van Buren is a small town. Old-fashioned values, perhaps. However, I found its citizens very cooperative. Especially the bank employees. I also had some informative conversations at the Southland Furniture Factory across the river in Fort Smith, domain of the famous hanging judge. Then I had the pleasure of meeting your former parole officer, a Mr. Jasper Gant of Tahlequah."

"You must've had to kill a lot of whiskey at night to tolerate all that."

"I correlated the various, shall we say, testimonies I received and examined certain pertinent documents and discovered, alas, that you quit your job at the furniture factory the very day People's Bank and Trust Company was robbed."

"I hope it was a friend of mine that pulled the bank job and I hope he's lapping up tequila down in Mexico now."

"You moved to Stilwell then, I believe, and lived there for several weeks in the apartment of a woman named Anna Lee Yancey. According to her, you were carrying an impressive amount of cash."

"It don't take much to impress her."

"Apparently not."

I wondered if Anna Lee had ever met a decent man. We all wanted something from her, and she was so simple she thought giving us what we asked for would make us happy.

"The backgrounding I gave you and the subsequent offer I made you in the parole office were more for Mantis's benefit than yours. The offer stands, of course. But I fully expected you to refuse it. I was merely covering him for you. Now that you have been given a more accurate view of the strength of our bargaining position, you can accept our offer, go to Florida, and Mantis will suspect nothing."

"Oh, I do see. First, you tried to strong-arm Gonzalo, but he kept slipping your holds. Then you figure, hell, you might just as well try using somebody else on him, and there I was, sitting up like a duck in a washtub. Then you just sniffed around till you came up with some shit you could sling on me. But your aim's off some. I never robbed that bank, Pancho."

As we passed the medical center, he pulled over into the left lane and I dropped my Lucky on the floorboard and rubbed it out with the sole of my shoe.

"Hardly matters, does it? Guilt or innocence seems irrelevant." He stopped for a traffic light and flicked on the left-turn signal. "The bank was robbed. I assure you of that. I can place you near the scene. I can show that you left town almost immediately afterward. I can demonstrate that a week or two later you were, though unemployed, carrying a suspiciously large quantity of cash."

He made the left and we cruised up a hill toward War Memorial Stadium, home of the football Razorbacks, pride of the state.

"I've done my time for that money," I said. "I took it from liquor stores. I don't trust banks."

"The man who will rob a liquor store will rob a bank. And the fact that you have served time makes you more suspect. And certainly more vulnerable. Even if the information I have gathered is insufficient to convict you of bank robbery, I think you'll have to agree that it is surely more than enough to persuade Mantis to revoke your parole."

"Pull over into that football lot. I'll walk from here."

"Certainly."

Before I got out, he said, "I'm a man of my word, Durham. If you cooperate with us, there will be no trouble. You can have the money and the job in Florida. I'm sure we can find something for a man like you to do. We'll even leave you here to play your game in peace, if that's what you want. But if you remain stubborn, there will be retribution. You mean nothing to us. We want Gonzalo. But we'll run over you to get him. Think it over. I'll be here through the home stand."

"Thanks for the ride," I told him. "It was white of you."

After I got out, he leaned across the seat, picked up the butt of my Lucky, raised it up, and dropped it out the window on his side.

I stood there a minute, watching while the big silver hearse floated back down the hill.

Part III

18

The morning after Ratoplan tried cutting me up for trap bait, I drove the co-op pickup into Little Rock and went to Barry Rotenberg's office. He was part of the firm of Whistler, Rotenberg, Newcome, and Chance. Rotenberg had founded the firm, the first integrated one in Arkansas, with Lincoln Whistler, a slick, sharp, stubborn black that had left Helena twenty-five years ago with nothing more than a head full of angles and a gut full of gall, bluffed his way into Harvard and studied his way out, and then came back down to Little Rock carrying the law degree he was going to use to plague all the Old Guard, razor-backed white folks.

The firm had its offices in a big white house in the Heights section, a quiet part of town, with tall trees and old houses. I suspect that Whistler had been the first black to do any business there other than a little cleaning and catering. But others had followed him, and all the good Rotarians and Jaycees had picked up, moved west, and built new churches.

"Is Mr. Rotenberg in?" I asked the slim, pretty, chocolate-colored receptionist.

"Is he expecting you?"

"If he is, things are worse than I thought they were." I tried a smile out on her, but she didn't seem to care much for it. The belted-up, efficient kind you'd have to catch outside of office hours to get any life out of. "Well, I'd've called, but I was coming in anyhow and figured I'd just come a little early and drop by and see if he's in. If he ain't, you can just mark me down for another morning. There's no big hurry and I won't need but a few minutes of his time. Hog Durham's the name."

"Hog?" You'd've thought I'd said my name was Piss Breeden,

who, by the way, drives a school bus in Locust Grove, Oklahoma.

"Yes, ma'am," I said. "Hog. Head cheese, chitlings, cracklings, ribs. I'm a friend of Lefty Marks."

"Oh, Mr. Marks," she said, as if that explained it all.

She buzzed Rotenberg and told him who I was.

"Durham? Get his autograph, Bethlyn. The bastard's a slugger. The Babe Ruth of Little Rock. Show him right up. We don't want the police to catch him before he gets to me."

Bethlyn led me halfway down a hallway and then motioned toward the stairwell. "His name's on the door."

The only time I'd seen Rotenberg before, he'd been neck-deep in that whirlpool, grinning at the way Lefty was gigging the preachers. He hadn't stood then, so all I remembered of him was his curly hair and the way his sharp, dark eyes stood out so clearly against his pale, square face. But now, as he walked toward me in a gray, paint-spattered sweatsuit, I saw how short he was, and lean, and how much too big his head was for his body.

The office was cluttered in a systematic way. Old newspapers and magazines were stacked head-high all along one wall. Shelves filled mostly with paperback books ran about halfway down the wall directly behind you as you entered. A stereo system (amplifier, turntable, and two speakers the size of doghouses) occupied what floor was left along that wall. An electric coffeepot sat on one of the speakers, a hot plate on the other. Two saucepans and an iron skillet hung from the wall. His desk, a sheet of varnished plywood supported by two Army-green two-drawer filing cabinets, was pushed up against the one window in the room. When he sat at his desk he'd have his back to the door and be looking out through the tops of the trees in the backyard and maybe on good days he'd be able to see all the way down to where folks were hustling their cars up and down Markham after a buck or a fix or a way out. A floor lamp stood just to the right of the desk and next to that was an old brown couch. Two pillows stacked on one of the couch arms told me that the couch let out and that Rotenberg lived here.

But what really struck me was the wall to the right. Jelly jars filled with paint lined the floor a few feet in front of the wall and the handles of paint brushes stuck up out of coffee cans. A nearly finished crucifixion scene covered the wall. He'd finished the two thieves—one of them a black man in a pair of overalls and the other a spindly, wasted white kid that didn't have anything on but a Janis Joplin T-shirt and a Texas Rangers baseball cap. The two of them were looking up bug-eyed to where Jesus ought to have been, but there wasn't anything there yet except the cross.

"I'd shake your hand," Rotenberg said, "but I've got paint on mine."

I was studying the crucifixion. "Nice place you got."

"They do say a white man has to be crazy to be a civil-rights lawyer in Arkansas."

"I don't doubt it." I kept turning my head to study the painting. Three big stage lights shone down on it from the ceiling. It pretty well buried everything else in the room.

"Like it?"

"I don't know." I stood there staring at it for a few seconds more. "It's more than I can take in all at once. And then this is the first wall art I ever saw, outside of the slam, where some of the boys used to draw wide-open women next to the head of their bunks. And most of them boys had been in so long they had a hard time doing a woman justice. It might take me a while to get to where I can wrap my mind around real art."

"Oh, I don't know much about art," he said with a kind of a shy, kid's smile. "I just paint. It gives me satisfaction. Takes my mind off the courts."

"Maybe I ought to take it up."

"Come over here and take a good look at it. I don't get many honest opinions. From what Lefty tells me, you'll give me one."

I went over and stood about ten feet away from the painting. Rotenberg sat on the couch smoking a cigarette and watching me.

The three crosses grew out of a bare dirt hill. Several buzzards and a formation of fighter planes rode the gray air above the hill. The Marine Band, a few yards downslope, faced Jesus's cross and played their mocking instruments. I pointed at them. "They playing 'Hail to the Chief'?"

Rotenberg laughed. "It might not be a bad name for the painting."

Just to the right of the band, four men in ribboned-up military uniforms sat, all puffed and preened, on white horses. I walked up next to the wall to get a closer look at their faces—Eisenhower, MacArthur, Westmoreland, and Haig. Behind them and a little to their left, there was a decrepit old soldier in a wheelchair—Omar Bradley, drooling. Jimmy Stewart stood behind him, holding the wheelchair handles, proudly looking up at the fighter planes.

To the left of the Marine Band, Orval Faubus and George Wallace played cards on the hood of a fire-gutted school bus. They were using food stamp coupons for money. Three women, a black man, and a half-dozen starved-looking kids squatted together in a half-circle next to the carcass of the bus and stretched thin, charred arms toward the center cross. Two young soldiers, lusting together over a *Penthouse* centerfold, stood guard over them.

Meadow surrounded the hill. Here and there you could see a patch of grass or a clump of daffodils, but most of the meadow was covered with clusters of people, some of them in lawn chairs, many of them around barbecue grills. I didn't recognize most of the people, though I could identify enough of them to suspect that almost everyone in the picture was based on somebody real.

The good Reverend Dr. G. Forrest Bushrod stood at the head of an aluminum picnic table saying grace over a suckling pig that a bindfolded, dripping-wet Mexican had just laid on the table. One of the men around the table—every head bowed and every eye closed—was Mayor Jess Godley. Right next to them a group of white-robed women were clubbing a monkey with their hymn books.

Dead fish floated on the scum-covered stream that cut across the far left end of the wall. A swarm of hippies had claimed one bank of the stream. Some of them were naked and wrapped around each other in a big, free, any-hole-will-do pile. The rest sat empty-eyed and lotus-legged, holding flowers, passing joints, and listening to their musicians—John Lennon, Mick Jagger, and a white-bearded Indian guru that was playing something that looked like a cross between an organ and a giant cash register. Just across the stream, Richard Nixon was shaking hands with Mao Tse-tung while Leonid Brezhnev was having his blood pressure checked by Dr. Che Guevara.

At the other end of the wall, a group of women, all of them wearing wrinkled, outsized cop uniforms and Dallas Cowboy football helmets, were banging on pots and pans. One of them was holding up a sign that said: "Lesbianism Is The Answer."

Just above them, standing by himself, wearing a Baltimore Orioles uniform, was Brooks Robinson, drying tears from his eyes with a fielder's mitt.

The figures in the painting seemed a little flat to me, and the expressions on most of them were exaggerated, but I was impressed by how many people I had recognized and by the fact that when you got close each little scene seemed to stand by itself, but when you backed up some, it all flowed together. Playtime in the looney bin.

"Well," I told Rotenberg when I finally got through sizing it up, "I like the shit out of it, but I don't suspect anybody'll ever build a baptistry in front of it."

He didn't make much effort to keep pleasure from taking over his face. "I've worked on it now for nearly two years. It's come to mean more to me than the law."

"It ought to."

He pointed at the chair beside his desk and told me to sit down. I did.

"I was wondering what the baseball player was doing in it. Brooks Robinson, isn't it?"

"I think I just wanted one normal human being in it," he said. "A good man, healthy and well fed, somewhat innocent and still capable of being moved by the horror. I went to high school with Brooks. He's a nice man."

"Maybe you ought to just let the man looking at the picture be that man."

"Maybe."

"I'd like to see it when you get Jesus up."

"So would I. I'm not sure how to paint Him. I haven't been able to portray the proper combination of hope and despair." He told me his parents were Jewish but had become Methodists before he was born. A time or two in the last few years he'd considered going back to Judaism, but it had seemed to him finally to be more history, bad history, than religion. If suffering was the only answer, he'd already found it on his own.

He laid his head back on the ridge of the couch top and sighed. "I don't know why I'm doing it anyway. When I finish it I'll have to find something else. Probably end up painting something over it."

"You can get rid of them newspapers and paint that wall.

The Resurrection or maybe The Fire Next Time. And then there's the ceiling—all heaven opening up to you."

"A life's work." He raised his head and showed me a grin full of weariness, then looked over at the stacks and shook his head, as if befuddled by another man's foolishness. "I've been collecting those since the day John Kennedy was assassinated. I was still young then and believed in both Camelot and democracy. The rich young ruler would lead his people to equality. God." The tough, hard lawyer in him laughed once at the young romantic he had been and was, in some measure, still. "When he was killed, I thought the best in us all had died with him. I wanted to surround myself with a daily record of the decline of my country and the dream it represented. Now, I haven't the faintest idea whether things are getting better or worse. I save today's paper because I saved yesterday's. The boys are grown and gone. Ann left me for a psychiatrist. You live by yourself, you play games with your mind. And talk to strangers. You want some coffee?"

I didn't. He got the cup off his desk, took it over to the speaker and filled it. When he came back to the couch, he said, "You shouldn't give a burnt-out lawyer a chance to talk about himself. He'll go on forever."

"Lefty says you're damn good."

"I am. I'm just tired of riding out armed with nothing but a law book. It isn't an entirely reliable weapon."

"I don't know," I said. "The sons of bitches have dropped me with it every time they took aim."

He took a sip of his coffee, then smiled, easily this time—back to work. "They aiming again?"

I shifted my eyes away from him and looked out his window. I had my doubts about whether this was the best way to go about slipping Ratoplan's sleeper hold. Rotenberg wasn't like any lawyer I'd ever been around, but still he was a lawyer. And none of the others I'd dealt with had ever given me more than a limp hand-shake and a stiff shaft. Ratoplan was threatening to strangle me with the law, though, and I figured if I was going to try to stand up against him I'd need help from somebody that understood how to break that hold. The most promising of my other options was to take off at a dead run for Mexico. But it would pain me to have to skip town when I was hitting so good.

"I got a feeling they might try to revoke my parole," I told him.

"I've stayed on this side of the law since I got out. But that don't matter. I think they're wanting to stick me for something they think I did before I went in. I had a visit with my parole officer yesterday and he acted like he was setting me up."

"Mantis, I believe Lefty said it was. Right? I know the bastard. What is it he thinks he has on you?"

"Well, you know, I don't know for sure. They'll try anything. Maybe they think with a man like me if they look hard enough they'll find something."

"What exactly did Mantis say that gave you this, uh, feeling?"

"He offered me a job. He's done that twice now, and I turned him down both times. But when I said no this time he started hinting around about my past. He didn't think I was in any position to be vetoing his offers."

"What kind of job?"

"First, it was driving a bookmobile. This time he had some kind of thing lined up for me in real estate."

"Real estate." He repeated the words calmly and gave me a couple of slow nods, as if that had been exactly what he'd expected me to say. "Here in town?"

"Well, no. It was out of state. They're just wanting to get me plumb out of sight."

He finished his coffee and set the cup back on his desk. I waited for him to say something, but he seemed to be thinking it all through. So I said, "I'm not sure what's going to come of it. All I wanted to do is come in and see if you'd stand by me if anything did happen. I don't know how much I could pay you, but I'd give you what I had."

Rotenberg turned his head away from me and focused his eyes on the wall painting for what seemed to me like a full minute. Maybe he was using that minute to say farewell to art for a while and bracing himself to reenter the world he'd just got through saying he was so tired of. When he turned back to me, it was a lawyer's face I saw. "The first thing I need to know," he said, "is whether you robbed that bank."

"Bank?" I tried to work up a laugh but didn't manage anything but a little bubbling sound in my mouth. If I'd've been on trial they'd've hung me.

"When Bethlyn told me you were here, I knew what you'd come for," he said. "But I spent a long day in court yesterday before a judge who tends to nod off, and, well, if my leading you into a discussion of the painting seems to have been a lawyer's way of relaxing you before springing the surprise question, I apologize. The truth is that I just wasn't quite ready to talk about cops and robbers."

"It's all right. I did like the painting."

"You see, Lefty called me last night. Yesterday afternoon, while Eversole was shutting out Milledgeville, Lefty went out to the parking lot to check on his load of vegetables. Cesar Ratoplan approached him and asked to have a word in private." Rotenberg ran his left palm back across his bald head. "I think you can guess what was said. Ratoplan wants Lefty to cut Pinzon from the team. If Lefty refuses, Ratoplan will tell your parole officer about the bank robbery. He wants Pinzon off the team by the end of this home stand—not quite three weeks from now."

"Yeah, that's how much time he gave me too. I wonder why he doesn't just ask us to hand Pinzon over right now."

"He doesn't want Pinzon to know anything about the deal. He plans to spend another week in town trying to talk Pinzon into quitting on his own. But he knows there isn't much chance of that. That's just to make things look right. He wants Pinzon to believe he's being cut solely because he isn't good enough to play professional baseball. So he's giving Lefty three weeks to convince Pinzon of that."

"Goddam his gunslit eyes," I said.

"Lefty, of course, will not do what Ratoplan wants. He was planning to talk to you and Pinzon after today's game. But you're here and I gather that Ratoplan isn't the type to issue idle threats. So we may as well use this time to see just how bad things are. Now, did you rob the bank?"

I didn't see any point in lying. He already knew the answer. "It was over four-and-a-half years ago. I didn't hurt anybody. Besides, I've done time for more stickups than I've pulled. Hell, they used me for the solution to half the unsolved crimes in Muskogee."

"I wanted only an answer, not an apology. When I started practicing law, I believed that guilt and innocence mattered to the courts. And because I was that particular kind of fool, two or three of my early clients who I believed to be clearly innocent were convicted and served time. I've since learned that what you have to do is not so much to make your man look innocent as to make the other side look guilty. It's a game—like the one you play. Except the rules of mine don't make as much sense. There's nothing in the law as beautiful, as perfectly proportioned as the ninety feet between bases."

"Does that mean you'll be my lawyer?"

"I'm Lefty's lawyer. I'll be yours because you're on his team. He doesn't think you belong in prison, and that's good enough for me. He's a better judge than any I practice before. All I ask of you is that you tell me the truth."

I leaned a little forward in my chair and gave him my position as straight as I could. "All right," I said. "I want to play ball for the Reds. I damn-sure don't want Pinzon to have to go back to Miami on my account. So if it looks like I got a decent chance of beating this bank rap, I'll stay and fight it. But if it don't look that way, I'll fucking jump parole. That game you were talking about turns into something else when you hear the slammer iron clanking to."

Bethlyn's voice came through the box on Rotenberg's desk. "Mr. Rotenberg, Mr. Tucker is here."

Rotenberg told me to punch the button and tell her we'd be through in about five minutes. I did.

Then he asked me for details about the robbery—date, time of day, take, witnesses, possible alibis. I gave them to him: five years ago come September 17; about a quarter to six—just before their Friday closing time; $3,600 and change; five tellers, three or four up-and-comers with desks of their own in the lobby, and maybe twenty-five customers; no alibis. I even told him about Anna Lee Yancey. He wrote it all down on a yellow pad.

When he finished writing, he laid the pad and pencil on the couch and then spent a few seconds fingering a spot of reddish-brown paint on his sweatshirt. "We have a little time," he said when he looked back up at me. "Maybe we can figure a way out. You and Lefty and Pinzon talk it over and see what you can come up with. It's possible Pinzon knows something about Ratoplan we can use. Meanwhile, I'll check up on Mantis—find out who he's been leaving out on parole and who he's been calling in. When we've done that, you come back here and I'll tell you what I think your chances are."

"Fair enough," I said.

We didn't talk on the way to the door. He started to open it for me, then pulled his hand back, straightened up, looked me square in the eye, and said, "You don't have to tell me the game stinks. The entire apparatus is rotten. They'll send you back to jail if they can, not because you robbed a bank—though that's a damn handy excuse—but because Ratoplan wants Pinzon back in Miami and Mantis doesn't want you playing for Lefty. And I'll get you off if I can, not because I approve of bank robbery, but because Lefty's a friend of mine and because you seemed to understand my mural and because every time I beat the sons of bitches I feel like a kid on the Fourth of July. If you stay, I'll represent you. If you run, Godspeed."

19

Pinzon started the game that afternoon against Milledgeville and was as wild and loose as the devil's daughter but not nearly as successful. His earlier stint in the minors must've convinced him that his fastball and his curve weren't enough. He didn't last quite four innings, but that was time enough for him to show the Peacocks at least one specimen of every kind of pitch—palm balls, fork balls, screwballs, spitters, knucklers, even an eephus pitch every so often. He'd quick-pitch one time, rear way back and high-kick it home the next, and then maybe do his Luis Tiant whirligig after that. Cantwell said that he didn't always have enough fingers to give him the right signal and would have to get the umpire to stick his hand down there too. Pinzon did entertain the few hundred fans that were there watching, but it was more in the way of an acrobat than a pitcher. For he had a flashy kind of grace and now and again he made one of the Peacock hitters look like a hyped-up kid on the verge of a seizure. I think it pleased him so to make one guy look bad on some clever trick pitch that he could overlook the fact that the next one had doubled off the wall.

Coming underarm, sidearm, three-quarter, or straight up, from a big windup or none at all, too many of Pinzon's pitches had too little on them. And too many times his aim was anywhere from a few inches to a foot off. Pinzon either fooled the hitter bad or got burned. And what a pitcher that lacks the big jumping stuff has to learn to do is to fool him just a little bit every time. What Pinzon lacked was the concentration—and probably the desire—consistency requires. Even when it leads to excellence, consistency tends to get a little boring, and boredom, I think, is one of the things Pinzon had spent most of his life fighting against. I'll have to admit that it occurred to me a time or two while I was standing around first base watching line drives ricochet around the outfield that I might be doing the team a favor if I were to help herd him onto Ratoplan's cattle car. It's no trouble to find an excuse to skin the other fellow's ass if that'll make your own sit a little easier.

Lefty went out to the mound after Pinzon had given up a run-scoring double to their right-fielder, Rufus Jimson, with two down in the fourth. Joe Buck Cantwell came out from behind the plate to offer the receiver's opinion. I walked over to hear the conversation.

"What's he got?" Lefty asked Cantwell.

"Imagination."

Pinzon said, "I still feel strong. Let me get out of this inning anyway."

The scoring was already 6–1. Lefty said, "I'd like to get finished before dark."

Knowing it was over then, Pinzon flipped him the ball, grinned, and said, "I might could get the fuckers out in the dark."

"You'll be fine, Gonzalo," Lefty told him, "as soon as you can make yourself remember the difference between gymnastics and pitching."

"I been selling real estate too long. Now that I'm free I can't keep from dancing."

Lefty brought Dummy Boudreaux in then, his way of admitting we'd lost and were just going to play out the game. Dummy was a helluva lot better at cooking than at pitching. At that point in the season Lefty didn't have much choice. Bullet Bob was really our bullpen, but it would've been stupid to waste him by bringing him into the fourth inning of a game where we were already five runs down. Even a damn butterfly arm can get tired.

But it wasn't just pitching that lost that game for us. We didn't hit either. The Milledgeville pitcher, a weathered veteran named Mason Love, just kept flipping his cute little sinker at us and we kept beating it into the ground. It was a legitimate sinker, I think, nowhere near as hard and sharp and startling as Eversole's spitter, but just before it got to you it would jerk down just enough to cause you to top it. Every time I came up I was convinced I would nail the fucker. But that just caused me to swing a little harder and all that did was to hand the shortstop or second baseman an easier hop than he'd had the last time.

We took an 11–2 drubbing. I was afraid it was a sign of things to come.

20

In my room at the home that night after supper I admitted to Lefty that I had robbed the bank and told him that Ratoplan probably had enough evidence to get me convicted for it and certainly had enough to get my parole revoked. Then I gave him an account of my meeting with Rotenberg. When I'd finished that, I said, "I'll wait a couple of weeks to see what's happened. But if I'm still seeing the slam at the end of this road then, I'll have to take off running the other way. I figure I owe it to you to tell you that. I don't want to embarrass you if I can help it, but the pen's already cankered too much of me for me to stand for another dose of it. I'd rather run than rot."

He looked at me through sad, tired, tolerant eyes. "You owe me nothing. I helped you get out of jail because I thought you'd help the team. You've done that." He paused, studied his shoes, shook his head slowly. "But I would like you to give us at least those two weeks. When he wants to be, Rotenberg's as good a lawyer as there is in this state. And I'd like to think that if we keep looking at Ratoplan long enough, we'll find a weakness."

"Throw it under his chin," I said. "Make the bastard fall on his ass and soil that suit."

Lefty grinned briefly, then stood. "We'll talk to Pinzon in the morning. He's out tonight. And anyway, I'd as soon not put this on him so quickly after the shelling he took this afternoon."

"Fine," I said. "Maybe an alibi'll come to me in the night."

He gave me a look with a question mark at the end of it. I answered it with a shrug. He turned to leave, then looked back at me. "You and I both know that as a ballplayer you're more valuable to this team than Pinzon is. But I hope you understand why I can't

allow myself to sacrifice him so I can keep you." He sounded like
he was apologizing for his principles.

"It's not Pinzon that robbed the bank," I said.

He nodded twice, slowly. "Well then. Tomorrow we'll talk to
Pinzon and see if the three of us can't begin to find a clean way out
of this."

"It don't have to be clean."

21

But the next day Pinzon was gone.

I didn't think much about him not being at the home in the
morning. I figured he'd just laid out all night somewhere drunk or
found him a hustle he wanted to see through to the end or maybe
even picked him up a twitch sweet and generous enough to take his
mind off his pitching. I thought he was too stubborn to let himself
get talked back to Florida and too smart to let himself get kid-
napped.

When our bus pulled into the parking lot at the field, though, I
saw Ratoplan standing straight and clean and grim at the stadium
gate. And it occurred to me that I might have either overestimated
Pinzon or underestimated Ratoplan. In just a couple of weeks,
Ratoplan had dug up enough of my past to cover my future. There
was no telling how much dirt he had on Pinzon. Looking out my
bus window at him, I thought maybe he'd managed to scare Pinzon back to Miami without my help. Though it shames me a little
to say it, the thought cheered me some.

Lefty gave the gate key to Woodrow Ratliff and hung back with
me so that we'd be the last ones to Ratoplan. Pansy wanted to walk
with me, but I told her to go on. "Me and Lefty have some business
with that tan manikin yonder."

She looked at Ratoplan, then back at me. "Go on," I said. "I'll
explain it later."

She turned to Lefty for reassurance. "It's all right," he told her,
using a gentle father's voice. She hurried on ahead and caught up
with Bobbie Sampson just outside the gate. She gave Ratoplan a
long look when she passed him.

"What do you intend to do about *her?*" Lefty asked me, still being a little fatherly for my taste.

"God knows," I said. "She's more woman than I deserve."

"Ah," he said, "the gentleman's way out. It doesn't suit you."

Ratoplan stepped out and blocked the gate. "Where's my car?"

Lefty and I glanced at each other but said nothing. I felt a laugh stirring in me. I wasn't certain where Pinzon was headed, but I was pretty sure how he was getting there.

I saw anger, barely controlled, pulling at the smooth beige skin around Ratoplan's mouth and eyes. A couple more licks, I thought, might drive the bastard to his knees. Pinzon had stolen his car; now all we had to do was piss on his suits and kill his barber. I couldn't keep from grinning.

"The situation is not humorous, Mr. Durham," he snapped. "Especially from your point of view."

"Aw, hell, Pancho. Everything's humorous from my point of view." I gave him a short laugh, most of which was real.

"You may be laughing your way back to prison." He seemed to be getting his anger under control. His mouth smoothly rationed those words out, letting us see the poison that covered each one of them. Making threats seemed to ease him.

"It won't be the first time a man got sent up for laughing. But I do realize how the sound of it must grate on a man that spends his time developing land and blackmailing innocent folks." I knew I was talking a little harsh to the man that held the keys to my cell, but I had a bluff I wanted to try on him. Besides, I never have mastered any other way of talking to his breed of scum.

"Innocent?" He tilted his head a little to the right and arched his eyebrows.

"Yes, by God, innocent. I got a little something I think might throw a rod in that mechanical spic brain of yours. I got me an alibi." I let him look at a broad, confident smile. "It's ironclad, Pancho. Ironclad. Now, if you'll just move your immaculate ass, I'll be about my business."

We stared hard at each other from opposite ends of the world, both of us doing all we could to look invulnerable. But I didn't think he quite pulled it off. I thought I saw a little sprig of doubt poking up through the manicured landscape back of his eyes. I can't say what he read in my face. I've pulled some bluffs in my time. Some worked, some didn't.

He didn't move, so I walked around him. I was a couple of steps inside the gate before he spoke again. "I suppose you were dining with Mr. Marks here at the time of the robbery. Discussing the pennant races perhaps."

I turned back to him. "I don't recall Lefty being there," I said. "But I did have a good-sized crowd around me. Oh, and by the way, coming in town just a minute ago, I saw a carload of niggers riding a big silver Imperial up Markham. Already had stuffed dice dangling from the mirror. Brand-new bumper sticker said: 'I'm Hung and I'm Proud.' Their eyes were all lit up and their teeth just ashining. Goddam, if it wasn't a sight. Slinging chicken bones and wine bottles out the window as they roared along."

I went on down and entered the clubhouse. I took a good look around on the off chance that Pinzon had come in early and climbed the fence. I was all but certain he wouldn't be there, and he wasn't. I sat on the stool in front of my stall and started pulling at my shoes.

"Who was that at the gate?" Julius Common Deer asked me. He had the stall to my right.

"Used to be Pinzon's keeper," I told him. "Rich prick from Miami."

"What's he want?"

"He liked that keeper job, so he wants Pinzon back." I set my shoes on the floor of my locker. "You didn't see Pinzon last night, did you?"

"Not after he left the house. Him and Bob said they were going to The Tank. Wednesday night fish fight."

Bob had made it back and looked as good as he ever did this time of day. He sat on the floor, his legs stretched out, his back against his locker, his chin on his chest, his eyes closed. His right hand was wrapped around a pint bottle of Dr. Pepper.

I walked across the room and sat on his stool. "Rough night?"

"Nothing special," he said without opening his eyes. "Selma win last night?"

"Haven't heard."

"Ole Bull's the one we got to watch out for." He stuck the first two fingers of his left hand in his mouth and rubbed his tongue. "Damn shot of whiskey do me a world of good right now. But I guess if I started it there wouldn't be no end to it."

"What become of Pinzon last night?"

"Damned if I know." Then he raised his head and uncovered his bloodshot eyes. "You know what that bastard did?"

I could sense a story behind his question. "No," I said. "But I was wondering."

He put the Dr. Pepper to his lips and sucked it about halfway dry. It seemed to give him a lift and he started in. "When we went on the road, I just about had them fish timed to the second. Oh, now and again the big un'd have a off night, but not often and nothing like what he done last night. And there's an ole boy name of Blurb Porter hangs out at The Tank I paid a little something to to write down the winning times for me when I was gone. So I go in there last night and I'd just cashed my retirement check and I figure I pretty well got it figured. Figured I'd clean up." He shook his head disgustedly and took another, smaller, swig of soda.

"Pinzon, now, hell, he ain't been in there but the one time before and he didn't see the fish then. But he won't listen to a thing I tell him. They put them fish tanks out on the bar a few minutes early where a man can look 'em over good before he puts his money down. But the bartender, ole Harry Vetch that owns the place, he's standing right there keeping an eye out making sure don't nobody mess with 'em. I show Pinzon the list of winning times, but he don't pay the least mind to that. Says to me, 'Look at that piranha, Bob. Just as still and quiet and lazy. He's not going to eat.' And that's how he wants to bet. I tell him it ain't never happened before, but he won't listen to reason. He asks Vetch, he says, 'What's the odds on nothing happening?' And he says it like the Rio Grande's still dripping off his back. You heard him talk that way?"

"Yeah," I said.

"Vetch, he don't know what he's talking about. 'Won't happen,' Vetch tells him. But Pinzon wants special odds and Vetch won't give 'em to him. House policy, you get five-to-one and you got to come within five seconds. Pinzon ain't satisfied with that. By this time he's raised ruckus enough that most of the boys is looking him up and down." He stopped there and kind of half-laughed—in spite of himself, I think.

"Goddam if Pinzon didn't look like a plumb fool. He's wearing checked Bermuda shorts and a bright red shirt and them thin socks that pull damn near to your knees and some lily-white loafers with a gold buckle on their top. And well, anyway, a bunch of them bet him ten-to-one, his five to their fifty. I'm just like the next man; I figure a man wants to give me five dollars I'll take it. Ever' time I been there that fish would've eat your momma if you'd throwed her in the tank with him. But not this time, by God. Vetch drops that goldfish in there with him and that goldfish skitters this way and that from corner to corner like a quick queer in a boxing ring. But that big fish just floats there lazy as you please, flapping a fin now and again and looking as fat and content as a preacher after Sunday dinner. Shit, we waited and waited. One of the boys even reached over and shook the tank, which is against the rules, but it didn't do nothing but scare the goldfish. After a while, the goldfish relaxed some and swum right up head-to-head with the big fish and started nuzzling. For a minute there I thought he might eat the piranha. Finally, we just had to give it up. More than a few of us hollered that it was rigged. But Vetch is known to run a honest game and couldn't none of us figure how Pinzon could've rigged it. We was still mulling it over when Vetch give Pinzon the money we'd given him to hold. And Pinzon was gone before you could open your mouth. We all just stood around quiet then, looking at them fish and shaking our heads. After a while, Vetch got a little net and dipped that goldfish out and put him in his own tank. Some of us wanted to dip that piranha out and kill him, but Vetch wouldn't have it."

He tilted the Dr. Pepper up and finished it. "Beat any damn thing I ever saw. I know he fixed it some way, but I don't know how."

"He just knows his fish," I said. "You know where he went after that?"

"To buy him a goddam catfish farm, for all I know. He had the money for it." He stood then, unbuttoned his pants, pulled them to the floor, and stepped out of them. "I'm thinking about asking Lefty to let me be a starter," he said. "What do you think about that?"

"You're our bullpen, Bob. Nobody else out there can take your place."

"We ain't got but Eversole starting, though."

"The others'll get better. Say, you notice that Cuban standing by the gate just now? You didn't run onto him last night, did you?"

He took his undershorts off and put his jock on. "Yeah, matter of fact we did. But I'd've never pegged him for a Cuban. Way he dressed I figured he was from someplace overseas. It was early, though, when we saw him. I felt like having me some barbecue, so I had Pinzon pull the truck into this little nigger dairy queen and I got out and ordered and I'm standing there waiting when I see this silver Imperial that's as long as from here to yonder pull up beside us. Your Cuban gets out and goes over to Pinzon and says something to him. Then Pinzon gets out and goes over and gets into the Imperial. I get my sandwiches and get back in Lefty's truck. I'm damn near through eating when they finish talking. Pinzon comes back and the Imperial leaves. I ask him don't he want nothing to eat. He says he's done got more on his stomach than he can keep down. Then he drives us on into town and that's it."

He pulled a pair of Astro gym shorts on. I got up off his stool. He fumbled around in his locker until he found his socks and sanitary hose. Then a thought came to him. "You think that fucker in the Imperial had something to do with them fish?"

"God only knows," I said.

Just before batting practice Lefty and I sat in the dugout and together tried to figure out what Pinzon was up to and what Ratoplan might do about it. We didn't get far. But we did agree that Ratoplan probably wouldn't move on me until he'd gotten some kind of line on Pinzon. There wasn't any point in Ratoplan playing his ace until he had to. Of course, we had no way of knowing when that'd be.

"By the way, you don't actually happen to have an alibi, do you?" Lefty asked me.

"I was laid up with a little coed in Tahlequah."

"Name?" I figure he knew about what was coming but couldn't keep himself from asking.

"Escapes me now. Pretty little thing, though. Nice legs. Long brown hair. Kind of a hippie. Smoked dope, dropped acid, worshipped the sun. Put out like a manure spreader."

"You were like a father to her, I suppose."

"Yeah," I said. "Spare the rod and spoil the child."

Lefty laughed, shook his head, and raised himself up off the bench. "I doubt if our Cuban friend fell for the bluff."

"Well," I said, "it's about all a man can do when he's got no hand and he's in too deep to fold."

22

Things seemed to get just a little worse every day for the next couple of weeks.

After Eversole had shut-out Milledgeville to open the home stand, we'd lost six in a row—four to Milledgeville and then, after a day off, two more to Asheville. Eversole broke the streak by beating Asheville 3–2, but, hell, he had to drive in the winning run himself. And then we turned right back around and lost the last two games of the Asheville series and the first two against Memphis. Except for Eversole and Bullet Bob, our pitchers were usually either walking folks or wishing they had. Even Eversole lost two games during that stretch. The first one he lost—the last game of the Milledgeville series—wasn't his fault. He held them to two runs, just one of them earned. But still he lost, and I think most of us had gotten to where we expected him to win every time out. As for Bullet Bob, he never had a really bad outing, but usually by the time he entered a game, we were so far behind, there wasn't much he could do.

I still figure Ratoplan's scam pretty much accounted for the slump I went into. But I don't know what came over the rest of the team. All of us slumped except Jefferson Mundy and Julius Common Deer, and they spent a lot of time standing on base waiting in vain for one of the rest of us to drive them in. Well, I guess you couldn't say Worm Warnock slumped, but then he wasn't but a .250 hitter to start with. It wasn't the pitching we saw. Hell, there weren't that many good pitchers in the league. Nobody had more than one, two at the most. And we had the only Eversole—the kind of pitcher that could go out on even just a fair day and damn near beat you all by himself. Still, we sure enough made some of them little sloppers look good. We got shut out by a kid from Memphis named Jaybird Lane that couldn't've beaten that slammer team I'd played for in McAlester. Christ, if he had we'd've all stabbed one another before they got us locked back up good.

I had one spell where I went 5 for 30, all of them singles, and didn't drive home a damn run. In the bottom of the ninth of that game Eversole lost to Milledgeville, I came up with one out, us one run down, Mundy on second and Julius on first. Their pitcher, a little rubber-armed junker named Turpin Parrum, served me up a hanging curve that should've made me famous, at least locally, but I swung just as hard as I could and hit the son of a bitch straight up. The third baseman caught it between home and the mound. I walked over to the dugout and splintered my bat on the roof. I guess it's a wonder I didn't miss that.

Attendance dropped steadily. Lefty had that produce truck come in twice a week and it drew a pretty good crowd. But most of them just took what they wanted off the truck and went on home without ever entering the stadium. God's little gash battalion came back once and howled and sang at us, but there weren't enough souls there to occupy them long. They left before the game got started good and we didn't see them again during the rest of the home stand. I suspect that the decent folks started figuring that if they'd just leave us alone a while, we'd do our own selves in. I knew, though, that if and when we did drop over, they'd do the Christian thing and kick the hell out of us one last time before we died.

Evenings after the games, I'd either sit around the house and sulk and snap or go out to a bar and drink till I fell off my stool. I kept thinking I ought to light out for Mexico but kept putting it off. Ratoplan came to every game and I tried to keep up my bluff, but a lot of the verve had gone out of it. I figured Ratoplan attended the games because he expected Pinzon to return, and I was fairly sure he wouldn't sic his dogs on me until he'd given up, one way or another, on treeing Pinzon. Now and then he'd take time out to remind me what a short drive it was to the penitentiary. I'd give him a brave hooraw, then strut out onto the field and go 0 for 4.

Mantis and I went through our tired old routine a couple of times. It was easy to see that my batting slump pleased him. The poorer I hit, of course, the less attention he'd get when he dragged me back to the slam. His pleasure irked me, but I was so low on hope I had a hard time talking back to him. I saw a grim truth in his eyes and in his smile: If I fought I'd have to win every round. If I ran I'd have to run forever.

And then on the twenty-second of May, less than a week before the home stand would end, Eversole, pitching the last game of the Memphis series, made me think that even when you knew they were apt to beat you, you might ought to stand and fight them until it was over. Since coming off the road, we'd fallen to third place in the standings, and sometimes it looked like we might have trouble ending the season ahead of Plaquemine. But Franklin Brown had won the day before, pitching his first decent game of the stand, and we were fairly confident that Eversole would make it two in a row for us. But that day, for the first time all season, he didn't have good stuff. Memphis didn't just beat him; they got eight runs off him. Eversole's control was off a notch or two and he kept throwing his spitter in the dirt. After the first inning most of the Kings managed to discipline themselves to lay off anything low. So over the course of the game, Eversole walked six or seven guys, beaned one, and had a couple of others get on on swinging third strikes that skipped past Cantwell. If he'd had his good fast-ball, he could've relied on it and just shown them the spitball now and again as a reminder. But even early that day you could tell he was missing about a foot off his hummer. By the fifth the Kings were laying for it and hitting it. We weren't much help to him in the field either. Jew Bernstein, in left, got turned around on a slic-ing liner and let it get past him for a triple. Rainbow Smith came up with what should have been a double-play ball and sailed it high over second base and into our bullpen down the right field line. The two third strikes that got past Cantwell were in the dirt, but Cantwell should've been able to get down and block them and then throw the men out. But Eversole never changed. He kept coming at them, and when they hit him he came right back.

I think there are days when you can see courage on a ball field. And I think I saw it in Eversole that day. Even when he knew he'd lost, he refused to be humiliated. With the score 8–2, the bases loaded, and two out in the eighth, Lefty walked out to the mound, clearly intending to remove Eversole. But they never said a word to one another. Lefty looked up at Eversole and started to say some-thing, but Eversole turned to him, shook his head once and finally, and finished the game without yielding another run. In our end of the eighth, Lefty even let Eversole bat for himself. Jew Bernstein and Mike O'Bryan, hitting for Cantwell, led off the inning with back-to-back singles. Most of the few fans there booed then when we didn't send up a pinch hitter. We were too far behind for Ever-sole to sacrifice, and I don't think he would have done it anyway. Ordinarily, he didn't pay much mind to his own hitting. Every so often he'd get a pitch he particularly liked and take a cut that would damn near suck all the air out of the stadium. But most of the time he'd miss it or foul it or pop it up. This time, though, he spread his feet a little farther apart than was his custom, went into a crouch, and choked up a couple of inches on his big bat. The first pitch was a hard one just off the inside corner. He whipped his bat around and lined one their left fielder was lucky to backhand on one hop. The run he drove in wound up not mattering to the game—we lost 8–4—but it was his way of saying that he might go down but not easily and not for long.

I didn't feel like eating that night—a bad sign with me. Part of my mind was telling me I ought to take a lesson from Eversole's performance. But another part was saying a man shouldn't apply ball game lessons to life, especially not when taking that lesson too seriously might land him in the slam. I got tired of arguing with myself and decided that an hour's worth of honest sweat might do me good. I backed the Gravely tiller out of the shed and pushed it to the garden.

I'd been working the soil maybe half an hour when I felt a hand on my shoulder. It was Pansy. I shut the motor down. "I didn't hear you coming," I said.

"I stood by the fence and watched you for two or three minutes."

"Christ, I'm ripe to be ambushed."

"Is there something I can do out here to help you?"

"Not till dark," I said. "I was just needing to get my mind off my hitting." I wanted to keep her convinced that my hitting slump entirely accounted for the foul moods I'd curdled the last two weeks with.

We stood there together a minute looking over the garden. "We need a rain," I said.

She hooked her arm under mine and leaned against me. The western sky was red and dying. The air was still and beginning to cool. When she spoke, her voice was part of the evening. "Sometimes I think I'd like to have a little house in the country. A big garden, a milk cow, a couple of horses to ride."

I'm sure she felt my arm tense some then, because she let go of it, put her palm on my cheek, and turned my face toward hers. Then with an easy smile that let me know she didn't mean to threaten, she asked, "Would you build your woman a farmhouse, Hog Durham? And bring me fresh sweetmilk in the morning? And in the evening go horseback riding with me across the meadows?"

I brushed a strand of hair out of her face, then bent down and kissed her forehead. I said, "Well, I could probably rustle the cows and horses for you. And if I set my mind to it I might could farm well enough to keep us from starving. But I never was much hand at carpentry. Probably the best I could do for you there would be to throw up a tent."

"We'd be pioneers," she said. "You look the part. And I'm a tough woman." She let out a graceful, happy laugh.

I smiled down on her. "Pioneers are folks that are too stupid or too strange or too stubborn to fit into the world the decent God-fearers have made. So they have to go out and find them a world that's so old it's new to them and makes stupidity and strangeness and stubbornness seem natural."

Pansy's face turned serious and I figured I'd better lighten it up some. "Now me, you see," I said, "I been rehabilitated. It took them a while, of course, but they finally corralled the pioneer in me and gave him a good pistol-whipping. So here I am, out in society, happy and wholesome."

She didn't laugh. "Do you ever really think about what you'd like to be doing in a year or two?"

"Sure," I told her. "I'm as American as the next man. What I want to do is hook on with some kind of sleek business rig and draw me an easy salary and have me a long-legged secretary that hollers and rakes her nails slantwise across my back when I make her come and I want to live in a big-windowed, architectured house with a prim little woman that cooks good and dresses nice and takes proper care of the younguns. Every night before turning in I'd walk out on my patio and look down at the city lights and up at the big round Dixie moon and then haul out my old cock and piss the martinis that had seen me through the evening down the hill toward the poor. How about yourself?"

"I'd like to be your secretary," she said. And then she laughed.

"Couldn't do it," I said. "Your legs aren't long enough."

She gave me a play slap and then we stood there and grinned at each other like teenagers. After a minute of that, I put a hand on either side of her waist, held her at arm's length, and said, "You know what, love? The simple, shameful, God's truth of it is that all I want to do is to hit .400 forever."

And she looked right back up into my eyes and, without a hint of either threat or calculation, said, through the purest mouth you ever saw, "I love you, Hog Durham."

I pulled her tight against me and wrapped my arms around her, partly because I needed her there and partly because I didn't want her to see my face. And I thought to myself, Of all the goddam times for this to happen. Even in the best of times it was a bigger idea than a man like me could ever quite get his mind around.

23

Lefty scheduled a workout for the morning of May twenty-third, an off day between the Memphis and Oxford series. I came in early to have one last talk with Rotenberg before deciding what to do.

"I've gone in with less and won," he told me.

"And gone in with more and lost," I said.

He nodded. "Four months from now, of course, it would be different. I could almost guarantee you wouldn't do a day of time."

He was talking about the statute of limitations, five years, which would be up on September 11. I was aware of the time limit, but hadn't figured it would make much difference in my case. They didn't have to convict me; they just had to revoke my parole. They could make me serve time for the bank robbery without ever trying me for it. I didn't see how they could lose. If they convicted me of the bank robbery, they could have the judge declare me an habitual, and then he could give me life. If I was acquitted, Mantis could still revoke my parole and make me serve out the rest of my liquor store sentence.

Rotenberg didn't see it quite that way. He told me that if they arrested me for bank robbery the next thing they'd try to do would be to hold me without bail. If they couldn't get by with that, they'd set bail so high I'd have no way of making it short of buddying up with little Winnie Rockefeller. And if and when I did make bail, Mantis would revoke parole and send me back to McAlester to await trial. One way or another I was likely to be in jail from the time they arrested me until my trial ended.

"Chances are they'll find a way to keep you locked up for most or all the rest of baseball season. But that's it. I'll make them bring you to trial. And then I'll beat them. If Mantis tries to revoke your parole after that, I'll not only stop him, I'll get him fired." Rotenberg said all that as if he were just reciting facts.

"I might stick it out if I could be pretty sure of that. But the slam's full of people that have been convicted on less evidence than they'll have on me."

"You're paranoid," he said. "And maybe that's a sensible attitude most of the time. But in this case they don't have much to use against you. First, you were in the general area at the time of the robbery. But you were just one of about 100,000. Secondly, you never returned to your job at the furniture factory after the Friday of the bank robbery. But three other people quit their jobs at that factory the same day. In fact, Southland Furniture Company has the second-highest rate of employee turnover, among factories, in the state of Arkansas. They pay the minimum wage and working conditions are abominable. If I have to, I'll take the jury in there and show them why people quit."

"You been there?" Well, he was the first lawyer I'd been around that did anything but plea-bargain and cash checks.

"No. But I had it checked. My description of it was accurate, wasn't it?"

"Oh yeah," I said. "The place is enough to drive a man to bank robbery."

He smiled. "Perhaps we should avoid leading a jury along that line."

"There were eyewitnesses," I reminded him. "And the girl. She saw me with the money."

"What the eyewitnesses saw happened nearly five years ago. If what you've told me is true, none of them had ever seen you before you entered that bank and none of them have seen you since. Since then People's Bank and Trust Company has been robbed two more times. If one of the eyewitnesses has nerve enough to definitely identify you as the thief, I'll have him crying before he gets off the stand. And then when our turn comes, I'll put another eyewitness on the stand who'll contradict everything the first one said. I am very good with eyewitnesses. It's not always an honorable talent. But then we all have to find our own way to justice, don't we?"

It wasn't a question I thought needed answering, so I just grinned.

"And as for the woman, the lovely, promiscuous Mrs. Anna Lee

Parsons Yancey Whitfield Shickembush Syrock. Well, I might be
able to persuade a jury that she is capable of lying. If I can't, *I'll* go
to work at the Southland Furniture Company."

And, looking at the confidence in Rotenberg's face, I actually
felt a little twinge for poor ole Anna Lee. "You know," I told him,
"Anna Lee's not a bad woman. She just scares a little easy and so
throws herself at too many men hoping that sooner or later one of
them will take care of her."

I guess Rotenberg was like an old, smart boxer who knows that
when you get inside them ropes what matters is who wins. He said,
"If they put her on the stand and she merely testifies that you had
what seemed to her to be quite a bit of money, I might let her tes-
timony stand. It could actually help us. You came out of prison.
You took a job at the furniture factory. You worked there twenty-
three weeks, putting a substantial part of each paycheck in a
shoebox or something. When you had saved enough to cover a
month-long fling, you quit the job. Happens all the time. But if she
testifies that you had $3,600 and that you told her you got it rob-
bing the bank, I'll make the jury think she's a lying whore who
wants to punish you for refusing to marry her.

"I don't argue that the system's good. I just say that you can
beat it and sometimes even change it a little if you're smart enough
and mean enough."

"Ain't you heard the song, lawyer? Love is all you need."

"That's not even true in bed."

24

Actually what we were having at the field that day was less
workout than tryout. Lefty was making some adjustments, taking a
look at two new prospects for the team. One of them was a twenty-
three-year-old pitcher from Texarkana, Arkansas, who called himself Genghis Mohammed, Jr. The other was Susan Pankhurst.

By the time I got to the park, Lefty was already hitting infield. I
decided to just have me a seat and see how Susan Pankhurst handled herself around first base. Bullet Bob was sitting on the dugout

bench having a beer. Since there'd be no game that day, he had no reason to stay sober.

He gave me a disgusted look and shook his head. "The bastard's gone too far this time. Christ. A damn twat and a Mohammedan."

"They'll draw fans," I said. "Or at least Susan will."

"Why don't we train us a dog to shag flies and stick him out in center. Maybe we could find a monkey that could pinch-hit for him."

I watched Susan go to her right, field a tough hop, and flip the ball to second. "She don't look bad."

"For a woman."

But she didn't look bad, period. She danced around the base, fielding sharp grounders flawlessly. She handled wild throws (a lot of them, I figured, were intentional) with the nerve and skill of a veteran, coming off the base to catch the ones that were way off line. Her arm was too weak for short or third or the outfield, but it looked like it would do at first—and maybe second. Once Rainbow Smith made a throw she had to field on a medium hop. Those are the toughest kind. A kid can handle the long hop, and on a short hop you just give it a scoop and hope the ball sticks in your glove. Most of the time it will—given a little luck and a good glove. But the medium hops will handcuff you if you don't keep your head down, make a quick adjustment with your hands, and keep your body from flinching. Susan did it as well as I could have.

I started to point that out to Bob, but then I realized it would just rile him up more. Instead I asked him about the new pitcher, who was warming up down in the bullpen with Stump Guthrie.

"You mean fucking Ali Baba? We need pitching, but I just as soon Lefty didn't get 'em out of the asylum. Sumbitch come in here while ago with some kind of silky black thing draped around him. Looked like he'd run plumb out of clothes and wrapped his-self up in a black sheet. Shaved head. Big damn gold earring dangling from his left ear. Reckon he'd lost the other one—or pawned it somewhere. First thing he done after he finished talking to Lefty, he went over and started in on Mundy and Flood and them boys. Trying to make Mohammedans out of 'em, I suspect. Now me, I might not always act it, but I'm a Christian man." He coughed up a hocker and spit it on the steps. "I got nothing against niggers, but I can't see no call for that kind of shit."

"I didn't know you were a religious man, Bob," I said, trying to keep back a grin.

"I ain't the kind that goes around broadcasting it. But chewing on the notion of having a outright heathen on the team has kind of brought me back round to my upbringing."

To tell the truth I wasn't much on the Muslims myself. Of course I'd never met any outside the slam. Most of them didn't find their way to Allah until after they'd gotten shut up in the joint. My guess is that what they knew about the Muslims was that white men hated them and they had pretty names. And I suppose they were aware of the promise that if and when they got out they'd have holy authority for shitting on their women. I figured the same was probably true of our new pitcher. Though I will say he was the first one I'd come across that had the imagination to tack the "Jr." onto his name. Clever way of giving himself roots.

After infield, several of the boys rolled the cage out to the plate so that batting practice could commence. And our man Genghis Mohammed, Jr., swaggered to the mound.

"I believe I'll go have myself a closer look at him," I told Bob.

"I done seen all I care to. I'm just hanging around for the vote."

Mohammed must've thrown for twenty minutes. He was a tall left-hander with that easy, loose-jointed delivery you have to be born with. One of them guys God made and said, "You're a pitcher, son. Throw strikes." His fastball was good, if not quite overwhelming. He kept it down and when it came up to the plate it jumped away from right-handed hitters. He had a big, wide-breaking curve that a good right-hander could probably handle, but it would cause a lot of left-handers to start having spasms all down their front leg. But his best pitch was a screwball. Actually he had two of them. One was the slow one he'd use for a change-up. And the other one came in hard and had a short, sharp break on the end of it, like a good slider except it broke in the opposite direction. I'd never seen one like that before. None of the boys trying to hit against him had much luck.

I found Lefty and asked him where the kid had been.

"I don't really know," Lefty said. "Couple of years ago he was pitching for San Antonio and doing damn well. Then he just up and quit. Religious crisis, he says. When he called me a couple of nights ago asking for a tryout, I couldn't remember anything about him until he told me he used to be Nathaniel Bates. When I was a kid I used to play ball against his grandfather. They had a pretty good black team that played out of Hope. Then I remembered reading about Nathaniel in the *Texarkana Gazette*."

Susan Pankhurst, carrying a bat, came over and asked Lefty if he wanted her to hit now. He told her to wait. He wanted his regulars to have several turns apiece against Genghis.

"If you get a hit off of him, it's apt to shake his faith," I said.

She looked at me as if I'd insulted her, and walked back to the batting cage.

"What did you find out from Rotenberg this morning?" Lefty asked me.

"Well, he thinks he can beat the bank robbery rap if it comes to trial. And if they arrest me, he plans to make it come to trial. But he figures they'll delay trial as long as they can and keep me locked up while they're diddling."

"What about your parole?"

"He swears he can keep Mantis from revoking parole without giving me a trial. I don't know about that."

"If he said he can do it, he can do it."

"I guess," I said. Then I looked off out at the freeway for a minute and sighed. "I've about decided to stick it out."

"I thought you would," Lefty said. "It's the right decision."

"Doesn't seem like right and wrong have much to do with it," I said.

"Sure they do. They always do," Lefty said. "But sometimes you have to cock your head just right to see how."

Then he left me and sent Woodrow Ratliff out to take Mohammed's place on the mound. Joe Buck Cantwell took a few licks before Lefty told Susan it was her turn. She made pretty good contact, spraying the ball around, but had no power. She used a thick-handled bottle bat and kind of poked at the pitch. But she didn't back off and she looked like she'd be hard to fool. I doubted whether she'd be able to get around on a good fastball, but Ratliff didn't have one, which, of course, is the real reason Lefty'd had her wait. You couldn't say she hit like a good man, but then she didn't hit like a woman either. If Lefty used her right, she probably wouldn't embarrass herself.

After the workout everybody but Susan and Genghis went down into the clubhouse to vote. We started with Genghis, that being the easier decision. Whatever else he was, he was clearly a pitcher.

Everybody knew that was what we needed. Everybody voted for him but Bob.

Then Lefty stood and started to make a case for Susan Pankhurst. Bob stopped him.

"If Ali Baba's on the team now, he's got a right to vote. You got to call him in."

I saw what Bob was up to, but I was surprised he had that much sense. I'm sure Lefty saw through it too, but being a man of principle, he went ahead and fetched Genghis.

When Genghis came in, he gave us this baleful Sonny Liston stare and said, "You have chosen well."

Arguing for Susan, Lefty never mentioned politics or the rights of women. He stuck mostly to the financial aspects of the move. Attendance would increase. We'd sell more beer and dogs. And since this was a communal outfit, that'd mean more money for each of us. "And she can play baseball," he said. "You saw her."

"Well, she does all right at it," Rainbow Smith said. "In the field anyway. I was a little surprised at that. I tested her with a couple of throws and she handled them okay. And she ain't a automatic out at the plate. I expect, though, that they'll blow high, hard ones past her without much trouble."

Lefty explained that she wouldn't be hitting much. He planned to use her almost entirely as a defensive specialist when we had a good lead in the late innings.

"Shit, man, they start off like that, taking just a little. Then before you know what come down, they done took it all over, running the whole show. It's against my religion. I won't pitch when she's on first." It was Genghis Mohammed, Jr., doing just what Bullet Bob had hoped he would.

A big, sure voice came from over by the showers. "She can play when I'm pitching," Eversole said. I don't think we'd've been any more surprised if it had been Dummy Boudreaux.

After that, Lefty wanted to call for a vote right quick. "Is there anyone who won't go along with the will of the majority?" he asked.

"I won't quit the team," Genghis said. "I just won't pitch when she's on first."

"We won't ask you to do anything that violates the precepts of the Glorious Koran," Jew Bernstein said, with more humor than anger.

Bullet Bob wasn't quite ready to give it up. "It's old Hog's job she's after," he said. "I know he's been in a little slump here lately, but still he's won more games for us than any hitter we got. I don't see that we got any call to go insulting him like this. And O'Bryan. What about him? We all got to ask ourselves how would we feel if it was our job she took."

Mike O'Bryan said, "Don't worry about me. I can't complain about the way Lefty's been using me. And I'm never going to be anybody's defensive specialist." Since I'd beaten him out at first, he'd become our main pinch hitter. And once or twice a week he'd take Jew Bernstein's place in left.

Then it was my turn. I stood up. "First of all, I think Lefty's probably right about Susan helping us at the gate. And the way we been going, we better do something or we're going to drive the poor bastard into bankruptcy." I stopped there a second or two and hitched up my britches. "Now, boys," I went on, "I've never given much of a good goddam one way or the other about women's liberation. Seems to me like most of them women are trying to figure a way into a system I've spent a lifetime trying to stay clear of. But I can damn well understand a woman wanting to play baseball for the Reds. That's not wanting in; that's wanting out. And out's where freedom is."

I stood there a little while longer, looking around at my teammates and realizing I'd gotten carried away with myself some. Before I sat back down, I said, "I'd appreciate it if you good folks would remember me at the polls Tuesday. Name's Hog Durham."

"Anybody else have anything to say before we vote?" Lefty asked.

"While we're at it," Bullet Bob said, "why don't we go on and vote Bobbie in too? She looks like she'd make a helluva catcher. I don't see no reason to go about this half-assed. What about Pansy, Hog? She interested?"

"It's against her religion."

We held our little election then. Bob and Genghis were the only two no votes. Strange bedfellows.

Lefty, followed by Julius Common Deer, headed out to give Susan the news. But when the door opened, in came, by God, Gonzalo Pinzon.

25

Three nights later we rode Lefty's truck into Little Rock for a showdown with Ratoplan. I drove, Pinzon sat in the middle, and Lefty rode shotgun, looking out the window at the rain. "When it comes, it comes all at once," he said.

It had rained a couple of times in Little Rock several weeks earlier, while we were on the road, but up until three days ago we hadn't had to postpone a game, home or away, all year. Now we'd canceled three in a row and the next day would make it four. We'd played one inning of the first game of the Oxford series, last of the home stand, when black clouds whipped across the sky, thunder rattled the stands, lightning shot everywhere, and it commenced to piss and pour. After that it had been one thunderstorm after another. Tornadoes had chased one another across the state. Yesterday one had dropped down in Hot Springs and leveled Bathhouse Row.

"Doesn't it usually come earlier than this?" Pinzon asked.

"Yes," Lefty said, "but it always comes."

"Ain't nobody loves a practical joke like the Lord," I said.

I drove down Cantrell Hill. Brown water streamed out of the rising woods to our right and then came together and formed a sheet over the road and rushed toward town.

Since Pinzon's return, I'd alternated between wanting to kiss him and wanting to strangle him. He'd told us he'd gone down to Miami to set up a deal that would keep Ratoplan off our asses. Before leaving he'd given Ratoplan a warning that kept there from being any chance of me getting turned in. When I'd asked him why he hadn't given us some word about this before he left, he just said he'd wanted to keep a free hand. There'd been things he hadn't been ready to tell us. I could see why. Because what he did tell us, finally, was that both he and Ratoplan were working against G. Harold Carney and, indirectly anyway, for Fidel Castro. Pinzon had hated Carney so much that, after getting waived out of baseball that first time, he'd let Ratoplan recruit him as a kind of half-assed spy. They embezzled what they could of Carney's money and sent it to Cuba. They informed the Cubans every time Carney had one of his harebrained terrorist schemes. They infiltrated anti-Castro paramilitary groups. After a couple of months, Pinzon realized he despised Ratoplan as thoroughly as he did Carney. But it wasn't until boatload after boatload of Cuban refugees started washing up on the docks that he decided he wanted out. He thought he would come to Fort Chaffee and work with some of the refugees. He hoped that way off in Arkansas he'd be invisible to Ratoplan. Who ever looked for anything in Arkansas? And maybe he'd've been right, but when Pinzon got here he read about Lefty and the Reds and decided to give himself one more shot at playing the only game he'd ever really cared about. After hearing all that, I'd asked why he hadn't played under an assumed name. Just hadn't been thinking, he'd said. Just been too eager to start playing.

So Ratoplan hadn't had much trouble tracking him down. The first thing he'd suspected was that Pinzon had gone back to baseball. He'd checked around here and there, with this team and that, until he got wind of the Reds. Then he'd known he had his man. After trying threats and bribes on Pinzon without success, he'd come at him the roundabout way, through me and Lefty. But Lefty wouldn't deal with him, wouldn't trade him Pinzon for me. And I was unpredictable, and even if I'd decided to cooperate, there was no way of knowing how effective I'd've been. Finally, it came down to him looking Pinzon in the eye and saying, "If you stay here, Durham goes to the pen." So Pinzon had taken off to Miami and worked us out a deal. All we had to do to get them to call Ratoplan off was to let a couple of Castro's boys play for us. They'd guarantee us A-1 ballplayers.

At first the deal had infuriated Lefty. Hell, he even threatened to solve the problem the easy way—by cutting Pinzon from the team. But over the next two days I could see him softening toward the idea. Anybody could see that for drawing fans Susan Pankhurst wouldn't make a patch on them Cubans. So he'd agreed to the meeting with Ratoplan. He was willing to listen, but he hadn't made any promises yet.

I wouldn't be surprised but what Ratoplan was the first man that ever walked into the Terminal Bar wearing a three-piece suit. He stood in the door a minute, letting his eyes adjust, then looked around at the long, narrow, dingy room filled with faded hippies and semi-enlightened rednecks. I figured he probably chewed on a

little thought about the nature of decadence. He carried a look of
refined disgust across the joint.

"I suppose this is your idea of a joke," he said to Pinzon. We had
a corner booth. He brushed the seat off with a napkin before sitting
down next to Pinzon.

"The place is full of Castro sympathizers," Pinzon said. "Get
yourself a mug and we'll pour you a drink." We had a pitcher of
dark beer.

"I'll abstain, thank you," Ratoplan said.

But the bartender, a small, dark, wiry, bearded guy that had a
patch over his right eye-socket, brought us another mug.

I poured Ratoplan a beer, letting the foam slop over the rim of
his mug and onto the table. He raised his eyebrows, started to say
something, then held it. Pinzon finished his beer and poured himself another one. I lit up a Lucky. I didn't feel much like drinking.
Somebody played the jukebox. It was one of them high-voltage
bands whose main appeal is that they're loud and simple and that
the lead guitarist is apt to set fire to his instrument when the song's
over.

"If they're good enough, your boys can play for the Reds," Lefty
said. He didn't raise his voice, and the three of us who made up his
audience had to lean toward him to hear him over the music. "You
get them into the country, take care of the paperwork, and send
them to us. Then they'll have to try out for the team just as anyone
else would. We'll vote on them. If we accept them, they'll be paid
the same money as any other player. During the games, I will use
them as I think fit." He paused, glanced at Pinzon, and then focused his eyes on Ratoplan's. "You're vulnerable now. I know who
you are. If you try any tricks, if you come back with any more of
your threats, I'll come down on you like a hawk on a field mouse."

"There is no longer any need for hostility," Ratoplan said.

"I think that concludes our business," Lefty said. And he got up
and walked toward the door.

We watched him and then looked at each other. Pinzon said,
"By God, Cesar, how's that for getting down to business?"

"The two of you have been extremely fortunate up to this
point," Ratoplan said, "but I'll be surprised if your luck lasts until
the end of the season."

"Leave a tip," I told him.

Pinzon laughed.

We followed Lefty out into the rain.

Part IV

26

It was Police Night at Patriot Park in Selma, Alabama. The first 2,500 people in the stadium were given a little American flag on a stick; a bumper sticker that said: Help God Save His Country/Support Your Local Police"; a black Styrofoam nightstick; and a paperback book called *The Handy Dandy Evolution Refuter*. Cops and their families, straight-A students, disabled veterans, boy scouts, and Vacation Bible School students got in free. The stadium had spaces for about 10,000 fans, but after all those seats and the aisles between them had been filled, another couple of thousand folks were herded out to some temporary bleachers that had been set up just beyond the outfield walls.

The show was supposed to commence at seven-thirty, but it must've been closer to eight by the time they got the fans seated and the cops scrubbed down and juiced up. But sitting between Lefty and Pansy in the visitors' dugout, I enjoyed myself. Ever since Pinzon had come back and helped pry Ratoplan's fingers off my neck, things had been easy and good between Pansy and me. I hadn't told her about the bank robbery, but I had told her that Mantis had been threatening me with another McAlester vacation and that that at least partly accounted for the foul moods I'd been subjecting her to. We'd spent the last couple of nights in Little Rock laying together in her room and, among other things, listening to the rain hit the roof. And we'd spent a good part of this day touring Selma with Lefty, walking, like King and his folks had done an age ago, from Brown's Chapel to the Edmund Pettus Bridge, where the cops had turned them back. The name of the road we followed had been changed from Sylvan Street to Martin

Luther King Drive, but there was still a stiff view of suffering on either side of it. A block south of where Martin Luther King intersected with Jefferson Davis Avenue was a housing project, bleak and battered. We stood outside a chain-link fence a few minutes and watched black kids shoot goals.

When we'd entered Patriot Park, Pansy had managed to talk one of the Selmans into giving her samples of the free paraphernalia. Then while I was in the clubhouse getting into my uniform, she'd stuck the bumper sticker onto my bat. Now Bullet Bob was parading in front of us with the toy nightstick protruding up out of his fly. Pinzon was at the far end of the dugout with my bumperstickered bat in one hand and the little flag in the other. He sang a tune he'd composed for the occasion.

> My name is Teddy Roosevelt.
> I am a bully man.
> I have shot Injuns in the West
> And spics in Greaserland.
>
> Now I am the president
> Of this Almighty land.
> God, I know, is on my side.
> His stick is in my hand.

When he finished the song, he stretched himself belly-down against the dugout steps, put the bat to his shoulder like a rifle, said, "Don't let them take you alive," and commenced taking play shots at the crowd.

Lefty had gotten *The Handy Dandy Evolution Refuter* from Pansy, and now and then I heard him laughing over parts of it.

"Educating yourself?" I asked him.

"In the beginning was the word and the word was wrong," he said.

Then we heard sirens and looked across the diamond and saw a gate swing open in the fence down the right-field line and in came the Dallas County Honorary Posse, riding at a gallop, three abreast, in uniforms of Confederate gray, a pistol in each holster, a rifle brandished high in each right hand. There must've been 150 of the stupid fuckers. They circled the field twice, getting further and further out of formation, and then rode out the hole they'd come in. Going out the gate, each rider fired his rifle into the air. And the delighted crowd roared.

"The South will, by God, rise again," I said.

"Several times a day," Lefty agreed.

When all the posse had cleared off, two groundkeepers, dressed for the night in old police uniforms, trotted out of the Selma dugout and set up a microphone on top of home plate. Then they left and the sirens commenced again. This time a cop car, red and blue lights flashing on top, flags flapping from the fenders, led the procession through the gate. It was followed by three motorcycles and four more misery wagons. When the lead car passed our dugout, I saw that Bull Cox himself, wearing his sheriff's costume, was at the wheel. They circled the field just once, slowly. A high school band, sitting in the section of seats directly behind home plate, played "Dixie." They sounded like they'd been bribed by yankees.

Bull parked beside the pitcher's mound and strutted to the mike. The other cop cars took the infield positions, first, second, short, and third, and faced homeward. The three motorcycles positioned themselves in the outfield, one in left, one in center, one in right. Each of the drivers—helmeted, legs spread, arms folded across chest—stood just to the left of his vehicle. Bull stood at the mike and watched his men get into position. Then he turned, waved his Stetson at the crowd, and whooped and hollered a couple of times. They waved their little flags and whooped right back at him. The band kept trying to get "Dixie" right and had finally got within hailing distance when Bull shoved his hat back on his head and held out a palm for silence.

"You got to hand it to ole Bull," Bullet Bob said. "You can't beat him for putting on a show."

"Wait till I get him in Little Rock again," Lefty said.

"Shit, it'll be over by then," Bullet Bob said. "That's the last series of the year."

"The pennant race may be over," Lefty said, and then paused. "One way or another. But I'll give them a show that'll make this look like a wake."

"Man, there's no way you can top this, Genghis Mohammed, Jr., said. "They gonna end it by hanging a nigger boy from the rafters."

Pinzon favored us with another ditty:

> Niggers from a rafter.
> Meskins from a tree.
> Let's bring back the poll tax
> And set this country free.

Bull thanked the crowd for showing up and making the night a success. "It does my heart good to know that I live amongst folks that still honor two of the things that made this country what it is today—law and order and baseball." Here he stopped and tried to make his voice take on the weight of thought. "And if we didn't have law and order we couldn't have baseball. In some of the big cities, folks are afraid to leave their homes and go to the ballpark. They're afraid they might get mugged on the way to the game or come back home to find out that a burglar has busted into their house. It's not a fit way to live, and, thank God, we've managed to keep it from coming to that down here."

Bull rambled on for a while about hard work and safe streets and Sunday school. Then he told the crowd that it was time to present the annual Law Enforcement Officer of the Year Award, which this year was going to a rookie deputy—born, raised, educated, and born again right there in Selma—named Junior Boggs. Junior was president of the Bearcat Boosters, coach of the midget league Amvet Warriors, and a member of the Sulphur Springs Freewill Baptist Church. His wife was the former Joy Lynn Biggerstaff. They had two fine children, Billy Bob and Bitsy. One Saturday back in February, Junior had rescued the local TV weathergirl, Lornetta Gooch, daughter of Harley and Viola Gooch from over by Marion Junction, from a man who'd escaped from a Florida insane asylum and was holding Lornetta hostage, demanding the TV station give him an hour of prime time so that he could present his plan for achieving world peace. Well now, ole Junior wasn't having none of that. He sneaked in the back way, somehow managed to slip up behind the lunatic, sunk a .38 slug in the back of his head, and saved the evening for "Love Boat" and "Fantasy Island."

Pinzon said, "Ah, to be in Selma, now that Junior's there."

"Lornetta Gooch herself will present the award," Bull announced.

Lornetta sprung up out of the American dugout and sashayed to the microphone. She had her feet in patent leather spike heels, her face under several layers of Max Factor, her frosted hair in a $75 frizz, and her body in a white one-piece bathing suit with a banner slantwise across her chest that said "KALA TV 5." The fans moaned and whistled and waved their flags.

"Damned if that ain't a prime piece," Bullet Bob said.

"Fucking her would be an act of patriotism," I said.

When Lornetta got to Bull she went up on tiptoes and gave him a sweet little kiss on the cheek. Bull grinned like a stump freak in an amputee ward. Then he leaned down to the microphone and said, "Lordee, I do hope Beulah ain't here."

The crowd laughed. Lornetta giggled and worked up a blush. "Well, Lornetta," Bull said, "we're getting off to a late start and these folks're apt to miss the ten-o'clock edition of "Eyewitness News." So I wonder if you wouldn't be good enough to go ahead and tell us what the weather's going to be up to?"

"Fair to partly cloudy," she said, just as cute as a button on Peggy Lou's Easter dress. "Highs in the low nineties. Lows in the high seventies. Ten percent chance of afternoon or evening thundershowers."

She smiled. Bull smiled. I suppose the crowd smiled. Bullet Bob said, "I bet ole Bull's getting him some of that."

"Lucky girl," Genghis Mohammed, Jr., said.

Bull walked back to his car and dragged out a trophy that was about the size of a healthy midget. On a pedestal a bronzed cop stood in full regalia, chest out, legs spread, hands on hips. He carried it to Lornetta and was going to give it to her, but she shook her head and stepped to the microphone.

"A family of four could set up housekeeping inside that trophy," Lefty said.

"It'd be hot in there this time of year," I said.

"Ladies and gentlemen," Lornetta began, in a serious speech-class voice, "it's a great honor for me to be here tonight for Police Night. And it's a special thrill to be able to present this award to Deputy Junior Boggs. I owe my life to his bravery." She extended her left arm toward the Selma dugout. "Junior . . ."

Junior looked to be about five years and forty pounds beyond the high school football field. Bands of fat had formed around him but hadn't had time yet to do much serious falling. Swollen with ignorant pride, he long-stepped his way across the infield. When he reached Bull and Lornetta, he stopped, turned, and looked back at the dugout, out of which a choir appeared, wrapped in robes the color of old blood. They lined up, joined hands, and, to the accompaniment of the ball park organ, sang "Let the Lower Lights Be Burning." I joined in on the chorus.

> Let the lower lights be burning!
> Send a gleam across the wave!
> Some poor fainting, struggling seaman
> You may rescue, you may save.

"Why, Hog," Pansy kidded, "you have the voice of an angel."

"I sung bass, Hon, in the Slammer Tabernacle."

The choir doused the lower lights, and Lornetta returned to the mike. "For outstanding service to your community, for courage far beyond the call of duty, Deputy Sheriff Junior Boggs, I do hereby present you this award as Law Enforcement Officer of the Year."

Trophy extended, Bull stepped toward Junior, but Lornetta slipped between the two lawmen, wrapped her arms around Junior's neck, and kissed him flush on the mouth. "Junior," she said, letting him go, "thank you so very much for saving my life. I'll be grateful to you forever."

Junior laid his right hand on the butt of his holstered pistol, wiped his eyes with his left, and said, "Why, you're quite welcome, Miss Lornetta."

Then he accepted the trophy from Bull. I don't think he much wanted to make a speech, but Bull and Lornetta pushed him forward. The trophy was so big that he had to hold it off to one side to keep it from blocking him away from the microphone.

"Some of y'all that know me know I ain't never been much on public speaking. But I would like to take this chance to say how proud I am to accept this award. I never expected ever to get such a honor. I just go along doing what I been trained to do and what I know way down deep in my heart is right." He stopped, swallowed a time or two, looked at the trophy, and then switched it from one side to the other. "I'd just like to thank Sheriff Cox for being so good to me, and my momma and daddy—Mr. and Mrs. Burl R. Boggs, Star Route 1. Most of y'all know them—for raising me up the way they done." He started to let it go at that, then thought of something else. "And I'd like to put in a good word too for Coach Buster Spoon. When I's in high school Coach Spoon always taught us that if you wanted to amount to anything you had to put out 110 percent effort 110 percent of the time. I just really do hope I can go through life that away." He raised the trophy a little and took another look at it. "I thank each and ever' one of y'all for this very much. I won't never forget it."

Lornetta hooked her hand around Junior's free elbow and turned him toward the choir, which roared into "Stand Up, Stand Up for Jesus."

Bull stretched both arms, palms up, out in front of him, and the crowd stood and began singing with the choir. Everywhere the little American flags, held tight in fevered hands, jumped jubilantly back and forth, up and down through the bristling air.

I don't know whether Eversole had been sitting quietly all along at his end of the bench or had just then been drawn out of the clubhouse by the sound of the rising tumult. I just remember that suddenly there he was, the huge dark man, standing, just off to my right, on the first dugout step. His long, thick arms hung down at his sides, a glove on one hand, a ball in the other. I leaned a little to my left to get a clear look at his face. I didn't see anger in it, but I sensed that it was there, that Eversole had simply covered it with several coats of determination. And not a grim determination either. There was almost a satisfied look to the face. I thought it was the face of a man who, after a long search, had finally found the perfect enemy and was now ready to go out and do them in.

The choir began the final verse. Lornetta, as formally as she could, led Junior toward them. I wish I could have seen their faces. I imagined the light of heroism glowing through the faint pink of Junior's man-child cheeks. I imagined Lornetta, Miss America for the moment, smiling all over herself while tears streamed down her face, dredging rivulets through the makeup. Southern man, stout and strong, southern woman, meek and mild, lost in similar delusions.

It was farce, all right, but for just a minute there I felt a rush of sympathy, an urge toward brotherhood. Folks get by however they can. They do work they don't like to feed their kids. Year by year, the work grinds them down. The kids grow up to be strangers. Husbands and wives cling together out of habit and fear and sometimes love. Or they break apart because one or the other or both suddenly feel for somebody else the stirring of passion, almost forgotten, always confusing. And when and if they ever stand back and take a hard look at it all, none of it seems to make any sense. So they need patriotism and they need religion. They need ceremony, then, even if the ceremony is a farce, so that they can fool themselves into believing in something. And, hell, anyway, their ceremony was no bigger a farce than anybody else's.

Oh, they were enemies to me, but not in the pure way they were to Eversole. Sitting there on that dugout bench, I fancied I had some understanding of them. And I knew that a part of me would always be kindred to them. But I knew too that another part of me—I think it's the best part, I know it's the strongest—would have to fight them for every breath. Because their ceremonies, and everybody else's, have made it a world of cops and robbers. And I'm one of the robbers.

When Lornetta and Junior had disappeared and most of the din had died down, Reverend Cotton Edmunds came to the microphone and prayed. It was their typical prayer, beginning in mercy, working its way into belligerence, and ending in gratitude.

Before leaving, Reverend Edmunds reminded the crowd that he was sponsoring a trip to the Holy Land and that they still had ten days to make their reservations. Then Bull got in his car, switched the siren on again, and, followed by the other cars and the cycles, circled the field one more time before heading out the gate. The crowd cheered for a couple of minutes before settling down. The groundkeepers removed the microphone and then came back out with rakes and began to smooth away tread marks and hoofprints.

We ventured out onto the edge of the field, stretching, running a little. All of us, that is, but Eversole. Stump Guthrie was waiting for him in our bull pen, but Eversole had time—he could finish getting warm while we batted—and he used it in his own way. He stayed on that first dugout step for several more minutes, looking out over the crowd, priming himself. Tonight, in the heart of vigilante country, he would be riding point for the Marks Gang.

We'd gone 3 and 12 during the home stand, falling from 15-5 to 18-17, from first place (three games up on Selma) to third (four games back of Selma and one behind Nashville). I'd hit .216 (13 for 60) during that spell, and my average for the season had fallen from .521 to .305. I hadn't driven in but five runs in those fifteen games, and it had been so long since I'd really jacked one I sometimes had trouble remembering what it felt like. I knew Ratoplan had twisted some of the snap out of my bat, but I couldn't lay it all onto him. The pitchers had had time to get a book on me, and they'd begun to feed me more breaking stuff, keeping the ball away from me. Now and then, when they caught me leaning over, they'd bust one in on my hands, but other than that they'd quit trying to tie me up with the hard one inside. They weren't great pitchers, but they were professionals, and they (and Ratoplan) had turned me around enough so that I was trying to hit their pitches instead of waiting for them to fuck up and give me mine. To do that, to wait for his pitch, a hitter needs concentration, patience, and confidence. So it did me more than a little good when Eversole, on his way out to the bull pen, walked over where I was horsing around with Julius, laid his hand on my shoulder, and said, "Get me a run."

I told him I'd do what I could. But I was flattered that I was the one he'd come to.

"I want this game." And then he stared down hard at me, like Sitting Bull at a reluctant brave.

"I'll get you the run." A fool's promise, maybe, but I felt good giving it.

Minutes later Selma took the field, the high school band ambushed "The Star-Spangled Banner," and Junior Boggs, sitting in a box seat beside the American dugout and surrounded by his wife, his kids, and Lornetta Gooch, threw out the first ball.

Jefferson Mundy lined Whitey Shelton's first pitch up the middle for a single. Worm Warnock, on a hit-and-run, got under the ball and sent a little looper out to short right. Their right fielder, Jake Moreland, had to come in hard to make the catch. At first it looked like they had Mundy doubled off first, but Moreland hurried his throw and Axe Heflin had to come well off the bag to field it. So it was one down and Mundy still on first when I came up. For the first time in a while, I felt good at the plate; the bat felt like a weapon. Chief Eversole, here comes that run, I thought. Shelton started me off with a pitch that came hard at the center of the plate, about halfway between the knees and the belt. Good-bye, motherfucker. But no. Just as I began my swing, the ball jumped away from me, a sharp four-inch break. My hands adjusted some, but not enough. I still hit it pretty good, but my cut was all arms, no body behind it, a defensive swing. Two hops, right to short. Double play. I'd been easy meat for Whitey Shelton.

Eversole started his game by playing a little chin music for

Jimmy Stennis. The first pitch came right at the kid's fine, firm FCA jaw. Stennis jerked his head back just in time to save it. He backed out of the box, but then made a show of digging in again. The crowd, glad the opportunity had come so quickly, booed. The second pitch was the first one's twin. Stennis bailed out fast. The boos became threats, curses. Eversole's not going to beat them, I thought, he's going to kill them—which is, of course, one way of doing it.

Bull Cox, still in sheriff's drag, stomped out, wagging a bent finger at Eversole, and had a talk with the umpire, on the topic, I'd guess, of gratuitous violence. The high school band played "Hail to the Chief." It occurred to me that it was right decent of them to salute Eversole that way. Bull said his piece and marched off the field to a round of applause. Knee-high spitter over the outside corner. Called strike one. Another one—same place, same result. Stennis stepped out of the box and prepared himself for the next spitter. Instead he got the hard one, over the inside edge just above the knees. He half-fell away from it and then kind of golfed at it, like an old woman trying to sweep a rat out an open door. Sit down, Little Jimmy.

Eversole got the next two hitters in the first and all three in the second without allowing any of them to hit a ball out of the infield. He looked as sharp as I'd ever seen him—which was going some.

I drew a walk my next time up, with two down in the third. Rainbow Smith followed that with a long single that sent me to third. But then Julius flied to center and stranded us.

Bucky Bilbo led off their half of the third with a Texas Leaguer to center that I thought was going to fall in, but Julius got a good jump, dove, caught it, somersaulted, and popped to his feet, waving the gloved ball. Bilbo and, seconds later, Bull rushed the base ump and claimed that Julius had dropped the ball and then scooped it back up during his somersault, but the ump knew better and they probably did too. They just figured their protests and the crowd's boos would intimidate the ump into giving them a break later.

Shelton got out of the fourth by getting Joe Buck Cantwell to bounce into a double play, 5-4-3. I kept studying Shelton and I saw that whenever he needed an out pitch, he'd either cut the ball or scuff it. That was the pitch he used on both Cantwell and me. It's easy enough to throw. You just hold the ball in your hand with the cut or scuffed side opposite to the way you want it to break. Then you throw it like a half-assed fastball and it'll break anywhere from four to eight inches. It's hard as hell to hit because you can't pick up the spin on it the way you can with a curve or slider. I figured the smart thing for me to do would be to lay off that pitch until I had two strikes on me.

That worked when I led off the fifth. Shelton threw me one that jumped in at me and I took it for a strike, but then he fed me a regular curve, just off the outside corner but up a little, and I stuck it in the gap in right-center. The ball took a righteous hop off the fence and I rolled into third, winded and proud.

Shelton toughened up then. He threw Rainbow Smith five good pitches. Two of them were just off the plate, and Rainbow swung from the heels at the other three and walked back to the dugout cussing himself.

I guess Rainbow's striking out the way he did caused Lefty to decide to just go ahead and steal the run, because he gave the suicide squeeze sign before Julius even got into the box. Now, I've never been known for my foot speed, but you don't have to be fast to score on the squeeze. You just break for home as soon as the pitcher goes into his windup and if the bunter gets the ball down and fair, you score. Julius was a good bunter, so I figured we'd pull it off. But I have to hand it to Shelton—when he saw Julius square around, he did just what he had to do. He sailed the ball right at Julius's chin. If Julius had just stood there and let it hit him, he'd've gone to first and I'd've still been on third. If he'd ducked the pitch, it would probably have gone all the way back to the screen and I'd've trotted home with an easy run. Even if Iron Joe Talmadge had managed to catch it, he would've been off balance and I'd've knocked that son of a bitch for a pretty little loop. But when you're trying to squeeze, you've got it in your head that you have to bunt the ball, get it on the ground, protect the runner. So Julius went for it, and in spite of the ball being up in his face the way it was, he almost pulled it off. The bat met the ball a little too flush, though, and straight on, and Whitey Shelton, rushing from the mound, dove and caught the thirty-five-foot line drive just before it hit the grass. Then he stood up and threw casually back to third. Three outs, no runs, inning over. The crowd gave him a big ovation, and I'll have to say he deserved it.

Eversole just kept right on—1, 2, 3, inning after inning. It was

his illegal pitch against Shelton's. The spitter is the tougher one to
throw, of course. In fact, it may be the hardest pitch there is to
master. You have to grease the part of the ball you're holding—
you can use sweat or spit or vaseline, anything slick; that's the easy
part—and then when you let it go you squeeze it between your
thumb and first two fingers and kind of squirt it out of your hand,
like you might with a bar of soap. If you don't do all that just right
the pitch won't break. And the spitter that doesn't break is as sure
a home run ball as there is. You throw two of those a game, you're
a loser.

Shelton kept getting into trouble and working his way out. I
came up again in the seventh with one down. He threw me a good
curve for a strike, then brushed me back and followed that with a
scuff ball that caught the outside corner. I asked the ump to take a
look at the ball. He did, found the scuff, tossed that ball out of the
game, and threw Shelton a fresh canvas to work on. Shelton
wasted a fastball outside. With the count two and two on me, I set
myself for the out pitch. But Shelton decided to punish me for
going to the ump and threw me one as hard as he could and just a
little behind me. I backed into it, twisted clockwise, and caught it
square in the middle of my back. It hurt like hell. I stood there a
minute, threw a glare out at Shelton, then looked down at Iron Joe
Talmadge. I could see him grinning under his mask. I said to him,
"You tell your tough little friend out there on the mound that if he
ever does that to me again, I'll jerk his head off and take it home
and feed it to my hogs. They're used to eating swill."

Then I went on down to first. Most of the Reds had come out of
the dugout and were yelling at Shelton, who just stood there on the
mound looking right pleased with himself. I'm sure my teammates
were expecting me to go out after him, and the crowd must've been
looking for that too, because they were on their feet, jeering, hungry for blood. After all, it was Police Night. And any other time I
probably would've given them what they wanted. But right then I
didn't want to risk getting thrown out of the game, not that game.

Lefty started toward first to see if I was hurt, but I waved him
back. The fans sat down, the boys went back into the dugout, and
Rainbow Smith grounded to short. I broke up the double play by
throwing a cross-body block into their second baseman, Punch
Lurleen. It didn't do any good though. Julius popped to third for
the last out.

Eversole set them down in order again in their seventh. In the eighth they began to ask the ump to check the ball after almost every pitch. But Eversole was the absolute master of the spitter. He didn't need but just a touch of grease to throw it—so little that by the time Joe Buck Cantwell caught the ball, twisted it around once in his glove, and showed it to the umpire, it'd be dry. Hell, everybody in the park knew Eversole was throwing the spitter, but I don't believe Gaylord Perry could've caught him.

After Iron Joe Talmadge fanned for the second out in their eighth, Bull, High Sheriff of Hazard, blustered up to the home-plate ump and tried to get him to go to the mound and search Eversole. Sweat had soaked completely through Eversole's uniform, from neck to crotch. His hair was sopping wet. His skin was drenched. So both Bull and the ump knew a search wouldn't find anything. Bull was just trying to upset Eversole, get him out of his rhythm, trick one fat pitch out of him. When the ump refused to cooperate, Bull commenced to give him a long, thorough cussing. I'm sure Bull knew he wouldn't get thrown out of that game for anything short of assault. So he went on and on, singing his loud, abusive song at the ump, while the crowd hummed harmony. The two base umps came in to help their partner and the high school band played "Three Blind Mice." Just before heading back to his dugout, Bull reached into the plate ump's ball pouch, took out a new baseball, spit on it several times, and threw it to Eversole, who caught it, looked it over, and nodded thanks.

The ump got that ball back, of course, and rolled it out of the game. But it didn't matter. Eversole threw nothing but spitters to Bimbo Helms, who took one for a strike, one for a ball, and then chopped one to me for the third out. If we could get him a run in our half of the ninth, Eversole would be three outs away from perfection.

Shelton had retired us in order in our half of the eighth, so Eversole led off the ninth. With the count two and one, Shelton grooved a fastball and Eversole took it up the middle for a single. Mundy then tried to sacrifice him to second, but he bunted it too hard and Shelton's good quick throw just nipped Eversole at second. Worm Warnock flied to short left and Mundy had to stay at first. Then I was up again, two down and Mundy three bases from home. Shelton surprised me with his first pitch by throwing his scuff ball over the middle of the plate and making it break in on me. I hit it off the bat handle, but luckily it was foul, on the ground outside third. I took the next two, both of them breaking down and away, one for a ball, another for a strike. One ball, two strikes. I stepped out of the box, knocked the dirt out of my shoes with my bat, and decided to tempt Shelton—or Iron Joe Talmadge, really, who would be close enough to see what I was doing and would call the pitch. When I got back into the box, I crowded the plate more than I usually do and leaned forward just enough to make Talmadge think I was concentrating on the outside corner.

They fell for it. Shelton threw me a pitch almost identical to the one he'd started me off with. I stepped in the bucket, saw the pitch start to break, felt my power travel from legs to hips to shoulders to hands, and, head down, eyes wide, saw the perfect instant, hickory on horsehide, and heard the sharp, clear crack. It was out of the park, about thirty feet or so to the fair side of the left-field pole, before I left the box. Pick Maddox, their left fielder, didn't even start after it, just turned and watched it, a rising line drive, clear the fence and the temporary stands and then disappear into the darkness.

As I started toward first, Shelton kicked the dirt once and then flung his glove to the mound. I imagine the crowd was quiet, but I couldn't have heard them anyway. As I circled the diamond, I felt like I was floating through a world, still and quiet, where everything was frozen in a soft, white light. It wasn't much, and it didn't last long, but it was as close to rapture as a man like me ever gets.

I touched home plate, and Mundy brought me back to earth by throwing his arms around me and dancing a reel with me. Then the others were there, pounding my back, slapping my helmet. I thought, Where are you now, Cesar Ratoplan? Ole Hog's asnorting again.

Pansy met me at the top of the dugout steps and gave me a kiss that would've been fit for a soldier just home from the wars.

Straight-faced, Pinzon sang, " 'He has loosed the fateful lightning of his terrible swift sword.' "

Lefty laid his hand on my right shoulder and said, "You're back."

"ARMED ROBBER GUNS DOWN AMERICANS," I said.

Eversole walked over and thanked me. "I knew you'd do it," he said.

"Finish them off," I told him.

Before I got sat down good, Rainbow Smith had doubled down the right-field line. Bull Cox plowed out to the mound, where Shelton was standing with his hands on his hips, looking disgustedly up at the Lord.

Bull brought in Suitcase Poff, and Julius lined his third pitch hard but right at Bimbo Helms in center.

I was a little flutter-bellied when I took my position in the bottom of the ninth. It calmed me some to look at Eversole, who seemed as mean and hard and sure as ever, ready to come after you with everything he had. But then Bucky Bilbo, leading off for them, about a quarter of a plug of tobacco stuffed in his right jaw, looked sure of himself too. Bilbo was a big, slow, lefthand-hitting third baseman, and I was pretty sure he wouldn't be bunting, so I played him well behind the bag and to pull. Speck Anderson, who'd come in for Rainbow at third, played him up even with the grass, just in case. Bilbo took a ball, a strike, then grounded the next pitch, a spitter, a couple of steps to my right. I moved over in front of it, took the big hop, and flipped to Eversole, who was covering first. The fluttering in my stomach eased off some. I'd handled the ball without trouble; with the pressure on, Eversole had remembered to cover first. I thought we'd make it.

Azbell Camp, small and quick, stepped into the box, pinch-hitting for old Jake Moreland. I knew he was up there to walk if he could, bunt if he couldn't. I moved up about three steps in front of the bag and yelled over to remind Worm Warnock to cover first on a bunt. Over at third Speck Anderson cheated in even further than I did. He was so close to home he could've damn near spit in Camp's face.

Eversole knew Camp would be taking a strike and so got the preliminaries out of the way by gutting a fastball. Then Camp surprised us by taking a swing at the next pitch, a high, tight hard one Eversole fired up against the expected bunt. But it was a poor, late swing—a good idea badly executed. I wasn't sure whether Camp was really as bad a hitter as he'd looked to be on that pitch. It could've been that he'd come up prepared to bunt and then got the hit sign and was still wondering about the rightness of that when the pitch was on him. Whatever, the swing had more thought than wrist in it. I had to think that even with two strikes on him Camp's only hope was to bunt.

The crowd was stone quiet and I could hear Lefty, all the way across the field from me, yelling for Speck Anderson to move back a couple of steps. Speck did it, but I don't think he wanted to. I think he figured it the way I did—we ought to get right in Camp's face and make him swing at the ball.

The count was way in Eversole's favor and he decided to take advantage of it. His two-strike pitch to Camp was a fastball high and a good foot outside. Camp took it for ball one, but before doing that he shortened up on his bat. He would've bunted that time if he could have. The odds were good, then, that he'd try it on the next pitch too. That next pitch came in high and tight again, just off the plate. Camp showed bunt early, but then drew his bat back and punched at the ball, hoping to slap it past Anderson, who was coming in on him from third. Another good idea, this time better executed. But not quite well enough. Camp got too much bat handle on it, and Speck was able to short-hop it and nail the little bastard at first. One more out to go.

The last man up was Tree Folsum. Twenty years earlier, he'd been the pride of the Dixie Association. He'd been, they say, easy-going and full of life, with a swing as swift and sure as doom. One year he'd hit 56 home runs, still an Association record. After that he'd played with the Yankees, but he'd lounged too much and laughed too loud, and after two good years and two bad, he'd found himself in Kansas City and then Saint Louis and then he'd just gone ahead and drank himself the rest of the way back home. Now he was a sort of freak that Bull trotted out onto the field every so often for the edification of the home folks, who could see him as an example of the evils of easy freedom and hard liquor.

He was a big man, nearly as tall as Eversole, and the old, long muscles were not yet completely hidden. Now and then—four, five, six times a year, even yet—he would step into the box and, with fathers pointing at him and lecturing their sons, see just the right pitch and feel the gift come back to him and send the ball arcing long and high across memory to link that present with a hopeful past. And this night, sent up to face Eversole, he was nobody's freak, nobody's object lesson. He was Bull Cox's last hope, the last man in Selma standing between Jeremiah Eversole and one night of absolute perfection.

Maybe Eversole underestimated Folsum some, or maybe he figured Folsum would be taking a strike, like Bilbo and Camp had done, like the book said you should do. Whatever the reason,

Eversole's first pitch to him was over the inside part of the plate and about letter high, a gopher ball to a power hitter, but a pitch an old man with whiskeyed hands shouldn't've been able to get around on. Folsum actually got around too quick. He jacked it down the line toward the right-field lights, but it began curving and ended up twenty or thirty feet foul. He'd given it a ride, though, and that livened the crowd, pumped a little hope into them, and they began to urge him on.

Eversole bore down. He threw a spitter low for a ball, another one at the knees for a strike, then wasted a fastball outside for ball two. Folsum stepped into that fastball, started his swing, but checked it at the last second. You could see then that he'd come to the plate looking for the fastball, telling himself to lay off everything else until he had two strikes on him. But now, two strikes and two balls, Eversole having just tantalized him with a hard one, Folsum had to set himself for the out pitch. He didn't figure to be the kind that would end a game by being called out on strikes. So he had to be ready to swing at the spitter.

He didn't get it. Eversole came in high and tight with a fastball almost identical to the one Folsum had knocked the bejesus out of But Folsum had guessed right that first time and this time he was surprised. His big bat flashed around, but late. Joe Buck Cantwell looked down at his mitt, saw the ball secure there, then jumped straight up—not high, but an old catcher with bad knees like Cantwell had to've been completely snookered by the moment to have jumped at all.

It seemed like a full minute passed before any of us rushed Eversole. Cantwell started toward him but stopped about halfway. Eversole, still grim, lifted his hands above his head and glared at the Police Night crowd, which sat and silently watched. Slowly, arms still high in triumph, he began turning to his left. Fuck this, I thought. When you beat them, you laugh. When he'd turned enough so that he was almost facing me, I ran to him, jumped into him, and wrapped my arms around his neck, my legs around his waist. He staggered back a couple of steps, then braced and caught himself. "You did it, you goddam muleheaded savage," I shouted, laughing, at him. And then he threw his great, round head back and laughed with me.

The others followed me, swarming the mound, knocking us over, jerking us up, exultant, oblivious to everything outside the walls of

Patriot Field. Tree Folsum, bat in hand, a big smile creasing the worn face, came out to the mound to take Eversole's hand and say, "It was a pleasure, big man, just to be part of such a game." And Eversole, with right good grace, nodded thanks.

After a while, I noticed the crowd, or some of it, was applauding. Not many baseball fans ever get to witness a perfect game, at any level, so these were lucky and had the sense to know and appreciate it. I told Eversole to tip his cap to them and he looked at me kind of funny, but then he said, "Aw, what the hell," and did it, lifted the cap high and waved it. And as their applause grew louder, it occurred to me that Eversole had not defeated these people. In spite of himself, he had made the night a gift to them, a gift fashioned by endurance, control, determination, and intelligence, a gift they couldn't keep from accepting any more than he could keep from sharing. His victory was everyone's. They could preserve it in their minds as the final act of Police Night. "And after all that," they could tell their friends, the memory warming them, years later, "this big Indian from Arkansas came out and pitched a perfect game." It was pure baseball, pure art, and changed nothing but that one night, when a man's right arm delivered us all for a while from ourselves and the mean world made by men who, in the name of God and money, conspired to keep us at one another's throats.

27

I guess it's only fitting that the first time a woman played in a professional baseball game nobody noticed her. Susan Pankhurst claimed a little piece of history for herself by coming in for me in the bottom of the eighth of the game the day after Eversole's masterpiece. She handled two chances, good throws from first Mundy and then Worm Warnock. She didn't bat in that game. Atticus Flood, Jew Bernstein, and Mike O'Bryan went down in order in our ninth. We lost, 9–5.

The other thing about that game was that it was Bullet Bob's first really bad outing. He relieved Franklin Brown with one out in the seventh, the score tied, and a man on second, and before that

inning ended we were behind 8–5. Bob claimed he couldn't concentrate on the hitters for worrying about having a woman behind
him. But the truth was simpler than that. Due to the Little Rock
rains and all, Bob'd had a long layoff, and he needed to throw
three or four times a week to stay sharp, the knuckleball being a
pitch that requires touch rather than strength. Still I felt a little
twinge of sadness for him as he stood out there looking like a middle-aged fat man throwing batting practice and having to take the
jeers of his ole buddies on the Selma bench. I wondered, for a minute, what would become of him.

Susan played again the next day, when Genghis Mohammed,
Jr., made his first start and we beat Jigs Thurmond, 6–2. Oh,
Susan and Genghis were never on the field at the same time. Lefty
limited Genghis to fifty pitches, a limit that would be raised ten
pitches for each of Genghis's next several appearances, until Lefty
was sure Genghis's arm was in shape. So Genghis left his first game
leading 4–1 with two down in the fourth and a 2-2 count on Bimbo
Helms. Then Pinzon came in and pitched through the seventh,
giving up just one run. Bullet Bob, Susan playing first behind him,
finished up, yielding nothing but one walk in the last two innings.
In the eighth, after getting two quick strikes on Axe Heflin, who'd
been the loudest of Bob's hecklers the day before, Bob ambled up
to home plate and held the ball up in Heflin's face, as if to say,
"Here it is, Axe. This is what you're trying to hit. Just a little white
ball, coming up there nice and easy." Heflin, who seemed to've lost
his appetite for comedy overnight, told Bob to get his ass back on
the mound. Bob did, then threw Heflin a floater that looked like it
was changing its mind every few inches about where it was headed.
Heflin took a swing that lifted him plumb off the ground and
didn't come within a foot of the ball. Bob gave him a horse laugh
you could've heard in Georgia.

In the ninth Susan made her first appearance at the plate. She
was announced as S. K. Pankhurst, the name Lefty had used on
the official roster to snooker the league office, and Bob bet me
twenty dollars that before she was through batting Selma would
find her out. They had their junker, Suitcase Poff, mopping up,
and I figured Susan would get around on him all right. She looked
at three pitches, one of them a strike, then swung at a curve,
bouncing it to second. She ran hard and well to first but was, of
course, thrown out. The Selmans didn't notice a thing unusual.

Bob paid off after the game, but he bitched first. "They knew," he said. "They just couldn't fucking believe it."

But the truth was that Susan wasn't noticed because she wasn't something they were looking to see. If somebody had told the Americans we had a woman on the field, I'm sure they'd've been able to narrow it down to Susan. But they'd've had to study it close, because, in uniform, she looked like a ballplayer. She stood about five-ten, she'd strapped her tits down tight, and she'd let Bobbie Sampson mow on her hair until it was nearly as short as mine and a good deal shorter than Julius's. It wasn't that she was trying to disguise herself as a man. As far as I know, that never occurred to anybody. Susan just knew she'd have to do a lot of jerking and stretching at first base and she didn't want to be bothered by the flapping of her hair—or her tits. And if you'd watched her play first a while, you might've wondered why somebody as lean and quick and graceful as that wasn't at short or second or in the outfield, but then you'd've said to yourself, "No arm probably," and let it go at that. A good close look at her face might've been enough to make a hard man rethink the ethics of faggotry. But if you hadn't expected to see a woman—and how could you have—I don't think you'd've seen one.

The way it worked out surprised all of us. Lefty, and the rest of us too, had taken it for granted that the first time Susan trotted onto the field she'd be recognized as a woman and all kinds of hell would be raised immediately. If it'd been Bobbie Sampson, we might've thought differently. Hell, with a cap on, Bobbie looked a lot like Stump Guthrie. But Susan! Christ, I thought they'd do more than just see that she was a woman; I thought they'd start lusting after her.

All during the time Susan was playing in her first game, I kept thinking one or another of the Selma boys would any second jump up and start screaming and maybe sic the dogs and hoses on her. But after she entered her second game and still wasn't spotted, it occurred to me that she might just pass for male all season. Something like the same thought must've come to Bobbie Sampson too, because when a bunch of us went out for beers after that game she told Lefty he owed it to Susan to go to the press with her story. Lefty argued that sooner or later Susan would get more publicity than she'd want and that the longer she could play with what

amounted to anonymity, the better chance she'd have to show she
was a legitimate ballplayer and not just a gimmick.

"She's already played," Bobbie said. "They can't change that.
The more publicity we get, the harder it'll be for them to stop her."

"She hasn't got a hit yet," Lefty said. "She hasn't had to field a
tough chance. All I'm saying is that we should let her play a little
more before calling attention to her. If we fill the stands with reporters and Susan has a bad game, she'll wind up being the butt of
one of those cute human interest stories at the end of the evening
news."

Susan and Pansy were at the other end of the joint shooting
eight ball with Julius and Pinzon. Bobbie turned her head and
watched them for a few seconds. Then she looked across the booth
at first Lefty and then me. "What do you think, Hog?"

"I don't know," I said. "Maybe we ought to just leave it up to
Susan."

"Susan doesn't know either. She's so grateful to Lefty for giving
her the chance to play that she's willing to leave the rest of it up to
him." She lifted our pitcher, refilled her mug, and took a sip from
it. Then she put her thumb against one side of the mug's base and
her second finger against the opposite side and began slowly, ab-
sentmindedly turning the mug counterclockwise. She looked up at
us and grinned. "Do you think it might be possible that you men
overestimate the difficulties of baseball?"

Lefty waited a beat or two as if thinking the question over, then
smiled and said, "No."

Susan played two and a half innings in the fifth and last game of
that series in Selma, a game Eversole won, 6–zip, to give us a 3–2
edge in the series. She came to bat again in that game, this time
against Pettus Edmonds, a hard-throwing reliever that Bull Cox
had on his roster to satisfy the league regulation requiring at least
one Negro on each team. He fanned her, but she managed to
foul a couple of two-strike pitches before going down. She hadn't
been impossibly overmatched. It was encouraging that she'd gone
up there and struck out like a man. As soon as she learned to slam
her helmet against the dugout floor after striking out, she'd fit
right in.

She'd played in five games—three in Selma and two more when
we were in Milledgeville—and been to the plate four times without

a hit when, against the Asheville Wolves on the twelfth of June, she lined one up the middle off Catawba Joiner, who, after shooting two fastballs past her, tried to fool her with what looked to be a palm ball. An out later, Julius doubled her home. We were already up by five runs, so the one she scored didn't matter—except, of course, to her and the women's movement. The record books wouldn't be able to reduce her to a woman's name followed by a string of zeroes.

Lefty went to the press.

Reporters from everywhere swarmed us after that, with their notepads and their tape recorders, their tired eyes and their cheap clicketyclack minds. They came from every town in the league and from Atlanta and New Orleans and Knoxville and Birmingham and God knows where else. The *Arkansas Chronicle* sent their sports editor, Wilbur Haney, but he got fed up with the company after a few days and had himself replaced by Joe Bo Corker, who five years earlier had been a tight end for the Arkansas Razorbacks and now ordinarily covered high school football. There were even a few slumming yankees, come down to do another piece on another version of The New South. The first couple of days it was just newspapermen, but after that here came the damn TV crews— stoned cameramen in jeans, jogging shoes, and jaybird T-shirts, beaming, blow-dried, bright-blazered announcers swelled up with a local celebrity.

They were mostly interested in Susan and Lefty, of course, but there were so many of them that some were always lurking around ready to leach on to any of the rest of us that would hold still long enough. I got considerable attention from them on account of my record. No matter what they asked me—what I'd done, what I'd learned, was I grateful—I told them the same thing. I figured I had an obligation. I told them that the prisons I'd been in were filled with poor whites, blacks, and, in Oklahoma, Indians. I told them that the guards were stupid, fat, and vicious, and that, as far as I could see, that was the way the system wanted them.

The reporters didn't print much of what I had to say, and they framed what little they did use so that it sounded like the whining of an ungrateful parolee. It didn't matter. You just say what you have to say.

I wasn't the only one that tried to use the reporters to his own interest. After telling them he was against having Susan on the team but admitting that so far Lefty seemed to be using her right and that she hadn't hurt the team yet, Bullet Bob told them he'd been unfairly drummed out of the big leagues. "I ought to be up there right now," he said, "but they're prejudiced against knuckle-ballers. That's all there is to it. Look at my record here. I'm the best reliever in this league. But do you think I've heard anything from any of the big clubs? Why hell no. That'd mean they was owning up to being wrong in the first place and they ain't about to do that. Not yet. But they're going to have to set up and take notice before I'm done here. A knuckleballer don't hit his stride till he's my age. Look at what Wilhelm done and them Niekro boys. It won't be long till them big boys'll be coming to ole Bob and asking for his services. They know that a good short reliever is a prime piece of property and I'm here to tell you that ole Bullet Bob Turner is God's own short reliever."

Genghis Mohammed, Jr., swore he would only speak to an authorized representative of *The Scorched Truth,* or whatever it is that the great American prophet Rastus Muhammed calls his propaganda rag. But Genghis wasn't the kind that could resist an audience, and when, after a day or two, no Black Muslim sports reporter had come forth to take his statement, he heard the sweet, eternal voice of Allah telling him to go on ahead and lay a line on the heathen. During our last two days in Asheville, Genghis rewarded the press with long harangues about the purity of the black race, the proper role of women, and the evils of pork.

"I can understand the rest of it," I said to Pansy, who'd gotten a little riled listening to one of Genghis's rants, "but how can a man let religion stand between him and barbecued spareribs?"

Several of the guys on the team—Joe Buck Cantwell, Worm Warnock, Rainbow Smith, Speck Anderson, Mike O'Bryan, and Stump Guthrie—either didn't talk to the press at all or just gave yes or no, it's-O.K., or I-don't-mind answers. I think most of them just didn't care to say anything that they might have to see printed up in the paper, but Stump Guthrie had the best reason. One evening Stump and Bullet Bob and I were out in our bullpen idling the time away while Asheville took batting practice. Stump said he thanked God the bullpen, at least, was off limits to the reporters. There was still one place a man could have him a chew and look out at the world without some damn fool coming up and asking him a question about it.

Stump's silence didn't bother the press, of course. He wasn't the sort of man they paid attention to anyway. And, like I said, they didn't pay much heed to my rants about the jails or Genghis's about Islam. They were used to people like Bob trying to use them to promote themselves. They didn't even seem to mind Eversole pushing them when they got in his way, though it didn't take them long to learn to stay clear of him. No, they got pretty much what they needed from Lefty and Susan and livened it up by throwing in a little color from the rest of us. They wrote Susan up and the fans came out to see her and Lefty obliged them by playing her at least a little in every game, though in one close game she didn't do anything but pinch run for Joe Buck Cantwell. She caught some jeers and a few wolf-whistles, but most of the fans seemed to like her well enough.

And I guess it would've gone on like that, getting a little quieter each time Susan played, if Franklin Brown hadn't told an Asheville reporter something that charged the air up all over again, something that didn't have a thing to do with Susan. Franklin answered a question about what it had been like to go to the co-op's high school. That had led him around to the subject of racism in Magnolia, Arkansas. He said it was still around, just dressing better and going to bigger churches. Then, warmed up good, he went on to say that the new right-wing white fundamental Christians weren't new, fundamental, or Christian, just white and right-wing.

And he was talking in the heart of enemy country, Asheville being headquarters for Dr. J. Raymond Whiteside, ringleader of the Christian Caucus, pastor of the Holy Light Baptist Church whose Sunday morning services were televised nationwide to millions of frothing crusaders, and founder of Vigilance Mountain Baptist College, a fully accredited spawning pool for pastors, missionaries, youth directors, song leaders, and other censors.

So, anyway, Franklin's comments, which probably would've been ignored in most other places, made headlines in Asheville. The *Mountain Clarion* sports page said: REDS PITCHER CALLS AMERICAN CHURCHES RACIST. The article gave Reverend Whiteside the last word. "Apparently, Franklin Brown is a young man who has recently graduated from a self-proclaimed secular humanist school. I do not wish to hold him responsible for his remarks. He has been brainwashed. His comments are totally in error, of course. How can anyone call God's church racist when the simple truth is that the vast majority of American blacks are members of that church? In fact most of them are Baptists. I hold Mr. Lefty Marks, whose school Franklin Brown attended and whose baseball team he now plays for, responsible for this slander of decent Christians everywhere. An apology is in order, but we cannot expect one from a person so young and wrongly educated as Franklin Brown or from so fierce an opponent of traditional American values as Lefty Marks. May God have mercy on them."

I was sitting next to Lefty in our dugout before the last game of that Asheville series and listened to him answer the reporters' questions about Whiteside's statement. I could tell he enjoyed himself. To him, Whiteside represented the old enemy and was a proper, fat target.

Eversole pitched another shutout that night, his fourth in a row, leaving him just twelve innings short of the Association's consecutive-scoreless-inning record set in 1924 by a Memphis sidearmer named Barefoot Billy Waters. I hit a three-run shot to dead center in the top of the seventh. Susan played the last two and a half innings and made a good diving catch of a line drive off the bat of their left fielder, Choo Choo Charlie Olsen, who'd just been called up from the Black Mountain Warblers.

Afterwards, a few of the more persistent reporters tried to talk to Eversole, who gave them nothing. A couple interviewed me. I told them that the pitch I'd hit had been a fat slider out over the plate and that the American prison system sucked. Susan was up in the press box with the editor of the Lifestyles section of the *Atlanta Constitution*. I didn't see Franklin Brown in the clubhouse, and then I noticed that none of the blacks were around, except Genghis, who was over in his corner putting on a dashiki. I figured Atticus, Jefferson, and Franklin were dressing in the manager's office, which Lefty never used.

Lefty dressed with the rest of us and right then was surrounded by half a dozen reporters who were trying to get him to take some shots at Whiteside. I was close enough to see him moving around as he undressed and to hear his voice. He gave them more or less what they wanted, I guess. Once I heard him tell them that Whiteside was the kind of man Jesus had chased out of church with a whip.

When he stood and took off his uniform shirt, I could see the reporters staring at his stub of an arm, which was just a narrow six-

inch flap with three little fingers and a thumb gouged into the end
of it. He could wave it a little and wiggle one of the fingers, and he
did that for the newsmen. They were quiet for maybe a minute
and then one of them asked him why he was called Lefty when his
right arm was the good one.

"I write with this left one," he said. "The ordeal of it makes me
choose my words with great care."

They laughed some at that, nervously, still embarrassed by the
arm. The same guy asked him what sort of writing he did.

"Just the occasional aphorism," Lefty said, "and, once or twice a
year, a clerihew." He unbuttoned his pants, pulled them to his
knees, and sat down. "I thought that was a helluva play Susan
made on Olsen's line drive in the ninth, didn't you?" he asked
them.

28

It's something like 650 miles of Interstate 40 from Asheville to
Little Rock and Bobbie Sampson drove it straight through except
for a gas-and-piss-and-breakfast stop around daybreak at the
Music City Truckstop in Nashville. We had to get off 40 and go
into town a ways to find the place and when I saw that it looked
like just another of those big, ugly, especially American rectangles
where truckers stretch and eat and meet up with pushers and
whores, I wondered why the hell we'd gone to the trouble of getting there. The food usually runs from indifferent to god-awful, a
dose of speed was the last thing I wanted right then, and they
usually keep the whores pretty well penned up out back, away
from the general public.

But this place did turn out to be special. Oh, the whores were
probably around somewhere doing their part to keep the teamsters
moving and if you'd've asked around you could've probably lo-
cated a man that would sell you a pill you could've rode to Panama. But somebody there knew how to cook real food I had the
breakfast special—country ham, red-eye gravy, a heap of grits,
three eggs over easy, homemade biscuits, a bowl of cereal, and coffee. I ate at a table with Pansy, Pinzon, and Jew Bernstein, who

took turnabout making jokes on my table manners. I didn't pay them any mind. I just ate and listened to Lefty, sitting at the table just behind me, tell Susan and Julius and Bobbie about his last year in the minors. The year was 1948 and Lefty was with the Amarillo Gold Sox in the West Texas–New Mexico League. Lefty said they had a big, bald center fielder named Bob Crues, who that year batted .404, hit 69 home runs, and had 254 RBIs in 140 games.

"What ever became of him?" Julius wondered.

"I don't know," Lefty said. "Bob was a little old for a prospect—not too old really, but old to a scout's eyes. And it was a hitter's league—short fences, thin air, not much good pitching. Half the regulars in the league hit over .300 and there were three or four besides Bob who went over .400. Still nobody's ever had a year like that anywhere. Driving in almost two runs a game." He paused a few seconds, maybe for a drink of coffee. "The scouts have a way of saying this man or that one can't hit major-league pitching and then proving themselves right by seeing to it that he never gets the chance."

"Well," Julius said, "he had that good year to remember the rest of his life."

"Yes. But you have to wonder if that's a blessing or a curse."

That wasn't something I wanted to wonder about just then, so I concentrated on eating. When I finished the special I got me a side order of biscuits and gravy, a fried peach pie, and a Dr. Pepper. Sunrise in Tennessee, a batting average on the rise again, a pocketful of change, nobody stalking me, and a gutful of God's own grub. Why worry over what happens after baseball?

"Freedom, Lord, freedom," I said out loud.

"It'll make you fat and soft," Pinzon said. "Only the threat of tyranny can keep you fit."

"I can take care of that," Pansy said.

"I have serious reservations about that." Pinzon fingered his chin, cocked his head, raised an eyebrow, became a psychologist. "You are much too benevolent, much too generous, far too—if you'll pardon my using the term—easy. I daresay you would be the ideal complement to many men, perhaps the majority. But with one such as Hog, ruled as he is by purely physical appetites tempered only by a strangely provincial sort of paranoia, a benevolent dictatorship, I fear, would only exacerbate his already alarming anarchical tendencies. I have seen his type before. All that will suffice for him is outright repression punctuated by rare, unpredictable moments of relative lenience. Look at him now. Only years of being fed the penitentiary's gruel could have produced such raptures over a simple meal of ham and gravy."

"The grits ain't bad," I said.

He reached across the table and laid his right palm on the back of Pansy's left hand. His brown eyes looked solemnly into her green ones. Not knowing whether to laugh, she turned to me. Pinzon said, "I do hope you will forgive me for speaking with such candor, but over the years I have come to believe, my luscious sweet, that the truth will set you free."

She laughed at him then and said, "Well, it's been a long ride, Gonzalo, and I realize that you're nuts."

"I knew you'd understand," Pinzon said.

I lifted my glass of Dr. Pepper. "Ladies and gentlemen of the Reds, I toast Gonzalo Pinzon, who could have been the chief of American psychologists but wisely chose instead to become a master car thief."

Pinzon said, "One does what is most useful."

That was about as lively as the way home got. The road had been good; but wearying. We'd gone 11 and 4 on the trip and that had restored our confidence. But the bus itself was no longer the rolling honky-tonk it had been earlier in the season. It had become a hideout, a refuge, a place where you could gather yourself before having to face the light again. There was a little card playing and some quiet talk. But Bullet Bob drank his beer by himself this time, and most of us just rested, read, or thought. Ratliff did play his guitar a couple of times, but he didn't sing, or if he did it was to himself, and the tunes he played were sad and slow and seemed mostly just to purify the silence.

I may've been the only one that felt this way, but it seemed to me that by packing us all so close together inside itself and showing us the outside world through windows, the bus freed each of us from the rest of us and from everything else except his own mind. Pansy sat beside me and now and then she'd lean over against me and sleep a while and I was glad she was there, but I had a strong sense of being almost entirely separate from her, and right then I liked that too. I needed the space to think in. In my mind, freedom and movement had always been tied up together. But the bus let me move and belong at the same time, gave me freedom and family both. I wondered if I could keep feeling free after the bus stopped. Maybe, I thought, that's asking too much. Maybe we've made us a world a man can't be free in. But I knew I couldn't let myself believe that. Because if there is such a thing as freedom, it begins, like grace, with the simple, stunning faith that you can be free, that you can live a life that's tied to the life around you and yet remains your own.

Oh, I knew I hadn't yet figured a way of living that kind of life. The slammer years had made me want freedom, had caused me to do some hard thinking about just what freedom was and how you got it and how you kept it, but they'd also worn serious holes in what faith I had in myself and my fellow man. A long stretch of hard time may be enough in itself to keep a man from ever being free. But I could hope, I told myself. I could dream.

29

The morning after we got back to Little Rock I came in and took my seat in Mantis's office. I'd already talked on the phone with Rotenberg, who'd told me that while we were on the road he'd had a long lawyerly talk with Mantis, reminding him that I'd been paroled into the custody of Lefty Marks and that Mantis had no moral right, so long as I obeyed the law, to try to force me to agree to a change of custody. "You've complicated his job," Rotenberg had told me, "so he doesn't much like you. But I think things may be more straightforward from now on."

I had my doubts about that. While I lit a Lucky, Mantis looked me over. He looked like he might be willing to give up part of his summer vacation to get me back in the slam. "Hoping I'd jumped, were you?" I asked him.

"I'm surprised you risked coming in without your lawyer," he said. "He off chasing ambulances?"

"Bureaucrats," I answered. "They're slower."

Mantis leaned forward, narrowed his eyes, and started to say something. But I didn't want to let him start in on how disappointed he was that I'd thrown away the opportunity to work for so fine a man as Ratoplan or how crude it had been of me to go to a lawyer. "We've been winning. I've been hitting. Lefty's been paying my salary. I've missed Sunday school a time or two, but other than that I've been a model citizen. I'm going to keep playing and I'm going to keep hitting. For the first time in my life, I've lucked into a real lawyer. I think I'll keep him as long as I can. And I'm not real interested in any job you might have conjured up for me while I was gone."

He showed me a hit man's smile. "Oh, I don't think there'll be any more job offers. I don't have any more time or energy to waste on you." That was fine, but he couldn't keep from trying to remind me that he was a righteous citizen and I was a hopeless thief. "You'd probably be surprised to learn that I have some parolees who actually want to be helped." He stood up. "Come back next week and let me have another look at you. I won't keep you long. I just want to stop you from getting more than a week's head start on us."

"Fair enough," I said. "A man ought to be able to do some tricks with a week's worth of slack."

I got up and headed for the door.

"Enjoy yourself at the circus," he said to my back. "It won't last long."

"Nothing does," I said, and closed the door behind me.

I felt good walking the three blocks up Capitol to the Quorum Cafe, where Julius Common Deer was eating and waiting for me. Things had clarified between me and Mantis, and right then it seemed to me that I had a little edge on him. It was clear he wanted me back in the slam. But he always had. He was just admitting it now. Thanks, most likely, to Lawyer Rotenberg, he was having to play it straight up. He'd be quick to hop on me if I fell, of course. But it looked like he'd quit trying to lure me into just folding up and laying down for him. If I could manage to stay on my feet just a couple of months longer, the statute of limitations would run out on that bank job. And then, Lord, I'd be damn near as free as the next man.

30

We drew a houseful for the game that afternoon—ten or twelve thousand, several hundred of them having to stand along the foul line fences. They had come to see Susan, and when Lefty put her in in the seventh with us up by a couple of runs, they cheered and hooted, whistled and booed. They seemed about equally divided, pro and con. She made her first error that inning—a wide throw that pulled Mundy off the bag on what should've been an easy force at second. That gave the folks that thought a woman ought to stay, one way or another, under a man a chance to pump some conviction into their jeers. It also cost us a run before that half-inning was over. But when Susan helped get the run back in our end of the eighth by bunting for a hit and then scoring from first on Rainbow Smith's double, the other half of the crowd, the part that thought any woman man enough to wear one ought to be given a uniform, got its chance to reply. And I don't think either side took it too seriously. They were mostly a tolerant, easygoing bunch, asking only the right to cheer or boo whenever they felt like it. There weren't any preachers or politicians there that day to set them against one another.

The crowds dropped off considerably after that, but they were still sizable—four, five, six thousand, I'd say. Every couple of days Lefty'd give away flatbed truckloads of fresh produce—tomatoes, now, and sweet corn, summer squash and cucumbers. And day in and day out we sold more beer than any joint in Arkansas. We sold so much, in fact, that Lefty had to take to hiring folks right out of the stands to help us hawk it.

Eversole pitched his fifth straight shutout against Nashville. Four days later, against Plaquemine, he made it six in a row and 55 consecutive scoreless innings, breaking the league record. He seemed capable of going on forever, immune to time, fatigue, and pain.

And all of us stayed pretty well clear of pain ourselves during the first part of that home stand. The Reverend G. Forrest Bushrod and his upright enforcers, having already persuaded the state legislature to pass a law requiring public school biology classes to replace Darwin with Moses, were now working full-time to shut down the city's porn houses. And they had, by God, closed one of them down good. One bright afternoon while we were playing Nashville, the Asher Avenue Adult Book Store and Peep Show burned to the ground. It was the fourth time that had happened in the last ten years. (Lefty claimed it was a record exceeded only by the University Baptist Church in Magnolia, which had been totaled by lightning five times in the last nine years, three times on Good Friday.) Neither Bushrod nor John Schicklgruber, fresh from winning the Republican nomination to the U.S. Senate, took personal credit for reducing the smut house to ashes, but both of them allowed as to how it seemed to be a clear sign of the will of God. As soon as the smoke had cleared there, Bushrod's patrol broke camp and marched south to the Chicot Cinema, which was running a sensitive little art film called *A Hard Man Is Good to Find.* Anyway, all that made things easy on us for a while. I was thankful that the Vigilantes of the Cross had decided a Communist baseball team wasn't as dire a threat to their New Jerusalem as those boys spilling their seed into fuck-film popcorn were.

Little Rock was modern enough and American enough so that news turned into history in a week or so and then quickly became irrelevant. So the reporters began to lose interest in us. The big city papers, except for the *Memphis Commercial Appeal,* which sold a lot of copies in eastern Arkansas, had, for the time being, actually finished with Susan and us by the time we left Asheville. But during our first few days back home, we had to put up with boys from all the little Arkansas papers—the *Texarkana Gazette,* the *Fort Smith Times-Record,* the *Pine Bluff Commercial,* the *Magnolia Daily Banner,* the *Northwest Arkansas Times,* the *Conway Log Cabin Democrat,* and others of less renown. But most of those reporters just made day trips, got their story (or concocted one that would do), and headed on back home. If it took you more than one article to say all there was to be said about a fallen woman playing for an agnostic baseball team, what kind of reporter were you? We did get some TV coverage. Each of the three Little Rock stations sent a crew out to interview Susan. Each of them edited its interview down to three minutes, cut that down into one-minute segments, and ran a segment a night for three nights on the suppertime sports report.

The *Arkansas Chronicle* did keep their man Joe Bo Corker on us full-time, but I don't know why. He would've had trouble interesting readers in an orgy at the Vatican. I guess that explains why he was assigned to us, actually. Old Wilbur Haney, their sports editor and that year's president of the College Football Writers Association, didn't want folks getting too interested in us. Wilbur did condescend to come out to the park once, for the second Plaquemine game, the one where Eversole broke the record. Afterwards he came down into the clubhouse and stood around a while, saying nothing, just trying to look moral and wise—which can be a job of work when all you know of morality and wisdom is what you've managed to pick up while kneeling before the coaches at the University of Arkansas. I considered having the team huddle around me while I sent up a postgame prayer, but I decided there wasn't much point in unduly provoking Wilbur. The closest any of us got to communicating with him was when Pinzon, coming out of the showers, went over to him, handed him a wet towel, and walked on to his stool. Wilbur looked down at the towel, then back at Pinzon. Then he carried the towel over to the hamper, dropped it in, and left.

I thought Wilbur might use his column as a platform to sling some shit on us from, but he didn't. His next column had to do with a study done by *Popular Psychology* which showed football players to be a cut above the common run of humanity. They respected authority, believed in a strict moral code, and thought that the man that worked the hardest won the most. And that's why, Wilbur concluded, football is such an important part of a good university.

We split with Nashville, two games apiece, and swept four straight from Plaquemine. On the road, away from the parish bookies, the Pirates' incompetence was too steady to be funny. They did have their radio crew with them, though, and I suppose that all the good loyal folks way down in ole Pumpsie Narvaez's domain circled their radios every afternoon and bet on each pitch. You had to be a gambler—and the kind that would bet, given proper odds, on just which day your mother would die—to tolerate that team. Just sitting in the stands and watching them must've been dull going, but playing them had to be worse. When you beat them, all you felt was the relief of not having to live with the shame of losing to them. Ordinarily, we wouldn't've drawn a thousand fans for that whole Plaquemine series, but at this time they were still coming out to see Susan. And one favor the Pirates did do for anyone that saw any of those games was to answer once and for all any question about whether a woman was good enough to play in the Dixie Association. Hell, Plaquemine could've used an *old* woman. If they'd had Susan, she'd've been their star.

I don't know what Pumpsie paid his players, but I figured if he paid them at all they got more than their due. I do know that the team traveled in an old school bus while Pumpsie rode ahead of them in a big red Cadillac driven by his toothless cook and crony, Tiboy Ledoux. According to Pumpsie, Tiboy had lost his teeth over a period of fifteen years at the Breaux Bridge Crawfish Festival. Each year he'd get up on a little platform they had there and pass the hat until it had a hundred dollars in it and then he'd haul out his pliers and, one at a time, jerk two teeth free. Fifteen hundred dollars altogether—which is a sight more than I'll get for mine. Still, it made you wonder, not so much about Tiboy's mind—I've seen smart men do worse for less—as about how well Pumpsie paid him. Whatever he was paid, though, Tiboy seemed good at his job, which was, depending on the time of day and Pumpsie's mood, cooking, chauffeuring, drinking, listening, and scouting out women.

Tiboy had found Pumpsie a Hot Springs stripper to see him through his Little Rock nights. During the games, she sat at the far end of the Pirates' dugout and smoked long cigarettes. Most of the time Pumpsie was down there with her, talking, sharing a smoke, rubbing her up a little. He introduced her to us once—after the first game of the series, I think it was. I'd just finished showering and dressing and was standing out in the parking lot talking to Lefty, Pansy, Pinzon, and some of the others. Tiboy pulled the red Cadillac over to where we were and Pumpsie got out of the back seat. I don't think the girl wanted to get out, but Pumpsie insisted. He bent into the open door, took her hand, and said, "Aw, come on now, Hon. Let ole Pumpsie show you off some. These here are folks that appreciate womanflesh."

She said something I couldn't hear, but went ahead and got out. Pumpsie closed the door behind her and she leaned against the big car, facing us. Pumpsie backed several steps away from her, then stopped and used up a minute admiring her, nodding his head every so often and making approving little clicking noises. She was wearing a pair of black high-heel lace-up boots that came right up to her knees, a black string-tied top you could see through without much trouble, and tight red shorts that let a few good inches of haunch show. Her hair was so dark the dye looked like it would come off on your hands. Her eyes were round and damn near purple—contact lenses, Pansy told me later—and she'd filled the space between her eyebrows and her lids with a streak of silver paint. A tattoo of a blue rose rode the upper part of her left breast, and a little red apple with one bite gone decorated the upper inside of her right thigh, just an inch or two below what she was selling.

"Boys, this here's Jo Ellen Shavers. Hails from Fordyce, Arkansas, home of Bear Bryant. I'm seeing to her while we're here in town and I ain't big on sharing my women, but after I'm gone you can catch her act down at the Black Orchid in Hot Springs. Works under the name of Scheherazade. Just tell 'em Pumpsie sent you. You treat her right, she'll do you some good."

Jo Ellen gave us an old smile. Pumpsie commenced telling her who we were. "Darling, ole one-armed Jack there's Lefty Marks. If he had his way we'd all be members of the lower middle class and have a little dirt under our fingernails. The big fellow there is Hog Durham, the one that stuck a couple of poor ole Walmsley Sims's curve balls out in the freeway just a while ago. The blood Indian plays center field for them. That Mexican boy yonder pitches for them now and again, I believe. And I forget your name, Sweetness. I'm thinking you're Hog's woman. Ain't that right? I hope you're doing him proud."

Pansy gave him a glower for an answer.

"No offense meant, ma'am," Pumpsie told her. "I just ain't much good with names. Never have been."

"How's Mary Belle?" Pansy asked him pointedly. I suppose she meant to be chastising him for being unfaithful.

"Just fine. She's home holding down the fort. I thank you for asking after her."

"I'm pleased to meet you, Miss Shavers," Lefty said.

"Same here," she answered.

Pumpsie smiled on her. "Aye God," he said. "Don't look a day over sixteen. And ain't she a picture leaning up against Big Red the way she is. Seems like they're making 'em better than they used to, don't it, Lefty?"

"They're made better," Lefty said, "because they have to put up with more."

"Yes, Lord," Pumpsie went on. "Fresh, firm buds and long, lean flanks. Makes an old man's cock so hard a cat can't scratch it."

Jo Ellen smiled with half her mouth. "I always get the charmers," she said. Then she got back into the Cadillac.

Pumpsie gave her a foreman's look. "They come cheaper here than they do in New Orleans," he told us, "but they ain't got the same class."

"Whatever you're paying her," Lefty said, "it's not enough."

Pumpsie refused to be insulted. "Well, I'll admit she is damn good at what she does, as long as you can keep her from talking." He gave that a short laugh that none of us added to, then let us watch his face grow serious.

"But, hell, Lefty," he went on, "I do enjoy talking. Sure, I got ole Tiboy, but I can foretell damn near down to the word what he's going to say and when he's going to say it. So now and then a yearning for fresh conversation comes over me. And what I stopped by to do, aside from giving y'all a gander at Jo Ellen, was ask you if you wouldn't like to ride down to Hot Springs with me this evening. Big Red rides like a damn dream and we'll glide along through them pines and pass a jar of whiskey around amongst us and maybe sing up some hymns. I told Jo Ellen I'd let her work tonight, so she'll be drawing two salaries. You ever been to the Black Orchid?"

"Hot Springs isn't my favorite town," Lefty told him.

Pumpsie grinned and shook his head. "You damn radicals. You spend all your time worrying about the poor and then if you ever take power the first thing you do is start passing laws to keep them from having any fun."

That was close enough to the general truth and yet far enough away from Lefty himself to amuse Lefty some. He returned Pumpsie's grin and said, "Aw, Pumpsie, some of my best friends have been sinners. You understand, though, that that's not to say I'd want my sister to marry one?"

"Well then, by God, let's leave your sister behind and ride on down to Hot Springs together. Bring you a woman with you if you got one that'll go. If you ain't I can match you up for the night with a little twitch that dances with Jo Ellen. From Calico Rock, I believe. I forget her name, but next to Jo Ellen she's the best thing they got. And both of them from Arkansas. Speaks well of the state. What do you say?"

"If I can't have Jo Ellen, I guess I'll stay home and read some poetry."

Pinzon spoke up then. "Ees that lovely, lovely woman in Plaquemine weeth the beeg, beeg teets that Meester Marks he hunger for."

At the time, I was surprised that that got to Pumpsie, but it did. "If you're talking about Mary Belle, Crisco, you might ought to keep a little closer watch on your mouth. That woman's dear to me and I'll not have her name drug through filth. You understand that?" For a minute I thought that was just another part of his routine, but all I could see on his face was a kind of low-rent righteous outrage, untainted by any hint of irony.

Pinzon said, "Si, Señor Narvaez. You macho, macho man."

"Ees true, Creesco," Pumpsie said. He turned and walked toward the Cadillac.

"I go too?" Pinzon asked.

"Not in my car." He opened the back door and got in next to Jo Ellen. Tiboy started the big, quiet engine. Pumpsie, apparently back to what he wanted to pass off as normal, lowered his window and said, "Lefty, don't you be reading too much of that damn poetry now. It causes suicide." They glided away.

We stood there watching them go. "The son of a bitch," Pansy said.

Julius Common Deer, maybe trying to impress Susan, gave us a moral. "Any time you put a dollar price on sex, no matter how high, you cheapen it."

"Well," I couldn't resist saying, "the cheaper the better."

Pansy glared at me.

"That's a fine man you have there," Lefty told her. "Such a sweet, lyrical bastard."

"He may be just a little better than Pumpsie," she said.

"I don't know," Lefty said. "Pumpsie is marrying his Mary Belle. We're all invited. September twenty-first, the weekend after the season ends, at the stadium in Plaquemine. He told me about it before the game today. This is going to be his last year of traveling with the team. He said he thought it was time he settled down." Then he got a card out of his back pocket and showed it to us. It was white with fancy gold lettering and announced the wedding.

I laughed. "The bigger they come the harder they fall."

Lefty stretched out his arm as if he had a drink in it and said,

" 'Here's to opening and upward, to leaf and to sap.' "
Pinzon said, "I wonder what the odds are on it coming off."

31

For a couple of days after that parking lot scene with Pumpsie, I wondered some about Lefty and women. Maybe he had one waiting down in Magnolia and just had sense enough not to talk about her. Maybe he'd had one and lost her in some way that pained him enough to put a fear in him. Maybe, over sixty now, he wasn't much interested in it any more. But I tended to doubt that. Lefty wore those sixty years well, and, anyway, there's men a lot older and tireder than Lefty that don't have anything left but a hard dick. So I wondered about him and, wondering, I realized again how little I knew about him. For, as Shakespeare Creel said in our cell one night, after we'd been told that Billy McRue, a teenaged car thief from Heavener who didn't have but a year to serve, had cut his dick off with a kitchen knife, "You can't understand a man till you know how he feels about his cock."

That was said in the crude, joking way trapped men use to get through bad times, but there was a truth in it that Shakespeare and I both recognized, a truth that sometimes now made me ask myself if all Lefty's good causes had cut him off from his cock.

Then one evening I got part of an answer. Oxford was in town to make up the four game series that had been rained out earlier. The league office had agreed to let us do it in two days, a doubleheader a day. We'd just finished splitting the first one and were back out at the home eating a supper of Dummy Boudreaux's chicken étouffée when the doorbell rang. "Pop Stone," Lefty said, getting up. "He told me he might come out tonight."

I figured he'd come to spend an evening out on the porch, rocking and talking the way he and Lefty had done down in Oxford back in the spring. And I was looking forward to sitting out there with them, weighing Lefty's radical hopes against Pop's ironic memory.

But Pop had brought a woman with him, a woman Lefty knew, or had known. From where I was in the dining room, I couldn't see

Lefty open the door and let them in, but I heard him say, "Tamara Burroughs?" That was followed by a pause, which the woman used, I guess, to nod. Maybe Lefty hugged her. "My God, it's been damn near fifteen years, hasn't it? Christ Almighty, where'd you find her, Pop?"

"She found me," Pop told him. He didn't sound near as pleased as Lefty had. I figured it was because he didn't want to have a woman spoiling an evening of good talk. Actually, there was considerably more to it than that.

"Come on in here and let me introduce you around." I knew Lefty was talking to the woman because, hell, we all knew Pop. It was Pop that answered though. "Not just now, Lefty. J. G. Flemson's out in the car. This all has to do with your man Eversole."

"Is he in trouble?" Most of the reunion joy had gone out of Lefty's voice.

"No. Not at all," the woman said with a professional sincerity. "We'd just like to talk to him about that incident back in Oxford."

Well, I didn't want to get up from my meal just then. Knowing we'd be tired after that day's doubleheader, Dummy had volunteered to stay home and cook us up a feast. And he'd done himself proud. But what that woman said took my appetite away from me. When they start telling you you're not in trouble, they'd just like to ask you a few questions, it's time to commence thinking about jumping bail. I got up, blessed Dummy Boudreaux, and went into the living room.

They were walking out the door. I caught them on the verandah. Lefty introduced me to the woman, saying that they'd taught together years ago at the University of Southern Arkansas.

"It wasn't a university then," she said.

"It's still not," Lefty said.

She was a tall, handsome, dark-headed woman, dressed in a gray pleated skirt and a white, silky-looking blouse. She had a navy blue scarf strapped around her neck, and she'd pulled her hair up and pinned it to the back of her head. She gave me her hand and showed me a packaged smile. I thought she might tell me to have a nice day.

"Lord, Tamara," Lefty said, "you do look good."

"Thank you. I've taken care of myself."

Three nights a week, I thought, at the Elite Career Girl's Greco-Roman Spa. Disco calisthenics. The tanning booth. The sauna.

The executive mind in the executive body. You've come a long way, baby.

And Lefty just stood there grinning at her. I was beginning to suspect his judgment in this matter. "You with Flemson," I asked her, using a tone a G-man might've tried on one of Pretty Boy Floyd's neighbors.

She turned to Lefty. "Could we do this without your friend? All I want to do is to talk to Jeremiah Eversole a few minutes. I give you my word I'll do nothing to harm him."

"He ain't here, lady," I said.

"Hog doesn't trust anybody wearing more than twenty-five dollars' worth of clothes," Lefty explained to her. "And not without cause," he added, in fairness. Then he turned to me. "I think we can trust Tamara. She may have changed, but I don't think she could've changed that much."

"Somebody comes in and makes a big point of telling you they mean you no harm, you better watch your ass. They'll be patting you on the back in one room and drawing up papers on you in the other."

The Burroughs woman said, "All I can do is assure you again that I pose no threat whatsoever to Jeremiah Eversole."

"You going to give him a trophy for being Player of the Month?" I asked her.

She looked me hard right in the eye. "I've been counseling Candy Commerce. She's had a difficult past. For the past ten years she's been drifting along without an anchor. But now she's trying to start a new life. As a step in that direction she admitted shooting a man in Oxford, Mississippi. Eversole. He wasn't seriously wounded, I take it. I merely want the opportunity to persuade him not to press charges."

"I'm sorry, ma'am. But the poor fucker's laid up in his room, strapped to an anchor. If we unchain him, he'll drift away from us."

J. G. Flemson had got out of his white Lincoln and walked from there about halfway up to where we stood. "They coming?" he said. "I got things to do besides sit here and look at the scenery." Then he turned around and went back to his car.

"There's one fine human being," Pop Stone said. "Last year he gave $1,000 to the United Fund and they gave him a plaque saying he was Oxford's Humanitarian of the Year. He's got it propped up in the middle of his desk. A man doing business with him has to look around the plaque to see Flemson."

"They always sell those awards too cheap," Lefty said.

"Well," Pop said, "he didn't think he could afford another one. He's let the United Fund people know that they've got all they're going to get out of him."

"Once a humanitarian, always a humanitarian," Lefty said.

"He may be cold," the Burroughs woman said, "but so far he's been far more cooperative with me than you have. It never occurred to me that I'd have any trouble getting to talk to Eversole."

"Every fourth day," Lefty said, "Eversole goes out and pitches a strong game. About all he asks in return for that is to be let alone. And, in case you haven't noticed, Tamara, Flemson is scum."

"And that's a generous way of putting it," Pop Stone said.

Tamara Burroughs reached out and touched Lefty's elbow, gently and briefly. She said, in a new, softer tone, "I'm not concerned with J. G. Flemson. I'm merely trying to help his son. You see, when Candy came to us she had Colonel Sanders Flemson with her. Though he's of age, he's legally incompetent. Candy could've been charged with kidnapping. However, I've managed to place them in circumstances that have proven beneficial to all concerned, including J. G. Flemson."

"I take it you got them in the asylum, then," I said.

She gave me a cold look. I gave her a reversible smile. She turned back to Lefty and said, "Since the last time I saw you, I've outgrown my idealistic fascination with the lower classes."

"It's menopause," I said.

"The poor have the potential to be as bad as the rich," Lefty said. "They just lack the necessary finances."

She looked right at him for several seconds, and I thought I noticed something like sadness in her eyes. "Lefty," she said, "I've changed completely since we knew one another." She stopped there to look at him some more. What had seemed like sadness in her eyes began to harden into defiance. "I'm the women's counselor at Vigilance Mountain Baptist College."

Lefty couldn't take it in immediately. After a hesitation, he asked, "Whiteside?"

"Yes." Her defiance settled into a calm stupidity. "He's a great man." As far as I could tell, she was dead serious.

"Prosecution rests," I said.

A minute or two later Dummy Boudreaux came out onto the porch and signed to Lefty that the pecan pie was being served. Lefty signed back that we'd be there in a few minutes. And that, no, the guests wouldn't be wanting any. After Dummy left us, Tamara Burroughs asked Lefty if he wouldn't at least go out to the car and talk to Flemson a minute. And she thought again that things might work more smoothly if I didn't go along. Lefty said, "So far this evening his judgment's been better than mine."

J. G. Flemson sat behind the wheel smoking a cigarillo. He had the windows up and the air conditioner going. The Burroughs woman got into the front seat with him. Pop and Lefty and I climbed into the back. Flemson gave us an over-the-shoulder, rubber-eyed glance. "What's the big guy coming for?" he asked Tamara Burroughs.

"I always wanted a big, white car like you got here. And I didn't want to pass up a chance to see how these leather seats felt rubbing up against my ass."

"This one's sold," he told me.

He put the car in gear. Lefty told him we weren't going anywhere. Flemson looked at the Burroughs woman. She nodded. He put it back in park. The Burroughs woman tried to fan the cigarillo smoke away from her face with the back of her hand. I lit up a Lucky.

"Why don't you switch on the radio and see if we can't pick up some hymns?" I asked Flemson.

"I don't like music."

"Tamara," Lefty said as if the rest of us weren't there, "I can't believe this has happened to you."

"Hell, it happened to Eldridge Cleaver," I said.

"And Saint Paul," Miss Burroughs added.

"You'll understand it better by and by," Pop Stone told Lefty. Pop looked like he was starting to enjoy himself some.

I couldn't say the same for the Burroughs woman. But then she'd given herself over to folks that had been battling joy for two thousand years. She looked back at Lefty again, not just turning her head but twisting her whole upper body around, and began explaining herself to him—and only to him. Again it was like the rest of us weren't there. I could see that there'd been a time when pleasing him had meant a lot to her. She told about being a child welfare worker in Asheville. It was a tough, depressing job, but she thought she was performing a service, and she had always needed to feel useful. There was a fourteen-year-old foster child named Jimmy Childers that she'd counseled off and on for months and believed she was helping. Then one day he picked up a .22 pistol and sent a shell through his head.

"He left a note that said: 'I don't belong here. I'm sorry. Jimmy.'"

She paused there and let Lefty watch her eyes well up.

Flemson took advantage of the pause to provide us with a piece of merchant's wisdom. "Suicide is the coward's way out." Then he pushed a button and his window slid down a few inches. He flipped the butt of his cigarillo out. I reached across the car, just brushing the back of his head, and threw my Lucky out too. "You got your own window," he said. I told him I didn't know how to work the controls.

"Whiteside's religion isn't an answer," Lefty said to the Burroughs woman. He would've went on, but she held up a palm and stopped him.

"Yes, it is," she said. "It's *the* answer. I realized that all my life I'd been ignoring the important thing. The spirit. I tried to help Jimmy with practical things. I kept him in school. I got him a part-time job. All he lacked was a sense of worth. Nothing I did for him gave him that. And then I understood that it wasn't just my efforts for Jimmy that had been a waste, it was my whole life. I had wasted my life. And eventually—and this wasn't easy for me— eventually I came to see that the answer my parents had tried to provide me with, the one I thought I'd rejected forever when I was eighteen, was the only possible one. At that point, I still didn't know whether Christ was the answer, but I was certain that if He wasn't, there was only chaos, nihilism. I started going to church. I chose the Holy Light Baptist Church because it was active and because it was fundamentalist. I knew that Jesus was either the Son of God who gave His life to redeem us from the Fall or the greatest liar who ever lived. And I knew that if He could be found it would be in a church that took His word literally. The first few times I attended church I was more than a little skeptical, but gradually, Sunday by Sunday, my skepticism was worn away. I experienced a warmth and energy and certainty I'd never known before. And finally I knew that I'd become a part of a liberating truth much greater than myself."

Lefty reached up and touched her forearm. "Tamara," he said, "suicide is the coward's way out."

She jerked her arm out from under his hand. "It's not suicide!" She damn near yelled that, then caught herself and turned down the volume, if not the passion. "It's the very opposite. It's life. I tried logic. I tried reason. I worked with you in the civil-rights movement—and I'm not ashamed of that. But those old black preachers we used to criticize for being so timid, well, I've realized they were the ones who knew the truth all along. And the truth is in here." She jabbed a forefinger at a place between her tits. "And up there." She pointed the same finger at the roof of the car. "The humble, depraved human heart redeemed by our Lord and Saviour."

I started humming "Just As I Am." Lefty told me to shut up.

Tamara Burroughs went on. She was right proud of her humility. "I've read the books. I have a doctorate in sociology. I know the theories. And all of them are wrong, Lefty. It's all hollow, vain ratiocination. The solution to our problems will not come out of our heads but out of our souls. Man's reliance on his mind is what has made this century the darkest one in history. We've made a god of the state because we've turned our backs on Christ. We've made man the center of the universe and that has led to subjectivity and relativity. And man cannot truly live without an absolute."

"Bullshit," Lefty said. "It just takes a little courage, a little kindness, and a little consideration for the poor son of a bitch next door. I grant you it's hard sometimes, but it beats arming yourself to the teeth in behalf of the Good Fairy."

"Damn you," she said, her humility and pride having combined and changed into anger, in the traditional Christian manner.

Lefty smiled. "An excellent two-word summation of the fundamental Christian doctrine," he said.

She gave Lefty a Judgment Day look.

"Let's take care of the business we come on," J. G. Flemson said. I wondered if he ever changed expression.

The Burroughs woman looked down at her lap and smoothed her skirt. Then she looked back up at Lefty. "History has discredited humanism. For the race, it leads to social chaos. For the individual, it leads toward the empty self. It creates a vacuum at the very center of being." She paused for just a beat or two, but when she spoke again her voice was hard with arrogance, and, as if she had felt a call to show that her "damn you" hadn't been just a slip, as if to demonstrate beyond all arguing that a good Christian woman could have a sharp tongue, she said, "I'll put this in words you might appreciate: both literally and figuratively, humanism sucks."

"Well," I said, "anything that sucks can't be all bad."

Pop Stone gave me his good laugh again, but Lefty and Tamara Burroughs were fixed so hard on one another that they may not have even heard what I'd said.

"Tamara, you're still the same woman," Lefty said. "You always wanted the quickest answer. Back then I thought it was because you were young. But now I see I was wrong and I shouldn't be surprised you've come to this. You've found the easiest fix of all, the oldest, cheapest way to get rid of the pain of living. If that's how you have to manage, I guess it's O.K. It would be nice, though, if you and your friends would quit trying to force the rest of us to accept your jingo morality and your little chickenshit salvation." He opened his door and put a foot on the ground.

"I told you what kind of man he was," Flemson reminded Tamara.

Lefty said, "It was good of you to come by. I'll give your message to Eversole and I'll give his answer to Pop. I think it's safe to say he won't press charges."

"I got a form here I had drawn up I'd like him to sign. It's just a little something saying Colonel Sanders didn't have nothing to do with the shooting. Pore ole boy like that, you know, he's got no business being dragged into court."

"I don't think he'll be signing anything either," Lefty said.

"You just tell him then if he messes with me, he'll come up a loser."

"I don't want to scare him too bad."

"You just mind what I told you."

Lefty got out of the car. I followed him. We started up toward the house, but we hadn't gone over ten or fifteen steps before Tamara Burroughs got out her door and hustled up after us. We stopped and waited for her. When she got to us, she smiled at Lefty and I think that one was genuine. I figured it had risen out of memory. She said, "You're hard, Lefty, and you're wrong. But I know you're not mean." She looked down, then back up at his face. "I'm sorry our meeting had to turn out this way."

The way Lefty stared back at her, the sadness of memory making his face old and tired, gave me a minute of wanting both of them to throw off what they believed in and just settle for each other.

He reached down with his hand and took one of hers. "Maybe next time we can manage not to discuss religion."

"Religion is my life now," she said. But this time there was no pride in her voice and no anger. Something had changed, she was saying, that couldn't be changed back.

Lefty nodded and let go of her hand. "I was afraid of that."

They looked at each other a few more seconds and then she left him.

We watched them drive out of sight. I turned and took a step toward the house, but Lefty still stood there looking down the road at where they'd been.

"I was in love with her once," he said. I stopped and heard him out. "We both got fired by the college. She taught psychology. A bad sign, I guess." He paused there and grinned at himself. "I decided to stay in Magnolia. She wanted a bigger world than that."

"And got a smaller one," I said.

"She always had a religious side. I wouldn't've been surprised if she'd turned into Simone Weil. But I didn't expect Carry Nation."

32

We didn't see Tamara Burroughs or J. G. Flemson again in Little Rock. Eversole, of course, had no intention of pressing charges against Candy Commerce or Colonel Sanders Flemson, but he surprised me and Lefty by saying he wanted to talk to the Commerce girl face-to-face.

"We have a chance to win the pennant," Lefty told him. "But not without you. We need you on the mound every fourth day. I can't tell you what to do, but I'd appreciate it if you wouldn't throw this season away just so you could get some kind of personal revenge."

"I won't hurt her," Eversole said.

"You're giving me your word on that?"

"Yes."

So Lefty relayed Eversole's request to Pop Stone, who passed it along to Tamara Burroughs, who agreed, through Pop, to arrange a meeting between Eversole and the Commerce girl at Vigilance Mountain Baptist College sometime during our next stay in Asheville.

Several times Lefty and I sat together and tried to figure what it was Eversole had in mind. It was the first time either of us could remember that he'd actually asked to talk to somebody.

33

The league had always left the last week in June open. Up until about five years earlier, they'd played an all-star game during that period—matching the first-place team against the best players from the other teams. But there hadn't ever been much in it for the players, just a long drive for damn little money. More often than not the first-place team was Selma, and a trip to Selma wasn't many players' idea of a vacation. Though the league office, I'm told, threatened fines and suspensions, it didn't really have the power to force a player to go to the game or even to punish him for refusing. So it got to where more and more players started staying home or going fishing. The last time they'd held the game, the all-stars had been so short of players they'd had to fill out their lineup by borrowing a couple of Bull's reserves. Finally, the league office gave up on it and declared that from then on the open week would be used to make up any postponed games.

By using just two days to make up the four rained-out Oxford games, we got ourselves a long weekend off—our only one that summer. Lefty was going to spend that weekend in Magnolia and he invited any of us that wanted to to go along with him. He said we'd get a close look at farmers controlling their own land and workers controlling their own factories and farmers and factory workers cooperating for the benefit of both. "Sounds like I'll be missing a high ole time," I kidded him, "but I think I'll just stay here and drink." But Jew Bernstein, Woodrow Ratliff, and Dummy Boudreaux did take him up on the offer, and Franklin

Brown, Jefferson Mundy, and Atticus Flood rode down with them to visit their folks. They took the team bus. I figure Lefty had them pick up every hitchhiker they saw. Bobbie Sampson rode the Am-Trak to Saint Louis to visit one of her old tag-team partners.

Everybody went somewhere but Pansy and me. Joe Buck Cantwell decided to get up a fishing trip over to the Cossatot River in Sevier County. He and Stump and Bullet Bob and Rainbow Smith pooled their money—we'd just got our shares for June, $950 apiece, and it was going to get better—and paid $1599 for a 1972 GMC pickup, which they loaded up with liquor and grub and tackle and drove west. At the last minute, Pinzon, carrying nothing but a deck of cards, ran out and hopped into the back of the truck and rode off with them.

I wanted to go on the fishing trip, but I had Pansy to think about and what she wanted was a few quiet days of romance, which a woman's not too apt to get with a half-dozen drunks on a river.

Julius and Susan were the last ones to leave. They ate a late breakfast with me and Pansy that Friday morning and then went out and got into the co-op pickup and left for the Cookson Hills. Julius was taking his young woman home to meet old Ice.

That left Pansy and me alone with three whole days to fill. After Julius and Susan left, we walked up to the stand of pines above the garden and sat up there quiet for a while in the needles and the warm shade.

I took in what I could of the pine smell and the sunlight angling down through branches and the good view down on the garden and the house, and then I lit me up a Lucky and looked at Pansy. She had on a pair of cut-off Levi's and a blue T-shirt that said "Save the Seals" on the front of it. "Nice little seals you got there, lady," I said.

"Your wit's a little off today," she told me through a half-smile.

"Nice legs too."

"Your lines seem to be getting worse as you go along."

"Actually I've had that one work a time or two."

"Well," she said, "sometimes it's amazing how little it takes to please us."

"Women, you mean?"

"Any of us."

She was smiling at me then and I wanted her. "Yeah, sometimes. And other times there ain't nothing'll suit us."

"There's your line," she said. "True enough to make a girl stop a minute, but just common enough to let her go on afterwards. And maybe, if she's in the right mood, smart enough to let her fool herself into thinking that this time she might be getting herself a man with a little sense."

"What the hell does that mean?"

She rolled over onto her left hip, reached across me, took the cigarette out of my hand, stubbed it out, put her right hand on my shoulder and pushed me gently down flat on my back, and then both of us were as wild and hot as teenagers going at it in secret for the first and maybe last time, each of us given over absolutely to lust for the other, mindless and pure and perfectly alive, and she stood and pulled the shirt off over her head and slid the jeans down her good legs and stepped out of them, and, still on the ground, I took off my boots and my jeans and my shirt and she was on me and around me and rolling her hips and then pumping them up and down and me meeting her, moving with her and in her, without slack or thought, gone way beyond words, feeling nothing and everything, being part of the old, strong urge for life that made this world and gives it yet whatever hope it has.

When it was over, we lay there together, her head under my chin, her right leg lying leisurely across me—drowsy animals in the sun. But finally time came back to us and I felt some pine needles itching up in the crack of my ass and had to move to get to them and moving made me want a cigarette so I reached over and got the smokes and the book of matches out of my shirt pocket and became aware of being Hog Durham all over again.

Then Pansy sat up too. There was still some flush in her face. Pine needles stuck to her wet skin. Her hair hung limp and damp around her face. But right then I loved her, flush and sweat and limp hair and all, so I just, by God, took my old bent heart in my hand and told her so.

"It scares you, doesn't it?"

I nodded and took a pull off the Lucky. "It's not something I've had much practice dealing with."

"Me either," she said. "But I guess that's the way it usually is. We probably don't deserve more than one chance at it."

"Hell," I said, "we probably don't deserve even that."

And so from that Friday to the next Monday afternoon, when everybody started coming back, we practiced at it, tried to start learning how to make the most of our chances. We took turns cooking meals for one another and sometimes before the meal was over we'd be on the floor together—that being the one part of it we knew how to make the most of. Mornings after breakfast, we'd go out into the garden and hoe some and pick whatever was ready to be eaten. Afternoons, we'd go for walks or just lie together playing and taking each other easy, the passion partly controlled, temporarily muted, and then suddenly carrying us away again. We spent part of each of the evenings reading, each of us under a lamp, the living room between us, and we'd look up from our books at each other now and again with easy, almost civilized eyes.

One afternoon—Sunday, I guess it was—I spent a couple of hours writing a long letter to Shakespeare Creel. Earlier in the season, I'd sent him a few postcards, some newspaper clippings about the Reds, and a thousand-page history of Cuba by Hugh Thomas. (Shakespeare's reading consisted mostly of German philosophers, formal poetry, and long histories of foreign countries. He thought that almost all novels were trash and that almost all Americans, including himself, were romantic fools.) But the letter I wrote him that Sunday was the first thing I sent him that had much of me in it. I gave him an account of the season up to then, described Lefty and some of the guys on the team, told him (in a code we'd worked out years before) about my troubles with Mantis, and said there was a chance I'd be rehired, even before the season ended, to an old job I'd enjoyed when I was younger—which he would understand meant I was worried about getting sent up for the Van Buren bank job. And, finally, I told him, in one sentence, that I'd found a woman I liked being with.

It wasn't until I woke up about dawn Monday morning that it all began to worry me. I started thinking how it was that I'd always been a man who liked first things and last things, beginnings and endings, the road in and the road out, hail and farewell. Up until the time I started playing for the Reds and met Pansy, I'd never managed to get from hail to farewell with much grace. Whenever a place or a woman had ceased being new to me, I'd pulled away so that I could preserve the memory of newness. I'd never had the patience, the love, or the wisdom to ride things out and take a chance on seeing the bright flash of the new become the steady glow of the good. It's what had made me a criminal. Even now, I'll take the rush you get from robbing a bank over the one you get from being named president of it. So I'd taken a thief's chances and paid a thief's dues. For a few hours of excitement and maybe a few weeks' worth of drinking and whoring money, I'd risked and done years of slow time, years during which nothing was ever new, not even the occasional sudden burst of pointless violence. But I'd never taken the big risk; I'd never committed myself to anything or any place or anybody for any length of time.

But now, the early morning July sun slanting in on me beneath the half-drawn shade, Pansy sleeping beside me, I wondered whether this time I would do something other than reduce hope to memory. I didn't know if I could do it, and I was still more than a little scared by the thought of giving myself over to an idea of what life might ought to be. I didn't know if I had the courage to just stand on a piece of ground and live.

I lay there on my back, face turned to the light, and thought hard about what I wanted to do if I was still walking the streets when the season ended. If I tried real hard, I could hope I'd be offered a contract to play ball in a major-league organization. I did honestly figure that given the chance I could hit big-time pitching. My average might not be much more than respectable, but I'd hit the long ball and drive in some runs. But on account of my age and history, the chances of that happening were damn slim. I was a thirty-year-old minor-league rookie with a smart mouth and a record of armed robbery—not likely to be anybody's bonus baby.

No. And outside of baseball there weren't but two lines of work I knew anything at all about—farming and thieving. I hadn't done any real farming since I was sixteen and my grandfather died. Then my grandmother had let some kin of hers talk her into selling the place and moving out to Bakersfield to live with them. And hell, I wouldn't've stayed on it anyway. I was a kid in heat and wanted to see what was up the road, wanted to hear dancing music and share beds with one-night women. That was in the late '60s, Sun God Time, when stoned-blind hippies stood beside shorelines or waterfalls and stretched their arms out to the sky and then went home to some grimed-over room in some ruined city and talked of peace and of going back to the land and wired home for the money they needed to buy food and dope and records. I spent about a

month one spring back then in a commune in eastern Colorado—
there was a girl there I kind of liked that called herself Skyblue
Freewater—and one night they set a big wooden bread-bowl full of
seeds in the middle of the floor and all hunkered down lotuslike
around it and meditated on life and germination and smoked a
water pipe until they fell asleep and late the next morning they
took those seeds out and scattered them helter-skelter over ground
that was hard and dry and barely tilled and fertilized only with a
fool's hope. They were lost, and if I hadn't already figured that out,
I'd've seen it as soon as they started scattering those seeds. But
what I hadn't learned then was that they weren't any worse lost
than I was. Oh, I'd watched age and the economics of farming take
the heart out of my grandfather, so I knew that there was a damn
site more work than magic in coaxing a livelihood from the soil.
The last thing I wanted back then was a life filled with plows and
cultivators, discs and harrows, hoes and hay bailers, drought and
flood. I'd milked cows, butchered hogs, gathered eggs, spread manure, hoed corn, bailed hay, cut cabbage, staked tomatoes, broke
land, and sowed lespedeza, and I, by God, wanted off the land. It
didn't seem a fit place for a smart young hotblood like myself. I
wanted to buy tomcat nights with rainbow dollars.

I wandered for nearly a year, eating shoplifted food, getting
money when I had to by sweeping floors or washing dishes, sleeping sometimes with a woman, usually one that didn't think any
more of screwing a man than she would have of changing clothes.
Finally, I went back to Oklahoma because I was seventeen and
tired, because the few people I much cared to see again lived there,
and because I'd missed playing baseball in the summer. It wasn't
the land or any idea of working it that called me back. I got myself
a cheap room in Tahlequah, worked odd jobs, and got arrested a
couple of times for petty theft. When Ice Common Deer agreed to
let me rustle cattle with him, it was less out of any need for a partner than out of the knowledge that I'd get in worse trouble on my
own.

But lying in bed that morning in nearly the last space of quiet
before the team and the world came back, I did begin to think that
farming was the only decent choice I had left. It was either that or
follow some road that would just wind around a while before leading me back to the pen. I could maybe get me a few acres of scrub
rock in the Cookson Hills and work to build the soil up to where it

would grow all I'd eat and a little extra. Or maybe Lefty could help me find some place down around Magnolia.

I looked over at Pansy again, still sleeping, breathing through her mouth. "Pansy Puckett," I whispered to myself. Could a man settle down with a woman that had a name like Pansy Puckett? I'd been out of the slam nearly three months, and this was the only woman I'd had. She didn't know me, really, and I didn't know her. We just felt good together, and how long could that last?

I got out of bed and walked over to the window and looked out at the garden. You're a thief, I told myself, and you have been for nearly fifteen years now. Most of what farming you've done in that time has been in the last couple of months right down there in that little half-acre plot. But you're such a damn fool that a few nights with an easy-smiling, sweet-bodied, blond-haired woman and a few hours of tilling and pruning and such is enough to set you to dreaming of a homestead. How would you pay for the place, sod-buster? Rob another bank? And even if you managed to get some land, you'd probably wind up hating it and the woman. Every Saturday night you'd end up where you always have when you've been free to—drinking in some smoked-up dive and trying to pick up a piece of strange you could fuck and forget.

"Nice ass."

I looked back over my shoulder at her. She sat up, propping her pillow behind her.

"It's a pile driver," I said. I must've looked at her curious then because she pulled the sheet up over her breasts. I took a pair of underwear out of the drawer and put them on. "It's going to be hotter than the First Baptist hell today," I said.

"What were you thinking about?" she asked. "Standing over there looking out the window like you were a minute ago, you kind of looked trapped."

There was an old wooden straight chair over by the chest of drawers, and I sat down on it. I made a slow study of my hands. Then I looked up at her and said, "I was just wondering what becomes of old thieves."

"I thought they hit .400."

"Not for long."

"You're on your way back up to it." She smiled at me. I looked down at my feet.

"I don't know," I said, head down. "I woke up thinking about myself and it came to me that probably I'd fucked things up so thoroughly they were apt to stay that way."

"Have you done something? Is there some trouble with your parole officer again?"

"No. I haven't done anything lately. But then there's no way of getting around my past. And I don't know what I'm going to do. I know I don't want to end up back in jail, but I'm not apt to get offered any job I'd take either."

"If you're tired of me, Hog, or scared of me, just say so. I don't want to hear a long explanation of what a worthless bastard you are. I don't want your excuses or your pity. If you want to be free of me, then come out and say it. I'm not going to be your jailer."

She was sitting up then, the sheet up to her waist, her breasts against her thighs, her hands clasped around her knees. Her eyes were hard but calm. I tried to smile, took the few steps that separated us, and touched her cheeks with the tips of my fingers.

She pushed my hands away. "I won't be your play pretty either," she said. "I want you to sit in that chair and talk to me straight."

That whiner's corner of my mind was a part of me I liked even less than she did, and by the time I got sat down in that chair again I'd pretty well shut it down.

"Yes, ma'am," I said, being sure I let her see my fearless grin. "You're way too fine and purty a little ole thing to be messing with a scaly ole buck like me that the whole world's against and won't give a fair shake. We could try being Bonnie and Clyde, but there's more cops out there than there used to be and less sympathy for thieves and our run wouldn't last long. And anyway, I want better for you. You're the kind that ought to have long gowns and foreign meals and slow dances to orchestra music. Me, now, darling, I can't offer you nothing but a quick hand, a changing heart, and 3.2 beer.".

"I'll buy the beer," she said. Her face seemed to relax a little and her eyes may've softened some, and I think she started to just let it go, let me joke my way around the thing that mattered. But she caught herself. She'd raised a question she wanted answered.

She said, "You came along when I needed somebody. One man instead of one a week. I came along when you'd been a long time without. I wanted it to matter and maybe you just wanted it. After all that time you spent locked up, you probably wanted a woman a night for a while, and what you got was me for—what is it now? Almost three months? I've thought about it a lot. But it's not easy for me to talk about. And I think it's even harder for you. Maybe getting this started was a mistake for both of us. I hope not, but I can't help worrying. Because it does matter. To me anyway. And if you're not ready to deal with that . . . well, I don't know. Maybe you'd better do something about it."

I didn't say anything right off. I turned my head and looked out the window. But sitting the way I was, I couldn't see anything but treetops and sky, so I looked down at the floor. I thought for a minute about how it was that lust sometimes just rose up and spent itself and died but sometimes, not often but sometimes, kept right on rising until it was big enough to change everything in its shade.

I raised my head. Pansy was waiting. I said, "Well, it matters to me too. Though God knows I didn't want it to when it started. But now I can't say quit and, hell, I don't even know what going on means. It may be that if we go on together, it'll end up with two of us lost."

"And if we quit," she said, "we'd still probably end up lost, just in different places."

"That's the kind of lost I'm used to," I said. "I probably could handle it better."

She got up out of bed and came over to me. I stood and held her in my arms. She tilted her head back and looked in my eyes. "It has to be worth at least a chance, Hog." And then she smiled. "Because right now it's just me and you and the darkness left and all the light there's going to be is what we can make on our own."

"Nice memory you got," I said.

"It was the best line anybody ever gave me."

Part V

34

Lefty and those that rode the bus with him down to Magnolia got back to the home about noon that Monday, the thirtieth of June, all of them looking clean and refreshed and purposeful, like proper communalists. They were followed an hour or so later by Julius Common Deer and Susan Pankhurst, looking healthy and wholesome and just a little secretive, like proper young lovers. Old Ice, then, had approved of his son's young white woman, and she of him, and I foresaw a marriage and honest work and a string of the prettiest little half-breeds you ever saw.

Later that afternoon, in their pickup, which they'd pretty well scarred up in the brush, Joe Buck, Stump, Bullet Bob, Rainbow Smith, and Pinzon rolled in, all of them tired and grizzled and drunk (well, Joe Buck, the driver, was sober, but he was hungover like God on the Eighth Day), like proper weekend fishermen. They claimed they'd caught almost as many fish as they could eat, and all of them seemed pleased with the grand way they'd got drunk and told lies on the river. But their big story was about Pinzon, who'd talked them into dropping him by the Queen Wilhelmina Lodge, where he'd had himself a two-day golf and poker run that netted over $2,500. When they came back to pick him up, Pinzon had given the four fishermen $300 apiece, and they talked like they were right proud to know such a sporting, generous fellow. Pinzon himself didn't say much; he was passed out in the bed of the truck.

By suppertime everybody was back but Genghis Mohammed, Jr., and Bobbie Sampson. We already knew that Bobbie's AmTrak from Saint Louis didn't get into Little Rock until 1:00 A.M. (that being a system run, apparently, by people that hated trains). Julius and Susan were planning to pick her up at the station. But as the hours passed I began to wonder whether Genghis hadn't committed some religious offense and got his right arm hacked off, but he showed up whole about ten o'clock, I'd say, looking dark and solemn and mean, like a proper Muslim. The car he came in just stopped long enough to let him out. Four or five of us were sitting around in the living room when Genghis entered, but the first one of us he saw was Bullet Bob, apparently unconscious, sitting on the couch, a quart of Coors trapped between his thighs, his head lolled back, his eyes closed, and his mouth open. He did look like he might've recently got drummed out of the Hell's Angels for moral turpitude.

"I see nothing's changed here," Genghis said.

Nothing moved but Bob's mouth. "You hungry there, Mo, I'll see if I can't fry you up a bacon and tomato sandwich."

"It's good to be home," Genghis said, raising the right side of his upper lip. Then he went on up to his room.

After a minute or two, Bob collected himself, raised his head, and said, "Goddam Communist."

"They're not Communists," I told him.

He used up a couple of seconds thinking, "Same damn difference." He took a last pull off the Coors, let his head fall back where it wanted to be, and stayed there till morning.

35

We took back up against the Memphis Kings, winning on the first and second of July, losing on the third, then coming back strong on the Fourth, when we hosted the tenth annual Columbia County Co-op Goat Roast.

It wasn't much after sunup the morning of the Fourth when Lefty roared us out of our beds, hurried us through breakfast, herded us onto the bus, and took us out to the field.

"A ballplayer ought not have to keep these kind of hours," Bullet Bob complained as Lefty prodded him onto the bus. "Hell, the hours is the main reason I chose this as my livelihood."

"Like it or not, Bob, you're part of this co-op," Lefty, grinning, told him. "So you're obligated to celebrate."

"Shit, you can't make a man celebrate."

"Sure I can. That's how nations are built."

Bob stopped and stared back at him, then raised his right leg and farted. "That's what I got to say about your damn philosophy."

Lefty nodded, "Symbolic logic."

I don't know whether Lefty had got a permit for it all or whether he just figured the cops would be leery of stepping into the middle of a party of that many blacks, but for whatever reason, the law stayed clear of us all day long. That was something of a wonder too because it was well before eight o'clock when we rolled into the parking lot at the field and already the co-op folks were setting up their cooking rigs—old iron barrels which had been sawed in half lengthwise and which were set belly-down underneath spits contrived out of pipes and wire. They'd lined these big grills up side by side at the parking lot edge closest to the stadium. Behind them, strung between two poles they'd sunk into the ground, a banner that must've been thirty feet long said: "10th Annual Columbia Co-op Goat Roast and Independence Celebration. Everybody Welcome." Lefty had Bobbie Sampson park the bus right in front of them, and when we got out they were cheering us.

"Nigger heaven," Bullet Bob said to me.

"It's the only kind there is," I told him.

I saw Barry Rotenberg sitting in one of those long plastic reclining lawn chairs over behind one of the grills, so Pansy and I walked over to him.

Rotenberg stood and offered Pansy the chair. He had on a pair of army fatigue pants, a white T-shirt splotched with various blobs of dried paint, and a big, cheap straw hat. There was a bottle of beer on the ground beside him.

"I'll stand," Pansy said. "If I sat down I'd go right to sleep."

"We'll wake you when the goat's done," Rotenberg said, but he sat back down. Smiling, he looked at first Pansy and then me. Then he said, "You know, Pansy, I do believe you're getting lovelier by the week. It makes me wonder what you're doing with a thug like ole Hog there when you could have yourself an upright lawyer like myself."

She leaned over and kissed him on the forehead.

"I have this unnatural attraction for thieves," she said.

Rotenberg shook his head and laughed. "That's as fine a definition of love as I've ever heard."

I told him I'd never seen him looking so relaxed and happy.

"This is the one time of the year I'm sure to get a good meal," he said. "Ordinarily I either eat in my office or in the cafe closest to whatever courthouse I'm performing in." He paused and looked around him. "You know, I've never missed one of these things. The first one was a celebration of existence. The next few were celebrations of survival. Now it may be a celebration of triumph."

"Triumph's a little too grand a word, isn't it?" I asked.

"A local triumph," he said, "but a real one."

He talked a minute or two more about how fine a thing the co-op was and then asked me how I'd been getting along with Mantis.

"He's promised to quit trying to help me," I said.

"Well, that's good news."

"How's the painting?"

"The same," he said. "Too predictable, mildly funny, and unfinished."

"Still can't get Jesus nailed down?"

"Oh, sometimes for a day or two it seems I have Him. Then the next day He just seems to slip away from me."

After talking to Rotenberg, Pansy and I wandered around and socialized some. The co-op people, mostly fairly respectable-looking blacks, enjoyed talking baseball and I was a prime attraction for them, mainly, I guess, because I was an ex-convict and a home-run hitter. And when they found out that Pansy was from El Dorado, just down the road from them, they'd ask her if she knew old Ben Green or Jimmy Dunn or somebody, and now and again she'd recognize one of the names. "What's he doing now?" she'd ask, and they'd answer or say they didn't know: he'd gone North or West some years ago.

A few of the Magnolia people had brought guitars, there were a couple of horns and a set of drums, and an old upright piano had been driven up in one of the co-op trucks. Over at the western edge of the lot, next to the parking area for the zoo, the musicians had set up on the back of a flatbed truck and were playing old hymns, with a '60s civil-rights song thrown in now and then. Lefty said they called themselves the Co-op Earth Band and I accused him of thinking up the name himself. "On Sundays," he said, "they're still the B Street Baptist Singers. Their preacher didn't want them to use that name on secular occasions."

"You have trouble with preachers down there?"

"Not the black ones. Most of them like to see their people eat. They still don't take that kind of thing quite as much for granted as white folks tend to. The white preachers, of course, have been trying to preach us into hell ever since we started up."

"Well," I said, "they're having some success. They got you all the way to Little Rock."

We listened to a few songs and then walked over to where Genghis Mohammed, Jr., in dashiki and turban, was trying to show some kids (there were six or eight of them, none looking to be over twelve) the wisdom of the Glorious Koran by telling about the time he'd met Mohammed Ali. That was when Ali had been training to make an ass out of himself against Larry Holmes.

"I was a good brother to his sparring partner," Genghis told the kids. "Dude from Detroit named Abdullah Imeme. After the workout Abdullah introduced me to the champ. When Ali heard my name, he said, 'I'm proud we're brothers in Allah.' "

Genghis drew himself up and stared down heavy at them, letting them know that the Ali line he'd just quoted was something they ought to hammer into their memories.

One of the kids asked, "What else did he say?"

In a tone you might use to explain music to a deaf-mute, Genghis said, "He didn't need to say no more. There was a bond between us and him and we both knew it."

Then the same kid asked, "How come you wear that robe?"

I took in a minute or two of Genghis's answer, a lecture on black heritage, the nobility of black princes, and the glory of black civilizations. I might've taken in some more, but after that minute or two Genghis began to repeat himself.

A little later in the morning—ten-thirty or so; the game started at one—I was eating one of the ham sandwiches that were being given away when I heard one black kid ask another who that man was up on the roof of the stadium. I looked up there and saw Eversole, standing at the edge, looking down at the crowd. He had on the bottoms of his uniform but no shirt or cap. After a minute he sat down. I told Pansy I'd be back in a few minutes and got up, went into the stadium, climbed the grandstands, entered the press box, and went up the ladder that led to the roof.

He sat leaning back, the weight of his upper body on the palms of his hands, his legs outstretched and crossed. I'd expected him to be holding himself bolt upright, legs folded in front of him, like

Sitting Bull studying the cavalry from a rise. But he looked more like a sunbather on a solitary beach, holding himself up just enough to gaze out over the sea.

"Happy Independence Day," I said.

He didn't say anything back, but I couldn't see that he much minded my being there, so I stood next to him and checked the view. Looking out over and beyond the parking lot, I could see the zoo, open now, the chimpanzees, just beyond the gate, sunning themselves on their molded concrete hill, a couple and their son, four or five years old, stopping there a while, then going on up the curving walk leading to the duck pond, and then on to the bear and wolf and buffalo, the ostrich and the lion.

Then, turning just a notch to my right, I saw War Memorial Stadium, Little Rock's monument to her culture. Down the hill from that, traffic moved easy up and down Markham, the drivers released today from the grip of commerce. Turning again, slowly, I came to the state mental hospital, a few hundred yards east of me and standing on the edge of the same hill; its separate units, brick and square and flat and joined by wide sidewalks, looked like they had been planned by a hard, joyless mind down to the last detail—every detail perfect, calculated, and wrong. But then, what do I know about sanity?

Only a wide driveway separated the asylum from the University of Arkansas Medical Center, seven stories high and designed, I remembered reading somewhere, by a famous architect. To come up with the scale model for the medical center he must've had to fool with two cardboard boxes until he had them setting upside down and coming off each other at right angles.

About a mile further on east was the state capitol and I could see the dome that, over the years, had kept the sun and rain off of so many vicious fools. Though I couldn't quite see it from my stand, I knew that it wasn't but just a few blocks from the capitol to Central High School, where the Arkansas gunsels had set an example it would take the slickers in Boston and Los Angeles twenty years to learn to copy.

Turning again, I let my eye catch the Orval Faubus Freeway and follow it past the national guard ammunition dump and then on until it reached the left-field wall and screen, 400 and some odd feet of free ground from where I stood.

"Nice view," I said, and then sat down 'next to Eversole.

"It's good up here late at night," he said. "And early in the morning."

"Hell, it ain't bad now. The view makes you proud to be a ball-player."

"No," he said, "the field ought to be somewhere away from all this."

"There's no such place no more, Jeremiah. And the next best thing is to make you a place and keep it clean right in the middle of them."

"No," he said again. Then he looked at me and let his round weathered face relax. "You might make a place in the middle of them, but you can't keep it clean."

"You've made a place for yourself here," I argued. "And you've done it on your own terms. Every time you toe that rubber out there, the game, the field, hell, the whole damn day, is yours."

He looked away from me a second or two and then turned back. His eyes seemed to widen and lighten some and for a minute there I thought he was going to smile. But then he said, "If I couldn't pitch, I wouldn't have to be here at all."

I took some time thinking that over. Finally, I just decided to ask him what the hell he'd meant by it.

"I've spent most of my life training myself to do two things— take care of myself without anybody's help and pitch a baseball. Now I can do them both, but not at the same time. If I didn't need to pitch, I wouldn't have to be up here explaining myself to you."

He said that without malice, I think—or without any malice toward me in particular. And just to be saying something, hoping to keep him talking, I said, "Well, look at it this way. You're lucky you can pitch the way you can, else you wouldn't've ever got to know ole Hog Durham, philosopher and thief."

But just as final and matter-of-fact as you please, he said, "That's one way of looking at it." Then he stood and walked right to the edge of the roof and looked down at the crowd again.

Talking at his back, I said, "Hell, when a man can do something the way you can pitch, he ought to just do it and joy in it."

He turned around, ran his left hand back through his hair, and said, "It's a little thing."

I wasn't quite sure whether he was talking about baseball or joy, but what I said was, "So what?"

"That's one way of looking at it," he said again.

"By God, you're an agreeable son of a bitch," I said.

He came back to where I was and sat down again. I waited a minute for him to say something back. Then, seeing that he wasn't going to, I started rambling some, hoping to preserve the little connection we'd made between us. "It sort of puts me in the mind of my pore ole momma. She was the kind it was hard to argue with. You'd say something and she'd say, 'I can see that,' or 'That's not a bad way of looking at it,' or 'I guess so. I just never thought about it like that.' 'You got to learn to go along to get along' is what she used to tell me every time I hit somebody she thought I oughtn't to have. That saying was her idea of a piece of wisdom. She put a lot of stock in being agreeable. It got her into a couple of bad marriages and for a while it made her take responsibility for a kid she didn't much want."

"You?" Eversole asked.

He's interested, I thought. Then I figured I'd give him a piece of my history in hopes of getting a piece of his in return. "Yeah," I told him. "She did what she could with me for a couple of years. But having me with her had put her pretty much on her own. My daddy saw it as his responsibility to see her through the pregnancy and to give her his name. I hadn't much more than popped free when he jumped in his pickup and drove off. Bakersfield, California. A pretty little spot, where all the tired Okies go to die. After that it didn't take long for the shine to wear off of momma's little darling. I was going on three when a mechanic from Barren Fork, Oklahoma, named Vernon Haggard, said he'd marry her except he wasn't one to raise another man's child. Well, you got to go along to get along, and, being agreeable, momma turned me over to her folks and herself over to Vernon. They stayed around for another two or three years, but it grated on Vernon that all the yahoos he buddied with knew he was sinking his drill into a used hole, and Momma didn't much like living so close to a child she'd abandoned, so, finally, ole Vernon set fire to his garage, collected the insurance on it, and him and Momma packed up and went to Stockton, California. I'm sure they'd've preferred Bakersfield, but my dad was there. Momma used to come home all bruised up about once a year saying she was through with Vernon, but after a week or so she'd take a bus back to him—going along to get along. Last I heard, things was better for them—Vernon having lost most of the snap in his right, I guess. They had two boys, a girl, and a cinderblock garage on the outskirts of town."

I stopped and listened to the music coming up from the parking lot. Eversole just sat there looking off into the distance. I figured I ought to get up off my ass and go back down into the celebrating instead of staying up there sharpening my autobiographical skills. Having gone as far with it as I had, though, I decided to give it one more shot. "But then none of that has much to do with me. My grandparents were decent folks and they gave me as good an upbringing as a man has any right to expect. The trouble I been in, I found on my own."

I looked over at him and gave him a half-grin. "How about yourself? You don't seem like the kind that came out of a good Christian home."

I was just on the verge of leaving when he commenced to answer. "That's exactly what I came out of," he said. "The San Antonio Methodist Home for Boys." Then he laid flat down on his back and stared straight up, a little west of the sun.

"That an orphanage or some sort of a New Testament reform school?"

"Both." He stopped long enough there for me to think that was all he was going to give out. But then he went on. He gave me the story a sentence at a time, pausing after almost every one, sometimes for only a breath or two, sometimes for much longer, as if at any point he might change his mind and stop. Each of the sentences came out flat, almost without inflection. Still, I thought I could feel the rage underneath it all. I'm not sure what drove him on. Maybe something in him needed to say it all once and have done with talking about it. I was just glad I was there when it happened.

He was born, he said, forty-six years ago in a hospital in San Angelo, Texas. But his mother, Ruth was her name, had conceived him in Colon, Panama, where she was staying with her father, Commander Newman K. Eversole IV. She was eighteen at the time. Eversole thought she might've been pretty, but he hadn't seen her since his sixth birthday. One night, out of lust or curiosity or fear or rebellion or maybe even love (Eversole didn't speculate on motive, so I went right ahead on my own), she opened herself to a San Blas Indian, name unknown, fate unknown. Eversole's first

memory was of being four or five and living with his mother upstairs in a green apartment house in Odessa, Texas. The apartment
must've been just a few blocks away from the high school football
field, because he could remember the lights and the sound of the
bands and walking down there sometimes on Friday nights with
his mother and looking at the crowds and taking in the noise.
Never going inside, the white woman and her dark child, just
standing outside the gate, and watching and listening.

"Odessa, Texas," Eversole said as if those Friday nights pretty
well summed the place up.

He remembered houses after that and one man, Jim, tall and
fearsome through a child's eyes. Jim, who came and stayed and
then left. And he remembered knowing they were poor because his
mother told him they were, because now and again she would call
her father—the Commander, Eversole called him—and beg him
for a little money.

Finally, they quit moving. Ruth gave up and went home. She
took Eversole with her, on a bus from Odessa to Corpus Christi,
where the Commander was stationed then. A man in a gray car
met them at the bus station and drove them to a long, flat house.
The Commander wasn't there. They sat on the steps and waited.
Later—it seemed like hours, but they had had to wait in silence
and in fear—the Commander came up the driveway, driven by
another man, in a longer, darker car. Ruth stood and then Eversole
did too. He remembered the white uniform coming stiffly toward
them. And then the face, clean, hard, and thin-lipped. And the
words: "Get your bastard out of here."

His mother sat back down on the steps, put her face in her
hands, and shook. The Commander walked around her and entered his house. The driver sat inside the car and waited. Eversole
remembered just wanting to get out of the way and hide somewhere until it was over. And then his mother could find him and
they could leave and it would be all right. He went to a big shade
tree and sat under it, between two broad roots. When she stopped
crying, his mother went inside.

Again, he couldn't know how long he waited, running his palms
along the rough, twisted root-bark, but he remembered how his
fear focused on the driver, who sat in the car smoking cigarettes
and listening to a ball game. Given the time and place, I'd guess it
was a Cardinal game, but all Eversole could recall of it was the

way the sound came to him—a low, uneven static broken now and then by the crowd's roaring and the announcer's raving. That occasional swelling of noise reminded him of his sad Odessa Friday nights. This time, though, his mother wasn't there listening with him. This time there wasn't another hand to put his in. This time there was only the waiting driver.

When his mother came out, she called to him, and they got in the back seat of the car. They drove to San Antonio and spent the night in a motel—him and his mother in one room, the driver in the next. It wasn't until they were in their room that his mother began trying to explain what had happened and what would. Eversole wasn't sure she ever got all the way through it. What he remembered was the way she struggled with it, the way she started and stopped and started again, the way she would break and cry and then get up and wash her face and come back to the edge of the bed and try it again, saying what seemed to be the same thing over and over, apologizing for what she hadn't done yet, crying at her own weakness. But, for all his fear and confusion, what he understood was what there was to be understood: she was leaving him.

Next morning, the driver took them to the San Antonio Methodist Home for Boys. He and his mother went inside. He waited in the hallway while she went into a room. After a while, she came out with a tall, white-headed, gray-suited man. She went to Eversole, held him, cried again, then stood, looked away, and said, "Jerry, you go with Brother Overholster. He'll take good care of you." Then she ran out of the building.

"That's the last time I let anybody call me Jerry," Eversole said.

The good folks at the Home taught religion; Eversole learned self-reliance. They taught obedience; he learned rebellion. They taught patriotism; he dreamed of Mexico. But, on the playground, they let him play baseball, and he mastered that. As he talked, I could see him, the big, dark kid standing at the center of the ragged field, controlling his ferocity one pitch at a time. At thirteen he began teaching himself the spitball because it was against the rules. At fifteen, a year younger than the usual age limit, he played for the San Antonio Kiwanis Club American Legion team and won every game he pitched. At sixteen—already over six feet tall, as tough as Job but not as patient—he walked to Monterrey and began pitching in the Mexican League.

I waited for more, but this time he was through. When I was absolutely sure he wasn't going on on his own, I asked him what had happened later to ruin his chances of becoming a major leaguer in the United States.

"I didn't like them. They didn't like me."

I waited again. I could see him closing back up. "What became of your mother?"

"She went home to the Commander. She used to mail me fifty dollars and a fruitcake every Christmas." He stood up. "I never saw her again."

That was that. I stayed on the roof a few minutes more, watching him and waiting, running his story back through my head a time or two, taking it apart, using my imagination to fill it in here and there, making sure it fit good in my mind, because I was almost sure he'd never tell it to me again, might even come to resent my having heard it this one time. But whatever he was thinking or would think, I was glad I'd happened to catch him when he was vulnerable, glad I'd entered a moment when even Jeremiah Eversole, standing alone and apart and looking down on a celebration of a collective victory, was consciously longing to be a part of the rest of us.

Back down on the parking lot, I found Pansy and we wandered around together for maybe another half-hour, listening to more of the music, trading smiles and small talk with more of the people. I ate a couple of the barbecue pork sandwiches the co-op's head cook, a lean, heavy-eyed, middle-aged man named Gaylord Tucker, was handing out from the back end of a red-and-white reclaimed Holsum Bread truck. When I went back for the second one, I told Tucker he was a helluva man with a piece of pork and a pot of sauce, but he was too serious an artist to pay any mind to passing flattery.

About eleven-thirty the Memphis Kings came rolling up in their bus. Luther Ray, their manager, was the first of them off. He stopped, took a look around, then led his boys on down to the visitors' clubhouse. A few minutes later, Lefty rounded us up and by noon we were out on the field.

Kids from the ball teams sponsored by the co-op caught fungoes and took batting practice with us. Lefty had wanted us to play them in a two- or three-inning warm-up game, but there were too many kids for that, a couple of dozen anyway, ranging from about ten to seventeen years old, all rigged out in their co-op uniforms. And the kids seemed to enjoy just being on the field with us well enough. Since they acted as if we were something special, most of us enjoyed it too. Being treated like a hero won't do a man much harm if it doesn't last too long or happen too often. About thirty minutes of it once every ten years might actually do him some good.

We forgot ourselves and overstayed our time, so Luther Ray took his Kings out onto the field while we were still on it. "They's supposed to be a ball game sometime today, boys," he yelled at us as we finally cleared off.

The crowd was considerably smaller than what we'd been drawing. Lefty, figuring, I guess, he might run short of goat, hadn't done any promoting of the celebration. Some of our regular fans may've driven up intending to see the game, but then got scared off by the sight of all them niggers building fires around the parking lot. So we played to a crowd, mostly black, made up largely of co-op members or sympathizers.

After Memphis finished taking infield, the Co-op Earth Band took the field and played and sang first "The Farmer Is the Man" and then "We Shall Overcome." Then we came out and waited at our positions while Lefty, using the p.a. system, introduced Ernest Bell, who during the '30s had organized the Arkansas Sharecropper's Union. He paused there, then said, "Ernie, throw us a strike."

Ernest Bell stood and, with the game ball in his hand, waved at the applauding crowd. He looked more like an old, good, retired bartender than your standard model rabble-rouser—short, thick-armed, barrel-chested, a heavy fringe of white running back from temple to temple and framing a black dome. When he got through waving and smiling at the crowd, Ernest turned and looped a strike to Joe Buck Cantwell. Joe Buck walked back up to him and made him a present of the ball. After the half-inning, Cantwell told me that Ernest had said, "Still got my control, but the goddamned arthritis has taken some of the snap out of my slider."

Genghis Mohammed, Jr., determined to impress this crowd, pitched shutout ball for five innings, giving up just three scattered singles and a walk. We got a run in the third when Jew Bernstein singled, Genghis sacrificed him to second, and Jefferson Mundy singled him home. But then, when we had two outs on them in the sixth, Press Vernon, their first baseman, worked

Genghis for a walk, and Jazz Beale, who'd already amused the crowd by making a couple of nonchalant basket catches in center, drove a grooved fastball into the left-center gap and raced, with long, hurdler's strides, to third, where he hook-slid around Rainbow Smith's tag.

Genghis got the next hitter, Eldridge Colson, to pop to short and end that half-inning. Then he set them down in order in their seventh. With one gone in our seventh, I went with a 1–2 curve, drove it to the wall, and got myself a standup double. While they were giving Rainbow an intentional pass to set up the double play, I stood a few feet off second enjoying the smell of roasting goat in the air. I could remember long-ago Oklahoma Fourth of Julys like this—the kids playing workup in the pasture, the men laying around in the shade, smoking, drinking, watching, remembering, the women off stirring up the evening spread.

Atticus Flood spoiled their double-play strategy with a long single into right-center that sent me home with the go-ahead run. The first man up for them in the eighth dumped a looper in front of Jew Bernstein in left. Their pitcher, Jed Hooper, was due up next, and even though it was a bunting situation, Luther Ray sent a pinch hitter up. It didn't matter much though what Luther did right then because Genghis had lost it. He threw four straight balls to the pinch hitter and then four more to the leadoff man. When Lefty came out to the mound Genghis argued that he still had his stuff, that several of those eight pitches would've been called strikes by a less-bigoted umpire, and that it was his game to win or lose. Lefty nodded, held his hand out for the ball, and waved Bullet Bob in from the pen. Ignoring the applause he got for his day's work, Genghis stomped to the dugout, threw first his glove then his cap at the bench, turned and took a couple of steps back toward the mound, thought better of that, and finally stormed into the clubhouse.

I was standing out on the mound with Joe Buck and Lefty when Bullet Bob got there. Lefty handed him the ball and reminded him that the bases were loaded with nobody down. Joe Buck told him to be sure and cover home on a wild pitch. Bob said there wouldn't be no wild pitches. "And they better not be no passed balls."

"I can catch anything you can throw," Joe Buck said through a grin.

"Go to it then," Bob told him. Joe Buck trotted back to his position behind the plate.

Bob threw a warm-up pitch, caught Joe Buck's return thrown, and climbed back to the rubber. "You know," he told Lefty, "you might ought to see if you can't trade that Mohammed fucker to the asylum for a man that's got some sense." Bob threw again, came back again.

"Genghis pitched a strong game," Lefty said. "He just wanted to finish it."

"Man takes you out of the game, you hand him the ball and keep your damn mouth shut. What he done is horseshit."

"Maybe," Lefty said, letting it go. Then he walked away from the mound, about halfway out toward second, and set Mundy and Worm Warnock at double-play depth, meaning he was willing to concede them the tying run in exchange for a pair of outs.

But Bob kept talking all the time he warmed up. "Him taking a spell like that makes me look bad. Starter goes six or seven innings, he's put in a day's work. He can walk away and shower off with his head up. You get in a goddam tight late, you bring in your stopper. Lefty could've let the puffed up Mohammedan prick stay in and walk the ballpark or he can bring me in and win the game."

After he threw his last warm-up pitch, I said, "Genghis is just young and proud. I don't think the Muslims are real big on humility."

"I got my pride too," he said.

I nodded and jogged back to my position, thinking how it was that on the field, where he got to do the one thing he did well, Bob usually honored a strict, almost gentlemanly code. The rest of the time he drifted along from beer to beer. Baseball mattered to him. Life, on the other hand, was just something he had to tolerate between games.

And as if to point up the absurdity of Genghis's display of pride, Bob got out of the inning with five pitches. The first hitter he faced took a strike, then sent a two-hopper back to the mound. Bob went to Joe Buck, Joe Buck went to me, and we had us a neat little 1-2-3 double-play. That left men on second and third with two down. With any other pitcher on the mound, Lefty would've probably ordered an intentional walk to their next, and best, hitter, Jazz Beale. That would've set up the force at any base. But a good knuckleballer is more apt to give up a walk than a hit, and anyway a team's best hitter may not be their best knuckleball hitter. So Bob went ahead and pitched to Beale with a base open. In this case though, I don't think it would've mattered one way or the other. Bob was throwing his floater for strikes, and it was jumping around like a prayer in an air raid. He threw Beale a strike, a ball, then got him on a weak foul behind third.

That was it. Lefty let Susan finish up at first for me in the ninth, but Bob retired the side so quick—a swinging K and two rollers— that the fans hadn't much more than finished applauding Susan before the game ended. Right after the last out, several of the kids rushed to the mound and commenced slapping him on the back and ass and telling him what a helluva job he'd done. And Bob, his day's work done and order restored, smiled on them, tousled a head or two in passing, and, when he got to the dugout, picked up a ball and started showing them his butterfly grip.

We showered, dressed, and went back on the field for the goat-eating. In the outfield, the co-op folks were setting up makeshift picnic tables—big strips of plywood laid across two sawhorses and covered with butcher paper. They'd driven the flatbed truck through the right-field foul-line gate and parked it astraddle second base. With the Co-op Earth Band playing behind them, Lefty, still in uniform, and old Ernest Bell were up on the truck bed singing "We Shall Not Be Moved." I saw Pansy and Rotenberg standing together, clapping and singing along with the crowd that had formed around the truck. I walked over to one of the kegs and drew me a beer and then joined my woman and my mouthpiece.

Rotenberg sang through a happy drunk's constant grin. "Christ," I told him, "you're a disgrace to your profession."

"Thank you," he said. "But actually the one thing all us lawyers have in common is drunkenness."

"Well, lawyering is nasty work."

"Dark duty," he agreed. "But necessary."

"That just makes it darker."

"Ah, ole Hog, the thinking man's thief."

"Men," Pansy said. "You give them a couple of drinks and they start thinking they're smart. Why don't y'all just clap your hands and sing?"

"Aw, hon," I said, "it's such a womanish thing to do."

When the song had ended and the crowd was cheering the two

old agitators, Lefty climbed quickly down from the truckbed, leaving the stage to Ernest, who stood there a minute smiling. Then he pulled a white handkerchief out of his back pocket and wiped some sweat from his face. "Lord," he said, "this is no place for an old man." He walked to the end of the truck, stepped onto the back bumper, looked down, hesitated, looked up at the crowd, and said, "It's a long way back to the ground."

Lefty stepped up to him and stretched out his arm. "Hell, Ernest, I thought you could fly."

"I'm saving that."

Ernest kind of half-squatted, put one hand in Lefty's and the other one on Lefty's shoulder, and lowered himself to the ground. He laughed then and, looking at Lefty, said, "Just another case of the white man pulling us down."

"It's just too big a temptation," Lefty said, "when even a one-armed man can do it."

Well, the band played on, the beer held out, and the goat tasted good, covered the way it was with Gaylord Tucker's sauce, one of those small things that gives you hope for the race.

Folks sat around on the outfield grass, eating, listening to music, mixing and mingling, swapping yarns about crops and cops. A little before dark the traffic thickened on the Orval Faubus Freeway, most of the cars taking the exit just beyond us and then circling back around to War Memorial Stadium, where, at 9, the Little Rock Fire Department was to start lighting up the sky with hundred-dollar firecrackers.

For what would be the only time all that season, Lefty switched on our ballpark lights. Maybe one out of every three of them worked. You might've got hurt playing ball under them, but they were about right for a party. It prompted me to tell Pansy and Rotenberg about how it was to play at night in North Greasey, Oklahoma, where the lights were so bad you'd've been better off just strapping a miner's light to your cap. Rotenberg accused me of making up the name of the place. I promised to take him there sometime.

A band over at War Memorial Stadium started playing "My Country 'Tis of Thee." A few seconds later the crowd over there commenced to sing along. We sat quietly and listened to them a minute. While the last notes were dying away, the fire department shot up some exploding rockets.

I got up and headed for the clubhouse to have a quiet piss and a slow smoke. I thought maybe, if I could figure a way of doing it without seeming to intrude, I'd go back into the equipment room, where Eversole would be brooding in his hammock while he read his copy of *Darien Massacres*. I thought another look at him right then might brace me some.

But I got something even more bracing than that. I stepped down into the dugout and saw Pinzon slumped back into the out-field corner of it, one foot out in front of him on the bench, the other on the floor. His right hand was wrapped around the neck of a three-quarters-empty bottle of Four Roses. At first I thought he'd passed out and I wondered some at that—Pinzon ordinarily being a loud, colorful drunk, not the kind to drink himself under in a dark corner while a party was going on. I decided to respect his need, though, whatever it was. A fifth of cheap whiskey wasn't going to kill him.

But when I turned and started toward the clubhouse door, he spoke, "Hog?"

"Yeah. I need a piss."

"Wait up."

He studied his left foot, then with obvious effort, swung it around slow and let it drop to the floor. He set his bottle carefully in the corner, raised his head, looked out over the infield, sighed, and, finally, sort of swayed upward until he was standing. He walked deliberately toward me, seeming to concentrate on every step.

I went on into the clubhouse and held the door for him. He took a step inside, stopped, examined the room like it was the first time he'd seen it, then walked, carefully erect, straight to the urinals.

He pissed with his legs spread, both palms against the wall, his cock hanging free. If one of his hands had slipped, I think he'd've fallen forehead-first against the wall.

When he finished he raised his tired red eyes up at me and said, "I'm sorry."

"Aw, hell, everybody needs to get good and drunk now and then."

He nodded as if that had satisfied him and we started back across the room. When we were about halfway to the door, he pulled himself to a stop. "It's not that," he said. "It's the other thing."

As soon as he said it, I knew what he meant. But I asked anyway. "It's all my fault. I didn't want it. I offered to go back. But it was too late." His face was covered with drunken apology. I just stood there and waited for him to finish it. "I like you, Hog. I didn't mean it to come to this. There's not many people . . ." He shut up and looked away. Christ, I thought for a minute that he was going to cry. "Ratoplan . . ." The name seemed to ball up in his throat and he had to stop and come at it again. "He said it didn't matter. About me, I mean. They didn't care what I did any more. They had what they wanted." He stopped again. I watched anger drive apology off his face. "I just wanted out. They used that."

"The Cubans are here," I said.

"Fidelistas." He spit that out. "They'll be here anytime. Damned propaganda robots."

"We don't have to let them play."

He nodded slowly. "Either way, the season's ruined for me and you."

I left him standing there in the middle of the room, got what was left of his whiskey, walked across the infield, and took a seat in the visitor's dugout. The co-op folks were singing "We Shall Overcome" and the goddam fireworks filled the sky.

36

But we skipped town for a couple of weeks after that—Memphis and Nashville and Milledgeville—which gave me the slack I needed to set my mind for the invasion of the Fidelistas, as Pinzon called them. I managed to keep from doing much sulking, kept getting good wood on the ball, and went right ahead and let myself get more and more twined up with Pansy. Actually, they were good days. So maybe, without ever quite putting it to myself this way, I was having one more go at freedom, enjoying the space of each day as it passed into the next and carried me closer and closer to a return match with Ratoplan, a match that would be held in the shadow of the slam. If you can't live with the knowledge that it's all going to end, you can't live.

It had the opposite effect on Pinzon. He methodically drank

himself into a stupor every night, and every time he pitched he got shelled. Up till then, his main problem on the mound had been that he preferred flash to consistency, imagination to control. He would've taken a spectacular loss over a competent victory. But now he went out there and consistently served up one fat pitch after another. No trick pitches, no fancy windups, no laughter. He did everything right by the book—the fastball, the curve, and the change—pared down his delivery until it looked like Tom Seaver's, and took his beatings as if he expected them. When Pinzon denied himself flash, he denied himself life.

But our other pitchers more than made up for him. Eversole was Eversole. Franklin Brown was beginning to replace his here-I-come curve with the slider that would become his best pitch. And there were signs that he was learning the hardest thing of all—to win on the days he didn't have his good stuff. On the eighteenth of July, in Milledgeville, Genghis Mohammed pitched his first complete game, a shutout. Even Woodrow Ratliff had a complete game victory, beating Nashville 5–3 and causing their manager, Allie Ransom, to tell a reporter, "There's no way a man should win a game with junk like that." Ratliff took that to be a high compliment.

One night after a game in Milledgeville, Pinzon and I went to Lefty's room and told him it would be fine with us if he decided to back out of the deal with Ratoplan. "If it means I'll have to face that bank rap, then I'll just face it," I said. "It might even work out for the best. Rotenberg thinks I got a fair chance of beating it once and forever."

Then, in a tone so apologetic I wanted to hit him, Pinzon started in about how it was all his fault and how he figured that, no matter what Lefty did, the thing for him to do was to put as much space between himself and Miami as he could. "I'm just hurting the team anyway."

"Because you're going out to the mound with the intention of punishing yourself," Lefty told him.

"I'm no pitcher. Never have been."

"And now you've stopped trying to become one."

I stood up. "Well, don't do nothing on my account." I wasn't in the mood just then to sit around listening to an analysis of Pinzon's attitude.

It brought out the exasperated school marm in Lefty. "It's not *my* decision. Believe it or not, this is an actual team. And the team will make the decision. That's all I've ever agreed to."

"They'll be good players," Pinzon said. "But letting them play will cost you your idea of what a team should be. I've thought about it ever since I came back from making the arrangements in Miami. I made a mistake. I know those people. They're going to use you."

"For what?" Lefty asked him.

That was the question, of course. What good would it do Ratoplan or Castro's Cuba to have a couple or three certified third-world Communists play for a minor-league baseball team in Little Rock, Arkansas?

"Who knows?" Pinzon said. "When I went to them back in May I told them that having two model Cuban ballplayers on a team in Little Rock would counter some of the bad publicity they'd been getting over the Fort Chaffee refugees. But they swallowed it too easy. They must have their own reasons."

He gave me a hangdog look. I stared back hard at him. In an almost pleading tone, he said, "They don't give me explanations, just orders. I told Ratoplan I'd go back to Miami and stay if he'd take the heat off you and leave the team alone. But they don't want that now. They wait till something matters to you, then make you watch them ruin it."

"They won't ruin it," Lefty said. "If our idea isn't big enough to hold a couple of Cubans, we need to find a new one."

Pinzon shook his head. "You don't know them."

"I think they want it to work," Lefty said. "And I think it's Ratoplan's idea. He may believe a minor diplomatic breakthrough in the U.S. will be good for his career. A Caribbean version of Ping-Pong diplomacy."

"I'll tell you this," Pinzon said. "They'll try to run things. And they have no sense of humor."

"That's why they're funny," Lefty told him. Then he walked to the door and opened it for us. "Gonzalo," he said, "I'm not going to pitch you again until I see you laugh."

We closed out that road trip before a Sunday afternoon Ladies' Day crowd in Milledgeville, which seemed like a ladies' town. The stands were packed with girls on a lark from the Georgia State

Women's College and women on a guarded outing from the Georgia State Prison for Women. I hit three long taters for them. It wasn't all that big a feat considering that the Peacock's pitcher, Parker Sash, didn't have anything but prayer and gall. But I think it made the women like me and I felt pretty good about myself.

You live when you can, ready to fight when you have to.

37

Meeting at the frog joint was Cesar Ratoplan's idea. Chez Pierre was a piece of sham Paris that had been built in the center of Little Rock's downtown shopping center. We got there about a half-hour late, around eight-thirty, on account of having to wait while Pinzon worked his way up to the height of greaser chic. And there was so much greaser in that chic that we wouldn't've ever passed inspection at the Chez Pierre if Ratoplan hadn't vouched for us. Lefty looked passable; his suit wasn't exactly new, but it was gray and it was clean and it fit him. He could've been mistaken for one more rumpled liberal. I wore the suit Oklahoma had given me as a parting joke. I don't think the arrogant, bow-tied wimp that worked the door thought much of the cut of it, but he was so staggered by Pinzon's costume he didn't pay me much mind. He stood dumbstruck for what must've been a full minute, taking in the tight, cheap, shining sharkskin suit, the yellow shirt, the wide red tie with rows of white whales floating across it, the dark, slicked-back hair glistening with Brylcreem, the pointed-toed, gold-buckled, black ankle boots, the wide, ignorant, amazed immigrant's smile.

The gussied wimp turned to Lefty. "This one just off the boat?"

I answered. "Actually we just sprung him from Fort Chaffee. We came here hoping to find him a sponsor. He believes in God and hates Castro."

He looked at me then, raising a cultured eyebrow. "Ah. A local wit."

Pinzon tapped him on the shoulder and said, *"Comment allez-vous? Je vais très bien aujourd'hui."*

The quasi-frog said, "The young man has been studying, I see.

Very impressive." He hit the "very" hard. "However, delighted as we would be to serve you gentlemen, I'm afraid all the tables are taken."

"We'll just stand here and wait," Lefty said.

Pinzon tapped the guy. *"Cette cravate vous va à merveille."*

The apprentice frog looked at Pinzon's tie, then at Pinzon, then at me. "Do you think you could control your friend a moment while I summon the owner?"

"Hard to say. You know how emotional them fucking Latins are."

He sniffed twice and left.

Lefty grinned at Pinzon. "This seems to have done wonders for you."

"Les hommes aiment la vie."

"The good ones do," Lefty said, nodding.

By then Ratoplan had spotted us. He got to us just before the manager did. "Is there a problem?" he asked Lefty. Then he looked at Pinzon and shook his head. "Perhaps we should have met at the Burger King."

"Shit, you'd've got mustard all over your vest," I said.

Pinzon said, *"J'étais si maladroit. Il devait me prendre pour un sot."*

"I see you've had your little handbook out again."

"Ce qui me désole, c'est de vous voir si malhereux."

The doorman came back with the owner. He was a Jew in a blue suit. "What is the trouble here?" he asked Ratoplan.

"You Pierre?" I asked him.

He glared at me, rabbi to rabble. "I'm the proprietor, Isaac Morganstern."

"Please accept my apologies, Mr. Morganstern," Ratoplan said. "These men are associates of mine. I arranged to have a business dinner with them here. I assumed they'd have the decency to observe the appropriate codes of dress and behavior. Evidently I overestimated them. But I do assure you they are not the thugs they appear to be." Then he reached inside his suitcoat and hauled out his wallet. "If you could give us a quiet table in some secluded corner, I would be most appreciative."

The Jew didn't look at the wallet. He gave us all the once-over, starting with Pinzon and working his way to Lefty. When he got to Lefty, he knitted his brows, glanced down at the empty left sleeve, then back up at the face. "Aren't you . . . ?"

"Lefty Marks." Lefty stuck out his hand. The damn Jew shook it. I thought he might be stalling for the cops. "I'm honored to have you here, Mr. Marks. I admire the work you've done in southern Arkansas."

I looked at Pinzon. He shrugged. Ratoplan swallowed a mouthful of pride and said, "Lefty and I are associates."

"Not quite," Lefty told Morganstern. "But I have agreed to eat with him. This once."

Then Morganstern shook hands with Pinzon and me. Pinzon wasn't quite ready to give up his act. *"Je m'appelle Gonzalo Pinzon."*

"Enchanté," Morganstern said.

"They play baseball," Ratoplan told him.

Morganstern nodded, gave us a smile, and turned back to Lefty. "I'm not a baseball fan, but I've been told this team of yours is quite something."

"We're winning," Lefty said.

Morganstern led us through the restaurant to Ratoplan's table, telling Lefty on the way about his brother, a lawyer for the Connecticut branch of the ACLU.

It was a small place for respectable people. Tapered candles on the tables, crystal chandeliers from the ceiling. In the far right-hand corner, two old, overdressed fiddlers had a go at highbrow music. Neither of them would've made it with Bob Wills. The customers did what they could to ignore us, but several of them had some trouble tearing their eyes off of Pinzon. He treated a couple of them to a little passing French small talk.

The table was in the far left-hand corner, directly across from the fiddlers. Three guys waited for us there, a young, sleek Cuban, a heavier, older, tough-looking guy, and a well-fed, gray-headed fuck in a good black suit. I thought: An outfielder, a pitcher, and an umpire.

Before we could get sat down, Morganstern said, "We have a private executive dining room if you'd prefer more privacy."

"This'll do," Lefty told him before Ratoplan could say anything.

"Well," Morganstern said, giving us what came damn close to being a shrug. "When you've decided on a meal, I'll send you an appropriate bottle of wine, compliments of the house. Again, Mr. Marks, we are delighted to be able to serve you. And my apologies for the misunderstanding at the door."

He left. A waiter came out and pulled a folding wooden partition out of the wall, closing us off from the rest of the room. After that, he showed us a cute little bow and said, "I'm André. The menu is in French. If you like, I'd be happy to help you with it." He was about twenty and looked damn near as American as I am. He was probably ashamed of it though. I figured him for a French major at Little Rock University.

"I'm quite accustomed to French," Ratoplan said.

The waiter gave us each a menu and went off to conjugate some verbs.

As Ratoplan made the introductions, the Cubans stood to shake hands: Hagio Acribar, Ernesto Guerrero, Dr. Palacios Rubios.

I took in an eyeful of the doctor. "The two ballplayers sick?" I asked Ratoplan.

"Dr. Rubios is one of the preeminent legal and philological minds in all Cuba," Ratoplan explained.

"Not much competition though, is there?" Pinzon said.

Ratoplan showed us the smooth smile. "We believe in cooperation."

We sat back down. Lefty began asking Rubios something in Spanish, but Rubios interrupted him. "Your Spanish seems excellent, Mr. Marks, but this is your country and we shall speak your language."

"Dr. Rubios is fluent in seven languages," Ratoplan told us. I thought about plying him with a dose of Cherokee.

Rubios smiled as if he'd been applauded.

The student-waiter came back. Rubios ordered in French for himself and the two ballplayers. Ratoplan ordered in French. Pinzon ordered in street Spanish, scratching an armpit as he did. The college boy wrote it all down without batting an eye. Lefty ordered in English. I said I'd have what Lefty was having but with plenty of gravy. The waiter left.

Lefty asked Rubios if he'd been in the revolution.

"Only the latter part. I was, however, a longtime opponent of the tyrant Batista. I was forced to spend most of the decade of the 1950s exiled in Spain."

"Ah," Lefty said. "Under the umbrella of the benevolent Generalissimo."

Rubios leaned back in his chair, folded his hands under his chin, and looked down his nose at Lefty. "I procured a false passport and lived under an alias. Always I plotted with other expatriates for the liberation of my homeland."

The waiter came back with two liters of white wine. I ordered a beer. I drink wine when I run out of shaving lotion.

"What went wrong?" Lefty asked Rubios.

"Wrong?"

"With the revolution."

Ratoplan coughed. We sat through a nasty silence. Then Pinzon laughed.

Lefty said, "You seem to have got over your blues, Gonzalo. Might use you in relief tomorrow."

The waiter brought my beer.

Pinzon asked Ratoplan how he was getting along in the Miami drug trade.

Ratoplan gave him a cool, murderous look. "Gonzalo," he said, "you are a disgusting little punk."

"But punks are useful to you, aren't they, Cesar?"

"Only up to a point."

Pinzon put his elbows on the table and spoke directly to Hagio Acribar, the younger ballplayer. "You see, Cesar and his good comrades have determined that the need for hallucinogens, stimulants, depressants, painkillers, any kind of dope, is symptomatic of capitalistic decadence. They believe dope has, or will, replace religion in America. Do you agree?"

Acribar looked from Pinzon to Rubios to Ratoplan and back to Rubios.

"Shut up, Gonzalo," Ratoplan ordered.

"Religion will cease to be the opiate of the masses. Opium will be the opiate of the masses." Pinzon gave us a short, artificial laugh.

"These Americans are overly fond of irony," Rubios explained to Acribar.

"Irony?" Acribar turned a palm up.

"The disease of the pessimist," Rubios said.

"So far," Lefty said, "it's been the pessimist's century."

We sat back and let the waiter serve us some kind of onion soup and a basket of little bread loaves.

Pinzon leaned over his soup and took up where he'd left off with Acribar. "Well, not opium really. You don't handle opiates, do you, Cesar?"

"Gonzalo has always been a most imaginative liar," Ratoplan announced. "This soup is excellent."

"But dope," Pinzon continued. "Mostly cocaine. Planeloads and boatloads of it. They fully intend to cause the Great Imperial Beast to die in paroxysms of delight. Very neat, wouldn't you say? A real service to mankind. Cesar feeds the Monster's disease and at the same time makes the homeland's trade deficit a little less staggering."

"Small bowls," Ernesto Guerrero said, sopping up the dregs of his soup with one of the little loaves. He finished that loaf and reached out and got himself another. "Is your team a good one?" he asked me, then stuck the end of the new loaf in his mouth and tore off a bite.

"*Our* team," I said. "We're all comrades."

He laughed, short and low—but genuine, I thought. A big, irreverent man. A Cuban redneck. I might like him.

"We got a chance to win a pennant this year," I said. "God knows what we'll do after that."

"In the winter you should come to Cuba. It is good baseball there."

Ratoplan harrumphed through smirking lips. "Certainly that would be a relief to the Arkansas police."

"Oklahoma," I lied. "I'm clean in Arkansas."

"You know," Hagio Acribar said, smiling at his own ignorance. "I had thought this Arkansas was in Canada."

"It used to be," Pinzon said. "But they traded it for Saskatchewan."

Isaac Morganstern himself rolled the main course out on a big tray. Serving us, he asked if everything had been satisfactory thus far. Had we concluded our business? If we liked he'd remove the partition. Ratoplan politely declined. Well, then, would there be anything else? Another beer for you, Mr. Durham? You bet. Guerrero ordered one too.

I don't know what the others had. Lefty and I ate doctored-up summer squash, asparagus drowned in white sauce, and a young duck in an orange-looking glaze. It wasn't bad, but most of it would've been better rolled up in a good cornmeal batter and fried in hog fat.

"These restaurants are never quite French," Ratoplan said. "In a city such as this, the proper ingredients are extremely difficult to procure." He glanced at Rubios, who gave him a gourmet nod. "And in truth," he went on, "I daresay there aren't a dozen people within a hundred miles of here capable of appreciating genuine French cuisine."

"You get much beef in Cuba?" Pinzon asked Rubios.

"Some. Certainly. Enough. Our research has demonstrated that it causes potentially high levels of uric acid in the body."

"Ballplayers get meat," Guerrero said.

"And men who can follow orders in ten languages," Lefty added.

"How should I account, Mr. Marks, for your persistent rudeness?" Rubios asked.

"Indigestion," Lefty said, "compounded by intelligence."

Ernesto Guerrero, having finished everything on his plate but some of the sauce, broke one of the bread loaves in half and started sopping. I left the sauce on my plate and just ate the bread.

Ratoplan scooted his chair a few inches back, crossed his legs, folded his hands in his lap, and nodding toward his plate, said, "Quite acceptable."

"Cesar even eats like a revolutionary," Pinzon said to Acribar. "Notice how he saved a few bites of meat for the kitchen help."

The waiter cleared the table and then brought us each a piece of pastry and some coffee in a midget's cup. Ratoplan didn't want his pastry. Guerrero ate it.

"Well," Ratoplan sighed, giving his vested stomach a fond pat, "I suppose it's time we got down to business."

Guerrero lit up a cigar and asked me if ours was a fastball league. I told him the minors were mostly for young guys now and that young guys were signed because they could either throw or hit the hard one.

"Ah. I will win for you some games then, heh?"

"I'm certain both you and Hagio are well above the caliber of the players in the—what is it?—Dixie Association." Rubios ended that with a smug, professor's grin.

"Yes," I said. "Freedom will eat away at a man's skills."

Pinzon cleared his throat and rapped his knuckles three times on the table. "It has occurred to me," he said, "that no one has grasped the full moment of this historic occasion. Fidel Castro may finally be granted the opportunity to make his mark on American baseball."

Ratoplan nodded. "I see. Yes. It's your old Fidel Begs a Tryout routine."

"Glad you're so fond of it. When was it, Cesar? Forty-six, '47? Well, I don't suppose a year or so here or there matters much, does it? It has to be after '44, when he won his best all-around-school-athlete-in-Cuba prize. And before '48, when our Caribbean Messiah, then a law student at dear old Havana U, led the students in a street fight against the Fascist police. Defending university autonomy, I believe. Academic freedom. How bourgeois." He stopped, took a sip of wine, shook his head. "Pardon me, Dr. Rubios, while I savor the irony of that." Then he leaned forward, elbows on the table. "Now, of course, all students of literature are free to read either Sholokhov or Jack London."

Rubios turned to Lefty. "You are an amazing people. While millions of people starve, liberals in the United States wax eloquent over the right of some drunken novelist to describe homosexual ruttings."

"I also wax eloquent, Dr. Rubios, over the fact that while millions starve, socialist bureaucrats fatten themselves in French restaurants."

Before Rubios could reply, Pinzon said, "But, my God, I've digressed. Where was I, Cesar?"

"Lost." Ratoplan, who seemed to have resigned himself to whatever might happen, took a long drag off a Benson & Hedges.

"You were speaking about Fidel's time as a player of baseball," Ernesto Guerrero said. He looked to be enjoying himself.

"Ah, yes. Forty-six or '47. A year here or there. The rugged schoolboy athlete. So. Fidel sent a letter to Clark Griffith, the hardline Marxist owner of the Washington Senators. If you're going to play, play in the belly of the beast. 'I am one hell of pitcher,' he wrote. 'Please give me shot at bigs. I make you very happy.' The Griffiths, knowing Cubans work cheap, dispatch a scout. 'Fair fastball,' he reports. 'Average control. Poor curve. No change. Bad temper. Big ego. Belongs in the cane fields.'" Pinzon tilted his head to the right and shook it slowly and sadly. "And so, comrades, was the man who fanned Batista condemned to the bushes."

"Bushes?" Hagio Acribar looked from Pinzon to Rubios.

"A preposterous pun," Rubios explained, "to end a preposterous tale."

"Told by a preposterous fool," Ratoplan added.

"Thank you. There'll be nothing else," Ratoplan said. His tone threw me off for a second, but then I saw the waiter. Ratoplan lifted a long, sleek wallet out of the inside pocket of his suitcoat and gave the waiter an American Express card.

"A card-carrying Communist," Pinzon said.

"I have become tired a little," Hagio Acribar told us.

Pinzon nodded. "It's way past curfew in Havana."

"One sad joke after another," Ratoplan said. "Perhaps before we confront the business that occasioned this convivial evening, you could provide us with a final witticism and be done."

Pinzon raised his glass again. "Cuba libra," he said.

Ernesto Guerrero laughed. Ratoplan arched his aristocrat's eyebrow.

"Why do you laugh?" Rubios asked Guerrero.

"The beer is good for laughing."

Ratoplan set fire to another Benson & Hedges, then looked down and blew smoke in his lap. Looking back up, he told Lefty, "I've made arrangements for Hagio, Ernesto, and Dr. Rubios to reside at the Champ Hadley Hotel through the fifteenth of September. Your season ends, I believe, on the thirteenth?"

"What position does Dr. Rubios play?" Lefty asked.

Ratoplan flicked his cigarette over the ashtray. "Dr. Rubios will serve as their interpreter. Though, as you've seen, both Hagio and Ernesto speak English, neither has been in this country before and certainly cannot be expected to deal unaided with the intense media exposure that will now inevitably come to them. Dr. Rubios is a man of the world. He will be an invaluable adviser to them."

"I speak Spanish," Lefty said. "Gonzalo speaks Spanish. Woodrow Ratliff speaks Spanish. We don't need an interpreter."

"This has gone far beyond mere baseball. Ernesto and Hagio will be forced to become Cuban ambassadors, a role for which they have no training. Dr. Rubios . . ."

"Ernesto and Hagio can try out Thursday morning at nine. If they want to play for us and we vote to let them, they'll have to agree to live at the Home with the rest of us. They'll get no special favors. They'll be free to talk as much or as little to the press as they want. You and Dr. Rubios are free to come and sit in the stands, like any other spectator."

Ratoplan crushed his smoke in the tray. "We can't agree to that."

Lefty pushed back from the table and stood. "Fine," he said. "It would be simpler that way."

Pinzon and I glanced at each other, then stood with Lefty.

"What is this happening?" Guerrero wondered. "I have come for baseball."

"Nine o'clock Thursday," Lefty said. "Be glad to see you then."

"I will come."

Ignoring Guerrero, Ratoplan addressed Lefty. "Perhaps you should temper your haughtiness by reminding yourself of our friend Hog Durham's, shall I say, legal predicament."

"I'll take care of my own predicaments, Slick," I told our friend Cesar Ratoplan.

"Thanks for the meal," Lefty told Ratoplan. "Enjoy your flight home, Dr. Rubios."

"You are making a grievous error," Ratoplan threatened.

"Quelles que soient vos idées, vous êtes libre ici," Pinzon told the immigrants.

And we left.

38

"They think they can use us," Lefty admitted at the end of his pre-vote clubhouse speech. "But I think we can turn it around on them." He had left out Pinzon's part in it all and the effect the whole thing might have on my future.

There wasn't much doubt about the Cubans' ability. Hagio Acribar might've been born in an outfield. He went after a fly ball with a speed and grace and assurance that couldn't be learned— refined, sure, but not learned. With him and Julius and Atticus Flood in our outfield, we might never see another gapper bound to the wall. And at the plate he had the good quick wrists that let a man hold back until the last instant and then snap the bat at the ball, the kind of wrists that give you a chance even when you're fooled. Of course, you can never quite tell with a young hitter, but if you're scouting you bet on a kid with hands and wrists like Acribar's.

Unless you got in the box and actually tried to hit against him, Ernesto Guerrero didn't look like much. Even then you kept thinking it was more you than him, that you'd mash the next one he served up. I stood in against him myself for what must've been a good five minutes. Every so often, I nailed one, but overall I'd have to say he got the best of me. He threw a fastball (85 mph, tops) he could make sink or sail, a slider he jerked down, and a straight change, all of them coming out of exactly the same compact motion. The slider didn't break much, but it broke late. The change never came until you'd forgotten it. The fastball always looked just a little different than it had the time before. All a pitcher has to do is to keep the hitter just a fraction off. Guerrero played that fraction.

So, they were good. But then I didn't expect Castro to send us another one of his sisters.

A short, nervous silence followed Lefty's speech. Then Bullet Bob said, "We open it to these two fucks, it ain't baseball no more. We been going good. Hell, we got a shot at the flag. We need these boys like a whore needs romance. It might sound good, but it changes everything. It was bad enough when Susan started in. All them damn reporters and all. But this'll make that look like a high school homecoming."

Jew Bernstein said, "Look at it like this, Bob. The more attention we draw, the better your chance of making it back to the bigs."

"I got to use some damn Communist to make it, I'll stay where I am." Then he turned toward Lefty and went on. "There ain't no point in saying no more about it. Ain't even much point in voting. You got the votes. You got Hog out of jail, you got Susan on the team, you got them boys that's played for you for years. Ain't a one of us, really, that ain't obliged to you one way or the other. So if this is what you want, you'll get it. But I want you to know I don't like it. Don't like it at all. You got no call to draw us into this political horseshit. I think you might ought to ask yourself if maybe you ain't been taking too much joy out of seeing your name in the paper."

And then we all watched Lefty, who seemed to be taking the

charge seriously. After several seconds, he said, "I don't think that's true. But it could be. If you think Bob's right, vote no. If you just don't like the idea, vote no. I don't want to force this on anybody."

I noticed Pinzon looking around with his conscience in his eyes and I worried for a minute he might stand up and announce that this was all his fault, that it wasn't Lefty's idea at all. I didn't want that, and didn't like the serious way the boys seemed to be mulling over Bob's speech. I didn't want them voting me into Ratoplan's grip and I didn't want to tell them that's what they'd be doing, so I went into my stand-up con: "Boys, ole Bob there's drawing him a nice pension and probably the way he's going he'll get another shot at the bigs. Some of you have real lives you can turn back to when this folds up. You might even get yourself a job if you want one—though, mind you, I'm not wishing that on none of you. It looks like some of you young boys have a future playing ball. And I envy you that. Seems like a good life. But this here's just a little time-out for me. A year's dodge. And when it's over, it's back to the same old goddam dread and darkness. So what I'm telling you is I need the money. You saw what Susan did for us. It brought us an extra $350 a month apiece. I know it ain't much in this day and age, but the shameful truth of it is I've done years for taking less.

"Now I don't hold with Castro's politics, but I've met these two Cubans and they seem all right. We start judging a man by his government and we're all up Shit Creek. There's no doubt but what these boys can play ball, and if we let them play for us, Bob's right, there'll be fans sitting up on the roof. We'll be selling so much beer, Lefty's co-op is liable to have to set up a brewery. We'll be raking in the cash, boys, eating green and shitting silver. I can't see that the rest of it matters much. Whatever happens off the field, a baseball game's still a baseball game. I figure I can hit just as good with a houseful of folks howling at me as I can otherwise. Maybe better: I've done some of my best work out of spite. So what it comes down to for me is just money. I'm going to need me a cushion at the end of this little season of peace and monthly wages."

Well, standing in slammer shade will dim your view of duty. So, my spiel wasn't exactly high-minded. But it wasn't all shuck. And it carried the day.

39

LEFTY MARKS: THIS TIME HE'S GONE TOO FAR
By Wilbur Haney

There is an old line about sports and politics. They don't mix.

One is hard put to understand how it ever came to this. But then, no one has ever denied that Lefty Marks was shrewd.

He was allowed to have his team here in Little Rock because the city needed and deserved one. And because the Jackson Powerhouse folded, which left the Dixie Association with just seven teams.

Scheduling problems then, and the need for a team in a good baseball town.

"He conned us," a longtime city councilman remarked. "We knew his reputation, but he seemed to have mellowed during the past few years. No demonstrations or boycotts. Just that produce business down in Magnolia. He was smooth. He made us believe he'd always missed baseball. Nothing political about it, he said, he just loved the game and wanted back in. I don't know. Maybe we wanted a team too bad."

Maybe we all did.

The University of Arkansas gave us good football in the fall, good basketball in the winter. But after the Cardinals moved their AA team to Springfield, our summers seemed a little empty.

So now we have the cotton bowl, the Final Four and Lefty Marks.

And Fidel Castro.

Think about it. Fidel Castro.

No one should be surprised. From the beginning Dr. G. Forrest Bushrod has been warning that it might come to something like this. Too many dismissed him as a religious crank.

So the question has to be, what can we do now?

The city is considering revoking Marks's lease on Arkansas Field. But no one doubts that he would take them to court over that. And, most important, no one doubts that he would win.

First, a temporary injunction, then, most likely, the whole bag. Like so many radicals, Lefty Marks knows how to use the courts he so reviles. Unfortunately, he holds a lease which contains no provision against using the field as a center for communist propaganda.

Judge Lee Stuart Jackson, Commissioner of the Dixie Association and a man who has kept his league afloat while others sank, is powerless in this matter. He favors expelling the Reds and granting wins by forfeit to their scheduled opponents. Sensible, it would seem. But the expulsion of a league member requires the unanimous vote of the remaining owners. And Stephen Gabbard, the eccentric Oxford owner, has announced that he would vote against expulsion.

So that's that.

Do the two Cubans have their papers in order? If so, how did Marks manage that? The immigration authorities seem unwilling or unable to deport them. Why? And why does Lefty Marks wish to overthrow a system he uses so cleverly to his advantage?

So the question is again, and finally: what can we do?

For now, just this: stay away.

Maybe we can't stop Lefty Marks. But no one can make us support him.

40

It took the gleaming yankee TV boys a couple of days to bag up their cocaine and get to us, took them that long to realize this was actually happening in Little Rock, Arkansas, way down in barefoot Faubus country, that something new and maybe, by God, interesting was going on in that hick province.

But they made it down for Acribar and Guerrero's first game, Saturday the twenty-sixth of July, against the Oxford Fury before a packed and raucous house at Arkansas Field. And they interviewed the young Fidelista who looked like Valentino and told them he was proud to represent a new hope here in the dying heart of imperialism, and they interviewed the veteran Havana pitcher who told them you could break a great hitter's bat with a semi-pro fastball if you threw it to the right spot at the right time, and they interviewed the one-armed Magnolia Communist who offered them long ears of golden corn and lugs of bright-red tomatoes.

The crowd was so big that during batting practice Woodrow Ratliff took a brace and bit and drilled holes in the outfield wall so the kids out there could see in. And a few minutes later when I was out in right jacking around with Julius, Pinzon came up, handed me a pair of binoculars, and pointed toward the roof of the University Medical Center. Sure enough, up there in the rooftop chainlink cage that had been built for them to air out in, the boys from the moon ward looked down on us.

"They put me in one of those once," Pinzon said. "You could see the beach."

"Who do you think they're rooting for?" I asked.

"They're just hoping the stadium'll burn down."

Preacher Bushrod and his shotgun Christians, spurred some, I suspect, by Wilbur Haney's praise, had returned that day with their pickets and placards. But by game time the crowd had overwhelmed them, and finally even some of the faithful yielded to temptation and went into the park to see real Cuban Communists play real baseball. During the home half of the fourth inning, I heard a clamoring above me and stepped out to take a look and there was Bushrod, his proxy legislator, John Schicklgruber, beside him, standing on the roof of our dugout haranguing the crowd: " 'Woe unto them that call evil good, and good evil; that put darkness for light, and light for darkness; that put bitter for sweet, and sweet for bitter.' "

And so on and suchlike. In a cool blue summer suit, Schicklgruber stood short and stiff in the shade of his Republican prophet—the prim, outraged deacon and the middle-class messiah. Another laugh on the Lord. Then, from ten or fifteen rows back, somebody caught Schicklgruber just over the heart with a thrown hot dog.

Schicklgruber jerked back, looked down at the hot dog, fingered the mustard on his lapel, looked back at the crowd, and flashed a worn smile, then took it back and began glancing around nervously for a way out.

"Get your ass out of the way. We're trying to watch the game," somebody yelled at Bushrod. Not bad theology, I thought.

To his credit, I guess, Bushrod stood up to them, heaving chunks of scripture at them, threatening them with hellfire. Folks flung chunks of ice at him.

"Christ," Lefty said. "We don't need this. A dead preacher on the dugout roof might do us in." He got up and started trying to talk Bushrod down.

I noticed some of the Oxford players standing on the top step of their dugout and laughing at the goings-on.

Schicklgruber lowered himself into our dugout, brushed himself off, and spent a few seconds trying to wipe a look of confusion off his face. Then he looked up and down our dugout and apparently decided Stump Guthrie might be a sympathizer. He offered Stump his hand and said, "Hello, I'm John P. Schicklgruber, your Republican candidate for the U.S. Senate. I'd appreciate your consideration in November."

Stump shook the hand. "Stump Guthrie," he said. "I'm a catcher. I don't vote."

"Good. Good. Fine," Schicklgruber said through his worn smile.

"You can get out through that door," Ratliff told him. "Then go out the door to your right and you'll be on the ramp."

"Thank you." He gave us a big, openhanded, politician's wave on his way out.

Lefty wasn't having much luck with Bushrod. Atticus Flood stood at the plate trying to hit, but I doubt whether anybody in the place was watching him.

"You've picked a bad place. Let me help you down," Lefty said.

Bushrod kept ignoring him.

Somebody threw a handful of ice at the preacher. I stood on the edge of the steps with my back to the field and looked the situation over. Bushrod was reciting the Twenty-third Psalm as if it were a curse.

"Damn it, Bushrod," Lefty said. "If you have to preach, get down here and do it in front of the dugout. You're going to break your neck up there."

I leaned forward, put my palms down on the roof, and pushed myself up on it. I walked over to Bushrod, wrapped my arms around him, lifted him, carried him to the edge, and lowered him to safety. His sermon never slacked. The crowd gave me a nice hand.

A second or two after he hit the ground, Bushrod shifted into

Jeremiah. " 'Behold, I am against thee, O thou most proud, saith the Lord God of hosts; for thy day is come, the time that I will visit thee. And the most proud shall stumble and fall and none shall raise him up; and I will kindle a fire in his cities, and it shall devour all round about him.' "

He stopped for a breath. The iceman fired again. I grabbed Bushrod's elbow and pulled him down the steps and to the locker room door. When I reached for the doorknob, he jerked his elbow free and glared up and down our bench at all the laughing infidels. "Do you know what you're doing?" His voice boomed at first, then settled some. "This man"—he motioned toward Lefty—"is doing evil, and you're going along with him. Think, God help you, think." He focused on Stump Guthrie. "Isn't there one real Christian among you?"

Stump said, "Most of my folks are, but they don't yell about it."

Bushrod went into the locker room. I followed him and showed him the door to the ramp. His disciples were out there singing "Beulah Land."

And Guerrero went seven against Oxford, picking up the win, 4–2.

41

And so it went for nearly another week. Lefty started Hagio Acribar every other day and got him in for an inning or two in the other games. He was damned good at second or third and even better in the outfield. I thought he'd be a consistent line-drive hitter, but actually it was a little tough to judge since four of those games were against Plaquemine. Hell, Lefty started Susan against them one day, giving me a rest I didn't need, and she went 2 for 4, a bunt single and then her first clean double.

Ernesto Guerrero had an easy time of it in his second start. We got five runs in the second, two more in the third, and he coasted home from there with a five-hit shutout. Afterwards, in the clubhouse, the reporters couldn't get much out of him. He guzzled beer, sucked on a fat cigar, and no matter what question was asked, talked about the art of changing speeds. So they had to be satisfied with what they could get from Acribar: "We wish to be friends with United States." "In my country the poor are given food and have work and are not poor." "In Cuba the worker in the fields is as honored as the doctor of medicine." He said it all through a young, clean, earnest mouth. Nobody believed a word of it.

The rest of us answered questions in predictable ways: we didn't necessarily approve of Castro, but Guerrero and Acribar were good players and seemed like nice guys and anyway all we were doing was giving them a taste of freedom. Lefty, of course, tended to go into considerable more detail, sometimes beginning with the way we'd swindled Colombia out of Panama and then tracing our Latin American policy all the way up to the current thugs in El Salvador.

The stadium filled up every day with a crowd that was part hostile, part friendly, but mostly just amused, this being the kind of circus that didn't often stop in Little Rock. Bushrod's Christians kept coming, naturally, and howling about fire and retribution, but most of the fans just saw them as another part of the show. And Bushrod and Schicklgruber kept their act in the parking lot.

Pumpsie Narvaez came over to our dugout before one of the games and told us we'd abused his hospitality and would have to pay for it, but then he went back and commenced petting another one of the Black Orchid girls. So I didn't think much of his threat. With the team he had, what could he do to us except refuse to give us rooms at Fort Saint Ignatius when we were in Plaquemine?

During the game Susan started in my place, I spent a couple of hours hawking beer in the stands and I didn't see anything of either Ratoplan or Rubios. I figured they'd decided to give Lefty his way for a while, give Guerrero and Acribar room to prove they were ballplayers, and then make some kind of propaganda move. But I hoped that just having their boys here, playing in the U.S.A., would be diplomacy enough for them. And maybe they were just off somewhere together, sharing a bottle of good wine, cussing freedom in Latin.

Lefty gave Guerrero and Acribar a room together out at the Home, and they seemed to settle right in. Acribar was a notch too serious and polite for my taste, but now and again you could get him to laugh at himself, and it was hard to just dislike him outright. And Guerrero, he was another ballplayer, full of tales about old games and drunken fights over loose women. Except for his accent he seemed as American as the rest of us. About the fifth or sixth night after he'd moved in, he announced he'd gone as long as a man could without a woman and started trying to talk Pinzon into taking him downtown and helping him rustle up some whores.

It was after supper but before dark and we were sitting around on the porch. When he saw that Guerrero had Pinzon interested, Lefty stood up and said, "Don't take the co-op truck." Then he went upstairs to his room.

"You boys don't mind company, I got a notion to go with you," Stump Guthrie said. "We can take the GMC."

"Ay, cabellero," Guerrero said. "Come along, my friend Stump. The more the happier."

"Group rates," Pinzon said.

Joe Buck Cantwell gave Pinzon the cold eye for a second or two. "You sure you can get the women?"

"Police-inspected," Pinzon said. "I know every pimp in Little Rock."

Joe Buck stood up. "Well, I ain't been getting much offered to me free lately. Let me go up and hit my stash."

Pansy gave my thigh a possessive pat and got up and went inside. Julius and Susan followed her.

"That mean you're free to come along?" Pinzon asked.

"I'm afraid if I did it'd be whores for me from then on out."

"That way you get your money's worth," Stump Guthrie said.

"That goddam truck's part mine," Bullet Bob growled.

"Come along," Joe Buck offered. "A piece'd do you good."

"I never paid for it in my life," Bob told them. "And I damn-sure ain't going to start in by doing it in front of no Communist." He took a violent swig from his quart of Coors.

"I will not watch," Guerrero said through an easy smile.

"Aw, hell, Bob," I said. "It's pure capitalism. Your old pride'd be standing up for free enterprise."

"Everything's a goddam joke, ain't it?"

"I will tell Hagio," Guerrero said. "He wishes to learn United States way of life."

While Guerrero did that, Bob strung together a few warning sentences about patriotism and virtue. When he finished, I said, "And remember, boys, ever' one of them girls is somebody's sister."

Pinzon said, "You can pay extra and get an only child."

Guerrero came back down leading about half the team. "Hagio is tired," he said. "But we will have plenty for a good time."

I walked with them out to the truck and watched them pile in. Joe Buck, Stump, and Rainbow, being owners, rode in the cab. Pinzon, Guerrero, Jefferson Mundy, Atticus Flood, and Jew Bernstein got in the back.

"You should come with us," Guerrero told me.

"I don't like lines," I said. "What's wrong with Franklin?" I asked Mundy.

"Girl in Magnolia." He and Flood had a laugh at that.

"Won't be any lines where we're going," Pinzon said. He told Joe Buck to drive to the Champ Hadley Hotel.

A little off key, Guerrero started singing "God Bless America." By the time Joe Buck got the truck moving, the others had chimed in with him.

I watched them out of sight, trying to make myself take some pride in the fact that this was the first time I'd ever deliberately kept myself out of a whoremongering jaunt. I wasn't altogether successful.

Back in the house, I found Bob sitting glum on the couch. "Too much brooding won't do for a reliever," I said.

"That's the damn truth."

I guess I should've stayed down there, drank a few beers, and had a go at cheering him up. But I needed Pansy to show me I'd done right by myself, so I went up to her and, as a Tahlequah preacher I knew liked to say, wallered in the trough of sin. Because it was sin I wanted at the time. Not love.

It must've been one-thirty or two when the good-time boys came roaring down the hall to their rooms. I left Pansy's room, which I'd pretty well moved into by then, met Pinzon in the hall, and asked him how it had gone.

"Everybody's happy, everybody's broke. All the white boys had a black girl, all the black boys had a white one. Guerrero had one of each. Bernstein asked for an Arab but had to settle for a mulatto."

"How about yourself?"

"Sweet thing of French extraction named Lulu. She's saving up for a home in the country." He turned and took a couple of loose-jointed steps down the hallway, then stopped and turned back around. "Oh, Eversole was there. Seemed to know his way around."

"Eversole? You saw him?"

"Yeah." He gave me a drunk shrug and a big grin and headed on to his room.

A couple of hours later there was another commotion: a strong, loud woman's voice, something heavy getting knocked over, glass breaking.

I stepped into the hall just in time to see Bobbie Sampson push Bullet Bob out her door. He landed on his ass and skidded into the opposite wall. Bobbie was naked and all Bob had on was a pair of green nylon socks. She went over to him, jerked him to his feet, and caught him flush on the mouth with a good straight right. Bob bounced off the wall and fell facedown on the floor. Bobbie rolled him over with her right foot. Looking into his small, glazed eyes, she said, "Don't you ever try that again, you fat, stupid pig."

Bob opened his mouth and bubbles of spit and blood dribbled out. "Fuck you," he told her.

She drew her right foot back, but I got to her and pulled her away. "Don't kill him," I said.

She gave me a hard look. "Why not?"

"General principles." I tried a grin, realized it was stupid, and took it back.

"Goddam dyke," bubbled out of Bob's mouth.

She took a step toward him. I grabbed her arm. She spun and threw a right at me, a roundhouse I had time to block with a forearm. There was a time I'd've decked her then, no matter how right she was. "Don't hit *me*," I warned her.

"Don't get in the way."

She turned back around to Bob but saw Lefty standing over him. Bob had passed out. Lefty gave her a sorrowful look. "Shit," he said.

The sight of Lefty looking so weary took some of the anger out of Bobbie. "I forgot to lock my goddam door."

"Shouldn't be necessary," he said. He looked back down at Bob, a soft lump on the floor. "Shit," he said again.

"I'll drag him to his room," I said. "We can figure the rest of it out in the morning." I stepped between them, put my hands under Bob's arms, and started backing down the hall.

I heard Lefty say, "I'm sorry, Bobbie."

"I'm all right. He was too drunk to be dangerous. Anyway, I knew it was a chance we took when we stayed on." She went into her room.

As I backed through Bob's doorway, I looked up and saw Lefty, his back to me, his head down, his shorts drooping, an old, forlorn, one-armed figure under a dim light.

Bob, you son of a bitch, I thought, what a chickenshit way out.

42

Bobbie drove the busload of us to the park the next day, where, before another throng, we beat Plaquemine without any trouble. Bob didn't go to the game, though, and when we got back to the Home, he wasn't there either. I asked Lefty about it, but he claimed not to know any more than I did, said Bob had refused to talk to him that morning.

Then, about half an hour after supper, Bob called and asked me to meet him in the bar of the Champ Hadley Hotel. "Just you," he said. "I ain't ready to deal with Lefty yet."

I explained it to Lefty and then drove the co-op truck into town.

Bob sat at a corner table over a beer, smiling with busted lips at Bull Cox. It didn't take any gypsy to size it up from there, and I almost turned around right then, drove back to the Home, and left them to one another. But I decided I might as well go on and hear it said.

I took a chair at their table.

"Bull flew in special," Bob told me.

Bull pointed at his whiskey. "Drink?"

"No," I said. "I'm on parole." I looked at Bob. He studied his beer bottle.

"Good," Bull said. "It's a fine evening and I feel like a walk. Barmaid tells me there's a statue up the street I ought to take a look at. Cost the city a fortune." He shook his head.

They downed their drinks and we walked east on Capitol toward the Metro Mall, Little Rock's try at saving the center of its bad heart.

"They ought to've let the niggers kept it," Bull said. "They're just fooling themselves with this."

There were a few respectable whites headed for the frog joint, but most of the folks we saw were black and young, the girls in colored hose and platform shoes and tight, gleaming disco shorts, the boys caped and glad-eyed under wide-brimmed hats.

"Gonna dance all night," Bull said. "Then switch partners and go all day tomorrow. Forever and ever, Amen."

"Fat men ought not poke fun at dancers," I told him.

"Life ain't a goddam party," he answered. "They're dancing on food stamp money."

When we got to the brick-paved mall, we stopped a minute to figure out which way to turn. The plaza wasn't crowded—courting couples wandering whispering along, drunks on benches catching their second wind. Just across the way from us an old white man raised a brown paper bag to his mouth.

We followed Bull up to him. Bull asked him where the statue was.

The old man had himself another swig and said, "This used to be a bus stop." He offered the bottle to Bull, who shook his head. "I had a little business of my own, little laundrymat out on Roosevelt Road, just this side of the coliseum. But the niggers moved in and kept ripping up the washers and breaking into the change machine. The cops shot one one night, but that didn't stop them, just made them worse."

Bull shook his head in sympathy. "It ain't right."

The drunk went on. "My daddy was pastor of the Gaines Street Church of the Nazarene for twenty-seven years. Good church then. Ain't been a white man set foot in it the last fifteen years now."

"They probably turned it into a dance hall," Bull said.

The man held up his bottle. "This is all I got left. You want some?"

Bull shook his head again. "You ought to make a move," he advised. "Start over. No percentage in being a drunk." I guess Bull had tired of encouraging self-pity. "You know where that statue is?"

The drunk hung his head and sloshed his bottle northward. "It ain't worth seeing."

"I wouldn't be surprised," Bull said.

He started north and Bob followed. "It's the other way," I told them.

They came back. "You could've spared us that little scene," Bull said.

"Man needed counseling."

A cop guarded the sculpture.

"What the hell is it?" Bob asked.

"Beats me," the cop said.

It was a smooth dark-metal figure, fifteen or twenty feet tall. Bullet Bob tapped on it. "Hollow."

The inscription on the pedestal said the thing was called "Standing Figure Knife Edge" and that Henry Moore had made it.

"How much they give for this piece of shit?" Bull asked the cop.

The cop shook his head. "I can't recall offhand. It was a pretty penny, though. The chief said that for the same price we could've got a helicopter. Lot of people yelled about it."

"They ought to done more than that," Bull said. He circled the thing slowly, giving it his full attention. "Niggers like it?" he asked the cop.

"No. Far as I know nobody does. They got me guarding it to keep them from taking a hacksaw to it."

"Maybe they ought to paint it purple and stick a big hat on it," Bull said. He grinned. Bob and the cop laughed out loud.

Smiling, the cop said, "Then they could put a sign on the bottom of it saying 'In Memory of Martin Luther King.' "

They all laughed at that. Then a serious look came over Bob. "Didn't there used to be a Henry Moore that played for the Razorbacks a few years back?"

Bull ran it through his memory, then nodded. "Must've been a good twenty years ago. Good halfback. Got the first down when you needed it. Just fair speed, but tough as a Christian in China."

They studied the sculpture again.

"It can't be the same man," Bob said.

Bull shook his head. "I don't know," he said to Bob before looking straight at me and delivering the rest of his spiel. "Lefty Marks used to be a big-league ballplayer and look at him now. There's no predicting how a man'll turn out. The man that made this might've been a halfback in better days."

"Could be," I agreed. "It's the second law of thermodynamics. Sooner or later everything turns to shit."

"Not everything," Bull said seriously. He looked at the cop. "Is it the same man?"

"I don't know." He seemed confused. His memory probably didn't go back beyond Lance Alworth. "I never heard nobody say it was."

"They wouldn't," Bull said. "Nobody likes it when a ballplayer goes bad." He shook his head one more time. "I've seen all I care to. Don't let them get you down," he said to the cop.

"Y'all come back and see us."

"We got no choice," Bull told him.

On the way back, we saw that the drunk had passed out on his bench. "That's why it's going bad," Bull said. "We got too many that fold up like a damn accordion first time anybody gives them a little squeeze."

"How about you and me going over and seeing what's left in that bottle?" I said to Bob.

"I ain't no thief."

"Bob's going to straighten up," Bull told me. "And I'm here to offer you a chance to do it too. Bob says you got a good heart. Let's go back to the bar and talk about it over drinks. I'm buying."

"Aw, shucks," I said. "I guess I'd best be getting on."

"Made a little phone call to your parole officer," he said.

"Interested in criminology, are you?"

"Hell, I'm a sheriff."

"Bull's all right, Hog," Bullet Bob told me. "You'd like him if you got to know him." It was more of an apology than an argument.

"Bob," I said, "if you got to go down, just go down. Don't try pulling somebody else down with you."

"Parole officer—what's his name now?—he said things'd be a lot easier on you if you'd switch teams." He didn't even sound serious. I figured he'd just promised Bob he'd make the offer.

"You could bring Pansy along," Bob promised.

"I've ate some shit in my time, Bob," I said. "But I can't recall ever volunteering for it."

At the hotel entrance, Bull stopped, turned, and planted himself a couple of steps in front of me. "Could be I'm pissing in the wind; I don't know. Maybe with everything else curdling like it is, baseball ain't worth getting lathered up over. But it's about all I got left. And you can mark my word on this: I don't care what I have to do; I ain't losing no pennant race to no goddam Communist."

He entered the hotel leaving Bob and me together outside. "You're making a mistake, Bob," I said. "But I guess you already know that."

He looked down and rearranged his feet. "I don't fit in here no more."

"Well," I said, "most of us don't fit in anywhere."

He looked back up and offered me his hand. After a second, I took it.

"I wish it hadn't come to this," he told me.

"It didn't have to."

43

We didn't miss Bob the next afternoon. Eversole threw a shutout at Plaquemine, which he probably could've done left-handed. I jerked a couple out of the park and that might've dulled the edge of my anger and guilt if I'd been facing real pitching. The half-dozen pitchers Pumpsie Narvaez abused the mound with that day threw nothing but cripples. And Pumpsie himself didn't even bother to make the usual trips to the mound. When one of his jokes played out, he just waved in another one. He never moved out of his dugout, sat way off to the far end by himself, minus even the customary ostentatious piece that day, looking glum and vengeful.

After the game Lefty gave the reporters fifteen minutes with us, then, saying we were going to have a team meeting, shooed them out, called Susan in from the manager's office, where she was dressing, and told us what we already knew.

"Bob Turner has left us. I think you all know why. Both Hog and I tried to convince him to stay—Hog in person and me on the phone." Then he eased into reverse, went back several weeks, and told us how just after Susan had joined us, Bob had asked him to see if any major-league teams were interested in him. "Bob knew they weren't. He knew they had scouts down here. He knew that if they wanted him they'd be making offers. So *I* knew that what he was telling me was that he was beginning to want out. But I made the calls for him and got the answers I knew I'd get. Bob's too old for them to assign to one of their farm teams. To them, he's worth a salary only as a major-leaguer. And they didn't want him there, not just yet, didn't trust him. Last year he got caught drinking in the bullpen a couple of times and caused trouble with the blacks and Latins. They knew he could still pitch, but they didn't think he was good enough to compensate for the problems he would cause. They'd keep an eye on him, they said, and if he made it through this season without passing out on the mound or causing a race riot, well, maybe they'd see about giving him another shot next year in spring training. Might even consider signing him in September, this year, for the stretch run."

He stopped there, picked something I couldn't see off his lower lip, and went on. "When the season started we were the only team willing to give him a chance to do the only thing that matters to him. I'm not telling you anything you don't already know when I tell you Bob's a drunk with a big-league pitch. And I think you'll be honest enough to admit that if he hadn't played for us we wouldn't be sitting here now with a chance for the pennant. In other words, he doesn't owe us anything. We gave him a chance, but by doing that we certainly helped ourselves."

He lifted an eyebrow, lowered it, looked us over, and jerked the story forward again. "Now Bob wants to play for Selma. I could stop him, and I was tempted to. Like the rest of you, Bob signed a contract binding him to this team for a season. But that's just a technicality. The league required it. Even though he doesn't ap-preciate what this means, Bob, as far as I'm concerned, is a free man. I don't intend to do anything to keep him from exercising that freedom. Bull Cox has offered compensation, but that's money I'd as soon not take." He paused again, then finished it. "But it's your decision too. There's no question that his going to Selma will hurt our chances. But even without him, we're a better team than we were when we started."

We were quiet a minute. Then Ernesto Guerrero spoke up. "I am very sad this has happened. I did not wish to bring harm."

"It wasn't you," Franklin Brown said. "It was bound to hap-pen."

"Yeah," I said, "Bob was a drunk and a bigot and if he'd've had the strength for it he'd've been a bully. But by God, he could pitch. And that's all that mattered to us. He didn't like you, Franklin, and you didn't like him, but he saved damn near every game you've won. He's leaving a hole we ain't got anybody to fill and I think we ought to face up to that now and not just drift along and end up whining about it later."

"He might've stayed if we'd listened to him," Stump Guthrie said.

"Maybe," I said. "He might even come back yet if we'd just ship Acribar and Guerrero back to Fidel. But after that we'd have to get his O.K. every time we felt like taking a piss. Hell, he's gone, Stump. We're fools to sit around acting like we don't need him and we're fools to mope along wishing we had him back. I think we ought to sell him. Or, better yet, trade him."

I looked at Lefty. He didn't seem too pleased. "How much did Bull offer you for him?" I asked.

"Five thousand."

"It ain't enough. Bull has to be figuring this means the pennant for him and the shithole for us. I say gouge the son of a bitch. Get every penny you can get, then tell the papers you're donating Bull Cox's money to the ACLU or some such white knight outfit. I'd like to win this damn pennant and I don't think we can do it acting like the Goodwill Charities. Trade him if we can, make them pay if we can't. But Christ, let's don't just roll over."

Julius gave me a hard look. "Nobody's rolling over but you, Hog."

"I wish to offer myself to pitch the relief," Guerrero told us. "I am a starter more, but I have done this job well in my past."

"It is true," Hagio Acribar said.

Lefty nodded. "Maybe we won't need you to do that. When Julius was home over the break he saw a pitcher he thinks can help us. A relief pitcher."

I looked at Julius. He nodded. "How come you haven't said anything about it till now?" I asked.

"He was one of the refugees at Fort Chaffee. Bingo Montana sponsored him and got him a job at the air-conditioner plant in Fort Smith. He's been pitching a couple of nights a week and Sunday for Cherokee Nation. I talked to him about trying out for us, but he was afraid of leaving his job. And you know how Bingo is, they had a tournament coming up and he was doing all he could to make it hard for Jeronimo to leave. And anyway, as long as we had Bob, we really didn't need him."

"But now," Lefty said. "Rheems Air-Conditioning is laying people off and Fort Smith is not a pleasant place for an unemployed Cuban."

"How good is he?" I asked Julius. "Can he come anywhere near taking Bob's place?"

"I hit against him. He comes almost underhand. And hard. His ball jumps ever' which way. And he's just wild enough to keep you scared."

"Jeronimo Velasquez!" Guerrero damn near yelled it. "One goddam good pitcher."

"A traitor," Acribar reminded him.

Guerrero slapped him on the knee. "In this country they say live and let them live."

44

I got this from Shakespeare Creel.

Hog,

Always the same: boredom and sleep, twilight and darkness.

Stay clear.

New cellmate's from Stillwater: quiet, soft; works the crosswords, plays chess, craves sweets, reads Gurdjieff, Ouspensky, Thomas a Kempis, Revelations; stabbed his wife 47 times with a letter opener; she was unfaithful, he heard voices, saw angels with crimsoned swords, she laughed. They gave him a dime, he'll do three. Model prisoner. I let him win at chess and do not laugh.

Reading the Thomas *Cuba*. Up to 350: Hearst, Pulitzer, McKinley, Roosevelt, Spain. My gratitude . . .

Also an Oppenheimer biography. Superficial book. Curious man. Liberal Jew: wanted both power and conscience. Brilliant fool.

Found this: (Oppenheimer, circa 1930) "I have two

loves, physics and the desert. It troubles me that I don't see any way to bring them together."

The American Century, old chum, The American Century: Physics and the Desert.

The guards take Selma. We wager what we have. I bet on you and the straight up chance. Romanticism. Nostalgia. Hope. Lay off the sinker.

If the woman's good, hold on. Find a place and stand on it. Stay out of town. Study the old rivers. Thoreau: "Who hears the rippling of rivers will not utterly despair of anything."

Ergo: dams.

It goes on; maybe it comes round.

Come see me when it's over. I'll be here. Bring smokes and lawyer.

Go to it,
Creel

45

On the long ride out of Arkansas and across Tennessee, we studied the standings and figured our chances.

Team	Won	Lost	Pct.	GB
Selma Americans	53	36	.596	
Arkansas Reds	52	37	.584	1
Nashville Fugitives	48	40	.545	4½
Asheville Wolves	47	42	.528	6
Oxford Fury	45	44	.506	8
Memphis Kings	44	44	.500	8½
Milledgeville Peacocks	43	45	.483	9½
Plaquemine Pirates	22	66	.250	30½

Pinzon, sitting directly across the aisle from me, said, "Last year everyone in the league finished over .500 except Plaquemine. They went 25 and 101."

"Pumpsie's a saint," I said. "Giving himself up the way he does so everybody else can be a winner."

"The amazing thing is that they win one out of five," Pinzon said. "This year they've beat every team in the league at least once except us. Even Selma." He shook his head. "They do have that one hard thrower. But there's not a hitter in the parish."

We rode along quiet for a few minutes. It was hot and getting dark. Up toward the front Woodrow Ratliff started tuning his guitar. I could tell by the way Pinzon had his head cocked that he was calculating angles.

"A good team ought to beat Plaquemine every time," he said. "That's 18 games a season. You win those and split the rest, you finish 72 and 54. That might take the flag."

"Be close," I agreed.

He took a schedule card out of his wallet and studied it. Ratliff played "The City of New Orleans." When he began to sing, Pansy laid her head on my shoulder.

"Shit," Pinzon said. "We just have four more games with Plaquemine. I thought it was five. We'll need every break we can get to beat Selma."

"Aw, hell," I said. "We're going to win it all. I'm going to come in from the territory and settle down. And all the good guys will live happily ever after."

"Yeah," Pinzon said through a halfway grin, "and once upon a time in the land of dreams there lived a fool named Billy John Oklahoma."

46

And then we got to Asheville.

We played four and lost four. We didn't hit, we didn't pitch, we didn't field. Every time we saw a chance to screw up we jumped at it. We should've had the first one, but with one gone and men at the corners in their eighth, Guerrero's arm stiffened a little and, instead of Bullet Bob, in came Pinzon, who served up a gopher to their wasted-looking first baseman, Hawkeye Crawley. That made it 5–4 and that was that. Next day Genghis Mohammed, Jr., who usually put the ball about where he wanted it, walked everybody in the ballpark but the hot-dog vendor. Franklin Brown started the third game and gave up just three hits in six innings, but they were all taters—solo shots by Perk Maxwell and Elmer Jack and a wind-blown three-run job by Choo Choo Charlie Olsen. The two men Olsen drove in got on on errors, one of them mine—a routine chopper I caught, then dropped, then kicked. And finally, Ever-sole, our stopper, who'd lost only two games all year, went just two and a third our last day there—walked off the mound hangdog, trailing 4–zip.

But he did have some reason for not being up to form.

The second morning we were in Asheville, Tamara Burroughs, after making arrangements by phone the day before, drove up to our motel in a big white Vigilance Mountain Baptist College Dodge van that had chrome praying hands for a hood ornament and a bumper sticker that said: "In Case of Rapture This Vehicle Will Be Unoccupied." Lefty and Eversole and I were waiting for her in the motel restaurant.

When he saw Tamara, Lefty asked Eversole one more time, "You're sure you want to do it?"

"Yeah."

"Why?" That was my question.

"I like her." And that was all he would tell us. He liked her, he just wanted to talk, he wasn't after revenge. He wanted Lefty along to keep there from being any trouble, and he wanted me along, I guess, to hit somebody in case there was. And Lefty and me? Well, as much as anything else, we wanted a close-up look at Whiteside's spread.

I could tell the Burroughs woman didn't want me along, but she kept from saying it. In fact, there was hardly any talk at all on the way to the college, which had ruined a nice hilltop about fifteen miles southwest of town.

Miles of chain link topped with barbed wire fenced the place off from the world. An armed, uniformed security guard waved us through the main gate.

Lefty said, "Blessed are the peacemakers."

"Please don't start," Tamara Burroughs said.

Whiteside didn't go in for flash and dazzle like Oral Roberts, who'd blessed Tulsa with a Christian Las Vegas. But Vigilance Mountain Baptist College did what it was meant to do. One look at it put the fear of God in you—Whiteside's God, the foaming drill sergeant.

They'd scraped everything that'd grow off the top of that hill, set down identical four-story, white-brick buildings in four rows of four and, right dead center of that square of buildings, stuck up a forty-foot concrete Jesus, ringed by floodlights.

"Twelve of those buildings are dormitories," Tamara Burroughs told us. "And the other four contain classrooms. In the fall we expect to have 3,000 students enrolled. There are only a few hundred here now. We encourage them to do mission work in the summer."

The students we saw clipping along between buildings looked like Mormons, short-haired boys in slacks, short-sleeve white shirts, and ties, clear-skinned girls in prim skirts and wrinkle-proof blouses they buttoned to their chins. The boys looked like they might have to spend the best part of their lives resisting faggothood. The girls looked like they might have willed away all their pubic hair.

As we rolled down the macadam road, Lefty kept looking out his window and shaking his head.

Staring dead ahead, the Burroughs woman told him, "We're serving our God."

"Change gods," Lefty advised.

"There is but one."

Lefty relaxed then, smiled, realizing, I think, that it wasn't the place, this pious shyster college, that irritated him so much as the idea that this woman he'd cared for had given herself over to a system that methodically killed everything human and then jerked the gold out of the mouths of the corpses. My guess is that with that smile he let her go, left her to her one wrong god. He did, after all, believe in freedom.

We passed an intramural field where some students were playing softball. That was the first thing Eversole seemed to take notice of. "Softball," he said with the kind of disgust Mozart might've put into the word "disco."

A few hundred yards later we came to the gym and the church, which faced each other from either side of the road—the gym a heavy beige square of molded concrete built to spite nature, and the chapel an angular glass, brick, and steel atrocity that looked like it might sell pizza out the side.

The road led on. More forest turned to barren field. More signs of a plotted future.

Another fence enclosed Whiteside's headquarters. Another guard manned the arching iron gate, which, when we stopped, swung slowly outward. Macadam became concrete. Maples lined the drive. Two men on tractors were mowing acres of irrigated lawn. Off to our left, beneath one of the lawn's regularly spaced oaks, a German shepherd and a barefoot blacksmith-sized young man had squared off on one another.

"That's Sandy Flemson," the Burroughs woman told us. "Dr. Whiteside gave him the dog. They spend hours playing together."

Flemson took two steps toward the dog, who charged, sprang, caught a roundhouse right just below the ear, and went down like a bag of soybean meal. The Flemson loon started jumping up and down and laughing.

Tamara Burroughs stopped the van.

"Looks like you'd best buy him a new pup," I said.

She got out and hurried toward him. He took off the opposite way in a hard, clumsy run. She yelled at him and he stopped, turned round, and shuffled toward her. She knelt over the dog, felt its face, petted it a few strokes, then began trying to stand it up. By then Flemson was standing over her, his hands in his pockets, his upper body swaying. She looked up and said something to him. He nodded twice. After a couple of minutes, she got the dog to its feet. It stood spraddle-legged, took a step, tilted to its right, caught its balance, and finally wobbled off. She put her right hand on Flemson's left elbow and walked him to the van, talking into his down-turned face.

She slid a van door open for him and he got into the third seat, behind Eversole and me. He didn't look up. When she had the van moving forward again, she glanced back and said, "Sandy, these are some men who've come to see Dr. Whiteside." And I think she was about to start introducing us when I heard a sudden animal-grunt and turned just quick enough to see Flemson's big right hooking toward Eversole's head.

The easy way Eversole slipped it was enough to make you think he went through life always prepared to slip and counter. He jerked his upper body forward and to his left and the fist slammed into the doorframe between the windows. Eversole twisted back to his right, reached up with both hands, grabbed Flemson by the hair, and yanked him forward and down, pinning his neck against the back of the seat.

The Burroughs woman shouted "Sandy!" and the van left the road and headed toward the oak tree we'd seen Flemson and his dog under.

"It's all right," Eversole told her. "I got him."

The van stuttered, but she shifted, gassed it, and we shot back up on the road.

Lefty started laughing.

"He's upset," Tamara Burroughs said. Her hands clenched the steering wheel. "He thinks your friend has come to take Candy away."

"I have," Eversole said.

The half-wit grunted again, then went into a flailing, blubbering spasm. I caught a couple of glancing licks and I think Eversole did too, but he kept his grip on the kid's head, pressing down, cutting off air, and the spasm subsided into a strangling peace.

"Let him go," Lefty said.

Eversole eased up just enough to let Flemson suck in some air.

When we pulled up in front of the mansion, Tamara Burroughs damn near sprang out her door and scurried back to open Flemson's. Eversole kept one hand on Flemson's head, opened his door with the other, then let go of Flemson and stepped out of the van. Flemson lunged at him, rolled headfirst over the back of the seat, and landed on his side on the floorboard, his bare feet in my lap. I got out and left him to Tamara Burroughs, who knelt over him and began smoothing his hair and gently assuring him it would all be o.k., nothing would happen, they wouldn't let Candy go. Lefty stood and watched her and I could see his memory in his eyes.

When she had him soothed, she got him to his feet, asked us to wait there for her, and led him into the mansion.

Waiting, I took in my first good eyeful of the mansion. Two long, flat rectangles crossed each other, forming a ranch-style crucifix.

It wasn't much to look at, so I turned to Eversole. "You going to propose to that girl?" I tried to make it sound like a joke.

"I like her."

I took that to mean yes. "Chances don't look good."

"No."

Tamara Burroughs came out the end of the east-pointing cross-arm and headed toward us.

"I been going to whorehouses," Eversole said, as if that explained everything.

Lefty nodded like he understood.

"You come here to repent?" I asked Eversole.

The Burroughs woman motioned to us and we followed her down a flower-edged sidewalk to the other end of the place, where we entered a big room with white carpet and blue chairs. The wall opposite the door supported a painting of Whiteside standing open-mouthed on the edge of a cliff, wearing a three-piece pin-striped suit, hands raised toward a violent gray sky. One streak of sunlight slanted miraculously down from the fierce clouds, illuminating Whiteside's jowly face. It looked like he might be trying to interest God in a used car.

We went through a doorway to the left of the painting and then down a hallway past labeled doors: "Rev. Oswald Crutcher, Dean of Students"; "Rev. Coleman Marshal, Dean of Men"; "Judy Garr, Dean of Women."

We passed a conference room, then Studio A, Studio B, Studio C, two prayer rooms, and a snack center before finally entering a room marked "Private," which turned out to be a kind of den, ankle-deep carpet, color TV, plastic bubble skylight, dark, paneled walls studded here and there with plaques, shelves full of trophies. A Coke machine filled the far right-hand corner.

Two men and a woman were waiting for us—J. G. Flemson, Whiteside, and Candy Commerce. Whiteside and Flemson sat at either end of a long, low couch. Candy was in a stuffed chair to their right, hands folded in her lap. They had her trussed up in a starched brown dress, but even so, even with the best part of her tucked in and tied down, it was easy to see that what we had here was prime twitch. Long-legged, dark-headed, sloe-eyed.

"Gentlemen," Whiteside said. He motioned toward the chairs across from the couch. Lefty and I went over and sat down, but Eversole stood where he was.

"You coming?" he asked Candy Commerce.

Whiteside said, "Have a seat, son."

"I want to talk to her," Eversole said, staring down at Whiteside.

Then Candy said, "He's been good to me, Jeremiah. And I can't leave Sandy."

I lit up a Lucky.

Whiteside leaned forward. "Mr. Marks, would you be good enough to ask your man to sit down?"

"You agreed to let him talk to her."

"I'm fulfilling that agreement. From what Candy has said, your friend can't be trusted alone with her."

Who could? I wondered.

The Burroughs woman brought me a glass ashtray with a silver dollar trapped in its bottom, then went over and sat on a hassock next to Candy.

Eversole studied Candy Commerce hard for a few seconds before looking back down at Whiteside. "The idiot shot me. She came here to find shelter for him. You're using him against her."

The Burroughs woman answered. "Candace was no better than a prostitute when she came to us. Now she has a role in life."

I passed up the easy line, sucked on my smoke, and tried to piece it all together.

Lefty beat me to it. He stood up. "Jeremiah, they're not going to let you talk to her. There's nothing we can do now but press charges."

"You do that and you'll be one sad Communist," J. G. Flemson said.

Lefty gave Flemson a grin and started for the door.

"He won't hurt me," Candy Commerce said then. "I don't mind talking a few minutes."

"Well, then, preacher," Flemson said, "let 'em talk. Let's get this done with."

Whiteside hesitated, then nodded. "Take them to the women's prayer room, Tamara. Wait outside the door." He turned his gaze to Lefty. "If he tries anything with Miss Commerce, I'll have him in jail inside the hour." He stood and gave Lefty a short dose of his cold blue eyes. I snuffed the Lucky. Then the Messiah of the Deductible Dollar left us, went off, I guess, to loll around in the coffers.

Tamara Burroughs, Candy Commerce, and Eversole followed him out, leaving Lefty and me with good ole Jay Gould Flemson.

He focused his rubber eyes on me. "Why don't you go have yourself a look at the grounds?"

"Got a bum knee," I told him.

He got up and walked over and drew open the drapes that had covered a glass door. I could see about fifty yards of patio and then a swimming pool.

"That's my boy yonder," Flemson said. "He's happy here."

I could make out a man at the far end of the pool thrashing around with a red-white-and-blue beach ball.

"He's caused me and his momma a world of pain." He returned to the couch, sat down, and crossed his legs. "If it'd been just me, I'd've had him put away about the time he started learning to stutter good. They got some nice places, you know." He looked out toward the pool again. "Not up to this, most likely, but nice enough. His momma, though, she wouldn't have no part of that. Thoroughbred stock, you see. High strung and all. Got her a heart that pumps out Magnolia blossoms. And it was our only kid. Womb lays a little slantwise, the doctors tell me."

"If your son's happy, leave him here," Lefty said. "It'll give Whiteside legitimate claim to one piece of Christian charity."

"That's my intention. Though it ain't exactly charity."

"I see," Lefty said. "You buy a dormitory, they give your son a room full of play pretties."

"Nothing wrong with that. Makes everybody happy, including his momma. She'll be handing him over to Jesus. They'll even put her up too anytime she wants to visit. Course, she'd have to watch her drinking some."

Lefty said, "Well, then. It's all worked out."

"No, sir. Not quite." He jerked a corner of his mouth slightly upward. I thought he might be enjoying this—as much as he could enjoy anything. "You see, ain't no place'll suit poor ole Colonel Sanders that don't have that Commerce woman in it. She claims she aims to stay here, but a man that's known her as long as me would be a damn fool to put much stock in her word. One fine morning that itch in her britches'll need scratching and she'll be up and gone. When she does, that fool boy of mine'll be hotfooting it right behind her." He sighed and shook his head.

"If you pay Whiteside enough, he'll make sure your son doesn't get away," Lefty told him.

Flemson folded his hands together and tilted his head one notch back and one to his right. "I've made a long study of it, Mr. Marks, and I've got to the point where I can pretty well tell you just what you can buy with a dollar bill. Now, Brother Whiteside's a reasonable fellow—got nothing against accepting a sizeable donation. But he ain't desperate for it. There's a world of folks out there sending him ten, fifteen, twenty-five dollars a month in hopes he'll let them stand in line behind him at the Judgment. So, you see, what it comes down to finally is I need him more than he needs me. Not real good business on my part, but then he's got the only lot. I'd be a fool to think I could just buy him outright. I can't expect him to keep Colonel Sanders under lock and key. Word got out that he was padlocking an idiot for money, it'd cost him plenty. Folks'd be apt to start sending their little tithes off to Billy Graham or even Jimmy Swaggart. All I want is for him to do what he can for the boy as long as he can."

He leaned forward and showed Lefty his palms.

"I don't expect you'll believe this, but I want what's best for the boy." He leaned back, pursed his lips, slapped a thigh, and nodded. "I know he ain't fit to be running loose. And I don't have the time and his momma don't have the strength to give him the kind of care he needs at home. I don't mind telling you I'd just as soon he wasn't fixed on Candy Commerce. Why, ever' time he catches her laying with somebody he commences to howl and set things afire. That's why he shot your Indian. But he's a idiot and she's right pretty and when she ain't out servicing strangers she treats him decent, so there you are. Not much I can do about it. But if I can keep him here a couple of months, get his momma used to him being gone, why, maybe I could make some permanent arrangements without her squawking too loud."

"So you're worried about Eversole," Lefty said.

"There's nothing that woman would like better than to be sitting beside a nine-foot Indian surrounded by a busload of ballplayers and looking out into an open highway."

"We could make your son batboy," I offered.

"My guess is his momma wouldn't go for that."

"Nothing more dangerous than a Communist half-wit," I said.

"That's the way she'd see it, all right." He leaned forward again. "You boys don't think much of me, I know, and I don't reckon I'll be buying any ball cards with your pictures on them either. But you could do me a good turn right now without hurting yourself and I can more than return it."

Lefty laughed.

With all the calm of a man convinced that wasn't apt to be the last laugh, Flemson waited for him to quit.

Trying to remember if I'd heard Lefty laugh in just that way before—without anything like joy in it, out of a mixture of spite and disgust—I lit up another Lucky and looked out the window and saw the Flemson loon walk slowly out to the end of the diving board, bend over, study the water, then, very carefully, with both hands, arch his beachball out into the pool. Then he stooped, stared down at the ball, and made his calculations. His body, still bent, began tilting stiffly forward, and I thought he would just go in like that, not moving a muscle, but when his head was almost even with the board, he grabbed his nose with his right hand and pushed off, going out flat and knocking the ball several feet by hitting it with his head. He just barely went under, but came up spitting and thrashing, still gripping his nose. He sank.

"Christ, can he swim?" I asked.

"Like a dog," Flemson told me without even looking toward the pool.

And, sure enough, the fool bobbed to the surface, and, neck stretched straight up out of the water, face damn near parallel to the sky, he paddled to the ball and pushed it with his chin to the pool's edge.

"First time we threw him in he took off like a bird dog." He stood, reached down into his pants pocket, and pulled out a fistful of change. "You boys care for a Co-Cola?"

We turned him down.

"You know, Ty Cobb used to own a big part of this company." He dropped a couple of quarters into the machine. "Preacher Whiteside's a man that's got his mind wrapped solid around the workings of this system. A man's a fool not to." He got his Coke and returned to the couch.

I finished my Lucky, stubbed it, walked over to the glass door, watched Colonel Sanders go off the board again, and wondered what Eversole was saying to his girl and how she'd go about telling him no.

"Tell you what," Lefty said. "Why don't you just make your offer and be done with it?"

Flemson nodded, then set the Coke on the lampstand next to the couch. "You keep your Indian away from that Commerce woman and I'll see to it you get a ball team next year."

"Well, I've enjoyed it," Lefty said. "They should be through in there." But he made no effort to get up. I'm sure he wasn't tempted by the offer, but he was curious enough to want to hear it out.

"They're going to try to break your lease in Little Rock, and if you manage to stop 'em, why, Judge Jackson, he'll see to it the league gives you the boot. Gabbard's the only man standing between you and that right now, and he can be had. So, win or lose, Mr. Marks, y'all just got the one year. To my way of looking at it, that's a damn shame. Ever' owner in ever' town in this league has made money on account of you boys. But there's too many of 'em making the same mistake you're making: they letting politics foul their thinking."

Lefty cocked his head to one side. "Pop Stone tells me you've developed an interest in politics yourself."

"Why sure. I make no secret of that. I'm considering running for Congress on the Independent ticket. Don't have to dick around with the primaries that way. And you can win with about 40 percent of the vote. I figure I can balance that budget for 'em if they give me a go at it."

Lefty said, "Of course you don't want your son to burn anything down or shoot anybody during the campaign. And a voter might misunderstand if he drove past your place and saw him tied to a tree."

"Well, a man can't see that tree from the road, Mr. Marks, but, yessir, you got it about right. And then there's his momma too, you see. She won't let me put the colonel away and I'm afraid I'd have hell getting shut of her. Old Missippi. You know how it is. Honor and organdy. Slaves and mint juleps. Your common voter loves it. She's quality, you see, and I'm a damn Snopes."

Lefty studied him a few more seconds, then turned to me and said, "You about ready, Hog? It'll be nearly dinnertime when we get back to town."

Flemson stood. "You're one mighty smug bastard," he said without raising his voice. "You're an old man and this one last year in baseball may be all you want. But what's a man like Durham there going to do with himself when it's over? What's he fit to do? Who's going to hire him? If you're doing any good at all, it's in providing a place for men like him. Why quit it when you don't have to? I can give you a place to play in Greenville. Old ballpark laying pretty much fallow there. My name wouldn't be con-

nected to it. Be better that way for both of us. And I know enough
on Judge Jackson to make him go along. You're being stupid, Mr.
Marks, and selfish. You're going to muck up everything you done
on account of thinking you're too high-minded to deal with a man
like me."

Lefty stood and faced him. "I am old, Mr. Flemson. And I am
tired. Why don't you wander on down the hall and finish buying
Brother Whiteside?"

Flemson nodded and raised that same corner of his mouth
again. "I see. Well, I can't say I didn't expect it. But I always try to
appeal to a man's reason before I do anything else. Your Indian
won't be leaving with his whore. And you might be good enough to
let him know that the next time the guards see him on the grounds
here they'll have orders to shoot. Trespassing, you see. A man's
home's his castle."

Tamara Burroughs was waiting for us in the hall. "One of our
students will drive you back," she told us.

We didn't talk much on the way back to Asheville—or nobody
did but our denatured chauffeur. This would be his last year at
Whiteside U and, oh!, it had been a wonderful education. With
the Vigilance Mountain Choir, he'd sung in Taiwan, the Philip-
pines, Haiti, and Argentina. What wonderful people there were in
the world, so hungry for God's word.

As far as I could tell, I was the only one listening. Lefty sat and
calmly watched the edge of the world slip past his window. I figured he was thinking about Flemson, suspecting, like I did, that
when such a man as that makes a show of laying all his cards on
the table, he probably ain't playing cards. And Eversole just
rode on, stiff and grim in what I took to be defeat. It ain't easy, I
wanted to tell him, but it beats hiding. You got to hurt to live, old
stopper. You got to get down in the muck. Life springs up out of
manure.

But I didn't say anything, just kept listening to the voice of the
driver, a voice that had seduced so many out of life. And listening,
I understood again why. All I had to guide me was a bent mind, a
crooked heart, and a hard dick. But this boy, this Child of the
Faith, this radiant fool, had had all his questions answered and all
his fears removed by a black book and an empty tomb.

It surprised me some, but the truth is that right then a part of
me begrudged him his peace.

47

Late in the morning of the sixth of August, an off-day, at the park in Oxford, we had our first look at Jeronimo Velasquez, the refugee, Julius's Fort Chaffee reliever.

He was good. He didn't look like much, a skinny, five-ten right-hander with bug eyes and a nervous mouth, but he could make that ball dance. His delivery was a series of quick, strange jerks that made him look like he'd been wound up and suddenly let go. When he released the pitch, his head was down about knee-high, and his throwing arm was coming up from the ground at the hitter. The jerking, the bending, the odd angle of delivery, and the way he flashed his glove hand up and across his body just before letting the pitch go, made the ball hard to pick up until it was well on its way. He had a fastball that would come in damn near skimming the grass and then rise into the strike zone, another one he'd start just over knee-high and cause to break down and tail in to a right-hander, and a curve that, because of his underhand motion, rose. None of it was overpowering, just odd and quick, the kind of stuff it took a hitter at least one trip to the plate to get used to, and by then, Velasquez being the short man, the game should be over.

There wasn't any question about us needing him. While we were taking that dive in Asheville, Selma had split four with Memphis. So, three down and falling, we voted him in unanimously, though Acribar needed a little nudge from Guerrero. I had a qualm or two myself, for that matter. I didn't figure Ratoplan would be overly pleased by the team's newest addition.

While we gave Velasquez the glad hand, Lefty went out and told the reporters, who at that time were following us damn near everywhere but to bed, that in addition to two loyal Cuban nationals, the Arkansas Reds now had a Cuban refugee.

A half-hour later, I was in the parking lot giving quick answers to stupid questions when Sheriff Jim Tom Grimm tapped me on the shoulder and told me to come sit a spell with him in his car.

I looked at him. He wore a mean, snake-stomper's grin. "Nothing good's ever happened to me in one of them cars," I said.

"Oh, I ain't arresting you, Buck. Or not just yet. This has to do with your friend Crazy Horse."

Lefty, surrounded by reporters, leaned against the bus and issued statements. "This has nothing to do with Fidel Castro," I heard him say. "Our concern is with just three Cubans, two pitchers and an outfielder."

"Come on, Buck. Hell, I'll let you talk on the radio."

"Can I cuss?"

"You can blackguard." He laughed. "But don't you be taking the Lord's name in vain."

We got about halfway to his car before Pansy came trotting up to us. "Is it all right, Hog?"

"Sheriff here just wants to show me some of the knobs in his misery wagon. Trying to lure me into a career in law enforcement."

Grimm leered at Pansy. Her Levi's might've been a size too small and her T-shirt was right snug. "Still got your woman, have you, Durham?" he asked, sizing her up like he was fixing to make an offer.

"Yeah," I said. "But I'm always a little worried some smooth bastard like yourself will come along and charm her away."

Pansy took my arm. Grimm shook his head. "I guess there's no accounting for a woman's taste."

Grimm looked over at Pansy. "Now, you run along, little lady. Ole Buck here'll be back with you before you can get to missing him good."

I told her again that it was all right.

When we were in his car, Grimm said, "I hear tell you done had yourself a look at the religious life."

"Awful stirring," I said.

Grimm cut himself a piece off a plug of Day's Work, chewed it down, spit out the window, and said, "Ole Crazy Horse got him a letch on for Candy Commerce, has he?"

"I don't know. Might be the other way around."

"Wouldn't be surprised. She ain't particular." He commenced cleaning his fingernails with his pocketknife. "But I'm here to tell you, Buck, he better scratch another itch."

"Don't you believe in love, sheriff?"

"I ain't shitting you, Buck. You the one that can talk to him, you better do it. He keeps messing around, I'll have him so far back in the hole, we'll have to bring his meals to him on a golf cart."

This was all Flemson's doing, I knew, but I wasn't quite sure exactly what he was up to. What I was sure of, though, was that I was growing a little weary of threats. I opened my door. "I thank you, sheriff, and now, if you wouldn't mind too much, why don't you just go ahead and kiss my ass."

I started to get out. He grabbed my arm. I turned my head around slow and stared down hard at his big hand. He didn't move it. "The last thing that nine-foot savage told her was that he was coming back for her. Anything happens to her, Buck, it's his ass." He let go of my arm. "You boys have a nice stay here in Oxford."

"What was that all about?" Pansy asked when I sat beside her on the bus.

"He wanted to make me a member of the Williams County Honorary Posse."

48

If you spend your childhood on an Oklahoma farm and take the rest of your education from highways and jails, one of the things you'll get used to is heat. So when we came down into that Mississippi August with its blistering days and sultry nights, the kind of heat that can wilt a good man's bat and suck fifteen or twenty pounds off a pitcher in nine innings, I started jacking the ball around again, the way I had at the start of the season. I hit four out in five days, giving me 24 for the year, and had five doubles and three singles, went 12 for 23, and drove in eight runs.

But it wasn't enough. Three of the home runs were solo jobs, and four of the RBIs came in the one game we won big, a 9–3 for Eversole. Except for that game nobody hit much but me and Hagio Acribar. Jefferson Mundy was suffering his worst slump of the season. Rainbow Smith, ordinarily a fastball hitter, had developed a hitch in his swing and was going through a spell of fanning on high, tight, hard ones. And in the third inning of the first game of the series, Julius Common Deer had flung himself into the center-field wall trying to catch a drive off the bat of Joe Easter and had come up with an empty glove and a right shoulder bruised just bad enough to keep him on the bench for the next four days.

We wasted three strong pitching performances, Guerrero's, Brown's, and Ratliff's, losing 3–2, 3–1, and 4–2. Jeronimo Velasquez pitched his first two innings on Sunday afternoon, saving a 4–3 win for Genghis Mohammed. And Eversole, who used sweat as a weapon, looked strong again going nine in his game. He may've left his heart on Vigilance Mountain, but he was back in control of his head and arm. For our purposes, that'd do. Lord, that'd do just fine.

It was our last trip to Oxford and we filled the house for Stephen Gabbard. Flemson had been right: folks poured in to see our Cubans. The Fury played their Monday home games in the afternoon to avoid competing with the ABC Monday night games, and even though that was our fifth day there and a workday to boot, all but maybe a couple hundred seats were filled for that game. So, to thank us, to further demonstrate his support for Lefty, and probably to put a few more spangles on his reputation as an enlightened Mississippi liberal, Gabbard threw a lawn party for us Monday evening.

He had a place about ten miles east of town—rock and redwood house, swimming pool, tennis court, acres of lawn. Besides us, there must've been fifty or sixty people there, professors at Ole Miss, lawyers from Memphis and Jackson, a few doctors and psychologists, and maybe fifteen favored students, mostly female. Everybody treated me nice, the way people do with crippled animals. They deplored the brutal conditions in American prisons. They admired the way I seemed to have overcome my background. They were doing what they could in Mississippi, fighting people like J. G. Flemson and John Stennis and all the rednecks and yahoos, but it was such a tough journey, one step forward and half a step back, that you just had to fight them a day at a time and learn to be content with small victories.

It seemed to me that they were all living too high to be serious about changing much. And their compassion and admiration made me nervous and about half-mad, so I got me a beer and a steak and sat on a bench under a big white oak and watched Pinzon work his tennis hustle on a pair of lawyers.

After a while Pop Stone came over and sat down by me. "Feeling out of place?" he asked.

"I'd feel about as comfortable at a prosecutors' convention."

"Well," he said, "most of them aren't the kind you can depend on. But they're not out to hurt you either."

We were quiet a minute, chewing prime beef, medium rare. Then Pop asked, "Eversole serious about Candy Commerce?"

"Looks like it," I said. "But he may just be figuring a way of getting even."

"You might tell him that girl's not worth the trouble." Pop turned and looked toward the tennis court, where the crowd watching the Pinzon hustle had grown considerably. Then he looked back at me and went on. "Most people around here are quick to call her a whore. But it's not that simple. Ever since she was old enough to think about pain she's been trying to get clear of a bad, twisted past. She's defiant one week, repentant the next. She goes back and forth from the church to the road. Jason, her father, put her in the state hospital once for several months and they diagnosed it as manic-depression. That may be as close as you can get to summing her up in two words, but it's still damn simple. You don't cure history with lithium chloride. And then, of course, he has Flemson to contend with. It's just not worth it."

"I don't know," I said. "Flemson might have a hard time hurting Eversole. No car to repossess, no home to foreclose on. Comes to showdown, I think I'll put my money on Eversole."

"If he cares much for Candy," Pop said, "he can be hurt." He stood. "I'm going home," he said. "I stay, I'll get drunk. This isn't the place for it."

After I finished my steak, I got up and wandered around a while, listened while Ernesto Guerrero told an audience of postgraduate adultresses a story about Castro screwing a schoolteacher in a cane field, heard Hagio Acribar speak of material progress in revolutionary Cuba to a gaggle of cocktail cynics, smiled while Genghis Mohammed, Jr., trying to hide a leer, I thought, lectured the Lord's own coed (her fine, wet mocking body straining against an ensemble consisting of three patches and four strings) on the proper role of women, overheard Rainbow Smith deliver a very different lecture on the same topic to a similar coed, and caught pieces of other conversations, fine, sensitive discussions of the decline of southern fiction, the difficulty of working under an anal-retentive department chairman, the psychic benefits of ritual, the medicinal uses of camomile tea and ginseng root, the passionate art of Marilyn French, the playful esthetic of John Barth, the stunning size of a Jackson Pollock, the necessity of radical political commitment, the futility of radical political commitment, the ordeal of summer school, the spiritual liberation to be had through miscegenation, and the fierce joy of being fully alive in an age of decadence.

Well, I'd read some books, and I'd spent some hours kicking ideas back and forth with Shakespeare Creel, but this made me want to go over and piss off the diving board. But they would've tolerated that, led me politely to a chair, and poured me some coffee: "Four years in prison, you know. They do have such trouble adjusting." Pop Stone was right: they didn't do much harm; might even be of some use to some people. But I don't know, I can't explain it, the evil and the fear suddenly came down on me; these people's voices swelled and came together on me and at me—smooth sarcasm, schoolbook irony, wineglass laughter merged into the alien, soulless voice of Law: "You don't belong here. It's our world. We'll show what mercy we can." And I had to keep telling myself I was just as smart as they were and a whole lot tougher until I could find Pansy and take her away from some chinless Civil War historian who was telling her about chivalry and the Confederate officer corps, and then lead her around the edge of the crowd and out into the woods past the westernmost house, where I laid her down and, desperate with fear and love, had her beneath a shagbark hickory tree.

49

"Well," I said to Pansy the next afternoon as she drove me into Little Rock and the parole office, "unless everybody's lying, we're partly responsible for getting about half the team laid."

"You always set a brave example." She didn't smile, didn't take her eyes off the road.

"Guerrero got his first free American piece—or so he says. Pinzon had a little blonde from Indianola, though she may've been after the money he made playing tennis. And, hell, ole Joe Buck spent most of the night with an associate professor of home economics."

"Everybody loves a ballplayer." She looked at me then. Hard. Out of the side of her mouth, in a heavy redneck twang, she said, "Bunch of drunk professors standing around kissing hands and talking about truth and beauty and the role of women in the modern world and, why, hell, ole Hog, after a while he gets sick of it all and just grabs up his woman and swaggers off into the bushes with her and goes to laying pipe."

Arkansas had gone a good while without rain. Patches of meadow grass were turning brown. Leaves hung limp from branches. The sun was like a curse. "People see it the way they want to. Those rubber-legged Oxford gentry brought the fear on me. I know it. You know it. I don't have to wear a sign, do I?"

"Just wear that hell-for-leather grin and keep swaggering."

We rode quiet a minute as Little Rock, ugly and swelling, came at us. Roadrunner, Burger King, Evangel Temple, Elysium Hills Homes. Fill up, eat up, dress up, and die.

I reached over and touched her arm. "You ever wonder how people live this way?" I motioned out the window.

Her face seemed to soften some. "Sometimes I wish I could do it."

For the next minute or two, the silence took us again.

The buildings got higher. The air got worse. Heat rose from the pavement. People hurried here and there, caught up in a fast game they played to keep from thinking.

"I'm thinking about leaving for a while," she said. "Going back down to El Dorado maybe. See some people. Think things over."

"You hate El Dorado."

"It used to be home. Maybe I could remember what that felt like, back before Jimbo got killed."

We turned off University and headed east on Markham. I told her I wished she wouldn't go.

"Why not? Maybe you could try that little blonde from Indianola. Get you a little *strange*."

She spit that last word at me. I tried touching her arm again, but she jerked it away. I said, "All I ever had was strange until I met you. And maybe that makes you the strangest one of all."

"Whatever that means."

"Pansy, goddamit, you're the one that said this was all we had so it had to be worth taking a chance for."

She pulled over into the right lane and then turned up toward the capitol building. "The talk this morning made me feel like a permanent prop in a bad Hog Durham story." She looked at me, then back at the road. "I just need to think. I'm tired of the road and the Home and the team. I'll be back."

I saw two black men, ropes around their waists, patching up the capitol dome.

"I'm thirty-two, Hog. I want a home and a family real bad. I've been in too many saloons and too many strange rooms. So I might be asking too much now. I might not even like it when I got it. But Jesus, I want it." She looked out her window, away from me, and wiped her eyes with her left hand.

"I been in the same saloons and the same rooms. I was sixteen the last time I rode a white horse or wanted to—and that was an old swaybacked gelding. But maybe I want the same things you do. All I can tell you for sure is that I need you now. I'm not real good at thinking past the next game."

She stopped the truck beside an Arkansas Industrial Development Commission car. I opened the door and stepped down onto the street. "I won't be long," I said. "We can have a beer or something down at Friday's."

She gave me a broken smile. "I never mistook you for Sir Galahad."

"I'm just an old highwayman, but the king's dead and the knights have all gone queer and here I am."

"Yes." She shook her head. "There you are."

"Whatever that means."

I shut the door and watched the truck go to the end of the block and turn down the hill toward Friday's. God, I thought, what you going to do, Hog Durham, old vagabond thief, once Lefty Marks finally brings his rolling halfway house to a full stop?

The last few times I'd been in Mantis's office he hadn't done much more than frown and wave me out. But this time it was different.

As I approached her desk, Julie punched the intercom button and said, "He's here."

"Good," Mantis's boxed voice replied.

"Am I late?"

"Right on time." She motioned toward his door.

I figured Ratoplan was in there with him. It occurred to me that I could just walk out, head west, and live under a name I took off a tombstone. That would be fine with Mantis and Ratoplan. They probably wouldn't even come looking for me. And a few months earlier, it would've been fine with me too. But now I'd tied myself to a woman and maybe a world and I decided to stay tied. Or try to. I walked into the trap.

I was wrong about Ratoplan. He was way too slick to actually be there. The man with Mantis was big, lantern-jawed, and burr-headed. He wore a tight, cheap blue suit. When I entered he stood. My age, my size. I knew what he was.

"Hog," Mantis said through what looked to me like a triumphant grin, "I want to introduce you to Deputy Sheriff Lawson Maxey. He's going to read you your rights."

Maybe I couldn't handle a woman over a long stretch. Maybe I wasn't much hand at planning a life. But it came to me then that this right here was just the kind of shit I could deal with.

I said, "Hell, I know ole Lawson. He can't read."

Part VI

50

Hold on.

They let me call Pansy before they hauled me away, but they wouldn't let me see her—which was just as well, I thought. I told her to tell Lefty, to tell Rotenberg, to send me my box of books. "Don't forget the Yeats. It's on the nightstand." Bodily decrepitude is wisdom—yes, sir, Billy Buck, yes, sir.

"I'll bring it myself."

"No. Now's the time for you to do your thinking. Time to go to El Dorado. They're going to be doing this shit to me all my life."

"I'm going to be with you."

"It'll just hurt."

"Hurting's part of it."

"It ought not be the main part."

Let go.

Then Lawson Maxey handcuffed me, led me out back to his squad car, set me in the back seat, behind the grill, and shot off toward Van Buren. We said nothing as first Little Rock and then North Little Rock folded behind us. The future closed and the past opened up ahead.

Guiding us down 40 at a steady 75, Lawson began telling about having been an extra in a TV movie called *The Blue and the Gray* that had been filmed partly in Van Buren. "They covered Main with dirt from the depot down to the courthouse and brung in horses and hitching posts and such and before you knew it they had you thinking you really were in the War Between the States."

He shook his head in wonderment. "We heard about it ahead of time and, why, me and Sheriff Basham started growing our hair out early so's to be sure of getting parts." He paused there and glanced up at the mirror. "Back in them days, you know, they didn't have proper barbers. Soon's they finished up my last scene, I marched right down and had ole Holland Patterson cut mine off. Some of my kin had got to poking fun at me."

He checked me in the mirror again. There wasn't anything hard in his face. A big guy, a little slow, killing time with a prisoner. I said, "A man has to make sacrifices for his art."

Hold on.

My first morning there was a Wednesday. Visitation day. They let the preachers have first crack at us. Reverend Delbert Biggerstaff came into our cell and told us about the thief on the cross.

I was sharing the cell with three other losers, an eighteen-year-old car thief, a wandering hot check artist, and a Mountainburg dope farmer. The first two were backslid Christians. The third believed in reincarnation. But even he laid his hands in the stack with the preacher's and prayed.

The old scam. I watched and smiled.

"What do you believe in, son?" the preacher asked me when he'd finished humoring the sky.

"Locks and keys."

"He's a Communist," the car thief explained.

The preacher studied me a second. "Oh, the baseball player."

I nodded, "I believe for every drop of rain that falls a preacher dies."

Let go.

A few minutes later, Lawson led me down to a gray basement room, where I sat across from Pansy at a foldable Formica table. She took my hands in hers and commenced to cry.

At the other end of the table a black teenager was talking to a woman social worker.

"I told you it would hurt," I said to Pansy. "There's nothing you can do here." But I didn't move my hands.

"Barry Rotenberg said he'd have you out in a few days."

"I'll either be out quick or in forever."

The social worker stood and in a classroom voice told the black kid he needed to learn the meaning of the word "cooperation." The black kid said, "I ain't going back to no motherfucking honkie church home."

"It's Wrightsville then," the social worker told him, her voice firm, sure, cool, betraying no anger.

"Fuck it," the kid said.

I moved my hands and lit up a Lucky.

"Very impressive vocabulary." The social worker motioned to the jailer, who began turning the lock. "The hearing's at two," she told the black kid, then walked out of the room, glancing down at her watch. Lawson came in and led the kid up to his cell.

We waited out a quiet couple of minutes. Pansy had her palms on the table and was staring at the backs of her hands. I said, "If you're a tough kid and can't keep from snapping back at 'em, they won't give you but the two choices. You can go to Holy Joe's Mission Home for the Heathen or you can go to some pisshole they build a fence around and call a training school." I stubbed my Lucky.

The jailer opened the door and a woman, who looked to be a hard twenty, came in and sat where the social worker had been. She opened her purse, took out her compact, looked at her painted face, and, using thumb and forefinger, curled a few strands of store-bought blonde hair forward from either temple. A couple of minutes later Lawson came down with her man, wiry and somewhere in his thirties. When he laid his forearms on the table, I saw that he'd tattooed them the way country boys do in the pen— women's names, Ruby and Josie and, Lord, Imogene, cut into the skin with a filed-down spoon handle and made permanent with ink. Nothing was left in his eyes but a little of the kind of cunning that never starts working until you're already trapped.

"You get me another lawyer?" he asked her as soon as he got sat down good.

"Oh, Roy," she said, looking out sad-eyed past a heavy layer of silver mascara. "They want more than we got."

"You got to get it. I'm gone if you don't. That court appointed asshole'd get you the chair for a parking violation."

"I been hunting a job," she told him.

He gave her a sneer. "Do what you know how to do."

The woman looked down and fought her eyes.

He reached across the table, lifted her chin, and held it while he spoke. "Cut that shit. It ain't no use crying over what's already gone." He let go of her chin and stood up. "You come back when you got something to tell me."

After Roy left, the woman sat there dabbing the mascara with a Kleenex. Remembering she wasn't alone, she told Pansy, "He ain't that way much. Roy's got a good heart. He's just scared and that makes him mean."

Pansy nodded and was going to let it go, but I figured a little dose of truth couldn't hurt her—or Pansy either. "It ain't none of my business," I said, "but I've known a lot of men like Roy—good ole boys gone bad. You ought to get gone quick. He'll use you till you're used up, and the best he'll ever do for you is carve his name on your arm."

Her smile, generous and knowing, surprised me. "Nobody else ever done that much."

Then she stood, stuffed the Kleenex back in her purse, looked back at Pansy, and said, "Honey, you hold on to your man. They're not much, but there ain't nothing else."

"Christ," I said when the woman had left, "I was out so long I've started giving advice."

Pansy gave me her good smile. "It's not the first time you've underestimated a woman."

Hold on.

At two-thirty Barry Rotenberg told me he was going to get the arraignment delayed as long as possible. He thought there was a chance he could get the charges dropped before I was ever formally indicted. And at three, at the bail hearing, he and I rose up from behind the defense table and watched Judge William Jennings Bryan Tapp—he used the whole thing, of course—ascend, berobed, to the bench. He was gray, overfed, and bored. Rotenberg argued for bail, knowing he'd lose, citing my responsible behavior and twenty-four home runs since my release from McAlester.

The prosecutor, Sam Hugh Starbird, said that in view of the strong evidence and the parole officer's report no bail was justified. The judge had Mantis's report. Rotenberg had told me what it said: suspect is uncooperative, resistant to any authority figure, subject to fits of rage, has been diagnosed as sociopathic.

Parole revoked. Subject to remain in custody of Crawford County Sheriff's Department. Arraignment set for August 20. Next case.

Let go.

"That's some woman you got," Lawson said the next morning. They had me mopping floors. Lawson shuffled along beside me.

"Ain't she?" I said. I stuck the mop in the roller-bucket, pulled it through the wringer, and shoved the bucket behind me.

"She wanted to see you again, but it ain't the day."

I kept my rhythm, moving back, swinging the mop. Good eye, good hands. You can't get the dark one by him.

"I seen you on the late news last night. You looked good. None of that hiding the face they usually pull."

"Got nobody left to hide from," I said.

I pushed the bucket into the TV room and followed it. The boys were in there watching "Good Morning, America."

An hour later, my mopping done, Lawson, sitting across the table from me in the interrogation room, took up again as if he'd never been interrupted. Pushing me the *Chronicle* Pansy'd brought, he said, "Yes, sir, you looked real good on the news. Head up and proud-looking. But no show-off in it either."

"You should've had me over to watch it with you." I lit up a Lucky. He pushed me an ashtray. "How come they keep you at the jail most of the time?" I asked him.

"There's less trouble when I'm here. I get along good with people." I figured he was setting me up for a grilling. After he'd softened me up, they'd bring in some son of a bitch with filed teeth.

"You know, Durham," he went on, "you do seem like the kind a man could have over to his house without worrying. It ain't everybody here you can say that about."

"Well, I'm a plumb fool for popcorn and TV and teasing some with the womenfolk." Keep him wandering, Hog, keep him wandering. "But I do like a beer or two to grease things with. Reckon that'd upset the missus?"

"I don't mind a man taking a drink of an evening. Myself, I don't drink in the home on account of the kids an' all. But me and some of the boys I used to play ball with, we'll go out a time or two a year and tie one on. And Mitzi likes to drink on New Year's Eve."

"I knew you were a ballplayer as soon as I laid eyes on you."

He gave me a shy, proud smile. "I thank you," he said. "You play any football in school?"

"Lived too far out."

"You could've got a ride."

"Not that far," I said. "And baseball is the misfit's game."

He nodded as if that made good sense. "We used to play Tahlequah. Ain't that where you went?"

"*When* I went," I said. "I wasn't real regular about going." I crushed the Lucky. "She bring me some more smokes?"

"Cigarettes. Money. Reading matter. Sweet as she can be, looks to me like." He paused to give me a questioning look. He said, "Lot of books for a man that quit school."

"Oh, I may read too much, but sometimes it beats living."

"We'll have to let you have them a couple at a time."

"Sure. Give me the book of Yeats poems and one called *The Unsettling of America.*"

"That last book," he said. "Well, we don't want anybody getting stirred up."

"It's about farming, by an ole boy from Kentucky."

"Farming." He seemed to take comfort in the word.

We fell quiet. "Y'all beat Tahlequah when you played them?" I asked.

Memory brightened his face. "We took 'em easy my first two years. But when I was a senior they had this halfback, Eugene Crow, moved there from Locust Grove or someplace. Best I ever seen. You must've knew him."

"Just in McAlester," I said. "He escaped a few months after I got there." He had ridden away from the prison rodeo on a bay quarter horse named Rex. As far as anybody knew, he was still riding.

"He damn near beat us by himself," Lawson told me. "Gained over 200 yards. Nobody else that year gained as much as a hundred on us."

"At McAlester, he used to spend all his yard time running beside the wall, round and round. The rest of the time he'd be in his cell, sunk way back into the silence. I don't think I ever heard him say a word."

"We were lucky to beat them. Thirty to 27, I think it was. They didn't have much defense."

I said, "Lots of folks in Cherokee County still don't think he raped that woman."

He gave his head a slow shake. "He could've went to Oklahoma. Got offers from everywhere. I never understood it."

"I don't think football was ever much more than light exercise to him."

"It's a shame."

"How about yourself?" I asked him. "You play in college?"

"Oh, I went to Tech for a year, but it didn't suit me somehow. I'm a home boy, I guess."

"It beats drifting," I said.

He leaned forward then, folded his arms on the table, and furrowed his brow, and I wondered if, Christ, he hadn't brought the conversation, haphazard, around to where he wanted it. "You thinking about marrying Miss Puckett?"

"I was. But I'd just as soon not have to have a warden perform the ceremony."

"She's a fine woman."

"Yes," I said.

"Told me she used to be a cheerleader in El Dorado."

"I didn't know her then."

"You know, my Mitzi, she done that too. She was two years behind me in school, but when I was a senior I seen to it that the boys voted her into the Homecoming." He leaned back again, awash in memory.

I'd never been interrogated in quite this way before. "Lord, she just took your breath away. Her hair all done up like it was and that frilly white gown with the green sash running up across it. Little ole bitty thing she was. Mitzi Tull was her name back then. I'd've had to gone a long ways to do better. She's most of the reason I come home from Tech. I knew if I stayed gone somebody'd grab her up."

I lit up the last Lucky of the pack. I couldn't figure Lawson. Was he just wanting another man, a ballplayer, to tell all this to? Was he doing anything more than whittling away the slow slammer minutes with me? Did he think that by giving me so much of himself, he'd get me to say, "Aw, hell, Lawson, I'm guilty. Forgive me." There wasn't anything for me to do but ride it on out. "Y'all got any kids?"

And, sure enough, he pulled out his wallet. "Four girls," he said.

"This here's a picture we had took of us all this June when we went down to Magic Springs." He told me their names and ages: Michelle ("Mitzi loved that song."), Clarissa, Josette, and Brookie—from fourteen down to six. "I aimed to keep at it till I got me a boy, but then it got to where I couldn't afford no more. And, anyway, Mr. Tull—that's Mitzi's daddy—he tells me there's some men fixed so they can't make nothing but girls."

I told him they were awful pretty girls and gave him the picture back. He put it away. "Come from good stock," he said. "That's *Clyman* Tull I was telling you about. He's been an officer down at the People's Bank for nigh onto twenty years."

"You don't say," I said, seeing it all come round.

"He's got a long memory. Never forgets a face."

"Must be a burden."

"He takes pride in it."

"I knew an ole boy in McAlester that memorized the Book of Revelations," I said. "It won him a parole. Now he's pastoring a little church in Sapulpa."

"I'm glad to hear that. It's a gift is what Mr. Tull says, the kind a man's obligated to make proper use of."

"Sounds like a serious man. That's why he's in banking, I guess."

"He seen you in court yesterday. Mr. Starbird, the prosecutor, he had him there. Your lawyer talked to him yesterday evening."

"Must've been a big day for him."

"And then me and him watched the ten-o'clock news together."

"It's good to see a man get along with his father-in-law," I said.

"Like I told you, we was both struck by the way you held your head up, not hiding nothing."

"I got nothing to hide."

"There's them that think otherwise."

"You can say that about anything." I put out that last Lucky.

"Mr. Tull's a fair-minded man."

"He a baseball fan?" I asked.

"Not much on sports," he said.

We were quiet for a minute. Then I said, "You know, Lawson, that was my last smoke."

He nodded. "I figured you'd be curious what Mr. Tull thought about you."

"I didn't rob the bank," I said. "But they got witnesses that say they saw me do it. If they wanted to stick me for pulling a job in

Johannesburg, they'd round up half a dozen witnesses to that. We through?"

"Almost. I wanted to hear you say you didn't do it, face-to-face. Because it's been troubling me. I know all them eyewitnesses against you and I don't think they'd lie."

"They see what they're expected to see."

"What troubles me is that I like you. I like the way you listen. I like Miss Puckett. Your lawyer bought me a chicken-fried steak last night down at the Cottage Cafe. He was wanting to know about your state of mind. And I liked him too—wasn't nothing like what I'd heard about him. Don't none of that mean you couldn't've robbed that bank five years ago, it just worried me. Seemed like good people liked you. And then last night Mr. Tull asked me over to watch the news."

"That was nice of him. I hope he eased your mind."

"He said he wasn't sure it was you, said there was some resemblance, but he remembered a darker, burlier man."

"Can he swear it wasn't me?"

"He wasn't sure."

"What happened to his memory."

"He was worried about that."

Well, yes. Hold on.

A half-hour after breakfast the next morning, Lawson led me to a small office on the second floor of the courthouse. Rotenberg was behind a desk. Lawson went out into the hallway. I sat down and watched Rotenberg put a trophy on the desk. "At 5:37 P.M. Friday, September 17, four years and eleven months ago, the precise time and date you allegedly robbed the People's Bank and Trust Company of Van Buren, Arkansas, you were entering the city limits of Okmulgee, Oklahoma, in the cab of an olive green 1962 Ford half-ton pickup driven by Mr. Ice Common Deer. You were wearing the uniform of a semi-professional baseball team called the Cherokee Nation. You were the only caucasian member of that team. At precisely 6:00 P.M., by virtue of the fact that the team's manager, one Bingo Montana, meat-packer, had correctly predicted the outcome of a coin toss, the Cherokee Nation, with you at first base, took the field as the home team in the quarterfinals of the annual Okmulgee Invitational Baseball Tournament. Your opponents that night were the Kerr-McGee Oilers of Henryetta, Oklahoma. The highway distance from the People's Bank and Trust Company to the Okmulgee Municipal Baseball Park and Recreation Center, where you played that night, is 104 miles. In a vehicle of the nature of that driven by Mr. Common Deer, no less than an hour and a half would be required to cover that distance. Therefore, you could not have left Arkansas later than 4:30 P.M. Therefore, you could not have robbed the People's Bank and Trust Company."

He leaned back and beamed.

I studied the trophy, a two-foot-high statuette of a left-handed hitter. "I take it we won," I said.

"7 to 5. You went 4 for 6 with a home run, two doubles, and a single. You drove in five of your team's runs."

"That might be overdoing it."

He set his briefcase on the table and patted it. "We can't contradict the scorebook. Baseball is a historian's delight. Every pitch is recorded."

I grinned, shook my head. "Offhand, I can't recall the winning pitcher."

"One John Post Oak. With one out and runners on second and third in the eighth, he was relieved by a gentleman named Augustus Riverwalker, now deceased. Mr. Riverwalker got the save."

"Ole Gus," I said. "Overly fond of white port. Drowned two years ago last June in Red Horse Creek. I heard about it in jail. But when he was here, he was alive. On the day of his funeral, they played a ballgame and then got drunk."

We gave Gus and that game a moment of silence. Then I said, "I don't know if this'll work. But it'll damn sure gall 'em and that'll be a pleasure to watch. So I thank you."

"It was Julius and Ice Common Deer who remembered the tournament, and it was Gonzalo Pinzon who took time off to help round up witnesses. He and Ice found something like sixty people who remember you playing that night. I can't take any credit for that. What they've done would almost certainly be enough to clear you. But I haven't been idle. Over the last two days I've interviewed most of the people who were in the bank at the time of the robbery—customers, tellers, loan officers, vice presidents, 26 altogether. That's why you haven't had as much of my company as you probably wanted. Four people, not counting the prosecutor's three eyewitnesses, still work in the bank, two tellers, a loan officer, and a senior vice president. The other twenty-two were school-teachers, factory workers, secretaries, merchants, you name it. A fair democratic sampling. I hired a retired preacher and a notary public to witness the interviews. The presence of the preacher ensured maximum cooperation. I showed each of the twenty-six four photographs—one of you, one of Bullet Bob Turner, one of Pretty Boy Floyd, and one of Eugene Crow."

"Eugene Crow," I repeated. "Maybe that explains something."

"The consensus was that Eugene Crow robbed the bank. He received seven votes. Pretty Boy Floyd came in a strong second with five. You got three and Bob got two. Nine people abstained, saying, bless them, that it was hard to remember that far back."

"I was on TV two nights ago. Looks like that would've fouled your plan."

"I interviewed several of these people before you became part of 'Newscene 6.' But not all of them, by any means. It didn't matter. Most people don't remember what they see unless they see it several times. Yesterday a man named Bart Comstock, works at Whirlpool, pointed to the photograph of Eugene Crow and said, 'This is him. I saw him on the news last night.' None of them are reliable witnesses, neither these nor the prosecutor's three. And that's precisely the point."

"The senior vice president you talked to, was that Clyman Tull?"

"R. Clyman Tull III, president of the school board, thirty-second-degree Mason, deacon in the First Baptist Church, past president of the Rotary Club, chairman of the Crawford County Republican Party. Eyewitness to the robbery in question. And a man inordinately proud of both his integrity and his memory for faces. Ah, yes, the very man. I think he'd actually testify that Eugene Crow committed the robbery—in spite of the fact that Crow was still in the Oklahoma State Prison at the time." He folded his hands behind his head and gave me a confident smile. "You see, Hog, the prosecution hasn't done much work on this case. They just took what Cesar Ratoplan handed them. Not that Ratoplan did it himself. He hired a private detective, Charles Cavanaugh, to do the investigating. Cavanaugh gave his evidence to Randy Mantis, who gave it to the district attorney, who read it over and figured he had an easy win. While he is sitting around dreaming of higher office, we've drubbed his ass."

"You know," I said, "I've never beat these fuckers before. They're not holding something back? Setting us up some way?"

"I'm taking my evidence, several dozen Indians, and maybe Mr. Clyman Tull III to Sam Hugh Starbird's office. I think the good prosecutor will agree to drop the charges and to inform Mr. Randy Mantis of the happy news. And then you and Pansy and I are going to have supper with Ice Common Deer and assorted friends."

"What're we having?"

"Poached venison."

51

Around four-thirty I changed from county coveralls to blue jeans and then followed Lawson from the jail to the sheriff's office. Pansy ran to me, threw her arms around me, and commenced to laugh and cry at the same time. I held her and looked over her shoulder at Rotenberg, leaning against the tax collector's cage. This time I thought I saw as much resignation as victory in his half-smile. He had paid the old whore, Justice, and she had lain down, twitched cleverly beneath him, and then got up, douched, put on her robe, and walked to the lobby to offer herself to the next customer. I was just glad Rotenberg had known how to play her.

Sheriff Bus Basham set my cardboard box of belongings on the counter. "See if you can't get yourself untangled there, Durham, and come over here and sign for these valuables. I'd like to get you out of here before them damn Indians and reporters swarm us."

I walked over and checked the box—books (including Yeats and the Berry, which they'd never brought to me), Luckies, wallet, that same damn watch I'd been holding as insurance against bad times. I signed the form.

Pansy took my left hand. "Let's go home, Hog."

We started out, but Lawson came around me and stuck out a big hand. "Good luck to you, Durham," he said.

I let go of Pansy's hand, shifted the box into my left arm, and shook Lawson's hand. "I'll keep an eye out for a replay of your movie," I told him.

"Lawson," the sheriff said, "there's times a man needs to put a curb on his good nature."

Lawson stepped aside. I gave him a wink.

Pansy, Rotenberg, and I went out the door and into the newsmen. As they rolled film, snapped pictures, and shouted questions, we made our way down the grimed hall toward the afternoon sun and freedom. We pushed through the big double-doors at the end of the hallway and a great cheer went up. Joseph Hummingbird, in his AIM T-shirt, shook my hand and held it for the cameras. Then, with his other hand, he took Rotenberg's, and the three of us, Hummingbird in the middle, faced the crowd and raised our arms like heavyweight champions.

We lowered our hands and Joseph Hummingbird began telling a reporter that though I wasn't a Cherokee I had been part of their community for a long time and they stood by their friends. "We are here to demonstrate that we will not tolerate legal harassment of ourselves or our friends. We are here to celebrate a community victory."

They were asking me questions, but I didn't feel like answering. Just behind me, Rotenberg was saying this was not an absolute victory. "On the basis of very flimsy evidence, Mr. Durham was subjected to harsh publicity and held in prison for four days. We're considering a lawsuit."

I wanted to find Ice Common Deer, so I left the reporters to Joseph Hummingbird, took Pansy's hand, and walked down the steps and onto the wide sidewalk that had the names of the county's Civil War dead engraved on it and led to the big statue of Robert E. Lee on Traveler. A bare-chested Cherokee boy of about ten was sitting up there behind the general and kicking his heels into Traveler's stone flanks and yelling "Hiyee!"

Folks slapped my back as I passed by. And then I saw Anna Lee Yancey, standing off to one side by herself, holding a baby in her arms, looking bedraggled and beaten. I knew she must've come out of a need to apologize for telling about the robbery money, so I told Pansy to wait for me and went over and gave her the chance.

"How you, Anna Lee? Pretty baby you got."

"I named her Rebecca Ann." She started crying. "Lord, I always wanted one."

I remembered that. I nodded. She tried to wipe her eyes with the baby's blanket.

"It's all right, Anna Lee. You don't need to say anything. I appreciate what it took for you to come here."

She looked up at me, her eyes full of that childish gratitude that always seemed to make people want to hurt her. "I told your lawyer—he seemed like a nice man—I told him I hoped you got off and so he called me today and I thought I'd come." She looked away.

"It was good of you."

Looking down at her baby, she said, "That man that come a while back, Hog, he scared me bad."

"I know." I leaned over and chucked the baby's chin.

"He told me I could go to jail too."

"You could have. And all you did was tell him the truth."

"I didn't mean to hurt you, Hog," Anna Lee said. "You never done me harm."

"I was just there, Anna Lee. Nothing much mattered to me then."

"I best go on now. I just needed to say it." But she stood there like she always did, waiting for the man to either hit her or leave.

"I'll walk you to your car."

"That'd be nice."

I touched her elbow.

"It's over there." She motioned with her head.

It was an old red Galaxie 500. I opened the door for her. She leaned over, strapped the baby in a carrier, then got in herself and began fumbling through her purse for the keys.

"Anna Lee, you take care of that little girl."

She nodded and stuck the key in the ignition. "Sometimes I like to remember when we were together," she said.

I didn't say anything. She looked down, started the car, and shifted it into drive. "I didn't mean nothing by that. Leonard's been good to me. He works over at Horner Box. I got a family."

"Hold on to it."

Anna Lee gave me her doomed smile and drove away. I watched her go and wondered just how long it'd be before Leonard left her.

Pansy came up behind me and asked who I'd been talking to. I told her. "That was nice of you," she said.

"Anna Lee doesn't have a mean bone in her body. Or a smart one either. So sooner or later somebody'll break every one of them."

"Maybe she'll get lucky."

"They don't have a lottery in Oklahoma."

She took my arm and turned me around. "I think that's Ice over by the fountain," she said.

We were headed in that direction when I saw Pinzon drive the co-op pickup between two parking meters, over a curb, and up into the crowd. He killed the engine, got out of the cab, and vaulted into the bed, where I now saw Dummy Boudreaux, getting to his feet. "Barbecued pork," Pinzon yelled. "Cole slaw, lemonade, home-grown watermelon. Come and get it. All you want. Compliments of the Columbia County Cooperative and the Arkansas Reds."

Dummy let down the tailgate. Pansy and I went over to take a look. They'd gone out and bought special containers for the food. Two #3 washtubs for the pork and a big green plastic garbage bucket for the slaw. There were fifteen or twenty Black Diamond watermelons stacked up next to the cab.

When he saw me, Pinzon said, "Glad you could make it, Hog."

"Christ, they're apt to slap us all back in now."

"No, my man, that damn shyster lawyer of yours got me a permit." He handed me a watermelon. "Why don't you start carving these?"

Then he addressed the crowd again. "We got paper plates, paper cups, plastic knives and forks, trash bags—everything modern technology can bring you. Try to leave the courtyard clean. You never know when ole Hog'll have to come back."

I passed out pieces of watermelon for a while, then filled my own plate and went over to the fountain to eat with Ice and Mary and Pansy.

A kid played in the pool surrounding a winged water-spouting stone Angel of the Confederacy. "That little Jimmy?" I asked Mary Common Deer, a broad-shouldered, clear-eyed woman who wore her graying Cherokee hair pulled back in a bun.

"Yes. Can't keep him out of water."

"Shouldn't try," I said. "Looks a lot like Packy. How's she doing?" Packy was what they called their daughter, Elizabeth.

"She's studying science over at Northeastern," Mary Common Deer said. "We watch Jimmy for her during the day."

"Now why don't you ask Mary how her arthritis is and if the fish are biting? Anything to keep from saying thanks." That was Ice. A half-smile creased his dark, sun-cured face.

"Hell, Ice, you just saw your duty and did it. A man doesn't deserve any thanks for that. Anyway, you're getting all this barbecue and melon." I forked myself up a mouthful. "What you think about Julius's woman?"

"It's hard to think when you're looking at her," he said.

"She's not here now."

"It's hard to think when you're remembering what she looks like."

"Well, it ought to be a good marriage then," I said. "At least till time and gravity gets to her."

"Yes," he said.

"I think Julius has done well," his mother said.

"So has Susan," Pansy added. She and Mary swapped smiles.

"The little bastard never even told me he'd proposed," I said to Ice.

"He don't know you like I do, don't know what a fool you are for romance."

"Yeah, I've damn near gone broke buying roses and chocolates for Pansy."

Ice turned to Pansy. "What is it a good woman sees in a man like Hog?"

"I'm after him for his money?"

"Well, Hog, it's Friday," Ice told me. "I believe the People's Bank is still open."

52

The shindig on the courthouse lawn lasted another hour or so and then most of us piled in various trucks and cars and headed on out to Ice's farm, where we continued the feast with deer ribs and roasting ears. I talked to Bingo Montana some about the cattle business and about Jeronimo Velasquez, found a chance to thank Pinzon for his help in springing me, tried to answer Joseph Hummingbird's questions about the Columbia County Co-op, but finally tired of that, referred him to Rotenberg, and went down to the pond and sat with Ice, who was watching kids play in the shallows.

"It's not been too long ago we used to sit here in the evenings and drink beer and shoot cottonmouths with our .22's," I said.

"You weren't much of a shot."

"Hell, I didn't miss much. It's just that you didn't miss at all. Shame there wasn't a bounty on moccasins."

"Used to make belts out of the hides," he said. "Ugly bastards."

"That's why your people lost the country," I said. "Too romantic about nature."

"I didn't want my kids getting killed in a damn stock pond."

"Yeah, if you've done nothing else with your life, you've made this little brown hole of water safe for children."

He gave me that dry laugh of his that was so rare and good. "And what the hell have you done with yours?"

"I been hitting pretty good."

"Lord, you could always do that." He finished a rib and threw the bone to a yellow dog. Then he turned serious. "But that don't matter much, does it?"

"You find what you can do good and you give it your best and you hope it matters."

"It'd be fine if it was just people playing in country pastures and town parks," he said. "But the big leagues ruin it. Makes dreamers out of kids."

"Nothing wrong with dreaming."

"The world's been fouled by dreamers."

"Like Joseph Hummingbird?"

"Well, I like Joseph. He's got a bigger dream than just playing with the Yankees or getting rich. I think he's even done some good. But, yeah, like Joseph. He's nothing unless people follow him and that's always dangerous. And there ain't nothing but what's here and I don't think he'll ever be satisfied with that."

"I can understand that."

"I know you can. That's why you've spent half your life in jail."

"Bingo," I said.

He leaned back, put his weight on his hands. "Take a kid like Julius. He's got the talent and the will and maybe he'll make it. I hope he does. I wouldn't turn down a ticket to watch my boy play in the World Series."

"You might, you old bastard."

He gave his head a little shake. "But I worry about Julius. He might not make it. He could get hurt or find out he can't really hit the smart pitching. And he doesn't know anything but baseball and these hills, and these hills may look awful small to him when the baseball's gone."

"A kid grows up and goes off chasing a dream. That's the way it is and that's the way it ought to be."

"Everybody wants too much too easy," he said. "Everybody goes for the lights."

"And they're run by the electric company."

"Bingo," he said.

We sat quiet a minute or two and watched the light die out over the western hills. Mothers came down and got their kids out of the pond, reminding us as they did that there was plenty more venison and beer.

"I guess we ought to go up and be sociable," Ice said. "Let you play the freed hero a while." But he didn't move.

"It's good sitting here," I said.

"You look at it the way most people do, there's not much here. A house I built out of scrap lumber and creek rock, a barn, this pond, a few acres of truck crops, a few head of stock, some woods. It's hard work, but me and Mary put by most of what we eat. I sell four or five yearling steers every fall. I never took a dime of government money. I'd go back to rustling first. This place suits me, Hog. I take pride in being part of it and making it work. It's more than enough. I could make a good life out of less."

I looked up the hill at the people I'd known all my life, decent folks mostly, but many of their faces marked by alcohol and poverty, and most of their dreams bounded by these eastern Oklahoma hills. Very few of them had learned to plant those dreams in the ground beneath their feet. Ice was the exception.

"You're a good man," I told him. "Mary's a good woman. The two of you belong here. It's not that way with most of us."

"You always wanted excitement and it's always cost you," he said. "You never learned to pray for the possible."

"Yeah," I said. "Right now I want what you got, but tomorrow morning I'm apt to wake up wanting to be a stock-car driver in North Carolina."

"Well," he said, standing up, "that might be just the life for you—driving around and around real fast in the same damn circle."

"Bingo," I said.

53

That night after the folks went home and the fires went out, Pansy and I borrowed an old patchwork quilt from Mary Common Deer, walked across the half-acre patch of fall tomatoes Ice had recently set out, spread the quilt under a big red oak growing out of the top of a rise near the south edge of the farm, and then spent the best part of the night making love and slapping mosquitoes.

Just after dawn Ice's yellow dog woke me up by licking the sweat off my throwing arm. I coughed once and, reminded, got a Lucky out of my shirt pocket and lit up. It had been a dry summer and the pasture before me was more brown than green. Even that early the sun bore down hard. I got up, walked off a ways, and took a piss. The dog followed me, sniffed, and went over and marked a clump of Johnson grass.

If that dog had been an hour quicker about waking me, I'd've gone down to the barn and helped Ice with the milking. As it was, there wasn't anything for me to do but stand and think about life on this place—the long days and slow rhythms, the unforgiving hardness that could either bend a man to imbecility or straighten him to wisdom. I saw again why I'd left the farm, saw why I was tempted back, and saw too that it might be a life better suited to red Indians and yellow dogs than to an old, pull-hitting thief like me.

"Lord," I heard Pansy say behind me, "we should've brought some insect spray."

"I'm a little slow about licking on a woman that's covered with Off," I said.

"It's the slow licking I like."

I turned around and looked at the yellow dog. "What's a man to do with a woman like that?" I asked him.

He cocked his head, raised one ear, and let the other droop. After a couple of seconds he went over and stretched out, head between paws, a few feet to Pansy's right.

"You been working with that dog all night?" I asked her.

She looked at me sidelong, arched her back, opened her thighs. "I have a way with animals," she said.

I ran the dog off.

A half-hour later, over a breakfast of sausage, eggs, fresh sweet milk, biscuits and gravy, Ice, Rotenberg, and Pinzon gave Pansy and me a good kidding while Mary grinned and shushed them. I complained about the dog bothering us, and Ice said Pansy would've done better to run me off and keep the dog.

"In the long run," Pansy went along, "the dog might be the better choice. But, for a little while, anyway, it's so much easier to feel sorry for a man."

Mary laughed then, outright, and allowed as to how it looked like ole Hog had met his match.

"Be nice if you wouldn't insult her that way," Ice told her.

I pulled away from the table and said it seemed to be high time to clear out of Indian territory.

"Ball game at two," Pinzon said. "The prodigal thief returns to the one-armed grasp of his benevolent father. Good show. Big crowd. Some redeeming social qualities."

"Y'all ought to come," I told Ice.

"I got living to do," he said.

"But we're coming for the last one," Mary said.

"If it means anything," Ice added.

"Just being last makes it mean something," I said.

"It means you have to decide what to do the next day," Ice told me.

"Maybe we can have a pickup game," Pinzon said.

Out in the yard, Rotenberg shook Ice's hand and kissed Mary's forehead. "If you ever need a lawyer, . . ." he said.

"God forbid." Mary Common Deer laughed.

"Amen to that," Rotenberg agreed.

54

That Friday of my springing turned out to be a big day for Arkansas politics. It had nothing to do with me, of course. According to the Saturday morning *Arkansas Chronicle* I read while Pansy drove us toward Little Rock in the co-op pickup (we were fol-

lowing Rotenberg and Pinzon, who rode in Rotenberg's old white
Falcon, which sounded like a lawnmower with the croup), the
Honorable John P. Schicklgruber, member of the House of Repre-
sentatives and candidate for the U.S. Senate, had been one of
thirty persons, all members of the Ark-O-Roma society, arrested
by Pulaski County Sheriff Blanchard Pennecost during a Friday-
night raid on the top floor of the Champ Hadley Hotel. The
Chronicle reported that Pennecost, who was having some trouble in
his reelection campaign due to a few thousand dollars in missing
appropriations, a couple of kilos of vanished cocaine, and a few
dozen battered prisoners, had just two months earlier returned
from the Bahamas, where he'd attended an anti-pornography conference organized and hosted by the Rev. Dr. J. Raymond Whiteside. "Dr. Whiteside gave us a list of wife-swapping and smut
clubs. The Ark-O-Roma Society was on the list. I didn't think that
sort of thing existed in Arkansas. But I had a duty to investigate.
Two of my deputies infiltrated the club and then we just did what
we had to do. I'm sorry about Congressman Schicklgruber, but he
shouldn't have been there." Pennecost went on to say that there'd
been about 150 Ark-O-Romans on the top floor of the Champ
Hadley but that he'd only arrested 30 of them because he'd been
careful not to violate the Constitution by entering any unopened
doors. "But I don't play favorites either," he added.

It all made you wonder some about Schicklgruber. Why would
he take such a chance? There was the obvious answer, of course:
better men than him have thrown over bigger futures for a nice
piece of strange. And the Ark-O-Roma Society must've seemed
safe to him. Except for Schicklgruber's, the *Chronicle* didn't print
the names of the people Pennecost arrested. But it did print a
sampling of their occupations—doctors, lawyers, an insurance executive, several bankers, two delta soybean farmers, the principal
owner of a regional chain of discount stores, a former All-South-
west Conference football player, a former Arkansas Junior Miss,
and one chancery judge. Schicklgruber, then, was among his kind.
And they'd paid what they saw as their dues: "Sheriff Pennecost
exceeded his authority," the Champ Hadley's manager, Donald
Prudhomme, told the *Chronicle*. "He had no search warrant. These
are respectable people, prominent citizens. They paid their bill
and disturbed none of the other guests. We respect our guests' privacy and we think the sheriff should do the same."

"Respectable people don't go to orgies," Pennecost said. "There were naked dancers. There was wife swapping. They were using controlled substances and illegal paraphernalia. There was homosexuality. I don't owe any apologies." He and his men confiscated video cassettes of *Deep Throat, Behind the Green Door, Misty Beethoven, Eager Beavers, High School Snatch, Inside Seka, Debbie Does Dallas,* and *The Texas Chainsaw Massacre.*

"*The Texas Chainsaw Massacre?*" Pansy said.

"Foreplay," I told her.

Schicklgruber's only quoted comment on it all was "There's more to this than meets the eye," giving himself time to decide whether to plead alcoholism or to claim he was conducting his own investigation.

"You know," Pansy said after I'd finished reading her all the articles, "I actually feel kind of sorry for him."

"Yeah. I bet that party hadn't even got started good."

We pulled into the parking lot about noon and there was Lefty, in uniform, passing out peaches, okra, and purple hull peas. Three or four dozen people, I'd say, and a few reporters, stood around the trucks, waiting for food or quotes. When he saw us Lefty straightened up and waved.

I went over to Rotenberg and told him the only thing I didn't understand about the Schicklgruber scandal was why the two undercover deputies hadn't warned him. "You know they really didn't want to arrest Schicklgruber."

"You don't know Pennecost's deputies," Rotenberg said. "They probably didn't recognize him. And you may have Pennecost wrong. He's an irregular. He'd arrest Billy Graham if he thought it would win him a few votes." He stretched and sighed. "It's business for me, though. I'm sure some of the Ark-O-Roman socialites will be wanting me to defend them on constitutional grounds."

"Schicklgruber?"

"Oh, I have to draw the line somewhere."

Two reporters lurked just outside the clubhouse door, but I got past them without having to say anything more than that as far as I could tell, justice had gone 2 for 2 yesterday.

The boys gave me a proper welcome—lots of laughing and slapping and general hoorawing. I don't know how many of them knew I was guilty of robbing the bank—most of them, probably—but that had been five years back and I'd been straight enough

with them and I could hit and we still had a shot at the pennant.
Even Hagio Acribar seemed pleased. "I am truly proud you have
been unbound," he told me. I didn't figure he got that line from
Ratoplan.

After the commotion had settled some and I was in front of my
locker changing into my uniform and savoring the clubhouse
smells of oiled leather and yesterday's sweat, it came to me that I
hadn't seen Eversole. I'd've liked to've had his hand in greeting,
but I figured he was back in the equipment room brooding over
missed chances and lost civilizations. I decided to leave him be.

A few minutes later I was playing catch with Julius in front of
our dugout while the Nashville Fugitives took batting practice.
Lefty came over and stood beside me and told me that unless I
wanted to ease back into things, he would start me in the game.
We'd lost two more tough ones—Guerrero, 1–0, and Franklin
Brown, 3–1—and he wanted my bat in the order.

I said I was ready, thanked him for providing me with Rotenberg, and asked him where Eversole was.

"After he won Thursday, he asked for a couple of days off. He
pitches tomorrow. He'll be back then."

I threw him a look with a question in it. "Oh, Christ," I said.
Lefty nodded.

The house filled up a half-hour before game time. The Cubans,
revolutionary and counterrevolutionary, were still a curiosity, but
a sizable part of that crowd must've showed up because this
seemed like a good place to flick some jabs at John P. Schicklgruber. They'd brought banners saying, among other things: "Save
Our Families—Keep Schicklgruber in Washington"; "Politics
Makes Strange Bedfellows"; "Vote Schicklgruber—Make Love
and War"; and "Lonely Representative Loves Limber Lovelies,
Call 969-6969."

We got a nice hand when we took the field to start the game,
and Genghis Mohammed got an even bigger one after striking out
the side in the top of the first. Nashville threw Bells Whitson at us,
and Jefferson Mundy led things off for us with a line single over
second. Then, with Hagio Acribar faking a sacrifice, Mundy stole
second. Acribar worked the count full, then drew ball four. As I
stepped into the box, I heard a group of fans directly behind home
doing a variation of the Razorback hog call. "Wooo, Hog!
Sooeey!" And it did seem to me like a good time for ole Hog to take

one downtown. But I reminded myself to just meet the ball, a hit would mean a run, and Whitson didn't throw many gophers. He was what they like to call a stylish little left-hander. I looked at four straight pitches, sinkers and curves, just one of them a strike. Three and 1,.he's got to come to me now, I thought. So Whitson threw me another sinker, and I swung for the civic center and grounded into a 6–4–3 double play.

With Mundy on third, Rainbow Smith flied to center to end the inning, and that was as close as we came to scoring until the seventh. Genghis gave up a double to Dingo Donaldson in the third and a two-out triple to Cleon Crow in the fifth, but other than that it was all flyballs and strikeouts. His hard one was hopping good and the hitters that didn't miss it entirely got under it. By the end of the fifth, he'd fanned eleven.

"What's the record in this league?" he asked Lefty.

Lefty hesitated before saying, "Nineteen. But don't let thinking about it cost you the game."

Genghis gave him a cocky, one-sided grin. "I want my name in the white man's book. Ever' time he opens it up, he'll have to see it."

"It's not much of a book," Lefty said.

"Then how come you knew the answer?"

He kept challenging them, not mixing his pitches enough, coming time after time hard and over the top, set on the K. He whiffed the side again in the sixth, giving him 14, but not before Tate Fathers, their first baseman, parked one in the zoo and gave them a one-run lead.

Genghis fanned the first man up in their seventh, walked the next one, fanned the third one (giving him 16), then served a fat one to Stark Williams, who poled it high and long to dead center. Julius caught it on the run just before he crashed into the wall, then fell to the track in an awkward heap and lay there a few seconds before getting to his feet and holding up his glove, the third out still in it.

But still, the way Whitson was pitching, it looked like that one run might hold. He hadn't struck out a man; it was ground-out after ground-out: 4–3, 5–3, 6–3, 3 unassisted. It was damn near a hundred degrees on the field and that little left-hander didn't look like he was going to break a sweat.

But we got a break in the seventh. Hagio Acribar, leading off, shortened up to bunt, then slapped one past Dingo Donaldson, who was charging in from third. By the time their left-fielder picked up the ball, Acribar was on second. I came up then, and, after pulling two outside sinkers to short, I was determined to go with the pitch. I did. I sent the first sinker he threw me to second on one hop. It did move Hagio to third, though.

"Way to move him over," Lefty told me in the dugout.

"Hell, I was aiming for the wall in right," I said.

They kept their infield back, conceding the run on a ground ball to second or short. But Rainbow got behind 1 and 2 and then bounced back to Whitson. Two gone.

Whitson must've lost his concentration for an instant because his first pitch to Julius was over the heart of the plate and up. Julius stuck it in the left-field screen.

"Let up some, kid," I told him after everybody had shaken his hand. "You're making the rest of us look like old men."

"Some of you are," he said, giving me that young smile I wished he could keep forever.

So Genghis went into the eighth up 2–1 and 3 K's short of the record. After one batter, he was just two short. Then Allie Ransom, their manager, sent Jarrell Turrett up to hit for Whitson, and he doubled off the wall in left. Lefty came out to the mound to talk to Genghis and Cantwell. I thought they might give Drew Little, their leadoff man and a good contact hitter, an intentional pass. But Genghis hadn't thrown a double-play ball all day and probably wouldn't even try to now. A double play would just give him two less chances for strikeouts.

Genghis pitched to Little, but walked him anyway—four fastballs about eye-high. Jeronimo Velasquez started warming up in our bull pen. But Genghis got ahead of their next hitter and made him pop a 1–2 heater over by our dugout, an easy play for me. Waiting for it, I heard Genghis yell, "Let it go." I caught it, walked over to him, dropped the ball in his glove and said, "I get what I can get to."

Warner Penn put the next pitch in the freeway. Ball game, I thought. It didn't seem to bother Genghis, though. He fanned the next hitter, his eighteenth, pounded his fist into his glove, and strutted toward the dugout.

I sat beside him on the bench. "I hope he hits for you," I said.

"He won't," Genghis told me. "It ain't his way."

I watched Joe Buck Cantwell take a strike from their reliever, Billy Potts, a right-handed black fireballer.

Genghis wiped his face with a white towel. I felt like hitting him.

Cantwell sent a lucky little checked-swing looper over first, and Lefty had Mike O'Bryan hit for Worm Warnock. Genghis got his bat out of the rack and, before going to the on-deck circle, turned back to me and said, "This man's going downtown. It's my day."

And, sure enough, O'Bryan bounced Potts's 2–1 hummer off the right-field foul pole.

With the score tied, nobody on and nobody out, Lefty let Genghis hit for himself. He took three straight strikes. I caught myself hoping Potts would bean him.

Allie Ransom brought in Kenyon Earnhart, a southpaw, to face Jefferson Mundy. Mundy doubled. Acribar singled him home with the lead run. Then Earnhart hung a curve to me and I caught it flush, jacked it so high and long that I got to stand at the plate and watch it soar.

We scored three more times before they got us out, an 8-run inning, our biggest of the year.

While Genghis took his warm-ups for the ninth, Woodrow Ratliff used the public address system to tell the crowd about the record.

Nashville got two hits, a walk, and a run that inning, but Genghis put his name in the book, got two more K's for twenty and the record.

After the game-ending strikeout, he thrust his right fist into the air and stood on his hill, defiant in mild applause.

"Well," I told him when he finally got to the dugout, "now I can tell my grandkids I saw a man hold Nashville to five runs."

"You won't forget to mention your big tater," he said, and went into the clubhouse.

Lefty came up behind me and said, "You're awful high and mighty."

"Cocky black son of a bitch."

"Just looking after number one," Lefty said. "I believe I've heard you take that line."

I jerked my head back like I'd taken a punch. "But now I done seen that light," I said. "Which tends to turn a man into a horse's ass."

"Must've been neon," he said through a cracker-barrel grin.

55

When we got to the clubhouse the next day, a Sunday, Eversole was already there in full uniform. I asked him how the air had been in Asheville. He shook his head. "She left."

I studied his face, learned very little. "And the half-wit?"

"Him too."

Then Guerrero came up and said, "Aye, the man returns. We win easy."

And we did. Eversole beat them 5–2 with a six-hitter. I hit a three-run job off Spats Taylor in the third and after that the game was never in serious doubt.

That night, after filling up on fresh vegetables and some chicken Dummy Boudreaux had worked his magic on, I did the dishes and thought about Eversole's love life. I couldn't make sense of it— probably, I thought, because there wasn't any in it. Lefty came in, leaned against the counter, and talked to me about it for a few minutes. But he didn't know any more than I did.

We had the day off on Monday and I spent a good part of the morning setting out tomatoes and planting cucumbers, corn, and pole beans for the fall. I wouldn't be there when the crop came ripe, but maybe somebody would.

That evening Bobbie Sampson drove half a busload of us down to Pine Bluff to hear George Jones at the Convention Center. He looked too drunk to do anything but sing—though he did that right well. The whiskey, along with the paper mill smell that seeped into everything in town, just seemed to make the songs come out right.

The Milledgeville Peacocks came in Tuesday and over the next five days we took four games from them, bringing our record up to 60 and 48, just three shy of Selma. It rained-out the Thursday game, but Lefty and Mote Haze agreed to make that up with a Saturday doubleheader, which we swept. We drew an overflow crowd for the first game of the series, the one Guerrero pitched and won, 4–2, with ninth-inning help from Jeronimo Velasquez. After that, though, the crowds dropped off some—good houses still, but not quite full. Some of the new had worn off the Cubans and I

guess some of the vacationing folks that just needed to gawk at a
new roadside attraction dropped down to Hot Springs and took in
the wax museum or the IQ Zoo or maybe even drove all the way
up to Eureka Springs and caught the Passion Play and stood under
that big, stiff Christ of the Ozarks and thought about the meta-
physics of concrete.

The out-of-state reporters, having filed their quick stories and
quicker follow-ups, folded their clichés in their briefcases and flew
home. Anyway, for the time being, at least, we'd ceased to be the
big story in Little Rock. That honor went to John P. Schicklgruber
and the Ark-O-Roman scandal. It was the same old story, really—
another drunk congressman with a hard-on—but folks always get
a charge out of it, and I guess it's easy to see why. Comedy, pure
and simple. What I can't see is the tragedy some of the high-
minded want to put in it. You take Wilbur Mills, old and fat and
dull and surrounded by men just like him—hell, fucking Fanny
Fox was probably the smartest thing he ever did.

Just once it'd be nice to see one of those potbellied bastards that
had been caught red-handed shooting jism across a strobe-lit room
stand up and say, "Boys, I did it because I'm like most of the rest of
you. I like pussy a whole lot." But politicians are trained to eat shit
and call it sugar, so John Schicklgruber played it by the book. The
day we opened the Milledgeville series, he staged a press conference inside the Little Rock headquarters of Alcoholics Anony-
mous. According to the *Chronicle* I read the next morning, he traced
his alcoholism back to a July day in 1977 when he obtained documents proving the Russians had closed the missile gap. He had devoted his life to nuclear superiority. His failure drove him to drink.

In his despair, Schicklgruber said, he'd lost his moral compass.
But now, thanks to the diligence of Sheriff Blanchard Pennecost,
he'd found it again. He was withdrawing from the Senate race and
committing himself for six weeks to the Billy Sunday Sanitarium
in Gethsemane Springs, Nevada. When he emerged, upright and
forever dry, he would once again devote himself to the concept of
peace through strength, would do everything within his power to
help close the window of vulnerability. Then he kissed his wife for
the cameras and, I suspect, went off somewhere, laid himself down
beside his moral compass, and drank himself to sleep.

The Reverend Dr. G. Forrest Bushrod grabbed center stage the
next day. From the front porch of the old garrison house where

Douglas MacArthur was born, he told a crowd of newsmen and apocalyptics that God had told him to seize the fallen banner and lift it high. He wanted the Republican nomination, but if the party didn't award him that, his followers would go all over the state gathering signatures to put his name on the ballot. "We must choose between God and mammon," he said. Then he kissed *his* wife, and the faithful paraded across MacArthur Park singing "Onward Christian Soldiers."

I was sitting over breakfast reading the *Chronicle*'s account of all that Thursday morning when I got a call from Randy Mantis's secretary, Julie. She asked if a ten-thirty appointment would be convenient for me.

"No," I said.

"Eleven?"

"No."

"What time would be convenient?"

"It's raining," I said.

She put me on hold; I hung up.

A minute later the phone rang again. I had Pinzon answer. "Hog's taking a bath," he said. "Would you like to hold?"

I picked it up after I finished breakfast.

"Mr. Durham?"

"He ain't here. I'm his son."

"What?"

"You've got a bad connection."

Mantis came on the line. "Durham, I remind you that I'm still your parole officer. You're treading on thin ice."

"Summer's here. The ice is gone."

"I still have a responsibility. Unpleasant as it is."

"Take the day off. Go for a long walk. Think about the nature of responsibility."

"What time is convenient, Durham? It'll be brief." He paused. "You're in no trouble. I give my word. Maybe this can be our last meeting. I'm going on vacation."

"Twelve-fifteen," I said. His lunch hour.

"Earlier or later would be better."

"I got a game at two."

"It's raining," he said.

"It might quit."

"Earlier, then."

"My mornings are sacred," I said.

He paused again. "Okay. Twelve-fifteen. But you be here."

It kept raining hard enough that I knew there wouldn't be a game. So Pansy and I got to the parole office a little after twelve-thirty. She went in with me. "Last time they took you away," she said.

Julie was at her desk having a carton of yogurt and a can of Tab.

"Julie, this is Pansy Puckett. She's a kind of freehand social worker."

"Go right in," she told me.

Pansy started to follow.

Julie said, "Honey, you can have a seat on that couch. I'll get you a cup of coffee. Sugar? Cream?"

Pansy looked at me. I told her it was all right and went in.

Mantis looked up at me, then down at his watch. It took me a few seconds to recognize the big guy across from him. The beige leisure suit he was wearing threw me off.

"This is . . . ," Mantis began.

"I know him," I said. It was Lump Wingo, the Oxford deputy Eversole had kayoed that night way back in April. "Sucker for a straight right."

Mantis gestured toward the empty chair next to Wingo, who was showing off a mediocre snarl. "This'll do," I said, leaning back against the door.

Wingo turned his chair so that he could face me without twisting his neck. "I'd like to ask you a few questions," he said.

"I don't talk to just anybody. Why don't you write 'em down and mail 'em in?"

"The questions don't concern you personally." That was Mantis.

"The worst kind," I said.

"You seen Candy Commerce?" Wingo asked.

"We through now?" I asked Mantis.

"Mr. Wingo is investigating a possible kidnapping. It might be wise to tell him what you know."

"Oh. I'll do that," I said. "Candy Commerce is a good-looking whore that's shacked up with a rich preacher in Asheville."

"She ain't there now," Wingo said.

"Money ain't everything," I told him.

"I want to see that big Indian friend of yours."

"I'll tell him you been missing him."

Mantis decided to put some tone on the conversation. "Do you have any knowledge in regard to the current whereabouts of this Candy Commerce?"

"No."

Then he surprised me some: "I think that should be all, Mr. Wingo."

Wingo gave him a long, almost threatening look. "He's lying," he said.

I held the door open for him. He stopped when he got to it and said, "You tell Cochise I got my eye on him."

"He's such a flighty bastard I wouldn't want to upset him like that."

He showed me his slow nod and his mean grin. "You ain't got long," he said, and left.

"Nice crowd you run with," I told Mantis. "You come up with another deputy sheriff, be sure and call me again." I started to leave.

"I had nothing to do with that."

"Right," I said. "He just happened to be here when I dropped in."

We stared at each other, my hand still on the doorknob. Then he gestured toward the chair again. "As I said, I think this will be the last time."

I shut the door. "Sounds like a proper invitation," I said.

We took our respective seats and lit our respective cigarettes. "Actually, Mr. Wingo's temporarily on leave from the sheriff's department," Mantis told me. "He's working for a Jay Flemson."

It figured. I said, "Then he didn't have any business here at all."

He stared thoughtfully into the ashtray. "I wanted you to see him and take fair warning. He could cause you trouble. And as soon as he'd asked his questions I had him leave."

"You're getting mighty considerate here in the late innings."

He took a short puff off his cancer-proof fag, furrowed his brow, and leaned toward me. "This has never been pleasant, I know. For either of us. But you have a legal obligation and I have a job." He swiveled his chair a notch to his left and crossed his legs. "Probably the primary cause of recidivism is the parolee's inability to either arrange or accept a viable future."

"Say what you got to say, man, and be done. I been to this seminar."

He uncrossed his legs, stubbed his smoke, lifted a folder out of the wire basket to his left, laid it on the desk in front of him, opened it carefully, and turned a few pages, pausing briefly over each.

"It'll make a good story," I said. "If you can figure how to end it."

Leaving the file open, he leaned back. "Do you plan to marry Pansy Puckett?"

"Saturday night. Reception's at the national guard armory. Bring your own liquor."

He reached out with his right hand and closed the folder, back to front. "This is pointless."

"Amen to that." I snuffed my Lucky.

Drumming his right-hand fingers on the folder, he devoted part of a minute to thought. It seemed to piss him off. "Up to now, Durham, you've wasted your life. You've never trusted anything but your own smart mouth. And I don't think you have any intention of changing. That's a shame, too, because you're an intelligent man. Many of the men I deal with are just ignorant and mean. But you could make something of yourself, live a decent, productive life among respectable people."

I stood up. "I thank you for that," I said. "I'm going to run on out now and join the church."

"Diagnosis confirmed," he said.

While I was walking to the door, he said, "After the season ends, I'll need to know where you are and what you're doing. You can report by phone."

I left without looking back.

Two days later, after winning that Saturday doubleheader from Milledgeville, we got on the bus and took to the road again, for the last time, bound for Selma, the future Mantis had warned me about just three weeks away.

56

The crowd the next afternoon in Selma looked like it was made up mostly of hatchet killers and Klan snipers. But that might've been partly due to my own state of mind. I needed sleep and I didn't feel like standing out in the hot sun taking shit from fans in the middle of Alabama. We'd just driven most of the night getting there and the whole team looked pretty well dragged out. Just ride this one out, I told myself, one loss won't matter that much; we can get a good night's sleep and give them hell tomorrow. It ought to've been an off day anyway: the boys that make out the schedules don't worry overmuch about players: this was a Sunday, which usually meant a pretty good house. Play ball.

We were a quiet bunch in the dugout, just kind of seeing it through, nobody even seeming to pay much mind to the riding we were getting from the big Selma crowd. We didn't take batting practice or shag flies, just went out a few minutes before game time and loosened up our arms. I took maybe a couple of dozen easy throws. It would've suited me if Lefty had started Susan. I could've went back in the clubhouse and slept on the rubdown table until we needed a pinch hitter.

But then Bull Cox jerked us up out of the doldrums by sending Bullet Bob Turner out to give the home-plate ump the Selma lineup card.

"Look at this," Pinzon said. "Freedom lives."

"Christ," I said. "I hope I don't have to hit at that knuckleball today."

The fans cheered Bob, lightly at first, but, as they realized the significance of it all, more and more of them stood and their applause filled the house.

At the height of the cheering, Lefty climbed out of our dugout carrying our lineup card. He drew a loud round of boos. Halfway to the plate he stopped and tipped his cap to the crowd. The boos resounded. Pinzon stepped to the lip of the dugout and started applauding Lefty. One by one the rest of us joined him. Even Ernesto Guerrero and Stump Guthrie, warming up in the bullpen, stopped, took off their gloves, and clapped. Lefty laughed, gave us a bow, then walked on to the plate, gave a card to the ump and one to Bob, and made a show of extending his right hand to Bob. Bullet Bob hesitated, the fans, like a wrestling crowd, started yelling "No! No!" but Lefty kept his hand there, and after a minute, Bob, who was too simple to be an outright hypocrite, shoved his hand out and shook Lefty's. In the relative quiet that followed, we applauded Bob.

That got us primed, but we may've beaten them anyway. The biggest part of this game is pitching, and Guerrero had the kind of sinking stuff a little fatigue helps. He gave up five hits, got a couple of strikeouts, maybe a half-dozen fly outs, and the rest, the other 18 or 20 outs, he got on rollers or choppers. We only had five hits ourselves, but one of them was Rainbow Smith's leadoff homer in the second and another was Jefferson Mundy's two-out two-run triple in the fourth. Less than an hour and a half after the game started we were in the clubhouse with a 3–0 win.

We beat them the next night, too. Franklin Brown went seven good innings, mixing a hopping fastball with that slider he was beginning to master. Jeronimo Velasquez shut them down the rest of the way, and we won it 5–2, the difference being a three-run shot I hit off a 2-0 cripple Hoss Barnett served me in the fifth. The crowd didn't even have enough spunk left to boo Susan Pankhurst when she came in to finish up for me in the ninth.

Right then we were within a game of Selma and had Eversole scheduled to go for us the next night, and I went to sleep that night trying to remember just when it was we'd last been in first place— sometime back in the middle of May, but I couldn't remember the exact date. So, in the game I was all but sure we'd win, Selma beat us, clear and clean. They got a run in the first on two seeing-eye hits, a bunt, and a fly ball. We tied it in the third on back-to-back doubles by Mundy and Acribar. But with two out and one on in their seventh, Axe Heflin put it away with a shot over the left-field wall. Bull Cox brought Bullet Bob in then and we didn't put another runner on until Hagio bunted for a hit with two gone in the ninth. That brought me up with a chance to tie it. Bob threw me three knuckleballs I couldn't've hit with a tennis racket. I took the first two, both strikes, then swung from the heels at the last one, missing it a good foot.

I stood there cussing myself and whoever it was that invented the knuckleball until Iron Joe Talmadge, who'd been out to the mound congratulating Bob, came back and handed me the ball. "Here it is, cowboy," he said. "Regulation size."

Bob was behind him laughing. "You ought've come over with me, Hog. All y'all got's you and Eversole and he's getting tired."

"Yeah. He ain't but 27 and 4."

"Lefty's wearing his arm out. Early in the year he'd never threw that game ball to Axe. Right now when you're really needing him, he'll be slacking off. Arm's tired. Has to be."

"He was a little off today. And even at that you just got three runs."

"He threw the fat one when it mattered. How many times he done that before? Hell, Hog, come on over to Joe Bob's Lounge in a little bit and I'll stand you a beer."

"Reckon I'll drink with my own." I flipped him the ball he'd struck me out with.

He caught it and shook his head. "It's a shame," he said.

"Hell, Bob, if it don't hurt some it ain't real."

"You do need a drink, Hog."

Well, it hurt some again the next night. They shelled Genghis Mohammed, Jr., and we made four errors behind him and they won laughing, 10–5. Just to rub it in some Bull let Bullet Bob pitch the last half-inning. He set us down 1, 2, 3—two strikeouts and a damn six-hopper to short.

In the clubhouse afterwards we devoted a good half-hour to pure moping gloom. At the start of that series, we might've been willing to settle for a split, but getting it the way we had—drawing up to within a game of Selma, then falling back to where we'd come from—made us wonder whether we could actually win when it mattered. Getting close had given us the shivers and we'd commenced to play like the misfits we were—each of us working hard to find his own way to lose. I even wondered if Bullet Bob hadn't been right about Eversole. Looking across the clubhouse at him, I did think I could see a touch of weariness and maybe a hint of defeat in his face. We'd played 112 games and he'd pitched 31 of them, going the route 29 times. He was way better than this league, but he was forty-six, and it *was* possible he was finally beginning to wear down some. And God only knew what he was up to with that Commerce woman.

I went in and thought about that bet Shakespeare Creel had made with the guards, how he'd bet on me because he thought (or hoped) I could make something of a straight-up chance. I'd been lucky, I knew, to get that chance—lucky I could hit a hard ball a long ways, lucky the Reds needed somebody who could do just that and were willing to put a convicted thief in the lineup, and lucky, too, that through all the years of petty theft and barroom thrills and slammer payments, I'd managed to hold on to just enough sense to recognize not only that, at last and almost in spite of myself, I'd found something to belong to but also that belonging was what mattered, that you might have to start after freedom by breaking away but you couldn't get to it without joining in, that it was a thing of community, that it was not a separation but a union.

Lord knows, I told myself there under a shower all the heat had gone out of, that ought to be enough. If a man got that far, what difference could winning make? Up against that a minor-league pennant was just a cheap piece of cloth. In a world the pin-striped boys were conniving to scrape the life off of and cover with buildings the air can't get into, I'd found a place to breathe and be. Sure, it might all end with the season, 14 games away from gone and not likely to be repeated, but from then on I'd at least know what to look for, at least know that it was possible, at least know that, however much luck had to do with it, it wasn't something you could steal. And if I never found it again, I'd had it once. Just that much was worth being here for.

What do you say to that, Shakespeare, you old doomed thief?

And the ear in my mind heard his voice as clear as if he'd been showering next to me.

"Horseshit," it said. "Take the poetry out of it, and all you have is a two-game losing streak."

57

Pumpsie Narvaez was laying for us in Plaquemine. First, we had to stay in a motel just south of Baton Rouge. Pumpsie hadn't invited us back to Fort Saint Ignatius—and once had probably been plenty for Lefty anyway—so we'd made reservations at the Cajun Inn in Plaquemine. But when we got there, it was closed, and so were the others in town. We were lucky to find one as close as we did.

"I guess Pumpsie's not happy with us," Lefty said.

That was putting it mildly.

We spent our first day there resting and reminding one another that we couldn't let up against the Pirates, that we needed a sweep and all we had to do to get it was to play steady ball. That night, determined not to be lured into playing slack, Plaquemine-style baseball, we went out and took the field against a team of Mexican League All-Stars.

Just watching them warm up, you could tell they were good.

"These are the best in Mexico," Eversole told us. "Alvarado, San-
doval, Pedro Contreras, Guzman, Vasco Porcallo. Much tougher
than Selma."

Some of us were trying to talk Lefty into protesting when
Pumpsie came strutting up to our dugout. "It's all done up right,
boys," he said. "Had to waive most of my regulars. Damn near
broke my heart to do it, but I finally had all I could take of seeing
this league mocked by women and Cubans and Mohammedans
and two-bit Arkansas Communists. Anyhow, I'll fly these fellows
home in about five days and pick my regulars back up—or some
just like them. Got Judge Lee's signature on this paper here if you
care to check it out. I suspect your copy's back in Little Rock."

"That's all right," Lefty said. "I'm pleased we've won your respect."

He gave us the big smile and the sweep of a hand. "Just hang on
a spell longer, boys. You'll get to see some real ball here directly."

Pumpsie'd even brought a man up to manage them, Jesus Zumarraga from Mazatlan. Elegant, gray-headed, and imperial-
looking, he coached third when the Pirates were hitting, and when
they were in the field, he stood at the home plate end of their dugout, never pacing, never sitting down, coldly surveying the diamond, as if he were looking for a gap the barbarians might storm
through and retake the archdiocese.

As for Pumpsie, he sat at the other end of the dugout and poured
drinks for himself and his betrothed, the buxom, black-haired
Mary Belle Loudermilk, who wore a long, white slinky dress that
was slit from hem to crotch.

They started a six-foot-five sidewheeling right-hander named
Cuchilo Alvarado, who released the ball about halfway between
the mound and the third-base line so that, if you hit right-handed,
it gave your front foot a quick dose of the Saint Vitus' dance. If
you managed to keep your front foot in, he'd throw at your fists,
and when you started stepping in the bucket, he'd paint the outside corner. He kept everything but the brushback down and he
mixed just enough sliders in with that sinking, tailing heater to
keep you thinking. This here was hard stuff coming in at a bad
angle.

He shut us out through the first eight innings, yielding just one
walk and a couple of hits. The closest we came to scoring was when
Rainbow Smith doubled off the top of the wall. Ernesto Guerrero

kept us in the game, though. He got in trouble several times, but managed to work out of it, usually with a double-play ball, but in the seventh with two down and a man on first, Nuno Guzman doubled home a run.

So it was 1–0 when Jefferson Mundy led off our ninth by working Alvarado for a walk. Then he and Acribar worked the hit-and-run perfectly and I came up with men on first and third and nobody down. His first pitch to me was a fat slider, the one I'd been waiting for, and I nailed it, pulled it down the left-field line and over everything. But foul by about ten feet. Then he sailed one up under my chin. The next two came at the outside corner, the first one catching it, the second just missing. Go with it, I told myself, take it to right, the short, sweet stroke. But he threw me a pitch he hadn't thrown all night, a big, slow roundhouse curve. I strode twice, hitched twice, and ended up not being able to do anything but watch it come across the plate about thigh-high. A fat pitch, ordinarily, but under the circumstances it had made a damn twitching fool out of ole Hog.

A couple of pitches later, Alvarado got Rainbow Smith to two-hop into a double play, and that was the game.

In the locker room afterwards and in the bar back at the motel, we brooded over the game, bitching at the trick Pumpsie had played on us, but feeling a little proud too at the way we'd hung in against a first-rate team. Too much pride, really, in too little. We'd just been shut out, after all; hadn't even mounted a real threat until the ninth. But when you feel like you're sinking, you grab on to whatever's floating by.

Pinzon ran a finger around the mouth of his beer bottle and said, "A beautiful young woman, a rich, jealous old man, and a team of Mexican ballplayers all sleeping together in the same locked-up fort. Sounds like there could be trouble."

The next evening during batting practice, he mingled with the Mexicans, speaking quick Spanish with them, sometimes talking to one man at a time, sometimes drawing a group of three or four. Short runs of talk followed by nods and grins and little bursts of locker-room laughter.

"What was that all about?" I asked him while we listened to an old Cajun play the national anthem on a fiddle.

"Love," he said. "And manhood. Impotence and old age. The modern American woman's enlightened attitude toward sex. The loneliness of the immigrant."

"Ah. Real Philosophy," I said. "What did they think of it?"

"None of them were queer."

The Cajun finished the song and walked off the field. "Small crowd tonight," Pinzon said.

It was true. There couldn't've been over six or seven hundred. The old team had always filled the house. "You change all the horses," I said, "it fucks up the racing form."

Their pitcher that night, Antonio Mendoza, a big fluid left-hander, handled us easily in our first—Mundy chopped one to second and Acribar and I lifted petty flies to short center—and I went out to my position fearing that our only hope was for Eversole to pitch at least as well as Guerrero had the night before.

He hit their leadoff man, Luis Carvajal, square in the back. Jesus Zumarraga went to the plate, checked the bruise, sent Carvajal on to first, said something to the umpire, then took a few steps toward the mound, stopped, and spoke a sentence of calm Spanish to Eversole.

"Get out of my way," Eversole said.

Zumarraga shook his head once, then walked slowly back to the third-base coaching box.

Carvajal stood on first stretching his back. I looked at him. He motioned toward Eversole. "Loco," he said.

Eversole stretched, kicked, and hummed one just above the next hitter's head. The umpire came out and gave him the warning and the automatic fine. I wondered who the hell they'd send to collect it.

When time was back in, Carvajal took a big lead off first. "Loco," I said, making sure he heard it. He glanced back at me, and at that instant Eversole whirled and picked him off. Carvajal's hand was a good foot from the base when I tagged it.

From then on it was just Eversole—ferocity and art. Hummer away, spitter in at the knees, hummer on the fists, spitter away. Inning after inning, easy grounders, pop flies, and strikeouts.

That wasn't all he did either. When he came up to hit in the third and Mendoza sailed one at his head, Eversole didn't even flinch, just reached up with his left hand, caught it, turned, and handed it to their catcher, who looked at the ball, then up at Eversole, then back at the umpire, who looked down at the ball, up at Eversole, and then reached down, took the ball out of the catcher's mitt, put it in his pouch, threw out a new one, and said, "Ball one."

He was right. The rules say you can't have first after being hit unless you've made some effort to get out of the way.

Mendoza stood on the mound a good minute before throwing the next pitch. It was a curve, up and flat, and Eversole, grunting, pole-axed it. Propelled not by wrists, grace, timing, but by sheer strength, aboriginal muscle, the ball shot out in a high, rising line, cleared the wall in left center, and disappeared into the bayou wilds.

After Eversole had made his slow, defiant circle of the bases and acknowledged our congratulations with short jerks of his head, I went to his end of the dugout and sat by him. "I've never seen anybody do that before," I said. "Just reach out and catch a damn bean ball."

"He should've thrown at my legs," he said.

Mendoza, demoralized, broken, at least for the night, should've been jerked right then. But Zumarraga, who may have decided to just write this one off, left him in, and we had ourselves a five-run inning, two of the runs coming when I jacked a looping change. They ended up with two hits off Eversole, a broken-bat bloop, and a swinging bunt, and we coasted to a 9–0 win—or all of us did but Eversole, who wasn't much for coasting.

Still, we just had one Eversole, and we were scheduled for two more games against the Mexicans, two games we probably couldn't afford to lose.

58

We got to the park around four-thirty the next afternoon. It had been a blistering, humid day. All the gates to the stadium were locked. A sign over the ticket window said "No Game Tonight."

Hoping to rouse a groundkeeper or somebody, Lefty rattled the main gate and shouted a couple of times. Nobody came. Bobbie drove us to a gas station, from where Lefty called Fort Saint Ignatius. Tiboy answered and told him Pumpsie was busy. Then Pinzon called a bookie. "Tonight's game's canceled," he told us. "But we play two tomorrow. We're 2–1 favorites to sweep."

"Don't make no sense," Joe Buck Cantwell said.

"Sure it does," Pinzon told him. Then he slipped down into

Klan. "Them damn greasers is gone. I just hope the slimy sumbitches ain't took no white woman with them."

Lefty told Bobbie to drive us out to the fort. She remembered the way—the parish road into the bayou, the narrow private drive through the swamp to the gates of the fort.

I didn't think the guards would let us pass, but after a short talk with Lefty and a phone call to headquarters, they did.

Tiboy met us outside the main house. "Wait," he said.

We stood out there for what seemed like ten or fifteen minutes before Pumpsie appeared, wearing bathrobe and slippers, swirling whiskey in a glass, chewing on a cigar stub. "Glad you boys saw fit to drop in on us. It's always a pleasure. What is it you think ole Pumpsie can do for you?"

"You might tell us why the game was postponed," Lefty said.

Pumpsie examined his cigar. "Rain," he said.

Lefty nodded. "I see."

"I called the umps and they agreed it was pissing and pouring. Never seen the like of it. I didn't figure y'all'd even drive to the park in such a downpour."

Lefty stared at him a few seconds, then said, "I wonder what causes a rain like this."

"Oh, it was them goddam Mexicans. They brought the wrath of God down on me." He gave his head a solemn shake. "Years ago my ole momma told me not to have no truck with outsiders. She was on her deathbed then with the dropsy. Them was her last words, if I recall." He looked off to his right and shouted, "Fetch me a chair, Joe. A man can get to feeling mighty woebegone standing out in this rain."

Joe was a big, fat-faced, small-eyed thug carrying a rifle and wearing a black suit he must've bought at an FBI auction in 1957. He'd sneaked up behind us.

"That's Big Joe Landreaux," Pumpsie said. "Old friend of the family. And that handsome fellow yonder"—he pointed to his right—"why, that's Napoleon Kershaw. Claims he's kin to the fiddler. You believe that?"

Kershaw wasn't as big as Landreaux, but he was quite a bit uglier.

Landreaux brought Pumpsie a wicker chair, the kind Huey Newton liked to have his picture taken in. Pumpsie sat down, crossed his legs, and took a sip of the whiskey.

Lefty said, "We'll get out of the rain now."

"Aw, don't be leaving on me. I'd invite you in, but, Christ, the house is such a mess it'd shame me for you to see it. I wasn't expecting y'all for, oh, another half-hour yet. It wouldn't be respectful of you to leave before I got through telling you about them Mexicans. I had to mail 'em home early."

"Why is that?" Pinzon asked. He flashed Pumpsie a wide smile.

Pumpsie arched his brows, pursed his lips, and gave Pinzon a cool once-over. "I expect you figure you know the answer to that, don't you, Cisco?" Then he turned his gaze back to Lefty. "I had a notion them Mexicans would be hotbloods, so I hired some women for 'em. But, Lord, you know how they are, they wasn't content with that. They wanted the captain's piece. Kept rubbing on poor ole Mary Belle. And I'm damned if she didn't seem to take a shine to it. Now, I don't mind telling you, I been having my doubts about Mary Belle for some time now. Why, when y'all were here way back in May, Tiboy told me he seen her rutting with ole Cisco there. But Tiboy, hell, he'll take a drink now and again, and to be right frank with you, I thought he might be seeing things. I guess I just couldn't bring myself to think she'd sink that low. You know how it is when a man's in love. There wasn't no doubting it this time, though. The things she done, a Christian ought not have to witness. But then I had to see to believe. Then there wasn't anything for it but for me to cut her loose."

"Wherever she is," Lefty said, "she's better off."

Pumpsie nodded thoughtfully. "I reckon she might be. Having learned her lesson and all such as that. Still, it ain't in me to forgive her. All I want from 'em's big tits, a tight twitch, and fidelity. But I guess that's too much to ask this day and age."

"We *are* playing tomorrow?" Lefty said. "It might be easier for you to just forfeit."

"Aw, we'll play two. This rain'll blow over by then."

"Well, then," Lefty said, "if your friends can keep from shooting us, we'll leave now." He turned and started toward the bus. Big Joe Landreaux raised his rifle.

"I doubt he'd shoot," Pumpsie said. "But you never can tell about Joe. Everybody in this parish knows he's crazy. Ain't a thing in the world you could convict him of. So why don't y'all just come on back and humor a poor ole lonesome cuckold a while longer."

Lefty turned around and shrugged. "What's life without friends?"

"Why, there you go. I was saying the same thing to Tiboy just the other day." He sipped the whiskey again. "You know, Lefty, them Mexicans wasn't ever my idea. Judge Lee kind of wanted me to beef up my team for the stretch drive and some of the boys, you know, they don't think much of y'all and they were willing to help out, dollar here, dollar there. And, all in all, I guess it worked out for the best. See, I've had me another little woman for about a week now. And keeping her hid from Mary Belle the way I had to do was wearing on my nerves. This one comes from good stock. Real good stock. But goddamed if I ain't commenced to suspect my judgment's going slack on me, so I'd count it a favor if you'd give her a look-see and let me have the benefit of your opinion." He tilted his head straight back so that he was facing the sky and yelled, "Tiboy!"

Big Joe and Napoleon rushed up and arranged themselves—feet spread apart, both hands on their rifles, dead eyes dead ahead—a few yards to either side of Pumpsie.

We waited a minute. Nothing happened.

Pumpsie said, "That damn Tiboy's probably in there making free with her right now." He got up and opened the door. "Goddamit, Tiboy! Bring her on out here. We got company standing out in this rain to see her."

Tiboy brought her out. She couldn't walk on her own. Tiboy had an arm around her waist supporting her. She leaned against him, her legs kind of queasy beneath her. Still, for all that, they were nice, long legs. And you could see every inch of them. They had her in a pink robe but it wasn't fastened up. There wasn't anything under it but woman.

Her head was lolled forward and her long, dark hair hung down over her face, so I wasn't absolutely sure who she was until Eversole pushed past me. The two thugs jerked their rifles up and I grabbed the back of Eversole's collar and jerked as hard as I could. It stopped him, but just for a second. Then Lefty came over and stood in front of him.

"They ain't made one yet worth getting killed over," I said.

"Let go," Eversole said.

I did, ready to grab on again if he took off again.

Pumpsie said, "Well, now, I just had me a notion some of you might recognize her." He put a hand under her chin and raised her face.

And, yes, it was Candy Commerce.

She took us in slow, through wide glazed eyes, like an idiot child looking out at a new world from a safe place. When she recognized Eversole she tried to smile, but the necessary muscles wouldn't work, so she gave it up and slurred, "Hi." Pumpsie let her head fall back down.

Eversole said, "I'll take her now."

"Aw, now, son," Pumpsie said. "You'd be stepping in a mighty lot of trouble trying that. And, say you did get her out of here, which ain't likely, we'd have you for kidnapping. Her daddy's gone and declared her incompetent and signed her over to me. Least I could do for an old friend like Jason is see his daughter through the troubles. She's been through hell and part of Ohio, I don't mind telling you, and it's wearied her some, but I expect she'll come around any day now."

We tried to get Eversole to leave then, but he wouldn't. He just stood there glaring.

"The man's got a right to hear this out, Lefty," Pumpsie went on. "This lady's a friend of his and, why, Lord, there'd be something wrong with him if he wasn't concerned over her welfare. Jason tells me there was talk between them of latching on together permanent. So when Candy here and her poor ole brain-damaged cousin finally showed back in Oxford, why, their daddies knew they needed help with them and, me being known throughout the South for my openhandedness, Jason called and wondered if I might could see my way to turning him a favor and, of course, I was glad to help out any way I could. So here they are. I got the half-wit out back being looked after by one of them psychiatric nurses about the size of Joe here. That's why I was so pleased y'all dropped by this evening. Mr. Flemson, you see, he asked me special to make sure y'all seen what good hands she was in." He looked up at Eversole and smiled. "That ease your mind any, Geronimo?"

It took about half a dozen of us to hold Eversole down.

Candy Commerce raised her head a second, said, "I'm tired," and let it fall back down.

"I believe she needs another dose of that Thorazine, don't you Tiboy?"

Tiboy turned her around and started her back through the door. She said, "Bye-bye."

"We hoping to get her back on her regular medicine in a week or two, but Doc Rousseau tells us we need to keep her real calm for a good while yet." He had himself another sip of whiskey, then shook his head again. "Helluva woman though." Then he followed Tiboy and Candy through the door and closed it behind him.

I figured we'd have to struggle hard to get Eversole back on the bus, but we didn't. He went in meek and shamed. I followed him to the back of the bus and sat beside him, hoping I could come up with something to say.

"I need room," he said.

So I gave it to him.

To make sure Eversole didn't head back out to Fort Saint Ignatius, Lefty stayed at the motel with him the next afternoon and evening, while, before a big rowdy house, we drew what solace we could from taking two easy ones from the old Pirates, who, to keep things straight with the league office, played under the Mexicans' names.

We left the park as quick as we could, picked up Lefty and Eversole at the motel, and drove north, slow and sad, out of that godforsaken place, taking our last ride to Little Rock.

59

When we arrived in Little Rock the next morning, Lefty tried to get Eversole to stay at the Home with the rest of us, but he wouldn't have it. "I don't need to be humored," he said. So we took him to the field and he locked himself up in the equipment room and commenced to brood in his hammock.

That was a Wednesday and an off day, and most of us slept till way up in the afternoon. Dummy fed us a supper of catfish, hush puppies, country fries, and fresh tomatoes, and while we ate, some of the boys began asking Lefty and me what we knew about Eversole and the Commerce woman. We didn't know much and didn't figure it was our place to tell what we did, so we kept mum. Lefty managed to change the topic of conversation to Selma, who, while we were in Plaquemine, had taken five straight from Nashville and gone 3½ games up on us, 4 in the loss column.

"The scores weren't even close," Lefty said. "I think the fix might be in and I think they might want us to know it. I wouldn't've thought Allie Ransom would go along with that."

"Shit," I said. "When it comes down to crunch, you can count on them old southern gentlemen to roll over and plead patriotism."

"Not all of them," Lefty said. "Pop Stone won't do it."

Selma had to play five in Oxford before coming in to finish the season with us.

"If Oxford don't take them a time or two, we're done," Joe Buck Cantwell said.

Our one hope lay in the fact that we got to close out at home against the team we needed to beat, an advantage, Lefty told us, he had finagled by pleading poverty at the league meeting sometime way back in the winter. Judge Lee and several of the owners hadn't liked the idea of us both opening and closing at home against the league's best draw, but Lefty had argued that the weakest and poorest team, us, couldn't hope to survive without starting and ending well at the gate. But finally, it had been Bull Cox who had convinced the other owners to go along with the idea. "I want to hit them the first lick and I want to finish them off and watch them die and I want to do it all in front of their own home folks."

Lefty laughed and asked if there was more catfish. There was. "Those were his exact words," he told us when he'd returned with a new plateful. "So the owners who wanted us to fail voted with Bull, and Stephen Gabbard and Regina Pope voted with me and we all voted the same way."

Three and a half down with nine to go, but the last five against Selma. And our rotation fell in such a way that Eversole would be able to pitch three of the nine games, two of the five against Selma. A good part of what chance we had rode on his right arm. So, after supper, Lefty and I drove to the field to check on him. He was gone.

While Lefty checked both dugouts and the visitor's locker room, I climbed up on the roof to see if he might be up there taking the breeze. He wasn't, but I stayed there a minute, looking over the city and remembering the one long talk I'd had with him, almost exactly two months earlier. When they hurt you bad enough, I thought, you cover up. But you can't cover up forever. You beat them at the game you're good at, but sooner or later they'll trick you into playing something else. Old Bronc, I thought, after all these years of bucking in the daylight and hiding in the dark, you got rode down by an Oxford whore and a Louisiana lunatic.

"Well," I said to Lefty when I got back down, "if he's gone to Plaquemine, I hope he kills the son of a bitch."

"Yeah. And gets back here by game time."

When we got back to the Home, some of the boys were playing poker and listening to the Cardinals and the Phillies on the radio. I went up to my room without saying a word. I found Pansy reading *The Boys of Summer* in my bed.

She took one look at me and said, "He wasn't there, was he?"

"I'll tell you how it all comes out," I said. She laid the open book between her breasts. "Snider loses his ranch, Furillo gets screwed and goes bitter, Newcombe gets drunk, Campanella gets paralyzed, Hodges and Gilliam die, and Jackie Robinson, the proudest and toughest of them all, well, he dies too, but not before living long enough to be seduced by a Rockefeller, be called a Tom, and then see a son go to drugs, suffer through a cure, and get killed in a car wreck."

She studied my face, trying to judge my mood. "And what is the moral, Professor Durham?"

I jerked my right thumb toward the ceiling. "Big Zeke up there's hell on ballplayers."

"Maybe He was just a Yankee fan."

I lay down beside her. "How you figure He feels about spitballers?" I asked.

She gave a minute to silence.

"Eversole'll be back, Hog. This team's all he has left."

60

And she was right.

Bobbie drove us out to the park a couple of hours after breakfast the next morning and I went straight to the equipment room and there he was, reading *Darien Massacres* in his hammock.

He looked up at me and back down at the book.

"I came out here last night thinking we might talk some," I said. "You weren't here, I got a little worried. You all right?"

"I'm here now." He said it without looking up from his book.

So I left him. But a few minutes later, Lefty went in there, closed the door, and stayed a good half-hour. The rest of us killed time by playing gin rummy, trading lies, or reading the *Chronicle*. Selma had beaten Oxford last night 8–0, dropping us four full games back; the Yankees beat the Red Sox and went into first place; the Cardinals were beginning to fold; several Arkansas Razorbacks told Wilbur Haney they were ready for their opener Saturday against North Dakota State, a team, they said, no one should underestimate; the woman who claimed to be John Schicklgruber's primary mate in the Ark-O-Roma Society confirmed a report that she had signed to pose for a spread in *Playboy;* Reverend G. Forrest Bushrod, now the Republican nominee for the Senate, had received the endorsements of Orval Faubus, Charles Colson, and Tom Landry; the governor told a group of oilmen eating Springdale chicken at a hundred dollars a plate in Texarkana that he believed the Bible was the literal word of God and accused his opponent of being a Darwinian; Richard Nixon, preparing for a trip to China, said he held no grudges, had a clear conscience, and was writing a book on the proper uses of power; Norman Mailer punched Gore Vidal; the Secretary of Commerce said the economy would turn around in thirty days if every American would make an effort to consume more; the President told a group of Pennsylvania steelworkers that the workingman was the backbone of the nation, then flew down to the Bahamas, where he planned to recuperate from the pressures of office by spending a couple of weeks with his asshole to the sun; PLO terrorists had killed a woman and two children in Haifa, and Israel was responding by bombing southern Lebanon off the face of the earth; and in Mexico, before a crowd estimated at over one million, the Pope spoke out against birth control.

"Anything in the paper?" Julius asked me.

"Same old shit," I said.

He and I talked about his wedding some then. It would take place in nine days, at the field, on the Saturday we ended the season.

"Them assholes from Selma'll be giving you the razz," I said.

"We're going to get married early in the day, before they get here. The team brought us together. We want to marry on the field. We talked about doing it on Sunday, but we decided we wanted it to be part of the season."

"I expect you want me to perform the ceremony, don't you?"

"We'd sure like that," he said. "But I was afraid Joseph Hummingbird would be hurt if we didn't ask him."

"Were you able to keep Susan from crying?"

"She held it in."

He picked up a bat and studied the grain. After a minute he said, "I got an offer to play winter ball down in Puerto Rico. Me and Franklin and Atticus and Jefferson."

I nodded and gave him a smile. "All of you have a chance to make the bigs. It ain't granted to many."

"Daddy doesn't much like it."

"I know. He told me as much. But he'll keep that farm breathing good till you get back to it. And a man's a fool not to play while he can. Ball game in the sunshine, good woman at night, maybe a little garden spot and a collie dog. Shit, they can have the rest of it."

"Pretty Boy Durham's gone straight, has he?"

"Aw, hell, I'll probably have to hit Cherokee National now and again to keep myself in seed and dog food."

He let out a short laugh, then reexamined the bat grain. "You ought to talk to that man from Puerto Rico. He's going to be at that last game. They got a lot of teams there. It's good ball. You could bring Pansy."

"I might just do that," I said. "If the man'll have me."

I changed into my uniform, told Joe Buck Cantwell a rustling story, and then went over and listened to Guerrero tell about the year, 1970, Castro declared Christmas would be celebrated in July. "I was a rookie," he said. "It was the time of the big cane harvest. When we did not play ball, we worked in the fields."

"It was fair," Hagio Acribar said. "Fidel worked beside the people."

"My family grew coffee and fruit in the mountains," Guerrero said. "My heart was there and in pitching baseball. I did not like the cane."

Earnestly, Hagio Acribar tried to make us understand. "Our North Vietnamese comrades came to work beside us. And the Soviet Minister of Defense, Comrade Grechko. All of our government helped in the harvest. All of Cuba joined to save the revolution."

"You were a child," Jeronimo Velasquez told him. "It was an evil hour."

"I had nine years. I worked beside my mother. The people worked like soldiers. All were heroes."

Velasquez shook his head sadly. "All of Cuba became a plantation. Fidel became United Fruit."

"Aye, Jeronimo," Acribar said. "You are wrong about this."

Guerrero laughed and said, "I pitched a game on Christmas Eve of that summer. The crowd was happy but very tired."

"Christmas in July?" Stump Guthrie said. "Goddam, that's crazy."

"For the one year only," Acribar explained again. "Because of the harvest. The quota."

"It was Fidel who set the quota," Velasquez said. "Even so, we did not reach it."

"After July we were not made to work in the cane," Guerrero said. "The baseball was much better."

A few minutes later, we went out on the field. When I got the chance I asked Lefty how Eversole seemed.

"Tired but mean."

"That ought to do."

But it didn't, not for him anyway.

The crowd was smaller than any we'd played before at home in weeks. Bushrod's bunch—though their speaker's platform still stood at the parking-lot edge—didn't show. The only reporters around were the two sportswriters assigned to us by the two Little Rock papers. It was still a good crowd, about 3,000, and friendly, blacks in from the war zones out at Granite Mountain and College Station, lawyers, professors, college students, and liberals of various stripes who'd come more to show solidarity than to watch baseball, and a few hundred real fans, old-timers and their sons, who'd seen thousands of players here, some on the way up and some on the way out.

And when Eversole took the mound, those old-timers decided to show their appreciation of the kind of season he'd had (28 wins, an ERA of just under 1.00, 18 shutouts, a perfect game). They stood one by one and applauded him, keeping at it long enough for the rest of the fans to get the idea and join in, long enough for

Lefty and the boys in our dugout to climb the steps and applaud too, long enough so that those of us on the field stuck our mitts under our arms and cheered with everybody else.

I think all that may have thrown him off. Sure, Pumpsie and the Commerce woman were standing between him and his day's work too, but I figure his anger might've overcome that. Maybe not. But I do know that anger was as much a part of his repertoire as his spitter. An old anger, always just under control, but always there. And there's no doubt but that the crowd's, and his teammates', outright, enthusiastic admiration confused him. He stared down at the rubber for a long time, hoping to wait it out. But the applause continued, grew, and he raised his head, looked over at Lefty and the others cheering from the top of the dugout steps, then at me, and I thought his eyes showed the confusion of a warrior in a world gone friendly, and I wanted to tell him, "Just smile, man. Tip your cap. It won't be friendly long," but all I could do was make a fist with my right hand and hold it in the air. He turned back around toward the plate and motioned for Cantwell to squat and for the Asheville leadoff man, Elmer Jack, to step into the batter's box. With the crowd still applauding, he threw his first pitch. Fast ball, high and outside.

He walked Jack, got the next two, then fed a fat spitter to Hawkeye Crawley, who put it on the freeway. In the second he gave up another run on two doubles. Choo Choo Charlie Olsen started the fourth with a shot over the wall in right-center and they followed that with two hard line singles. Lefty came up out of the dugout and headed toward the mound, but Eversole didn't wait for him to get there. At the first-base line, he handed Lefty the ball and then went straight into the clubhouse.

It was too early to go to Jeronimo Velasquez, so Lefty brought Pinzon in, handed him the ball, and said, "Eversole's carried us all year. Let's see if we can't carry him once."

They had men at the corners and we were already four down, so we brought the infield in to cut the run off at home. Pinzon, pitching out of his old twisting, jerking delivery, but doing it, for once, with care and intelligence, got two quick curveball strikes on Hambone Rice, wasted a hard one and another curve, then got the whiff with a tailing fastball on the hands. Then Hawkeye Crawley bounced into a double play, and we were out of the inning.

We got a run in our fourth on Mundy's single and Acribar's

double. And in the seventh, with the bases full and one down, I jerked a great big 2-1 hummer out of the park, my thirtieth of the year. Pinzon pitched six innings of 4-hit, shutout relief, and we left the field with a 5-4 win and a feeling that luck was with us.

Late that night I called the *Chronicle* sports desk. "You got a score on the Selma-Oxford game?"

"Junior high?" It was Thursday night, junior high football time.

"Baseball. Dixie Association. Selma Americans. Oxford Fury."

"Let me see." I waited. He said, "4-2, Oxford."

We were still three down with just eight to go, but I said, "God bless the Fury."

61

We took two of the next three from Asheville, getting strong pitching from Franklin Brown, Genghis Mohammed, and Guerrero, and good relief from Jeronimo Velasquez, losing only Genghis's game and that due mostly to one fat pitch, a gopher to Hambone Rice that beat us 5-4. I jerked two more in those three games, giving me 32 and putting me three up on Axe Heflin for the league lead; Jefferson Mundy went 8 for 15 and drove his average to .346, five points ahead of Memphis's Jazz Beale; and all of us just generally rattled walls and rounded bases. Even Susan Pankhurst, who got in at the end of the two games we won, lined a sharp single to right.

At the same time in Oxford, Selma was losing two of three to the Fury, letting us pick up another game on them. Selma would be coming into town with a record of 69 and 52 to our 67 and 54. The math was simple now. If we won four of the five games, the year was ours. They only had to take us twice in five tries and they'd have their twenty-fifth Dixie Association title.

On Monday morning the eighth of September, a day of rest before the five-day showdown, Lefty asked me to ride with him to Rotenberg's office. We were going to pick up Eversole, take him to Rotenberg's place, and introduce him to Stephen Gabbard. "Gabbard thinks he can help him, and Eversole's agreed to the meeting.

But he wanted you there. With that many lawyers in one room, I guess he wanted a renegade to keep him company."

"Sure," I said, "I'd like to see how Rotenberg's painting's coming along anyway."

Driving us in, Lefty talked about women, ones he'd had and ones he'd let slip away, Texarkana whores when he was a kid, a high school sweetheart that had married a dentist when Lefty was in the low minors, baseball Annies when he was with the Browns, cocktail waitresses and college girls when he was tending bar and studying history in Albuquerque. But mostly he talked about Tamara Burroughs because she was the one that had mattered the longest and gone the farthest away.

"Well, you damn sure ruined her for the rest of us," I said. "She went straight from you to God."

I meant that to get a little laugh out of him, but it didn't. Then I realized that it was me and my woman he was thinking about.

"I'm only going to do this once," he said. "So bear with me."

I lit up a Lucky.

"I believe in damn near every simple old cliché you can think of. Having kids and setting a good example for them. Doing right by your neighbor. Opening your door to strangers. Refusing to take more than your share. I prefer mules to tractors, farms to factories, talk to television, singing to listening to the stereo."

He paused. I drew on the Lucky and waited.

"I've missed most of that," he said. "No wife, no kids, no farm. But I have taken some pleasure in watching other people find themselves a place and a reason. Young people, sometimes, who might otherwise have come here to Little Rock or gone to Dallas and started working for Timex or Texas Instruments—or mugging those that did."

"I grew up on a farm, Lefty. I know why kids get off of them first chance they get."

"These past six months I've watched you begin to come to terms with yourself. I've seen you with Pansy. I've noticed the care you put into tending that garden. And I know you have a past that doesn't leave you many options in the future."

We rode in quiet then for maybe a quarter of a mile. Then he said, "Part of the co-op's function is to help people buy farms."

I put my Lucky out. It looked like it was speech time, so I spent a minute composing one and then let it roll out. "I don't need to be told that Pansy's special and this team's special and I'm damn lucky to be part of it all. I want something that'll last, too, Lefty, but I'm not sure I can last with it. Every time something got to where it mattered, it scared me and I went back to what I was used to. Laying down with women I knew I wouldn't remember and didn't want to. Getting up lonelier than I was when I laid down. But not having to be responsible to anybody else. I've taken other people's money at gunpoint. And I've spent five years locked away, learning how to box up hope and how to fight fear with hatred." I tilted my head back and took in a big breath. "These six months may not be enough to undo all that. I ain't St. Francis you're offering to help get a homestead."

Lefty gave me his grin. "I'm not sure he'd farm it right. You have to be at least mean enough to keep the crows out of the corn."

A minute or two later we turned off Markham and headed up the hill toward the ballpark. I said, "Julius said there was a man from Puerto Rico coming to the game Saturday. I might talk to him about playing winter ball. I'm tempted by that."

"I don't blame you."

"Julius and Jefferson and them are a lot younger than me," I said.

We entered the empty parking lot and I watched the back of the grandstand rise toward us.

"Yes," he said. For a couple of seconds I thought he'd leave it at that. Then he said, "But you can still hit. Puerto Rico or anywhere else. If you decide you want to play ball again next year, I might be able to help you with that too. But the farm offer still goes."

"Give me a little time," I said. "I don't know if I can think about it right until we're done with Selma."

62

Rotenberg was showing his wall to Stephen Gabbard when we got to his office. Lefty and I shook hands with Gabbard and told him to thank his team for holding Selma at bay for us. Eversole, who hadn't said more than a sentence or two during the short ride from the park, stared at the painting. After greeting Gabbard, I did too. Christ was up there now, but he was on a chrome cross which was bolted to the original, larger, wooden one. Rotenberg's Jesus seemed to be made of plaster, white and crumbling, except where he had been wounded, hands and feet and crown, and there he was flesh, vivid, detailed flesh. And the eyes were real. Out of the face of a plaster saint stared the angry eyes of a man.

"What's the opinion of the sporting crowd?" Rotenberg asked. "Is it art?"

Lefty did his haughty professor. "It speaks, one must concede, rather directly to our national malaise. I am not, however, altogether certain that the parts, vivid as they are, coalesce into a whole."

"Ah, but Dr. Marks," Rotenberg said, going along, "that is our national malaise. Along with Astroturf and the designated hitter, of course." He walked over to his percolator. "Y'all want coffee?"

Lefty, Gabbard, and I did. Eversole kept looking at the painting. I took my cup, sat on the floor, and leaned back against the wall. Lefty and Gabbard sat on the old couch. Rotenberg pulled his desk chair over to that corner of the room. Gabbard talked a few minutes about a game in which Oxford had come back from three down and beaten Selma in extra innings. They got the winning run off Bullet Bob.

"We ain't hit him yet," I said.

"We didn't hit him," Gabbard told me. "He walked the run in. And, of course, he saved the two games they won."

Finally, Eversole came over and stood next to where I was sitting. "You should quit the law," he told Rotenberg.

"I have to pay rent on the wall," Rotenberg said.

Stephen Gabbard pulled out a pipe, filled it, tamped it, puffed it. "Do you know a man named Freeman Quick?" he asked Eversole.

Eversole didn't. I said, "He gave me a ride one time. He was on his way to buy a horse from Jay Flemson."

"If you stand on the road long enough, Freeman will give you a ride. And every time he'll be on his way to either buy or sell something from J. G. Flemson. And every time, buy or sell, Freeman loses." He crossed his legs and sucked the pipe again. "He's in jail now, charged with arson. I'm representing him."

"What did he burn down?" Eversole asked him.

Gabbard watched his thumb follow a carved line up the side of the briar bowl. "Flemson's mansion. Or that's what he's charged with. And maybe he did it. You see, that house stood on what used to be Freeman's farm. Flemson bought it for back taxes in 1952, when Freeman was in Korea. When Freeman returned from the war, he took a shot at Flemson, missing him, unfortunately. He spent a year in Parchman for it, and that seemed to cure him of violence. But he's never given up trying to salvage a part of his pride. Freeman's a simple man. I think he would've been content just to have gotten the better of Flemson in one deal. It hasn't happened yet. But I think there's a chance he will now."

He took a handkerchief out of his back pocket and wiped his brow.

"Sorry about the heat," Rotenberg said. "But Lefty shamed me out of my air-conditioning some years back. Told me Americans used more energy for air-conditioning than the Chinese did for everything."

Gabbard raised an eyebrow at Lefty, gave him an ironic smile, and said, "I'll try to hurry on through this, then. It's a long bicycle ride back to Oxford."

"I'll get Bethlyn to come up and fan you while you talk," Rotenberg said.

"You shouldn't tempt a Mississippi gentleman with a young black woman," Gabbard told him.

"What's all this have to do with Candy?" Eversole asked.

Gabbard glanced up into the dark, impassive eyes, then down at his pipe. "What do you know about Candy and Colonel Sanders Flemson?"

"She tries to take care of him," Eversole said. "It can't be done."

Gabbard puffed on the pipe, found it dead, relit it. "J. G. Flemson would've gotten rich, one way or another; but he got a fast start by marrying Howell Coldstock's youngest daughter, Varina. Howell Coldstock owned an old, proud name, a thousand acres of delta farmland, the majority interest in the Planter's Bank of Oxford, and every politician in northern Mississippi. Jay Flemson came from what most of Oxford would, and did, call trash. Howell refused to approve the marriage until he learned that Varina was pregnant by Jason Commerce. Jason was and is the husband of Margaret Coldstock Commerce, Howell's older, plainer daughter. At the time of Varina's pregnancy, Jason had a year-old daughter, Candace Varina Commerce." Gabbard sighed, shook his head, and went on. "I know this because some years ago Varina came to me wanting to file for divorce. She changed her mind, but not before she talked more than she probably wanted to. I'm not sure whether even Candy knows Colonel Sanders is her half-brother."

"She knows," Eversole said.

"Half-brother and full cousin," Gabbard said. "Jason Commerce and Jay Flemson owned a used-car lot together then, one of several Commerce enterprises, just the beginning for Flemson. Apparently, Jason told him about the pregnancy. Anyway, Flemson proposed and Varina managed finally to persuade Howell to let her accept. He presented Flemson with a dowry in the form of a $50,000 check, washed his hands, and spent the next, and last, ten years of his life on his verandah, drinking Tennessee whiskey and playing bluegrass on a phonograph. The last thing he did before he died was to make Varina promise never to institutionalize her son, the idiot, Jefferson Davis Flemson."

Well, Gabbard went on a while. We listened. Now and then, Eversole, seeming impatient, would put in a word or two.

Flemson prospered. Jason Commerce prospered. When Howell Coldstock died, his two daughters, their two children, and three Negro servants moved into the antebellum Coldstock home. Flemson lived in his mansion. Jason Commerce, after turning his family home into The Caddy's Rest, moved into an efficiency apartment above an office. On that basis, both marriages still survived.

But there were problems with the children. In 1967 a group of courthouse yahoos treated the idiot boy to a night in a Memphis whorehouse. A few weeks after that he hopped a passing schoolgirl and had to be gelded. At sixteen Candy converted to Roman Catholicism, spent nearly a year preparing herself for the nunnery, but then at seventeen, shortly after the idiot's operation, she suddenly began giving the aristocratic piece to any man that happened to ask. Jason committed her to an elite West Nashville asylum where they toned her down some with group therapy and lithium chloride. But when she came back to Oxford, she quit taking the medicine and became a baseball fan, saw every Fury home game, taking the idiot with her and sitting in boxes behind the home dugout. And in the autumn of her twentieth year she rode off to Mexico in a bright-red Mustang convertible driven by a twenty-two-year-old switch-hitting centerfielder named Julio Rivera. In the spring of the next year, in Aguascalientas, she left

Rivera in favor of a big pitcher, more than a decade older than her, whose name was Jeremiah Eversole.

"She liked the cities and the churches and had American friends," Eversole said, explaining why they stayed together little more than a year. "She would drink mescal and pray. I didn't have the patience for her or the understanding. She left and I went back to the solitude and the whores. She wrote letters, but I don't use the mail. When I was offered the chance to play in this league, I came and hoped it wouldn't be too late."

And while Gabbard went on with the tale, I kept glancing up at Eversole's face. But for all I could tell he had closed back up.

Since leaving Mexico, Candy Commerce had gone through two husbands and several religious denominations. The first marriage lasted nearly two years, but that was primarily because her man, a sewing-machine salesman, was on the road for much of the time. The second, to a psychiatric social worker, lasted less than a month. She sought comfort beneath virtually every branch of the Christian religion and even, briefly, tried Bahai. Nothing helped. She was never content for more than a few months at a time. She would be absurdly devout and then a man would come along with a car and a plan and she'd be gone.

With each of Candy's absences, the Flemson half-wit became harder to handle. When she was home she took him to the movies, cooked him fried chicken, watched the Saturday-morning cartoons with him, sat in a chair at the edge of his bed each night until he fell asleep. But when she was gone, he was alone. And he blamed it all on baseball because he had watched her drive away in that shiny car with Julio Rivera. He was nineteen the first time he tried to set fire to the grandstand at the field in Oxford. Varina bought him things, bright toys, music boxes, pets, had a Negro boy keep an eye on him and feed the pets, ordered the cook to prepare him fried chicken and mashed potatoes each evening. But he kept escaping and walking the ten miles to the baseball field, where he would be found hours later trying to set fire to the grandstand.

After about half a dozen of those arson attempts, Jay Flemson, hoping to humiliate Varina into allowing him to commit her son, went to court and had Jefferson Davis Flemson's name changed to Colonel Sanders Flemson. But because "Sandy" rhymed with "Candy" the new name pleased the idiot, and it was so appropriate that no one in Oxford, including Varina, ever again referred to him by his old name.

"Varina's only purpose was and is to atone for the disgrace she brought on her father, and atonement seems to have meant only one thing to her—keeping the deathbed promise. And she was the one person on earth who could hurt Jay Flemson without resorting to physical violence. If he committed her son, she would divorce him and claim in the settlement all the property she had brought to the marriage and half of what he had accumulated since. The wonder is that he didn't simply arrange for the boy to die in an accident, a fire perhaps."

"Or have *her* committed," Rotenberg said.

"Too old and proud a name—Coldstock," Gabbard said, "to be locked away in an asylum. Not even Flemson could have pulled it off, no more grounds than he had. And he wanted the name, the connection. Still does. I think he suspects that money alone can't keep him from being trash. No, there was nothing he could do other than try to reduce Colonel Sanders's chances of mastering the art of arson. So he took him to *his* mansion, the one he'd built on Freeman Quick's place, and Colonel Sanders spent most of his nights in a locked, windowless room and most of his days in the backyard Flemson had surrounded with a ten-foot cement wall and under the watch of the same hired Negro and sometimes, when the Negro was gone or Sandy was particularly unruly, leashed like a dog to the pecan tree in the middle of the yard. But neither hired boys nor walls are altogether to be trusted and once or twice a year someone would catch Colonel Sanders striking matches at the ballpark. Then, about eighteen months ago, Candy returned to the Coldstock home and stayed. Flemson delivered Colonel Sanders to her, and by this spring we had begun to think the four of them—the two sisters, the idiot, and the wild, God-haunted woman—would live out their lives together on that place, in that house, in the serenity just beyond despair."

Gabbard closed his eyes, ran his hand back through his hair, and waited.

"Then I came," Eversole said. "She saw my name in the paper, but I would've found her anyway."

"Yes," Gabbard said, opening his eyes to stare up at the ceiling. "And she remembered you slept in the locker room when you could. She came there and found you."

He looked at Eversole again, waited again. But Eversole wasn't quite ready, so Gabbard went on. "But Colonel Sanders saw her driving away and somehow knew and followed her on foot, carrying with him this time not just the box of kitchen matches but old Howell Coldstock's pistol too." He stopped, stared up at Eversole. "You know the rest of it."

"Yes," Eversole said. But that was all.

We waited.

"I need to know what happened," Gabbard said. "It's important."

"What good would it do?"

"It might free Candy. It might free Freeman Quick."

Eversole looked at Lefty, then at me. I said, "It might satisfy my curiosity."

Eversole looked toward the other end of the room for several seconds, then turned back and let it all come out. "He found us. We heard him and she went out and he was building the fire and she said something to him I didn't hear and he ran into the dark and shot the gun twice and then it was quiet in the dark and we couldn't find him. Then I heard him making noises under the bench in their dugout and I pulled him out and he didn't have the gun any more. There was just the loud moan that wouldn't stop and him hitting me, so I picked him up and carried him back and when I put him down he started hitting me again until I was tired of it and then I took his overalls off and tied him up with them. Then Candy was screaming too and we heard the police and I pushed her in the clubhouse and I was going to wait there and tell them to take him home, but one of them put his gun in my back and I had to hit him and I couldn't stay out after that. They tried to get in and we heard them talking until one of them left and took the boy. We waited. Then we heard Lefty and Hog and the other policeman and you and the Oxford manager and then everybody left and Candy did too. Just before light I heard a noise and opened the door and the bullet grazed my shoulder. He shot again and I jumped inside and he shot two more times. Then it was quiet. I went out and looked for him, but then I saw a fire behind the right-field fence so I put it out because I would pitch that night. So I didn't catch him, and him and Candy went to that place in Asheville."

We waited again, but he was through with storytelling.

So Gabbard took it up again. "Vigilance Mountain is neither wild nor austere. It is the sanctification of suburb and shopping mall—precisely the kind of place Jay Flemson or Jason Commerce would build if either of them decided to enter the business of religion. Raymond Whiteside had no chance of keeping Candy Commerce there long. She and Colonel Sanders caught a bus to Little Rock."

He wiped his brow again, relit his pipe. "It didn't work out in Little Rock either." He looked up at Eversole. "Because of Colonel Sanders, I'd guess." Eversole stared at the floor. Gabbard shook his head once and continued. "But there was Lump Wingo, too, who was in Little Rock working as Flemson's private eye. Sooner or later even a man as dim as Lump would've found the motel or house or apartment they were staying in. So Candy rented a car, returned to Oxford, took Colonel Sanders to Varina, and drove to the bank, intending to withdraw what remained of her share of the Coldstock inheritance and go back to Little Rock. Or maybe she wanted to get caught. Maybe it was easier that way. Jay Flemson had given his tellers orders to hold her if she showed up. One of them stalled while another called Jason Commerce, and before the day was out he had had her declared incompetent and committed to what he called the Saint Ignatius Mercy Home for the Disturbed.

"Nobody knows what Colonel Sanders did over the next few days, but we do know that Jay Flemson came and got him, telling Varina he'd hired a practical nurse to watch him. Flemson says he came home the next night and found the nurse drunk and Sandy gone. Later that night there was a small fire behind the home dugout at the stadium. No damage. Someone called the fire department and the sheriff's office, and while they were at the ballpark, Flemson's mansion burned to the ground. That afternoon, Sheriff Grimm found Colonel Sanders tied to a pole in an old barn on the abandoned Bodine place, not quite half a mile from Freeman Quick's house. So Grimm arrested Freeman and booked him for arson and kidnapping."

"They framed him," I said.

"Probably. But the truth is that Colonel Sanders, much as he loves the firelight, isn't capable of burning down a house the size of Flemson's. So, on the face of it, Freeman seems like the best suspect. It's common knowledge he's spent a good thirty years trying to exact some measure of revenge against Jay Flemson. Oh, he married a widow and sixty acres of scrub upland. But even then, even through two daughters and a grandson, he spent too much time trying to get the better of Flemson in a deal. It has never ceased to eat at Freeman. He became a poor farmer, a bad husband, and no father at all. It's not hard to believe he let it eat at him until there wasn't anything left but the violence again. Freeman says he's innocent, but Lord knows, there's reason to doubt him."

"Flemson did it," I said. It seemed clear to me.

"That's what Freeman says. But we'll never prove it. It makes sense. It's probably true. But we'll never prove it. Oh, he had the motive. You see, when Flemson began his petition drive to get his name on the ballot for congress, Freeman Quick started driving all over the district telling people how Flemson got his start. I think Flemson decided that if he set fire to his mansion and made it look like Freeman's doing, he might gain the voters' sympathy, if not for this election, then the next, and silence Freeman Quick at one stroke." He shook his head. "But we'll never prove it. I know Jay Flemson. We'll never prove it."

"So what did you come here for?" Eversole asked.

"Colonel Sanders shot you. We can prove that. And that gives us a way to get at Jay Flemson. He persuaded Varina to send Colonel Sanders to Plaquemine, where he could be with Candy. But that's merely a temporary out. He still can't commit him, especially not now, when he's hoping to win respectability at the polls. He's vulnerable and he knows it." He looked directly into Eversole's eyes and held the gaze. "That's why he's been frightened of you all along. That's why he went to Asheville. And that's why I need your help."

"What do you want?"

"I want you to say you'll press charges against Colonel Sanders Flemson for assault with a deadly weapon. Flemson can't risk seeing that go to court. This whole sordid history would become public knowledge. I'd make it clear to him that I intended to see to that. And if Sandy were convicted, the court would commit him. Or at least there's a good chance of it. And up would rise Varina, divorce, and scandal. I don't think it's a chance Flemson will take."

Eversole seemed to be considering it. Then he said, "I can't beat a man like that in court."

"It won't get to court. In exchange for your agreeing not to press charges against Colonel Sanders, Flemson will see that the charges against Freeman Quick are dropped and that Candy Commerce and Colonel Sanders are freed from that compound in Plaquemine."

Eversole just stood there staring hard at Stephen Gabbard.

Then I did what I was there to do. I said, "Jeremiah, the law's a horseshit weapon, but if it's all you got, you might as well grab hold of it. Your only other chance is to try shooting your way into Pumpsie's fort. If it was me, I'd go with Gabbard first and save the other for later."

He glanced down at me, then back up at Gabbard. "You tell him whatever you need to," he said. "But you tell him I want her here by Saturday. And you tell him this ain't Freeman Quick he's fucking with now."

63

The next afternoon Eversole beat Selma 6–0 in an hour and fifteen minutes. It was scoreless until our end of the third, when, with two down, Mundy singled and stole second, Acribar beat out a chopper, sending Mundy to third, I doubled them home, and Rainbow Smith hit a Whitey Shelton curve flush and drove it damn near to the zoo. After we got two more in the sixth, Bull Cox sent his one black man, Willie Gates, in to mop up. He made a quick, efficient job of it and Eversole kept getting them to beat the spitter into the dirt and it was over before some of the crowd of about 5,000 got sat down good. He might've beat them in under an hour if the Selma hitters hadn't kept asking the ump to check the ball. You couldn't blame them for doing that, but it was pointless. Eversole'd been throwing that pitch for thirty years. They weren't going to catch him dipping the ball in a jar of K-Y Jelly.

In the clubhouse afterwards, we were relaxed, confident, but pretty quiet. We'd pulled to within a game of the Americans, but to win it all, we still had to take three of the last four.

I took Pansy to a movie that night—they were showing *The Discreet Charm of the Bourgeoisie* in the atheist annex of the Unitarian

Church—and I just kind of rested in the dark and we left when the movie ended, missing out on the question and answer session. We went home, had a beer, and went up to bed. I tried reading for a few minutes but had to give it up. Pansy talked some about the movie, but I hadn't paid much attention to it, so there wasn't much I could say. She said she thought the Unitarians seemed to be performing a useful community service. I told her it seemed to me like they wanted to be religious without having to pay the price.

We lay quiet a minute. Then she said, "You think Franklin will beat them tomorrow?"

"Yeah," I said. "But I'm almost to the point where I can't tell thinking from hoping."

She turned over on her side, resting her head on the palm of her hand. "Is that good or bad?"

"Bad, I'd guess. Chancey, to say the least. But I'm not altogether sure. Never been there before."

"You know," she said, "during the game today I was looking at Bull Cox and thinking about him and it made me wonder what difference the score made. I mean, Lefty's right and Bull's wrong and we know that. We started from nothing and we've had a good year. Nothing can happen in the next four days to ruin that."

"Well, I'll have to get a ways past it before I can see it quite like that. I want to ride out of town with the pennant flapping from my aerial. This here's America, Love. We keep score."

Smiling, she laid her head on my shoulder. "And right now the bad guys are still one up."

"Yup," I said, "But we're fixing to bushwhack 'em."

Her breasts were against my ribs, and my old cock, interested in just the one race, started firming up. She reached down and took it in her hand. "Do you think it's wise for an athlete to participate in sex the night before a game?" she asked in a "Today Show" voice.

"I think he ought to keep at it right up till game time. Oral sex is best, of course. It keeps a man from talking his game away."

She rolled over on top of me and then I was in her. We were still a minute, just feeling one another, then, keeping me inside her, she sat up and started moving herself in that old, slow circle.

"Probably, though," I said, "he ought not let the woman get on top."

"It's too late now, Mr. DiMaggio. Marilyn's got you."

And the circle quickened.

A few minutes after we'd finished, I said, "If we have to lose, I just hope it ain't Bullet Bob that beats us."

64

The Reverend G. Forrest Bushrod was back in the parking lot the next day, stoking the holy fires, shaking hands and damning sinners, sticking the old hot shot to the rabble. But he and his several dozen disciples—maybe up to a hundred of them—had come not so much to rave about apocalypse and rapture as to work the crowd—the six or seven thousand that would show up that day—in behalf of truth and light and the Republican party.

The Selma bus pulled in right behind us, and Bull Cox and Bullet Bob and a half-dozen others of them went over to hobnob with Bushrod and some of the Arkansas Apostles. Pinzon sidled over there among them and I tried to keep within hearing range of him so I could catch what he was up to.

He slapped Bullet Bob's back. "Bob," he said, "you getting too high and mighty to even speak to your old friends? We've all forgiven you. You ought to come out to the place tonight and drink a while."

Several of Bushrod's best were staring at them.

"I don't need no forgiving," Bob said. "I done right."

Pinzon turned to a stern, lantern-jawed, rope-necked woman that had a "Vote Bushrod" button pinned just above the drooping right tit of her polyester dress and said, "You ought to see old Bob suck down the Coors. The rest of us are teetotalers, you know, but, Lord, Bob, he used to go through ten, fifteen quarts a day."

The woman turned away, then looked back at Bob, who explained, "He's a Cuban."

Bull Cox broke through the crowd that had gathered around Bob and Pinzon. "I don't like you, little man. Now, why don't you . . ."

Pinzon cut him off. "Why, you won't give me a chance, Bull. Me and you might get along just fine. Being a Cuban doesn't keep me from being a racist."

"These are good Christian people, son," Bull told him. "You might ought to learn to respect that." Then he took Bob by the elbow and led him toward the gate.

Pinzon turned to the lantern-jawed woman. "I'm glad to see you're trying to help old Bob." He cocked his head to one side and stared down at her through big, filmed-over eyes. "He's got a good heart. But sometimes the sadness of the world drives him to drink a little more than he should."

Later, while I was shagging flies during batting practice, Bob came up to me and said, "Pinzon didn't have no call trying to shame me before them people."

"He doesn't much care for the way you turned on us, Bob. I don't either. The pennant'd be ours right now if you hadn't done it. And this is likely to be the only season for some of us."

Mike O'Bryan hit a high fly and I moved a few steps to my right, settled under it, leaned forward a notch, and caught it behind my back. I threw it back in and Bob said, "I like a lot of you boys. It wasn't an easy thing for me to do. But I got a conscience."

I said, "If your conscience leads you to a man like Bull Cox, you might ought to find something else to follow."

He gave me a hard look out of them little eyes. "We going to beat Franklin today, Hog, and we going to beat Genghis tomorrow. You know that. Them boys can't hold us. Eversole might can do it again and maybe that Cuban can pull it off. But not them other two boys. They're young and they ain't used to this kind of pressure. I'm riding with a winner, Hog."

I was tired of him. "You beat 'em, Bob, and I'll be feeling low enough to buy you a beer."

That seemed to please him. "I'll meet you tomorrow night then, about seven at The Tank."

Well, they didn't get a run off Franklin Brown until the fifth, and that came off a leadoff double, a roller to second, and a sacrifice fly. We got to Ricky Russell for a run in the second and two more in the fifth—my thirty-third home run of the season—and we had a 3–1 lead going into the seventh. Then, after Franklin walked Tree Folsom, Jimmy Stennis hit a two-hop double-play ball to me. I kicked it, bigger than shit, and they had men on first and second and nobody down. Punch Lurleen moved them up a base apiece with a sacrifice. We gave Axe Heflin, a left-hand hitter, a pass to first to set up the double play that would get us out of it. Then

Lefty came to the mound, patted Franklin on the ass, told him he'd done a helluva job, and waved Jeronimo Velasquez in to face Pick Maddox. Maddox chopped one foul, took two balls low, then jerked a waist-high fastball into the screen. Grand slam. Five to 3, them. And if I'd fielded that two-hopper, we'd've been out of it clean.

They didn't get another hit off Velasquez. But it was over. Bullet Bob came in in our seventh and set down nine straight. I got the pleasure of making the last out again, a little squib back to the mound. Bob threw me out and yelled, "Tomorrow night, Hog."

I'd gone 2 for 5, with a big one and two RBIs, and I felt like stringing myself up from one of the shower pipes. The reporters kept asking me about the ball I'd kicked and how it felt to get beat by a former teammate and they asked Velasquez over and over about the pitch he'd served up to Pick Maddox. Lefty had to tell them the obvious several times—yes, if he had it to do over he'd leave Franklin in a little longer. There weren't that many of them—just the local writers, a couple from Memphis, and a few from around here or there, I don't know—but it was enough to sour a man on newspapers forever.

I noticed Franklin Brown sitting over in a corner by himself, still wearing his uniform, looking like a tired, sad, doomed nineteen-year-old kid. I walked over to him and put my hand on his shoulder and said, "Goddamit, Franklin, I'm sorry. You deserved to win it. I blew it for you. You went out there in the heat and pitched like a grown man and I got you beat by kicking a little-league grounder."

"Aw, hell," he said. And he looked up at me and couldn't get anything else out and just shook his head.

Then Pinzon did what needed to be done. He got up on a stool in the middle of the room and said, "Gentlemen, we've taken an informal poll and I'm pleased to announce that the Goat of the Day Award goes to none other than our own Hog Durham, the old thief who today rustled defeat right out of the green fields of victory." He held an empty Coors quart out to me.

I went up and took it. "Never a man deserved it more," I said.

"Don't be feeling too proud," he said. "We're going to win three straight and foil your criminal plans. I was raised a good Catholic and I know the good Lord won't turn his back on men like us for long."

"He better not," I said.

When we finally left the stadium, we found Bushrod and the born-aginners still in the parking lot, singing "Revive Us Again."

65

With just one gone in the top of the first the next day, I started to think Bullet Bob had been right. I started to taste that loser's beer.

Jimmy Stennis laid Genghis's first pitch on the chalk halfway between home and third, and Rainbow let it roll, hoping it would go foul. But it didn't. Stennis stole second, and Punch Lurleen singled him home. Bimbo Helms rolled into a force, but Axe Heflin, batting cleanup on account of Genghis being left-handed, shot a charge into a great big roundhouse curve, a damn kid's toy, and we were down 3–zip before it got started good.

Lefty came out to the mound, said something, and left. Then while Genghis was rubbing up the new ball and mumbling to Allah, I walked over and said, "You start pitching now and I'll get those three runs back myself."

"You on, man," he said. "I'm just now warmed up."

And after that he didn't show them anything but fire and ice. He kept the hard one down and most of the time it tailed away from the right-handers, but now and again he'd cut it and it would jerk in on them. And he'd feed them the scroogie too, both the darter and the one he used as a change. He had the good sense to shelve that big old showboat curve.

Their pitcher, Jigs Thurmond, didn't have anything that day but an old arm and a bad heart. Still, we spent the first two innings hitting line drives right at various Selmans. With two on and two out in the second, Jefferson Mundy hit one right on the nose. It went straight up the middle, never getting more than ten feet high, and landed right in Bimbo Helms's glove, damn near 300 feet away.

Joe Buck Cantwell buckled his chest protector strap and said, "Maybe the man up there really does like these assholes."

But Hagio Acribar led off our third with a double up the left-center gap and I singled him home. Rainbow's single chased me to third and they started heating up fast in the Selma bullpen. But not fast enough. Julius pulled Thurmond's second pitch into the screen and we were up 4–3.

Bull might've made a game of it if he'd come in with Willie Gates right then, but he went with Clem Farnsworth instead. We got to him for three runs in two innings and then rocked Suitcase Poff for two more in the sixth. Bridges was sharp over the last three, but we were laughing at them by then. Genghis went the full nine and looked like he could've gone that many more. Susan played the last inning and a half for me. After Bridges blew two by her in the eighth, she beat out a bunt and two pitches later stole second. The sheer feminine effrontery of it—we were up 9–3—sent Bull into a fine rage and we got the pleasure of watching him splinter a Louisville slugger against the dugout steps.

Well, reporters seemed like a better lot that day—though still a notch on the dull side. A couple of them talked to Susan in the manager's office Lefty never used, and the rest moved around among us, trying to act like part of the minor celebration and do their jobs at the same time.

Genghis, rightly pleased and proud, told them he hadn't quite got loose when he took the mound. "Man, when you got it, it's easy," he said. "Back 'em off. Keep it down, change it up, move it around. So sweet. They thought they had ole Genghis, but I showed 'em. You know it, Jack. Ole Genghis come back. Genghis done whupped them fat rednecks." And he gave them the sweet laugh. "You print it, Jack, like I say it."

When he'd finished with them, I went over and held my palms out to him. He slapped them and said, "You all right, Hog, my man. But after all that uptown jive there in the first I kept looking for you to jack."

I'd gone 4 for 5, all line singles. "It's all science," I said. "Punch and Judy. Ole Hog (Hit 'em Where They Ain't) Durham."

Putting on my jeans, I caught myself humming "Blessed Assurance" and decided that might be overdoing it some. We did have Guerrero and Eversole going for us the next two days, though, and Velasquez rested and ready in the bullpen. And the odds looked good right then, Lord, pretty good. But we couldn't let up. From then on, I knew, the first time they got a lead, we'd be looking at

Bullet Bob, trying to hit that floater, trying to wait for that one out
of a dozen that might turn over just one too many times.

That night about ten o'clock a taxi pulled up at the Home and
let Eversole out. When he reached the porch, where several of us
were still jawing about the game and eating homemade peach ice
cream, he asked me if Lefty had heard anything from Oxford.

"No," I said. "I don't think so. Not yet."

He nodded and climbed the stairs.

"Everything all right?" I asked.

"A rally out at the park," he told me. "Couldn't concentrate."

"Bushrod and them?"

"Selma too. Singing and lying," he said. "Is there a quiet room
in here?"

I gave him a grin. "I suspect you could have any one you wanted
to lay claim to."

He opened the screen door, then shut it again, gently, without
entering, and turned back to face us. "I've been paid to play this
game for thirty years. I don't know who's done it longer." He
stopped and we waited. "I've never pitched a game that means
more to me than the one that's coming Saturday."

"We got to win tomorrow," I said.

"We will." He took a long look around. "Nice place," he said.

66

They threw Hoss Barnett at us the following afternoon and he
and Guerrero traded zeroes for four innings. Atticus Flood led off
our fifth with a triple down the right-field line and, an out later,
scored on Joe Buck Cantwell's fly to center. Guerrero had been
sailing along, had just given up three scattered singles, two of them
seeing-eye grounders, and it looked to me like he might have the
game in his hand. Then, with one gone in their sixth, Iron Joe
Talmadge, their catcher, slapped a two-strike sinker to my right. I
moved over, backhanded it, and flipped it to Guerrero, who was
covering. He caught it, touched the inside of the bag a good step
ahead of Talmadge, then started to veer back toward second, out
of the runner's way. But Talmadge veered too, took a long jump,

and, coming down, raked the spikes on his left foot along Guerrero's right calf, tendon, and heel. They both went down hard.
Acribar, playing second that day, and I rushed to Guerrero and
saw the blood on the back of his leg. We helped him up, then
watched him take a step and wince. I looked over and saw Talmadge dusting himself off and wearing a proud bouncer's grin. I
started after him, but Julius Common Deer, seeing it coming, had
run in from center and he managed to get himself between me and
Talmadge. Julius put a bear hug around me and said, "Goddamit,
don't get thrown out." Both benches had emptied. I yelled at Talmadge, "Come on, you fat, stupid, chickenshit cocksucker." His
grin broadened. "Man was hogging the line," he said. Then somebody tackled him from behind and after that we all rolled on the
ground a while, cussing and pulling and doing very little harm.
The umps finally got it broke up, and, coming to my senses, I
started worrying about Eversole, afraid the Knights of Selma
might've got him down and stomped his throwing arm. I didn't see
him around anywhere, so I asked Lefty about him. "I sent him to
the clubhouse as soon as it started," he said.

But Talmadge had done the job on Guerrero. It was all he could
do to stand up, much less pitch. Lefty told Pinzon to get warm.
Pinzon went to the bull pen after his glove and I said to Lefty,
"Why not Velasquez?"

"Over three innings left," he said. "You save your ace." Then he
turned to Cantwell. "If he doesn't have it, you let me know quick."

I sat in the dugout while Pinzon warmed up. "Where's Guerrero?" I asked Worm Warnock.

"Susan drove him to the emergency room."

I shook my head and spit. "First chance I get, I'm going to level
Talmadge."

"Let's beat 'em today and tomorrow. After that, as far as I'm
concerned, you can go ahead and shoot him if you want to."

"I might not shoot him right off," I said. "I'd want to pistol-
whip him a while first."

Pinzon walked the first man he faced on five pitches. Lefty came
to the mound. "He's all right," Cantwell told him. "Good stuff.
Just off the plate." The next guy popped to short.

Mundy started our sixth by drawing a walk. Then he and Acribar worked the hit-and-run and I came up with men at the corners
and nobody down. I fouled two low sliders before taking my big

cut at a fat fastball. I hit it about 500 feet, 250 up and 250 down. Jimmy Stennis, the shortstop, caught it in short left.

"Good lick there, Big Time," Iron Joe Talmadge yelled as I headed toward the dugout.

I started back toward him, but Rainbow Smith on his way up to hit, grabbed my arm and said, "You go and sit down, Hog, where you can watch me drive them runs in."

I did and he did—a double off the wall. Pinzon went two more good innings, got the leadoff hitter in the ninth, then gave up a walk and a base hit. Lefty went to Velasquez, who threw just three pitches to Tree Folsom, the pinch hitter: a strike, a ball low, and an underhand sinker. Folsom one-hopped the sinker to Acribar, who fed it to Mundy, who sidearmed it to me, 4-6-3, and we were dead-even with the bastards and ready to show them our ace one more time.

67

Folks from all over came rolling up to the Home that evening after supper—two school buses filled with members of the Columbia County Co-op, flatbed trucks loaded with huge, hundred-pound south Arkansas watermelons, dusty old pickups and station wagons and long, oil-burning fifteen-year-old Buicks and Oldsmobiles carrying the eastern Oklahoma Cherokee wedding party. There were two bands—the Co-op Earth Band and one called Redskin Bluegrass. A couple of Genghis's old running buddies, not yet gone over to Allah, who looked like they might could make a pretty good meal of a small subdivision, rode in bare-chested and bareheaded on a pair of Harleys you could've jumped Lee Creek on. Twin brothers they were, Mule and Maynard Jackson. They'd played a season of football for North Texas State three years back, starting linebackers as freshmen, they said, but come that January they'd found themselves a little disenchanted with the academic life and so gave it up and worked on a gulf oil rig until they'd saved the money for the Harleys. From then on it had been the wind in their faces and the cops at their backs. They'd spent some time here and spent some time there and they didn't have a bad word to say about anything but the price of gas. Big old likable fellows without tie one in the world except to each other and their wheels. And I hadn't changed enough to keep a part of me from envying them. I wasn't much on a motorcycle, but by God, I could learn right quick. It made me take another hard look at Pansy and wonder about myself.

Ernesto Guerrero came up beside me. "You like the cycles?" he said.

"Yeah, I like 'em a right smart," I told him.

"For me," he said, "this is very pleasing." He made a sweeping motion with a bottle of beer. "The music. The dancing. The people very happy. Like Cuba when it is good."

"Like anywhere when it's good."

"No. I think some places they do not know this."

We stood and watched it all a minute. Then I asked about his leg.

"A cut here." He touched his right calf. "A bad bruising on the heel. Nothing is torn. It will heal soon. I wish to thank you for fighting him."

"Never got to him," I said.

He laughed. "But how you tried," he said. He took a drink of the beer. "I think we win tomorrow. It has been good here."

"You ought to stay," I said. "Maybe get yourself one of them cycles."

He shook his head. "Ratoplan and Rubios, they are not here, but they are watching. And Cuba is my home. Hagio and I, we wish to see the Grand Canyon. Then we return home."

"Maybe I can go down there and see you sometime," I said. "When the world changes."

"That would be good," he said.

And the lawn stayed full of the music and the dancing and the good slices of red melon. Kids of all ages and colors were throwing baseballs back and forth by porchlight. I danced some with Pansy and some with Packy Common Deer and took my turn with Susan and, Lord, it was fine, Lefty's dream come true for a night, dirt farmers taking over the mansion and singing while they did it.

I went over and sat by Ice and Mary Common Deer. "How come you ain't dancing, Ice?" I asked.

"Might make it rain," he said.

I laughed. "Well, hell, don't you need one?"

"I want to see my boy marry in the sunshine. Besides, we got over an inch Tuesday."

"Didn't get a drop here."

"Too close to Little Rock," he said. "No point in the Lord wasting it."

I stood and offered my hand to Mary. "You mind dancing with a white man?"

"Why, yes, I believe I'd like that, Hog."

Ice said, "You watch yourself now, Mary. He's a sly bastard."

They were playing something you could stomp to, and Mary lifted her skirts a little, and, laughing at herself, let the music take her. And when that was over, the musicians went into "Waltz Across Texas" for Julius and Susan and we all stood back and watched them.

Mary got Ice and brought him up to see it. He put his arm around her and she said, "Lord, old man, ain't they a fine-looking couple."

Ice didn't say anything, but I could see pride shining in his eyes.

I said, "That boy yonder came from damn fine stock."

Ice gave me his half-grin. "You trying to soften us up some before you ask us to give you his room?"

"God knows it might come to that," I said. "Right now, though, it's my time to do the offering. Why don't you and Mary sleep in the room me and Pansy been using?"

"I think it's safe to say I've spent a few more nights laying on the ground than you have," he said.

"Yeah, but that's because you're so damn much older. And because I've gone weeks at a time without ever laying eyes on the ground."

"One of the dangers of your old profession," he said.

"Mary," I said, "I wish you'd tell this old bastard not to shame me by turning down the little I got to offer."

Mary smiled at me, then at him. "A bed would be nice," she said.

I told them which room it was and how to get there and then went off after Pansy. I found her with Lefty and Barry Rotenberg and Joseph Hummingbird. Apparently, they'd begun by talking about our Cubans and worked their way to Castro. Joseph Hummingbird was praising him. "He had no choice except to turn to

Moscow," Joseph said. "Eisenhower and then Kennedy forced him to."

"Maybe," Lefty said. "But you have to wonder about a man who likes to stand on a platform before hundreds of thousands of people and deliver five-hour speeches."

"It's something every man ought to get to do," I said. "One time. Right before he dies."

Pansy took my arm. "What would you tell them if you had the chance?"

"Why, I'd talk about the things that matter. My hitting. Eversole's pitching. Dummy's cooking. This music. Your loving. Right at the end I'd have a fiddler stand up behind me and play and I'd go out doing a mountain jig."

Rotenberg said, "Christ, I'm tempted to build you a platform."

"We could do that easy enough," Lefty said. "But I'm not sure we could guarantee much of an audience."

"Aw, the truth is that just me and the fiddler would do."

I started to lead Pansy away, then stopped and asked Lefty where Eversole was.

"I gave him my room. I didn't want him out here where he might get good-natured before tomorrow."

"You hear anything from Oxford?" I asked Rotenberg.

"Nothing definite. Flemson's thinking. Gabbard says that if Flemson ever decides he has to call and admit defeat, he'll do it in the middle of the night."

Pansy and I got a quilt out of our room, went up to the stand of pines above the Home, and lay down fully dressed.

"Susan was hoping her parents would come," Pansy said.

It was a clear night. In the distance, I heard fiddles, banjos, and guitars.

I said, "They sent her here when she was seventeen and still in high school on account of her—what was it, now?—running with the wrong crowd? Then about the time she turns eighteen the wrong crowd just takes over the Home and moves in with her. Not many parents would want a daughter as pretty as her to end up playing first base. Now their golden girl's marrying a red Indian. Whoring might've been easier for them to understand."

"Still, she was hoping."

I looked up through the branches at the stars and something came to me. "Bull Cox should've gone to Bob in the sixth today.

We're one up, got men at the corners and nobody down. That's the kind of fix Bob can get you out of. If he does it, it's a new game."

She gave me a tolerant smile. "Wouldn't've mattered. They didn't score."

"Yeah, but Bull had to think they'd hit Pinzon, or even Velasquez. And maybe they would've too, if it'd stayed a one-run game with Bob on the mound. It changes the way both sides think. Now they have to beat Eversole."

She sighed, folded her hands behind her head. "I wish they had come."

I looked at her. "Who?" I asked. Then, "Oh." What I know about parents and children is mostly hearsay, so I didn't offer any more opinions on the subject. Anyway, I hadn't quit wondering why Bull hadn't used Bullet Bob. Then I knew. "Christ," I said.

"What is it?"

"He's going to start Bob."

"He's not a starter," she said. She sat up, laid her palm on my forearm, and looked down toward the Home. "Hog, why haven't you ever asked me what I was doing here in the first place?"

"It was easy enough to figure. You were tired and wanted out. Besides, I was more concerned about my past than yours."

"The bank robbery?"

"Among other things." I sat up beside her, held her face in my hands, kissed her. "How would you like to spend the winter in Puerto Rico?"

"Is that what you want?"

"I want you with me. I'm not sure about Puerto Rico. They play lots of baseball there. I know how to do that."

"I just want a home," she said.

68

We made do for breakfast: I crumbled half a pan of yesterday's cornbread into a quart Mason jar and poured buttermilk over it. It was about eight o'clock and the wedding was scheduled for somewhere between nine and ten, depending on how quickly the folks that wanted to could get shaved and showered in the ballpark dressing rooms.

It was close to ten before we all got out onto the infield and arranged ourselves. Joseph Hummingbird, in his jeans and his AIM T-shirt and with a book in his hand, stood on home plate. Julius and Susan, him in a brown suit I didn't know he had and her in a long blue gown with a big white flower pinned to it, stood directly in front of him, just on the grass, facing him. Ice, in his best overalls, and Mary, in her best gingham, were a step or two behind them. The rest of us, wearing whatever we'd got up in, rowed up a few feet back of that.

Joseph Hummingbird was right where he wanted to be: "Brothers and sisters, on this day when we have gathered to honor and make sacred the love of this good man and this good woman, I will begin by speaking to you of the wisdom and reverence and silence without which no love can endure."

He opened the book. "These are the words of Ohiyesa, sometimes called Charles Eastman, the Santee Dakota physician and writer. The words were written in 1911:

" 'The first American mingled with his pride a singular humility. Spiritual arrogance was foreign to his nature and teaching. He never claimed that the power of articulate speech was proof of superiority over the dumb creation; on the other hand, it is to him a perilous gift. He believes profoundly in silence—the sign of a perfect equilibrium. Silence is the absolute poise or balance of body, mind and spirit. The man who preserves his selfhood is ever calm and unshaken by the storms of existence—not a leaf, as it were, astir on the tree; not a ripple on the surface of the shining pool—his, in the mind of the unlettered sage, is the ideal attitude and conduct of life.

" 'If you ask him: "What is silence?" he will answer: "It is the Great Mystery!" If you ask: "What are the fruits of silence?" he will say: "They are self-control, true courage or endurance, patience, dignity, and reverence. Silence is the cornerstone of character." ' "

He closed the book gently, stared down at it a second, raised his eyes to Julius and then Susan. "I give you these words, my friends, because the world in which your love must survive is clamorous and violent. You must live among a people who believe in neither the past nor the future, who want only immediate diversion and comfort, who will rip away mountains and blacken whole seas to light their buildings and feed their machines, and who fear nothing more than the silence out of which can rise a full human being.

"So, I bid you, Julius and Susan, go forth together, preserve your love, yield not to the false gaiety of fools, guide your children toward dignity and courage and reverence, love the earth and dwell on it gently, delight in the mystery, and stand ever in awe of the silence at the heart of the world."

Well, you educate an Indian and you get a man that can talk like sweet Jesus about silence.

Then Julius and Susan pledged fidelity to each other and Joseph pronounced them man and wife and everybody wished them well. I asked Ice if he thought that was enough sunshine for his boy to marry in.

"Ought to do," he said. "Course, promising's easy."

Some of the Cherokees and co-op members began dragging and watering the dirt part of the infield. And the ball team went into the clubhouse and started suiting up—Julius and Susan now sharing the manager's office. I was just about in my uniform when Rotenberg came in. "Heard it was a splendid wedding," he said to Lefty. "Sorry I missed it." Then he and Lefty went into the equipment room, where Eversole was. A few minutes later they came out. Rotenberg left the clubhouse. I followed him out the door and up the ramp. Folks had fired up the grills and were cooking sausages and eggs. Rotenberg got in the late breakfast line.

"What happened?" I asked him.

"It worked. Or I guess it did. They're on their way. Gabbard's driving them up."

"Both of them?"

"Flemson gave Candy Commerce temporary custody of Colonel Sanders. Eversole can't have her without taking him."

"Eversole agree to it?"

"Sure. He's just another fool in love."

"Christ," I said. "He don't have a chance."

"Which one you talking about?"

"None of them have a chance. But it was Eversole I was thinking about."

"Oh, he might hold them until November. That's all Flemson wants."

I shook my head. "So they're coming to the game?"

"Gabbard said hold two seats for them right behind your dugout. The woman probably won't know where she is. They've been feeding her Thorazine like ice tea."

"And I guess we better hope the boy don't set fire to your seat."

Back in the clubhouse I found somebody's *Chronicle* and took the sports section out of it and carried it to the dugout with me. It said Eversole (29–4) vs. Shelton (14–9). I stretched out then, pulled my cap down over my eyes, and reminded myself that this might be my last game, that certainly I'd never play in one that mattered more to me, that I had to concentrate on every play, every pitch. Don't lunge, keep your weight back, hands back, head in, wait, look for the mistake.

I'd just about reminded myself into the shakes when Pinzon came out and said, "Selma's here."

I sat up and rubbed my eyes. "You nervous?" I asked him.

"No," he said. "I won't be playing unless Eversole has a heart attack."

I laughed and looked up at him. Gonzalo Pinzon, crazy-smart. "What you going to do when this is over?" I asked him.

"I think I'll hang around till Susan divorces Julius." Then he laughed. "I don't know. I liked the looks of those motorcycles last night. I think I'll buy one and head West."

"What's out there for you?"

"Roads," he said. "And Montana's a pretty word."

A couple of the Selma boys came out of their clubhouse and into their dugout. They sat down and commenced fondling a couple of bats and talking to one another.

"You know what the pretty word is?" I said. "Alabama. It's an Indian word that means 'Here we may rest.' A Birmingham burglar told me that. Shakespeare Creel, my old cellmate, said that was wrong, said Alabama meant 'thicket clearers,' but even if it ain't true, it's good."

Pinzon said, "Well, what does Selma mean?"

"Hell, I don't know. Probably Bull Cox's momma's name."

When Selma started taking batting practice, we went back inside. I played some gin rummy with Stump and Joe Buck and smoked a couple of Luckies. Lefty got up and thanked us all for playing for the Reds and for tolerating all the mistakes he'd made. "If you need a place, any of you, tomorrow or anytime, you'll be welcome down at the co-op. You'll have to work some, but we sing in the evenings." He lifted his cap, ran his hand back through his hair. "Now," he said, "let's go out and beat these sons of bitches."

We loosened our arms, took batting practice and infield, and watched the stands fill up. Lefty and Bull Cox brought their lineup cards to home plate. Lefty came back and taped theirs to our dugout wall. I went in and had a look at it. "I knew it," I said.

Lefty nodded. "Oh, yeah. It had to be Bob."

Eversole was warming up in our bullpen. Bullet Bob hadn't started yet.

I sat down. "Well, Christ," I said.

"Any way you look at it, it's a mistake," Lefty said. "If he was going to start him, he should've done it against somebody other than Eversole."

"I'd hate to have to remember losing it to Bob, though," I said.

"Don't lose it," he told me.

Just a couple of minutes before game time, Stephen Gabbard came into our dugout. He spoke to Lefty, who then went to our bullpen and told Eversole. I climbed to the lip of the dugout and looked. Candy Commerce and Colonel Sanders Flemson sat on either side of Rotenberg. She was sound asleep, her head on Rotenberg's shoulder. The idiot had a bucket of chicken in his lap.

It struck me funny. "Nice family you got, mister," I said to Rotenberg.

"Raised them up in the fear of God," he said. Then he laughed. "This goddam ball game better be good."

Eversole followed Lefty back toward the dugout, stopped, took a good look, nodded, and turned back to finish warming up.

We took the field. Woodrow Ratliff played "We Shall Overcome" on the organ. About half the crowd stood, joined hands, and sang. The place was full, people in the aisles and out beyond the walls looking through those holes we'd drilled weeks back.

Eversole seemed wild. He didn't walk anybody, didn't even get behind in the count, but his fastball was catching too much of the plate and he was getting the spitter up. Jimmy Stennis led off with a single to right. Punch Lurleen bunted him to second. Axe Heflin doubled the run home.

I went to the mound. "Maybe we ought to have Gabbard drive her back to Plaquemine."

He glared. "Cover your base," he said.

Then he got Pick Maddox to hit into a double play, but that was mostly Atticus Flood's doing. Maddox mashed one toward the gap in right. Flood caught it on the dead run and threw to Acribar at second for the putout on Heflin, who was rounding third by then.

"There's our break," Lefty told us in the dugout. "Good play. Bad baserunning. Now, make Bob work. Lay off the good knuckler until you have two strikes. Wait for the one with too much spin."

But Bob's butterfly was turning over once, then disappearing. He set us down in order. I made the third out, poking a little humpbacked foul to Axe Heflin behind first.

With one gone in their second, Bucky Bilbo tripled. Then Eversole walked Jake Moreland. Lefty set the infield at double-play depth for Iron Joe Talmadge.

They pulled the suicide squeeze and got the run. Talmadge bunted it hard down the first-base line. By the time I picked it up, Bilbo was across the plate and Talmadge was bearing down on me. I would've just had time to step out of the base path and throw to Acribar covering first. But I didn't do that. I braced myself, squatted, came up under Talmadge, tagged him hard on the nuts, and flipped him up over my shoulders.

He curled on the ground, holding himself. I walked over to him, looked down, and said, "Nice lick, Big Time."

Bull Cox came snorting out of his dugout, wanting me bounced from the game. The home-plate ump said it was an honest collision—two men with an equal right to the base path. Bull gave up the argument fairly quick. And nobody else came out of their dugout, except the trainer, who tended to Iron Joe. Bull must've ordered his players to stay back. With a two-run lead and Bullet Bob defying science on the mound, he sensed victory.

And it started looking more and more like he was right. Eversole became Eversole again, the spitter jerking down and the hard one riding in. But Bob was every bit as sharp and he had the two-run cushion. He retired nine straight before Jefferson Mundy, leading off our fourth, bunted for a hit. He stole second and, an out later, with me at the plate, took third on a passed ball. But then I fanned and Rainbow popped to second.

It moved along fast. The stands got so quiet I could hear Bushrod's Christians singing in the parking lot. We tried bunting Bob again in the fifth and sixth, but Bull had wised up to that, pulling his first and third basemen a couple of steps in on the grass. Julius, starting our fifth, and Mundy, ending the sixth, bunted into easy outs. And Bob, working on a one-hitter, had set down nine more in a row.

Then, with the fans chanting and Ratliff banging out "Keep Your Eyes on the Prize" on the organ, Hagio Acribar started the bottom of the seventh by whistling a double to left-center. The count went to 2 and 2 on me before I popped one in foul ground back of third. Jimmy Stennis and Bucky Bilbo both went after it, but Stennis, the shortstop, had the angle and caught it. Bob forgot to cover third, though, and Acribar, alert and fast, tagged at second and moved up a base.

"That may cost Bob the game," Lefty said.

It cost him a run, anyway. Rainbow lifted a high fly to right and Acribar scored easily.

When we took the field in the eighth, I looked over our dugout to where Rotenberg was sitting with Eversole's new charges. Candy was awake but seemed to be staring out toward the freeway traffic. The half-wit looked like he was into the game, though—pounding the top of the dugout while screaming "Win! Win! Win!" Rotenberg was helping himself to some of the chicken.

Eversole roared through the bottom third of their order, getting Jake Moreland to tap to short and fanning Talmadge and Bullet Bob. But our eighth went just as fast. Flood, Bernstein, Cantwell: 6–3, 4–3, 6–3.

Jimmy Stennis led off their ninth by bunting toward third, but Eversole got off the mound in good shape and nailed him by half a step. Then Punch Lurleen blooped a single over first and Axe Heflin sacrificed him to second. Lefty walked to the mound. Except for the Flemson heir's screams, the stands were silent.

"Let's put Maddox on," Lefty said.

"He can't hit me."

"Put him on."

Eversole did. Then he fanned Bimbo Helms on three pitches Ted Williams couldn't've hit.

As Eversole walked toward the dugout, the fans rose and applauded. His had been the finest individual season in the history of the Dixie Association. He owned almost every important one-season pitching record on the books. And all I could see ahead of him was misery—a woman who'd never been able to stay in one place for long, and an idiot who loved her, hated him, and carried kitchen matches. Oh, he'd bear the pain they'd cause him, close up again and bear it. He'd pitch somewhere until his stuff ran out, then just walk off into that silence Joseph Hummingbird had talked so highly of, that silence that can kill you, too. I sat down and listened to the cheering die. Lord, I wanted him to have this game.

Lefty did what he had to do. Eversole was scheduled to lead off our ninth, and Lefty had Mike O'Bryan hit for him. I don't think I'd've done it. O'Bryan was by far the better hitter, but Eversole could be a tough out when he concentrated on hitting. Jeronimo Velasquez started throwing to Stump Guthrie in the bullpen in case we got just one and went into extra innings. And Velasquez was a tough reliever. Still, I guess I'd've left Eversole in till he fell over. But then I'm a softhearted bastard.

I hadn't quite finished thinking all that out when O'Bryan lined a single up the middle. Lefty sent Pinzon in to run for him.

I got myself a drink of water, looked out at Bob, whose uniform was soaked through with sweat but whose face showed nothing. Calm, methodical, he had mastered the one thing. I closed my eyes and willed him to fuck up. He didn't seem to notice. I got my bat out of the rack and climbed up to the field. There were two hitters between me and Bob.

The crowd was roaring now, stomping their feet and roaring. Most of them were with us, I thought. A change since the season's start. And after all that had happened between then and now, it had come down to baseball, an inning, an out, a run, the way it should have. A pitcher and a hitter.

Jefferson Mundy twice tried to sacrifice Pinzon to second; both times the bunt rolled foul. Then he bouced one to short. Christ, I thought, double play. But Pinzon took Punch Lurleen out at second and Mundy was on first with one down. Moving to the on-deck circle, I noticed that Bushrod had his troops in the ramp above the Selma dugout, ready, I guess, to join Bull and his boys in the singing of the anthem.

Acribar took a strike, two balls, another strike, then popped to third.

And it was me and Bullet Bob Turner.

I don't know if the fans quit yelling, but they seemed to. I did hear Iron Joe Talmadge say, "Well, look what we got here. The old choker himself. Up to make the last out again. Ain't hit one fair all day, has he, ump?"

I was taking the first pitch. It started toward the middle of the plate, jumped in at me, then down. Strike one. Fuck up. Bob, I thought, fuck up. The next one moved just as much, but darted outside. I stepped out of the box, rubbed a handful of dirt on the bat handle. My teammates stood at the edge of the dugout, silent, I thought. The fans stood too, silent, I thought.

I stepped back into the box. Bob got his sign and went into his stretch. Just as Bob raised his front leg to go toward home, Mundy bluffed toward second and yelled "There he goes!" So it must have been that quiet. Because the yell broke into a silence. I *know* that. And I think it may have distracted Bob just enough. The ball came spinning toward home. *Spinning.* Not much. Just enough to keep it from floating or sinking. And I saw it clear. *Spinning.* And I moved into it, bat back, head down, weight rolling forward, and then the bat flashing at it, carrying all I had, and then, God Almighty, it was, Open your window, Jefferson Davis, and, So Long, Selma, Ole Hog done caught it all.

I watched it rise and rise, over wall and screen and Orval Faubus Freeway, and I ran toward first with my fists in the air and the roar came and I saw people coming over the walls and onto the field and I ran on, second and third, and they let me through them so I could make it all the way home, and Ratliff played "The Hallelujah Chorus" and I must've been crying then because Eversole picked me up and said, "When you beat 'em, Hog, you laugh," and I hugged him and prayed that it would work out with him and Candy and the idiot. Maybe it would. Anything seemed possible then. And they'd seen him pitch. Then Lefty was laughing beside me and I grabbed him and told him, "Take me to south Arkansas, Brother Marks. I'd like to go out of baseball with that swing." And Pansy came and I held her and held her and I wanted her forever and there was fiddle music then and people dancing and little kids trying to figure out what had come over their folks and Pinzon was dancing with Mary Common Deer and Ice with his son's bride and I thought, Let this joy last into the night and carry us to tomorrow. And then? What then? Well, this time, Ice, I'll pray for the possible, but all of it, every bit of it: May whatever grace yet abides in this most and least human of centuries be with us all, doomed dancers every one, until the last Amen.